Anna Jacobs is the author of over 60 novels and is addicted to storytelling. She grew up in Lancashire, emigrated to Australia in the 1970s, and writes stories set in both countries. She loves to return to England regularly to visit her family and soak up the history. Anna has two grown daughters and a grandson, and lives with her husband in a spacious home near the Swan Valley, the oldest wine-growing area in Western Australia. Her house is crammed with thousands of books. In 2006 one of her novels, *Pride of Lancashire*, won the Australian Romantic Novel of the Year Award.

You can discover more about the author at www.annajacobs.com

PEPPERCORN STREET

Three women find new hope in Peppercorn Street, a small village in a beautiful corner of Wiltshire. Janey is eighteen and living in a small flat with her baby daughter. Just as her new life starts to show promise, her past catches up with her. Nicole has just walked away from her husband and teenage sons, tired of being treated as a servant, and suspecting her husband of having an affair. Winifred has lived in her large family home at the top of the street for over eighty years, but it's all getting too much, though she doesn't want to leave. Things are not what they seem in any of the three women's lives; and to survive, they need good friends and courage — all freely available on Peppercorn Street.

ANNA JACOBS

PEPPERCORN STREET

Complete and Unabridged

CHARNWOOD
Leicester

First published in Great Britain in 2014 by
Allison & Busby Limited
London

First Charnwood Edition
published 2016
by arrangement with
Allison & Busby Limited
London

A catalogue record for this book is available
from the British Library.

ISBN 978–1–4448–3069–9

Published by
F. A. Thorpe (Publishing)
Anstey, Leicestershire

Set by Words & Graphics Ltd.
Anstey, Leicestershire
Printed and bound in Great Britain by
T. J. International Ltd., Padstow, Cornwall

This book is printed on acid-free paper

1

Janey Dobson heaved the buggy up the stairs while her social worker carried little Millie up to the first floor for her, opening the door with a smile and a flourish.

'Here we are, as far away from Swindon as we can place you and still keep you in our district. I think you're going to like this flat. It's been newly refurbished.'

Taking her wailing daughter into her arms, knowing she had no choice but to live here, Janey walked inside and turned round slowly on the spot, studying her new home.

The main room was bigger than she'd expected, with pale cream walls — new paint, too, from the smell. To her relief the bedroom she and Millie would share, though smallish, was completely separate. The kitchen was in a recessed corner at the back, consisting of a sink, a small gas cooker and a fridge, barricaded by about a metre and a half of freestanding bench top with cupboards underneath.

She breathed a sigh of relief. She'd been wondering how to afford a fridge. 'Thanks, Pam. This'll be great.'

'It'd be better if it was on the ground floor, but the other five flats are either occupied or assigned.'

'I don't mind. It's a huge improvement on the last place.'

'You've got Millie to thank for that. She cried so often the owners insisted we get you out of there. Grotty B&Bs like that one are only supposed to be used for emergency accommodation, but we're so short of places to put people they're nearly always full.

'Now, fasten Millie into the buggy and we'll bring up the rest of your stuff. The people from *Just Girls* will be delivering a cot this afternoon and a few other things to help you set up home.'

Janey helped bring in her meagre possessions, together with some bits and pieces Pam had given her today. Who'd have thought she'd be a mother and have her own home at this age?

Or that her parents would throw her out for keeping Millie.

She still hadn't got her head round their rejecting her and their granddaughter. People complained about the social services, but they'd been wonderful to her when she'd fallen through their local office doors, weeping and desperate, literally on the street with only a small suitcase. 'Thanks for all your help, Pam.'

'My pleasure. Look, let me show you how the heating works and then I'll have to dash. I'll pop round to see you next week but if there's any problem, get straight back to me. And be sure to register at the medical centre I showed you. They have an excellent child health clinic.'

'I will.'

When she was alone, Janey went to sit on the sagging armchair, rocking the buggy to and fro,

2

enjoying the quietness. She'd lived in lodgings until the birth, working at two or three odd jobs, washing up in a café, anything. When she'd started having her baby, she'd packed her bags and said goodbye to her landlady, a dour woman who wouldn't have her back with a baby.

No one except the social worker had visited her in hospital and she'd been glad to move to the *Just Girls* hostel afterwards. The matron there had helped her learn to look after her baby, but she was only allowed to stay for three months, hence the B&B and at last this place.

'We'll be all right here, Millie darling,' she said, but her voice wobbled. She'd never felt so alone in her whole life. No matter how kind social workers were, you were just a job to them, and even that was better than no one in the world caring whether you lived or died.

She was responsible for a child's life and everything else that went with that, but she still felt as if she was playing at being a grown-up.

Unstrapping Millie, she spread out a blanket on the floor so that her four-month-old daughter could kick, then went to investigate the kitchen. The cupboards were full of dust and odd screws or bits of wood from the installation and the fridge was new — and totally empty. She switched it on and put in her few bits of food.

Millie seemed happy so Janey quickly washed out the cupboards, then made a cup of tea while she waited for the shelves and drawers to dry. When the baby grew hungry, she prepared a bottle of formula. There was never any trouble getting Millie to drink her bottles, thank goodness. She was such a good baby.

Afterwards Millie fell asleep very suddenly, which made things a lot easier. Janey put her back on the floor and covered her with a blanket. Poor little love! She had a bright red patch on one cheek still which meant more teeth were coming through. She had the two upper front teeth already.

Janey tiptoed across to deal with the bedroom. There was enough room for a cot as well as the single bed, thank goodness. She pulled a face at the old-fashioned wardrobe against one wall, a huge thing with a mirror on the door and shelves inside it on the left. Since the baby was still asleep, she unpacked their clothes. Even combined, their things looked lost in that gigantic wardrobe.

She studied herself in the mirror. She'd grown her hair because it was cheaper and could just be tied back. It was a nondescript mid-brown but she couldn't afford streaks. Luckily she'd lost all the extra pregnancy weight and could get into her normal clothes again. Pam had persuaded her mother to hand those over one day when her father was out. He'd have refused just to spite her.

And she was learning a lot about charity shops, where you could find all sorts of things if you took the time to search.

If only her parents had let her have her computer! She could have played around on it even if she couldn't afford an Internet connection.

Someone rang the doorbell and as she went to use the crackly intercom for the first time, Millie woke with a start.

'Is that you, Janey? Dawn here from *Just Girls*. We've brought you a cot and a few other things.'

'Brilliant. I'm pressing the release button for the front door. I'm on the right on the first floor.' She picked her daughter up and shushed her gently, then went to open the door.

She knew Dawn, who had visited the hostel a few times, but not the other woman who was helping carry up the pieces of an old-fashioned cot.

Dawn looked round. 'Not bad at all. You should see some of the places where our girls have to live. We'll just fetch the rest then we'll help you set up the cot. Oh, this is Margaret, by the way.'

They brought up all sorts of bits and pieces, three loads in all. 'You never know what you need,' Dawn said cheerfully. 'If you find you don't need any of these, bring them back to our shop. You can't miss it. It's on High Street. One person's rubbish is another person's treasure. Some of the other girls go there on Tuesday afternoons for a cup of coffee and a natter. Now you're living in Sexton Bassett, why don't you join us? Do you think you could make it tomorrow?'

'Not tomorrow, no. I'll be too busy settling in here, shopping and catching up with the washing.' And she desperately needed some peace and quiet to get her head round what she would do with her life now.

'Well, don't forget to come next week. Since you're new to town, it'll help you to meet a few people.'

5

'I know. I won't forget.'

Janey was near tears by the time they'd shown her everything they'd brought, even a bundle of rags for cleaning, something she'd never have thought of. But she'd learnt not to give in to her emotions. Well, she didn't give in as easily as she used to, anyway. 'Thank you. I can't tell you how grateful I am. Um — is there a library near here?'

'Go down to High Street and turn right. It's about a five-minute walk on this side.' Dawn fumbled in her bag and produced a piece of card, scribbling on it. 'Here, give them this. You've no way of proving you live here yet, but they'll take my word for it that you're bona fide and let you join.'

'Thank you.' The tears welled up again but Janey blinked hard, refusing to let them loose.

As they got ready to leave Dawn asked gently, 'Are you sure you'll be all right, dear?'

'Yes. Yes, I'll be fine. I'm really grateful for all your help.'

But of course she wept after they'd left because one of them had given her a calendar. As she turned it to February and hung it up on a nail in the kitchen, today's date seemed to jump out at her and she started to sob. She'd hoped her mother would at least send her birthday wishes, because she had Pam's contact details, but she hadn't. Her father never bothered about birthdays, but her mother had usually managed to conjure up some small treats.

She was glad she'd told Pam not to give them her new address, though she hadn't explained the real reason for that: she was terrified of a certain person getting hold of it.

Well, she was eighteen now, whether anyone acknowledged it with a card or not, officially an adult — and still crying like a child. That had to stop.

Surely things would get better now?

★ ★ ★

Winifred Parfitt walked slowly up Peppercorn Street, glad of her father's old silver-headed walking stick these days. The houses at the lower end had all been converted into flats now, with ugly dormer extensions poking up to make full use of the attic space. No one cared two hoots whether the houses looked attractive, only how much money could be wrung out of a property.

Pausing for breath near a newly renovated house, she watched a woman with grey hair carry a baby inside and behind her a pretty young woman hauled one of those funny three-wheeled pushchairs up the steps. What did they call them? Buggies?

The girl didn't look old enough to have a baby. Children grew up too quickly these days, encouraged to act like women before they'd finished school even.

Just past this huddle of mass dwellings near High Street were more flats, but these were of better quality, older houses converted with an eye to street appeal. She sighed, remembering when this was the best street in the small town of Sexton Bassett. These houses had had gardens filled with flowers and lush shrubs in those days, not expanses of black tarmac with white lines painted on it.

Halfway up the sloping street Winifred stopped for another rest, because her shopping bag was heavy. She looked at the new group of retirement villas, finished only last month. The developer had made a little cul-de-sac off Peppercorn Street and called it Sunset Close. Of course! Everything was 'sunset' as far as old people were concerned. She got sick of the sound of that word.

The gardens of the villas were tiny and bare as yet. Well, no use putting plants in at this time of year. She sighed, remembering the huge old house that used to stand here and the lad who'd lived in it, a lad who'd asked her father's permission to come courting just before he went into the air force. Jack had been killed in the final year of the Second World War and she'd never found another young man to match him. She still kept his photo beside her bed. He looked so proud in his brand-new uniform. She was probably the only one who remembered him now. He'd been an only child. They'd planned to have four children. Now she had none.

A developer had wanted to demolish the old house a few years ago but had found it hard to get permission because it was heritage listed. Then one night last year it had burnt down. End of problem. There were now nine bungalows on the plot of land.

Over 55s only, the adverts had said. Her nephew had suggested she buy one and sell her home for development. Bradley had mentioned it several times and she was getting irritated by this. Why couldn't he understand that she loved the house she'd lived in all her life, however inconvenient and old-fashioned it was?

Lately Bradley had grown impatient with her, going on and on about how she wasn't thinking clearly.

Was she losing her grip? He hadn't said that openly, but she'd made one or two mistakes which he'd pounced on.

No, they had just been mix-ups. Mentally she was as acute as she'd always been. She could still do a crossword quickly and accurately, and answered most of the questions on quiz shows on the television, except for those about pop music and sport, of course.

She started walking again. The houses nearer to hers were semi-detached, Edwardian residences with large rooms and high ceilings. Most of them had been tastefully refurbished, she'd give the newcomers that, but these people didn't make good neighbours. They were so busy chasing money and ferrying their children around, they didn't have time to do more than nod at her. She missed having real neighbours to talk to or share a cup of tea with.

She missed having friends, too. Hers had died one by one over the past five years. So sad. The funeral of the final one had been yesterday and she'd been the only mourner because poor Molly had been a spinster like her. There were a lot of unmarried women in her generation, thanks to Hitler and Mussolini. After the war there simply

9

hadn't been enough men left to go round.

Molly's lawyer had asked Winifred to make an appointment to see him about a bequest, but he lived at the other end of town, so she'd have to take a taxi. More expense. If Molly had left her the books and bookcases, as she'd once promised to do, they'd be very welcome. You couldn't have too many books. They didn't die on you. She'd make an appointment in a day or two.

She paused at her gate, a little out of breath, and frowned as she looked at the garden. She really ought to get someone in to do the front. Gardening was far too much for her these days. But share values had tumbled and with them her income, so she simply couldn't afford it and that was that. The best she could manage now was to hoe the weeds along the path.

With a sigh, she pushed open the gate, closed it carefully and walked to the front door. It was dim inside because she kept the front curtains drawn for privacy. She shivered. The front of the house wasn't much warmer than outside. She'd be glad when spring arrived. Even if she'd been able to afford to have full central heating installed, she didn't have the money to run it.

Hanging her coat up carefully on the hallstand she went through into the kitchen and servants' quarters. She spent most of her time in here now in winter, because her nephew had found her a small oil-fired Aga second-hand a couple of years ago. He'd said it wasn't good for the house to get damp in the winter. It wasn't good for her, either, but he didn't seem to care about that. She was beginning to wonder about where Bradley's real interest lay: her or the house she'd foolishly told him he'd inherit one day.

Someone had to have the place and he was her closest relative. She'd not bothered to keep in touch with her other relatives and they'd not bothered with her, though one niece sent her a Christmas card every year. Families didn't stay together like they used to.

Bradley worked offshore but came to see her whenever he was in England. She made lunch for him and he did little repair jobs around the place, joking about keeping it weather tight.

In winter she now slept in the room off the kitchen, because it was warmer. She still thought of it as Cook's bedroom. She used the tiny servants' bathroom nearby, too. Her mother would have had a fit at that.

Thank goodness it was a huge, old-fashioned kitchen, with room for her favourite armchair as well as a small table and a television! She was very cosy here, really. She shouldn't complain. There were plenty of people worse off than her.

Pulling her library books out of her shopping bag Winifred debated which to read first, made a pot of tea and ate a piece of cake (home-made, she could still do the cooking, thank you very much).

As she settled down in the armchair, she felt guilty at how many romances she read — her father had always called them 'rubbish', though how he knew that with such certainty when he'd never read a single one, she didn't understand. And most of them weren't rubbish. Love was a wonderful thing. It made her feel good every time she saw a couple walking down the street hand in hand, with that luminously happy look on their faces.

Books with happy-ever-after endings had always been her favourites and if you couldn't read what you wanted at the age of eighty-four, it was a poor lookout. Picking up the new historical romance by her favourite author, she opened it and sighed happily at the description of the hero. He sounded just like Jack, so she gave him Jack's face in her mind.

★　★　★

When Millie woke up, Janey changed her nappy, gave her a drink and went out in search of the library and a supermarket. Pushing the buggy slowly along, she studied the high street shops with interest. Sexton Bassett was a smallish town but it seemed to have everything she needed. She'd begged Pam to move her as far away as possible from her old home. It hurt so much when her mother walked past her in the street, behaving as if she didn't exist and not even glancing at Millie.

Even before the woman behind the counter smiled at her, Janey could tell this was a good library. There was a feel to the good ones you simply couldn't mistake. They made you feel welcome, valued.

'Can I help you?'

'I've just moved to the area. I'd like to join the library and I want to find out as much as I can about the town.'

12

'Do you have proof of your resident status?'

'Not yet, but Dawn Potter gave me this.' She handed over the note just as Millie started to grizzle. 'I'm sorry. She's teething. I'll choose my books quickly, so I won't disturb you for long.'

The woman only glanced at the card before saying, 'That's fine. Look, why don't you put your baby's buggy in the children's area, then we'll take down the membership details. You'll be able to keep an eye on her as you look for books and she won't disturb people as much from there.' She indicated a glass-walled room to one side, filled with bright posters, toys and small chairs.

'Thank you. That'll be such a relief. I'm lost without a book.'

'You should join one of our reading groups.'

'Maybe I will.' Janey walked round the library, choosing the four books she was allowed, wishing it was more. Still, this library wasn't far to walk. She could come here two or three times a week.

As she waited to take out her books, the same woman who'd enrolled her, whose name badge said Nicole, came across with some brochures. 'I thought these might be useful to help you settle in. You must go and see the abbey ruins when the weather gets finer. You get such a sense of peace there.'

She pointed. 'There are some tatty paperbacks in those boxes over there. People bring them in rather than throw them away. You can take one or two each time you come in. Keep them if you like, but if you don't want them, we'd be grateful

13

if you'd bring them back again.'

'I don't have many books yet because I'm just setting up home. Can I really keep them?'

'Yes, of course.' She smiled and lowered her voice. 'Take half a dozen this time, as a welcome-to-the-town present.'

There! Janey thought as she moved across and found two of her favourite novels immediately. *I did have a birthday present after all.* It seemed like an omen.

Retrieving Millie, she walked out, feeling considerably cheered up. Now she'd have something to do tonight. You never felt as lonely with a book in your hand. She'd have somewhere to store books too. From now on she'd keep an eye on the cheap books in charity shops. She'd rather eat bread and jam for tea than not have a book to read.

There was a small supermarket on the other side of the street from the library, so she nipped in to buy some food for tonight. She'd do a proper shop tomorrow, make lists, be efficient. How her old home economics teacher would laugh at that! It had been her worst subject. Now, it was cook properly or eat rubbish.

She was tired but felt hopeful as she trudged home, even though it had started to rain. Her life was starting up again.

2

Nicole Gainsford watched the young mother leave the library, smiling now. Was the poor child raising a baby on her own? She must be if *Just Girls* was helping her. They took in young mothers without any support systems from all over the county.

She was going to make more effort to revitalise the young mothers' reading group at the library. These days you had to provide far more than a place to borrow books or go on the Internet. They had quite a few community groups going now. Some of the oldies had cheered up enormously at having somewhere to go and something to do.

Then another customer took her attention and she didn't think about the young mother again. What she did think about when she had a moment was the difficulty she was having with her teenage sons, especially William, who was going through an aggressive patch and was giving her a lot of grief. But also Paul, who had become very withdrawn lately and would hardly say a word to anyone.

She set off for home, on foot today because she had no shopping to do. Inevitably her thoughts turned to her husband. The two of them had drifted apart during the past few years, no denying that. She hadn't noticed at first and when she had, she'd tried to do something to bring them together. Only he didn't seem interested in his family any more.

In fact, she was wondering if he was having an affair. He was sometimes late home, sat staring into space a lot, had become very secretive about his emails, protecting his area of the computer with a password so that she and the boys couldn't access his stuff. Who was he emailing that was so secret?

She slowed down as she got closer to their house. She dreaded going home these days.

It was even worse that evening. William was outright rude to her and refused to gather his dirty clothes together for her to wash.

'All right,' she yelled. 'Let them stay dirty. Anything not in the laundry basket in the next five minutes you can wash yourself.'

Paul came down two minutes later with his dirty clothes.

'Where's your brother?'

He shrugged.

She waited a full ten minutes. No sign of William. So she set the washing off.

Five minutes later he sauntered into the kitchen and dumped his dirty washing all over the floor.

'Too late,' she said. 'You'll have to do it yourself.'

He kicked the nearest clothes across to her. 'You're the mother. It's your bloody job to do the washing.'

She kicked them back. 'You keep saying you're not a child. Well, grown-ups put their own things in the laundry basket.' She was sick of this argument which they had every week.

He moved across to her, towering over her

16

from his newly acquired six foot. 'I'm *not* — doing — the — washing.'

For a minute she thought he was going to hit her, but he just shoved her towards the utility room, knocking her against the wall, and kicking the clothes in her direction. Then he slouched off up the stairs, yelling over his shoulder, 'Call me when tea's ready.'

She went to sit down, feeling shaky. She'd really thought he was going to thump her. She'd been frightened of her own son. That was bad.

She didn't feel like cooking so hauled out some noodles and a jar of sauce and heated it up. That'd have to do.

She hesitated to call William, not wanting to seem as if she was obeying his orders, but in the end she stood at the foot of the stairs and yelled, 'Tea's ready.'

Both boys came down. Paul sat and ate quietly. She couldn't understand why he wouldn't talk to her. She kept meaning to get him on his own and insist he tell her what was wrong, but the opportunity had never seemed to arise. He made sure of that.

'There's no meat with this,' William complained.

'No. I didn't have time to defrost any. Your father's supposed to help with the shopping and cooking but he's been a bit forgetful lately.'

'That's women's work.' He stared at her challengingly.

She was too tired to take him up on that. How a son of hers had turned into such a male chauvinist, she didn't understand.

As he went to get the milk out of the fridge, she said sharply, 'Don't drink from the carton this time.'

He grunted and slammed a glass down on the surface so hard she expected it to shatter.

There was still no sign of Sam by the time the meal had ended, nor had he rung.

He didn't feel like part of the family any more.

★ ★ ★

The next morning Janey felt a lot better about the world because she and Millie had both slept really well in their new flat, right through the night. There were supposed to be some neighbours, but she hadn't seen anyone else nor had she heard a sound from the flat above hers or the one on the same floor.

She yawned and stretched, then crept out of the bedroom while her daughter was still sleeping and made herself a cup of tea.

After they'd both had breakfast, she made a careful list of the things she needed and went to check out the supermarkets properly, looking at all the specials before she made her choice. She came back with two loaded bags of shopping dangling from the sides of the buggy and a few big things in the tray underneath.

Carrots were two bags for the price of one, so she'd be eating a lot of carrots during the coming week. That was all right. Carrots were healthy. When she thought how fussy she'd been about eating before she left home she cringed, then smiled ruefully. Her dad only liked steak, chops or sausages with his nightly chips, so that was what they had.

At the *Just Girls* hostel, taking her turn to help in the kitchen, Janey had discovered that she enjoyed cooking, though she didn't know many recipes yet. She intended to learn more about cooking now she was on her own. It'd be something new to do and you could get books on it from the library and copy down recipes, so it needn't cost anything extra.

She left Millie in the buggy at the foot of the stairs with the front door locked, as she rushed up to the flat with the shopping. She only put away the frozen stuff because she felt so guilty at leaving the baby on her own in the hall. But how else did you get the shopping into the flat when you were going out straight away?

There was washing to do but she couldn't face it yet, so went down again and gave Millie a smacking big kiss on her fat, soft cheek. 'Shall we go for a walk?' She decided the gurgle meant yes. They both loved being out of doors and luckily it was fine today, if rather cold.

She thought she heard a door click shut upstairs and wondered if someone had been watching her.

She decided to explore her own street first, remembering the elegant old lady who had stopped to stare at her yesterday then walked on up the slope. Did someone like that live in Peppercorn Street too?

The street was about three hundred metres long, and went from rather shabby near the high street to marginally better where Janey's flat was situated, about a hundred yards away from the shops. She was surprised at how posh the houses were at the upper end and stopped several times to admire the older ones. Lovely, they were, with coloured glass in the doors and in the small windows on either side, fancy brickwork and big gardens behind low stone walls.

It would be nice to learn more about the history of architecture. She'd put that on her list when she got back. She was making a list of things she could learn about from the library, both to fill the time without costing anything and because she didn't want Millie looking down on her when she got older for knowing so little. As a result of getting pregnant she hadn't even been able to take her A levels.

She found that the street was a cul-de-sac, which was why it was fairly quiet, except for cars parking at the lower end and moving off after their owners had done their shopping.

She nearly missed the narrow path for pedestrians between the two top houses, then went back to peer down it. Curious to know where it led, she went along it. There was just enough room for someone on foot to pass the buggy. Two buggies would have had trouble squeezing past one another.

Halfway along someone had dropped a garish takeaway box, so she picked it up and put it into the litter bin at the end. There, that was better. The path looked pretty again. It had a low wall at the far end, where it curved to the right and opened out into another street, and surely those were daffodils poking up along its base? They'd look lovely against the grey, stone wall when they came into bloom.

The next street wasn't a cul-de-sac, but it also had a footpath between the houses at the top of the slope, so she followed that rather than going back down to High Street. This second path led to a small park at the end of the next street. Great! She and Millie could come here in the warmer weather. It'd be nice to walk under leafy green trees and look at flowers. Maybe there'd be a children's playground. She explored the park, which didn't take long, and sure enough there were a few swings in one corner, including baby swings. She thought Millie would be old enough to sit in one by summer.

Beyond the park was an area with one or two parked cars and a big gate at one end. Over it a sign said 'Grove Allotments. Owners only'. She went across to peer over the gate at the rows of neat plots, though there wasn't a lot growing in them at this time of year, of course. Some parts were covered in straw or a sort of matting, probably to protect the last remaining vegetables from frost.

Her granddad had always grown his own vegetables and she'd helped him from when she was little. He'd been dead for five years now but she still remembered how much she'd enjoyed gardening with him and how delicious the fresh fruit and vegetables had tasted. During the past year or two, she'd grown a few things in her parents' garden. Her dad hated gardening, hated anything that made him get out of his armchair after he got home from work.

An old man was working on one of the plots. He smiled and raised his hand in greeting, just like her granddad used to do. After a moment's hesitation, she waved back. You had to be careful who you spoke to these days, but he looked friendly and unthreatening, and he was quite old and scrawny, not really a threat to her because she was tall and quite strong, had been good at sport. That was another thing she missed.

Don't go there! she told herself firmly.

Turning, she walked back towards her street, wondering what to do with herself for the rest of the day. Washing, of course. There was always washing when you had a baby. She'd had to do a lot of it by hand because there was only one washing machine in the B&B, and times for its use were restricted. In the new flats there was a proper laundry room with two coin-in-the-slot washing machines and two separate tumble dryers, also some washing lines out at the back. That was luxury to her. Not that she'd be using the tumble dryers except in an emergency. Far too expensive.

There must be another woman in the flats because this morning there had been some women's clothes hanging outside, but Janey still hadn't seen anyone else going in and out.

Washing wouldn't take up the whole day, though. Nor would playing with Millie, who still slept a lot. Should she go to the meeting at the *Just Girls* shop? No, she couldn't face it yet. It was the time of day when Millie had a nap and she wanted to settle her daughter into a proper routine now. She sighed. Life felt so shut in lately. And boring. She could see why people living on their own got depressed.

The people from *Just Girls* had said they'd try to get her a television. That would help pass the evenings, but she wasn't going to watch it in the daytime like one of her mother's neighbours, who only seemed to be able to talk about the latest TV show.

If things hadn't gone so badly wrong for her, Janey would be at university now, meeting people, going out and having fun. It wasn't fair. It wasn't her fault she'd got pregnant. *He* had forced her.

But then, if it hadn't happened, Millie wouldn't exist. She had to remember that and not let life get her down. She hadn't expected to love her baby so much, given the circumstances.

The sky was darkening already, even though the days were getting longer now. She'd better go back.

She smiled, remembering what her granddad used to say about February: it might be the greyest, coldest month, but its arrival was a sign that spring was round the corner. Perhaps she'd be having a personal spring now that she was more settled, growing in all sorts of new ways.

Oh, she was being fanciful again! Hadn't she vowed to stay practical from now on?

★   ★   ★

Winifred stared out of her bedroom window as a movement caught her eye. The girl with the baby was walking along the footpath pushing the buggy. Definitely too young to be a mother.

Probably no better than she ought to be.

When the girl stopped to pick up some rubbish, however, Winifred got angry at herself for making judgements on no evidence. Whatever her faults, the girl had the right attitude to rubbish in this throwaway age. Most people would have walked past that garish cardboard box. Winifred had lost count of the number of times she'd picked rubbish up from that path.

She finished dusting her bedroom and sorting out her clothes, putting away the washing she'd dried in the kitchen yesterday. Then she made her way slowly and carefully down the stairs. At her age, you didn't dare risk a fall. Two of her friends had broken a hip in falls and one of them hadn't come out of hospital again. Winifred still missed her.

She went into the kitchen and got out the bones and shin beef she'd bought from the butcher that morning. There was nothing like home-made soup to warm you in the winter, and a good soup began with good stock.

She put the radio on to keep herself company then began to chop up an onion, wiping away a tear. It was caused by the onion fumes, she told herself fiercely. She hadn't been brought up to complain about life, however dull and lonely it had become, and she wasn't going to start now.

When the stock was simmering, she took out her diary and began her daily entry. Not that she had anything special to report for herself, though she did mention the girl with the baby moving into the flats and the way she'd jumped to conclusions about her. She also commented regularly

24

on the issues of the times: climate change, pirates at sea, demonstrations, terrorism, the more idiotic celebrities. There'd been a demonstration on the television news the night before. Had these young people nothing better to do than act like hooligans?

There had also been another young man killed in Afghanistan. Why did countries do this to their young men? How many of this generation's young women had lost loved ones in the current war? How many mothers had lost their sons?

She didn't know whether anyone would read her diaries after she was gone, but she'd asked in her will that they be lodged with the local heritage centre. After all, the diaries went right back to her girlhood before World War II, and she'd hardly missed a day in all that time. One day, perhaps, a historian would find them useful. Look at what had happened to the Mass Observation diaries from the War. They'd been turned into some splendid books.

★   ★   ★

Nicole got up early and tackled her husband after he'd had his shower. 'Sam, I'm getting really worried about William.'

'He doesn't look ill to me.'

'He isn't. It's the way he behaves. I thought he was going to hit me yesterday.'

That caught his full attention, which nothing much did these days.

'What! No, he'd never do that. Definitely not. We brought him up properly.'

25

'Since he met these new friends, he seems to have forgotten all we ever taught him. He's turning into a proper chauvinist. *Our son! A chauvinist!*'

Sam sighed. 'Give it a break. You're always on about women's lib. We're past that now.'

She stared at him indignantly. What was he talking about? She hadn't mentioned it for years because it always led to a row.

'William's just going through a bad patch,' Sam said soothingly. 'He'll grow out of it. Now, I have to get off to work.' And he was gone before she could stop him. He hadn't even bothered with breakfast today and he was usually ravenous in the mornings.

★ ★ ★

Dan Shackleton left his allotment at four o'clock on the dot, as usual. He called at the care home on the way back, to see his wife. He always did this, even though she no longer recognised him.

Peggy was going downhill fast now. Dementia was a dreadful thing. It tore families apart and stole the very personality from those who had it. She'd been such a lovely woman, kind and fun. Now she had a blank face that belonged to a stranger.

His sons thought he should still be looking after her at home. There had been a few arguments about that when he announced that he was putting her into care. They conveniently forgot that he was seventy, had his own health problems and had looked after their mother for much longer than his doctor thought wise.

26

He sat by the bed for a while, but Peggy didn't move, didn't look at him. He'd given up trying to talk to her. She didn't respond.

'Mr Shackleton? Could I have a word, please?'

'Yes, of course.'

He followed Matron into her office. She got him a cup of the horrible tea from the machine in the corridor and said in a gentle voice, 'I'm afraid it won't be long now.'

'I realise that.'

'Is your phone number still the same?'

'Yes.'

'We haven't got a mobile number listed.'

'I haven't got one.'

'Perhaps you'd better buy one, since you're out all day.'

'I'll give you my son Simon's number. He still lives in Sexton Bassett. My other son moved away. Simon can fetch me from the allotment if . . . ' He couldn't say the words. 'If I'm needed suddenly. I'm there till teatime every day, rain or shine.'

'You can buy a basic mobile quite cheaply these days, you know.'

'I'm not walking round like a dog on the end of a leash.' He realised he'd spoken aggressively and took a deep breath. 'Sorry. It's just . . . one of my little foibles. I don't like mobile phones.' Couldn't stand them, actually, but people looked at you strangely if you got vehement about the damned things.

'Very well.' She stood up, mouth a thin line of suppressed annoyance.

He sat in his car for a while, trying to calm

down. His heart was fluttering in a way that always upset him and made him feel precarious.

Eventually he drove home, hating to go into the dark, empty house. He went about his duties according to the routine he'd worked out. It was washing day. After he'd put a load on, he checked the fridge to see what was needed when he went shopping the next day. He didn't do housework in the daytime, but went to his little hut at the allotment as soon as it was light. He had a gas ring there to make tea or heat up soup, he could chat to anyone who turned up, and it was a rare day when he didn't see two or three people. He did whatever jobs were needed on the allotment, read the newspaper, listened to the radio.

Only there did he feel as if his world was still normal.

He suddenly remembered the girl he'd seen looking over the gate. Pretty little thing. No, not little. She was quite tall. But young. Even the police looked young to him these days. Was she the mother of that baby? She'd looked at him uncertainly when he smiled at her, and it had taken her a few seconds to smile back and return his wave.

What had happened to make the poor kid so wary? He couldn't imagine anyone being afraid of a skinny old chap like himself.

* * *

Nicole admitted to herself that she was starting to dread going home and that made her angry.

28

What she was really dreading was another encounter with William.

As she walked into the kitchen she caught him drinking directly from the milk carton, something she'd forbidden him to do several times. She hesitated, then anger took over and she surprised them both by rushing across the kitchen and snatching it from his hand.

'How many times do I have to tell you not to do that? It's a filthy habit.' She started pouring the milk down the sink.

'Let me finish it off, then. You're just wasting it.' He tried to grab it from her and the milk splashed the front of her blouse, so she shoved him away hard. As he staggered back with a shocked look, the final dregs glugged out.

'I'll do that every time I catch you drinking from the carton,' she snapped. 'The rest of us don't want to share your germs, thank you very much. And by the way, we now have no milk to put in our tea and coffee because I forgot to buy some, so you'll have to have it black, unless you care to get off your backside and cycle down to the shop.'

'No.' He turned to leave the kitchen.

'Wait! Have you emptied the dishwasher yet?'

'No. And I'm not going to. How are you going to make me?'

Once again the moment was fraught and he looked so ready for battle, she didn't dare challenge him further. 'Clearly I'm not able to make you,' she said wearily. 'But I'm not doing it for you.' She picked up her handbag and hurried out of the house.

'What about our tea?' he shouted after her.

'You keep claiming you're grown-up now. Act like it. Feed your bloody self!'

She bumped into Sam on the way out and yelled, 'They're your sons as well as mine. *You* deal with them!'

'Not again. Do you have to have these confrontations all the time?'

'Unless you want to live in a filthy pigsty, yes. And I'd appreciate a little support from you.'

'I'm tired, Nicole. I just want to rest.'

'Well, poor you! I'm not tired after being on my feet all day, am I?'

He turned away. It was too much. She yelled after him, 'I've had it with the lot of you. Feed yourselves or go hungry.' She got into her car and drove away.

She went to her usual refuge, the open space down by the ruins of the abbey. It was a beautiful place in summer, but rather spooky at dusk in winter, with bare trees scratching the sky around it. There was no one else nearby, so she locked the car doors carefully then let herself weep.

Since Sam had started his new job, he'd become very withdrawn. He stayed out late at night and said he was working. As if. No one worked till midnight.

She'd smelt perfume on him more than once. He said she was being ridiculous and how could he do anything if the receptionist wore a lot of perfume?

Of all the lame excuses, that took the cake.

He was unhappy at work, she knew, but he couldn't leave until he found a new job, not if they were to continue paying off the mortgage. The trouble was, he wouldn't even look for another job, said he couldn't face writing all those applications again.

He didn't touch her in bed and when he did come home early, spent most of the evening staring into space. He didn't help her in the house like he used to, either, not unless she nagged him.

And since he'd stopped helping, so had William. Paul was still doing his chores and hadn't defied her openly but he rarely said a word. Where were the two little boys she'd loved so much? How had they turned into these aliens?

What the hell did her family think she was? Their unpaid servant? She had to do something about that! Only what?

It wasn't the first time the idea of leaving home had occurred to her. She might actually move away, just for a few months, to give them a shock, bring them to their senses.

This was the first time she'd contemplated it seriously.

Only where would she go? How would the family manage without her?

How would she cope on her own?

When she got home, she slept in the spare bedroom. And Sam didn't come to look for her or ask what the matter was. That hurt so much.

★ ★ ★

The following morning Nicole got up, stared at the mess in the kitchen, which no one had bothered to clear up, and got ready for work in grim silence. She was out of the house before anyone else came down. She'd buy breakfast for herself in a local café.

Because she was angry at Sam for behaving as irresponsibly as the boys, she'd made no provision for their breakfast or lunch, and she didn't intend to make tea for them, either, not unless they started helping in the house. Let them manage for a bit without her shopping and cleaning for them! If that didn't bring them to their senses, nothing would.

And then what would she do?

Her shift finished at midday and she sat in the staffroom, staring into a mug of coffee, wondering what to do with herself for the afternoon. She wasn't going back and clearing up that pigsty. No way. She left a message on Sam's mobile to say he must come home on time tonight. She needed his support. Strange that he wasn't answering.

Her friend and colleague Helen came in, took one look at her and sat down beside her. 'Something's wrong. You're usually off as soon as your shift ends.'

Nicole nodded, tried to speak and gulped back tears.

'Look, why don't you come back to my place for lunch and tell me about it? I can offer you some true gourmet fare — sandwiches and tinned soup.'

When she walked into Helen's neat little flat, Nicole sat down and stared at her hands, trying not to cry.

32

'Tell me.'

She looked at her friend and began to sob as she told her what was happening. 'If I had somewhere to go, I'd leave them to it. I've had enough.'

'You don't mean that.'

'I do. I'm not going to spend my life like this. Sam hardly seems to notice I'm alive and the boys look at me so scornfully, you'd think I had an IQ of minus 10. Families are supposed to care about one another but mine's unravelling fast.'

'I didn't realise it was so bad. Look, you can come here in an emergency, but the flat isn't large enough for long-term dual occupancy, I'm afraid.'

'I'd not do that to you, Helen. I know how you value your privacy.'

'Well yes, I do. You're one of the few people whose company I enjoy. At fifty-eight I've given up pretending to be a social animal. I'm definitely a loner.'

Silence fell and Nicole tried to laugh as something occurred to her, but failed and another sob escaped instead. 'Amazing what a small thing it takes to push you over the edge, isn't it? A carton of milk, dammit. It ought to be something more important than that, don't you think?'

Helen reached across to squeeze her hand sympathetically. 'When I split up from Frank, it was shoe polish on the new carpet that was the final straw. But trouble had been brewing for a while. And it has with you, I think.'

She sighed. 'Yes. Things have been going downhill for a year or two.'

* ★ ★

William got home from school a bit later than usual. He stopped just inside the kitchen to stare round in annoyance. He'd been expecting to see his mother cooking tea, but she hadn't even cleared up the mess. He opened the fridge, his hand already reaching out for the carton of milk, then jerking back. There was no milk in the fridge door. In fact, there wasn't much food in the fridge at all.

His brother Paul came home shortly afterwards, looked at the kitchen and said, 'Isn't Mum back yet? She was supposed to be on early shift roster.'

'Not a sign of her. She must be working extra hours.'

'Well, I need to get something to eat quickly. I've got a rehearsal tonight.'

'Be my guest.' William gestured towards the fridge. 'There's sod all in it, though.'

'Mum's a bit edgy lately, isn't she?'

'Yeah. Must be her age.'

'You should have emptied the dishwasher yesterday. It was your turn.'

'I'm not into women's work and I'm not going to get into it, either, not when the world is full of unliberated chicks itching to do things for me.' He smirked at the thought of one particular chick. 'Anyway, Dad doesn't do much either. He's wised up, I reckon.'

Paul rolled his eyes. 'Heaven preserve me from arrogant shits who think the world is there to wait on them hand and foot!'

34

'I didn't see you volunteering to empty the dishwasher.'

'I did it when it was my turn. I'm not doing yours.'

'I've heard women go strange when they get older. She went ape about the milk yesterday. Tipped all of it down the sink.'

'I don't blame her. I don't like it, either, when you drink from the carton.'

'Whose side are you on?'

'My own.' Paul went to the freezer. 'Oh, sod it! We've run out of bread, too. Now what am I going to eat?' He went to the pantry and peered inside. 'Tins of fruit, tins of soup, tins of baked beans.'

'If you're making something to eat, make me something too.'

'Get it yourself.'

'I'm older and bigger than you. Do it.'

Paul shrugged. 'Nope. You can beat me in a fight but you still can't make me wait on you. I'm not a member of the William Gainsford Fan Club.' He found an apple, a chunk of cheese and opened a tin of baked beans, scarfing down the lot.

He was about to leave for rehearsal when their father came home and stared at the mess, not moving for so long that Paul looked at his brother, who shrugged.

'Isn't your mother back?' their dad asked at last. 'Did she say she was going to be late?'

'No, she didn't. I'm off to rehearsal, Dad. Don't forget to pick me up afterwards.'

'All right.'

Paul watched his dad rub his head, as if it was aching again, then walk upstairs without saying anything. On an afterthought he scribbled a note about needing to be picked up from rehearsal and stuck it prominently on the fridge where his mother would see it. His dad had been very forgetful lately.

William called, 'Hey, Dad. We're out of bread and milk, and Mum's not got anything in for tea.'

'She'll bring something home with her. She always does.'

Then his parents' bedroom door closed and there was silence, punctuated by a groan of relief from his father and the creaking of the bed as he lay down.

Paul shook his head, feeling really worried about his dad's behaviour, then caught sight of the clock and rushed out.

★　★　★

Nicole spent the rest of the afternoon at the cinema, because it had started to rain. She didn't get much benefit from the film because she kept getting lost in her own thoughts.

When she came out, it was getting dark, but at least the rain had stopped. She walked slowly home, stopping to gaze in the estate agent's window: *Flat to rent. Two bedrooms, Peppercorn Street, partly furnished.* She lingered for a moment or two, reading the details, dreaming of somewhere of her own, a peaceful orderly home where no one upset you. If only — no, she couldn't do it to them. It was just an escapist fantasy.

36

She continued along High Street to her end of town, stopped outside the house, took a deep breath and went in.

Not only had they not cleared up, they'd added to the mess, not even putting their crockery in the sink. Taking her favourite beaker, which no one else was supposed to use, she washed it out carefully and made a cup of coffee. She didn't feel at all hungry.

Footsteps thumped down the stairs. William. She could always tell.

He stopped in the doorway to look at her warily. 'Oh, there you are, Mum. What's for tea?'

'Nothing. I'm not cooking in this mess.'

'Huh?' He looked around as if searching for something. 'You usually go shopping on your afternoon off. We've not got much food left.'

'You didn't feel like helping round the house yesterday. Today I don't feel like shopping.' She went across, flipped open the dishwasher door and stood very still for a moment to hold in the anger. 'This hasn't been emptied yet. We'll be running out of clean crockery soon.'

'But what about tea? I'm famished.'

'What about it? I can't cook in a pigsty.' She left him standing with that sulky expression on his face that said he knew he was in the wrong but wasn't going to back down. But at least he hadn't threatened her today. Perhaps he realised he'd stepped over the line there.

In the bedroom she found Sam lying on the bed.

He sat up, looking dazed. 'Sorry. I must have fallen asleep. Did you work extra hours?'

'No. I just didn't want to come home. Comfy, are you?'

'I had a headache.'

'And did you have a headache last night too?'

'Come again?'

'No one cleared up the kitchen. And you didn't support me with the boys. William's still refusing to lift a finger.'

'Give it a break!'

'I am. A complete break. I am not doing all the clearing up after you three.'

'You always have done before.'

'More fool me. And actually, you used to help around the house quite a lot. You've hardly lifted a finger lately.'

'Since I got this job, I'm too tired with all the commuting.'

She glared at him. 'Has it escaped your notice that I work full-time too?'

'You've got an easy job compared to mine.'

'So I suddenly became the housemaid as well? No, thank you. Didn't apply for the job and I'm not being conscripted.' She began to tidy one of her drawers, not sure what to do next.

'Look, we'll get a takeaway tonight.'

'Not till that kitchen's cleared up, we won't. If you and the boys don't do that, I'm going out for a meal somewhere clean.'

He got up off the bed, frowning at her. 'Where? Maybe we could all go.'

'You lot have got clearing up to do at home.'

'Well, if you're going out, Paul needs picking up from rehearsal.'

'Glad you remembered. Don't forget to do it.'

She ran down the stairs, expecting Sam to call after her, say he'd organise the clear-up, but he didn't. She drove off slowly, tears blurring her eyes and making the street look surreal.

She didn't know what to do, where to go, just that she couldn't bear to stay in. Surely, surely, they'd clear up now?

The only thing she was certain about was that she wasn't going to touch the mess. She'd reached her sticking point. If she didn't stand firm, she'd lose all self-respect.

She was not only tired of what was happening at home, she was bone tired, period, and desperately needed a break.

She wandered round the shopping centre buying a snack for herself from a café, a piece of rather stale gâteau. Feeling defiant, she bought a glass of wine too. Why not? One small glass wouldn't put her over the limit.

Not until it was nearly time for the shopping centre to close did she go home.

Sam looked at her reproachfully as she announced that she'd be sleeping in the spare bedroom again.

'That isn't necessary.'

'I think it is necessary until we sort this out. I'm angry at all of you. And I'm not giving in.'

The boys rolled their eyes at one another but said nothing. They didn't go into the kitchen, though, just up to bed.

Sam went straight to bed as well.

She lay on the hard bed in the spare bedroom and cried into the pillow.

The kitchen stayed dirty the following

morning. Sam must have bought some bread and milk the night before when he picked Paul up from rehearsal, but at the rate her sons ate, they'd soon run out of butter and jam.

William gave her a sneering smile before he left, gestured to the mess and said, 'The earth hasn't fallen in, has it?'

She was still gasping with indignation at his insolence as the door slammed behind him.

Sam had already left.

How long could this continue? Would she manage to hold out against them? Should she just give in and do the minimum? After all, boys of William's age were noted for their macho behaviour.

No! She'd never forgive herself if she gave in. A saying someone had shared with her years ago popped into her mind: *If you want people to walk all over you, just lie down and become a doormat.*

She wasn't going to do that.

3

One of Millie's cheeks was bright red again and she winced when Janey put a spoonful of food in her mouth. When Janey put her to bed on Wednesday night, she didn't settle for ages. Then, at two-fourteen exactly, she began crying loudly. Janey jerked awake, terrified the noise would disturb the other tenants. She tried everything she knew to comfort her baby, but Millie refused to be comforted.

The hours of the night seemed to pass very slowly with darkness outside shutting her into a tiny, fraught world. Millie alternated her bouts of crying with shallow sleep, during which she whimpered and moved restlessly. Janey was so worried about her she didn't dare go to sleep.

There were gels you could rub on a baby's gums to help the pain, she knew, but she couldn't afford them unless a doctor gave her a prescription. She had trouble managing on social benefits without needing to buy extras, though she was better than she used to be.

She'd have to take Millie to the doctor's when they opened, just in case it was something more serious than teething. Pam had pointed out a medical centre just off High Street and said they had an excellent health visitor who also ran the Child Health Clinic. Surely they'd let her see a doctor without an appointment if Millie was still unwell?

Just before nine, Janey bundled her daughter up warmly and put her in the buggy, worried because the poor little thing was still crying, though in an exhausted way now. She hurried down High Street to what she thought was the turn-off, relieved when she saw the medical centre ahead, because she was so tired she wasn't sure she'd remembered it correctly.

Inside she tried to explain to the receptionist what she wanted, but Millie suddenly started screaming so loudly it was hard to hear what the woman was saying.

'I'm sorry. She's been crying like this for half the night.' Janey tried to disentangle her daughter from the buggy to give her a cuddle, but had trouble with the fastenings.

'Here. Let me help you. I'll deal with the baby. You bring the buggy through.'

Janey stepped back, soothed by the calm voice. Capable hands soon undid the safety straps.

Millie was soothed too, because she stopped screaming as soon as the stranger picked her up.

The woman led the way into a consulting room to one side. 'My name's Sally Makepeace. I'm a nurse and I'm the health visitor for the practice. Good thing I was here to help you today. She's in a right old state, isn't she? And you look exhausted. Been up all night?'

'Yes. She's teething, I think, but she's never been like this before and I'm worried sick. She's been crying since two o'clock this morning.' And it wouldn't take much more to make Janey cry too.

'I haven't seen you here before, have I? Are

you registered here?'

'Not yet. I've just moved to the area and my social worker, Pam Foster, suggested I come here. I don't know if she's sent the paperwork on yet.' She took a deep breath and steeled herself because she hated explaining this. 'I've just turned eighteen and I'm on my own, because my parents threw me out when I got pregnant. I moved into a flat in Peppercorn Street this week.'

'What about the child's father? Does he help you?'

'I don't talk about him, not to anyone.'

Sally's voice became gentler. 'That bad, was he?'

'Worse.'

'Well, if you ever want to talk . . . '

'I don't. Not about him, anyway.' She didn't dare. He'd threatened her if she revealed who he was, what he'd done.

Millie began to cry loudly again.

'Let's look at the poor little thing. The tooth is nearly through but her gums are very swollen. Some babies have it harder than others when they're teething. Do you have any soothing gel?'

Janey could feel her cheeks burning. 'No. I can't afford it without a prescription. I'm not extravagant but it's really hard to manage on benefits as well as setting up a home.'

'Don't your parents help you *at all*?'

She had to swallow hard before she could say it. 'They walk past me in the street as if I'm a stranger.' She felt comforted when the nurse laid a hand on her arm for a few seconds.

'That must be hard.'

'Yes. But I couldn't give my baby away like they wanted. And I'm getting better at managing, though I do worry about Millie. I've never had anything to do with babies before, you see. There weren't any others in our family. I've read some books about babies and *Just Girls* is helping me. I stayed in their hostel after Millie was born and they've given me a cot and all sorts of bits and pieces for the flat.'

'They're great. Look, I'll come and visit you, if that's OK, to see if you and Millie need anything else. I'm here to help, not criticise, so look on me as your support system in emergencies not an enemy. Right?'

Janey nodded. She trusted Sally instinctively, was relieved to have someone to turn to.

'Will you be at home tomorrow morning' — Sally consulted a list — 'say about eleven o'clock?'

'Yes. I take Millie out for walks in the mornings when it's fine, but we can just as easily go out in the afternoon.'

'Walks are good. You both need to get plenty of fresh air and exercise. And did they tell you about the meetings at *Just Girls*? You should go. You need to make some friends.'

'I will once I've settled in.'

Sally opened a cupboard and got out a sample of gel. 'Let's rub some on her gums now. If that doesn't do it, we'll give her some baby paracetamol. Can you wait here till this takes effect? There's a room you can sit in.'

'I'll do whatever's best for Millie.'

'Good. And I've got a great book about babies

44

that I give to new mothers. Want a copy?'

'Yes, please.' Janey was well aware that she was being observed and checked out, as well as Millie, in case she was a bad mother but she was cool about that. She didn't think she was doing too badly, actually. But just occasionally, when Millie cried on and on, she felt a failure or at best, a fumbling amateur.

Best of all, she left the clinic with a number to ring if she needed help outside working hours. It was such a relief to know she'd have someone to turn to if she was worried about Millie during the night.

It started raining as she was walking home, but strangely that seemed to soothe Millie rather than upset her and Janey didn't care if she got wet now that the screaming had stopped.

When she got back to the flats, she saw that someone else was moving in. She stood in the car park watching with interest as a scowling man with a pronounced limp opened the front door to two removal men, who at once started carrying his possessions into the ground floor flat underneath hers.

He had a lot more things than she did, that was certain, and what looked like a computer. How she envied him that!

She went into the building, intending to introduce herself to him, but after one quick nod to her and Millie, he started talking to the men again, so she left him to it. She carried Millie upstairs first and as she was opening the door, one of the removal men dumped the buggy on the landing with a grin.

'There you are, love.'

Even that small act of kindness made her feel weepy.

She hoped the flats were better soundproofed than the B&B had been. Millie could cry very loudly.

She'd not seen anyone around yet and if it hadn't been for that washing on the lines at the back, she'd have thought she was the only one here. The car park had remained empty, though that was nothing to go by because she had a parking bay too, only she didn't have a vehicle to put in it.

Please Millie, she prayed as she put her daughter down in the cot, *don't wake the man below tonight or he'll think we're the neighbours from hell.*

When her daughter fell asleep, Janey lay down on the bed nearby. She was so worn out she could feel herself falling asleep and didn't fight it.

★ ★ ★

During her lunch hour, Nicole went for a walk along High Street. She hadn't intended to succumb to temptation, but found herself stopping outside the estate agent's to read the *To Let* notices again. The flat was still being advertised. No, what was she thinking of? She already had a home. You couldn't just walk out on your family, however tempted you were.

She glanced at her watch and took a sudden decision to go and see whether the mess in the kitchen had been touched at all, because she'd been worrying about it all morning. If they'd just left it, she'd ask to see the flat. Just to have a look at it, see what you could get for your money. She kept dreaming of peace and it'd give her a threat to hold over their heads.

Surely Sam would have done something, at least? He couldn't just have gone to work and left the kitchen like that, with rubbish overflowing from the bin. And surely he'd said something to the boys about pulling their weight in future, as she'd asked him to do?

The house was empty and the dirty dishes in the kitchen had been shuffled around a bit, but nothing had been washed. The rubbish bin was still overflowing and the dishwasher hadn't been emptied, though there were a few gaps inside it where clean items had been taken out.

She walked round the ground floor, fighting tears, then stopped in shock in the living room. Her favourite ornament, which normally graced the window sill, lay in shards on the hearth. The little figurine had been all right when she left for work. It could only have got broken so badly by being hurled across the room.

She went across to look more closely. It had belonged to her grandmother and she'd counted it as one of her treasures. There were too many small pieces for it to be mended. It looked — as if someone had ground it under foot.

Surely not?

She backed away, not touching it.

William or Sam?

Without remembering leaving the house or

walking back along High Street, she found herself going into the estate agent's.

'You're advertising a flat to rent in Peppercorn Street.' She was pleased at how steady her voice was. 'I'd like to see it. Straight away, if possible.'

★　★　★

Winifred was glad it wasn't raining on Friday morning because she enjoyed her stroll down to the shops in fine weather. Today she needed her wheelie shopping bag, which she didn't really like using. It seemed to shout 'old age, infirmity'. But it was necessary for hauling back her heavier shopping. She also took her library books to change.

After she'd bought some food, she went to the library, looking forward to a chat with Nicole, who was such a nice young woman and was very good at finding new authors for her.

But today Nicole was looking wan and unhappy, clearly not in the mood to chat, so Winifred had to do the best she could to find some new authors herself. She saw a big sign on the noticeboard for the Golden Oldies Club, which Nicole kept asking her to join, but she wasn't the joining sort, never had been. She never knew what to say to strangers. The fairies who'd presided over her birth hadn't included the gift of small talk.

On the way back she saw a notice in the window of a charity shop that there was a book sale on, hesitated and went in. She didn't like using these places, knew her mother would have

48

disapproved of 'dirty' books, but was desperate for some more reading material. Sometimes she ran out of new books before she could get to the library.

To her delight she found shelves of romance novels on offer cheaply at four for a pound, tatty and worn but perfectly readable. She bought a dozen and had trouble balancing the carry bag on top of her loaded shopping bag.

'Shall I tie this on for you, dear?' the woman behind the counter said, smiling cheerfully.

Winifred hated being called 'dear' by complete strangers, but she understood that sometimes, as now, it was done with the best of intentions. 'Yes, please. I have a ten-minute walk to get home.'

'Look, I finish here in five minutes. If you like, I could drive you home, then you could choose even more books, if you wanted.'

This offer was so unexpected Winifred couldn't hide her surprise.

The woman smiled again. 'My mum has trouble carrying stuff home too. I take her shopping every week for the big stuff.'

'But you don't even know where I live!'

'If it's a ten-minute walk, it'll only be two minutes by car. No trouble to me.'

'Oh. Well, that'd be very kind of you, very kind indeed. I live in Peppercorn Street.'

'Oh, that's easy to find.'

'Thank you. I do miss being able to drive, but my eyesight isn't good enough nowadays. And I *will* buy some more books, in that case. Most kind.'

'There's a chair in the corner, if you want to

sit down. My name's Dawn, by the way.'

Winifred introduced herself but was too busy choosing books to sit. She indulged in a perfect orgy of book-buying, and all for a ridiculously small amount of money.

Her new acquaintance stopped the car outside the house. 'Do you live here? Lucky you. I've often admired this house and been glad it hasn't been converted into flats. Some of those developers are philistines and ruin beautiful old buildings, even if they don't knock them down. Come on, I'll help you carry your bags inside. You did go mad on the books, didn't you? You must read a lot.'

'It's my favourite pastime.'

When they were inside the house, Winifred nerved herself to ask, 'Would you, um, like a cup of tea?'

'Not today. I have to get on. But maybe another day, if you'd like some company? I could bring Mum round with me. She'd enjoy a little outing. Her best friend just died and she's lonely, poor thing. But I'll perfectly understand if you don't want to . . . ' She let the words trail away.

Winifred realised what Dawn was really asking and for once she let go of her mother's deeply inculcated training to keep one's feelings to oneself and said in a rush, 'That'd be lovely. I've just lost my best friend, too. How about Monday afternoon? Or Tuesday? Any day, really.'

'Monday, then. About three?' Dawn left with a cheery wave.

When she'd gone Winifred sat down on one of the kitchen chairs. What had she been thinking to invite complete strangers to tea? Accepting pity, that's what. Only . . . Dawn said her mother was also lonely, so that was probably why she'd made the offer.

Was it possible to make new friends at the age of eighty-four? Winifred took a deep breath and nodded to her reflection in the mirror. She was going to try. She really was.

She must work out in advance what to talk about, though. She was hopeless at thinking of things to say on the spur of the moment. And she would bake a cake, a chocolate cake. That at least she was good at.

She'd spent more than she'd intended on books, but it wasn't a lot really, considering, and she now had three whole bags of new romances to read.

She washed the dishes after tea, standing looking out at her back garden as the light began to fade, her pleasure diminishing slightly. What would her visitors think of such a messy garden?

But she didn't dare try to do any tidying up herself. Last time she'd made an effort to do any serious gardening she'd been in so much pain afterwards, hardly able to move, that she'd had to call the doctor out, then rest in bed for a few days. He'd talked about calling in a social worker to help her but she'd refused point-blank, terrified they'd try to get her into one of those care homes for the elderly. She'd kill herself first.

No, the garden would just have to stay a mess.

And her visitors would have to take tea in the kitchen because nowhere else in the house was warm enough.

Would that matter? Her mother would have thought so, but then her mother had always had fires blazing in each room and help with the housework.

* * *

Janey watched the old lady from the big house walk slowly past, going into town with a wheeled shopping bag. She always looked elegant in an old-fashioned way, her silver hair carefully knotted in a low bun, a severe style which suited her face, and her clothes immaculate, if a trifle old-fashioned.

She was so lucky to live in the big house at the posh end of the street, the one with the biggest garden. Janey had peeped over the wall as she walked along the path to the park. There was even a summer house in the back, rather dilapidated, but she supposed an old person couldn't keep up with the maintenance. Perhaps the owner wasn't as rich as she seemed.

If it was fine this afternoon, Janey decided, she'd wrap Millie up and go out for a nice long walk, but this morning she had the health visitor coming to see her, and check her out, no doubt. She walked round the flat, making sure everything was tidy and clean. She couldn't do much about the shabbiness of her second-hand furniture.

When the doorbell rang she pressed the button and invited the health visitor up.

'They should have found you a ground floor flat,' Sally said.

'I was lucky to get this one. I'd had my three months at the *Just Girls* hostel and Millie was making herself very unpopular at the temporary B&B.'

'Well, the flat's bigger than most, I will say, and they haven't spoilt the outside of the building. This must have been a lovely house in its prime.' Sally plumped to her knees beside Millie, who was lying on the blanket kicking and gurgling. 'She looks a lot happier today.'

'The tooth's through. I noticed it this morning when the spoon clinked.'

'Little minx! Did you keep your mummy awake?' Millie kicked even harder, panting happily in response to this attention. Sally smiled as she stood up. 'Do you mind showing me round? I might be able to help you get some bits and pieces.'

When she'd finished inspecting everything, she said, 'I think a playpen would be useful at this stage, then you could pop her in it while you carry up your shopping and the buggy.'

'Yes. But playpens are a bit expensive.'

'I know where we can borrow one, but you'll have to look after it and give it back when she grows out of it.'

'That'd be marvellous.' Maybe Sally really was here to help, not criticise. 'Would you like a cup of tea? I don't have any coffee, I'm afraid.'

'I'd love one.'

It was comforting to sit and chat about looking after Millie and by the time the health visitor left, Janey was feeling much better, less alone.

* * *

Nicole inspected the flat very carefully. It was partly furnished with reasonable furniture and had two bedrooms plus a decent bathroom. There was a nice large sitting room and a separate kitchen and eating area just off it, in an L-shape, so it didn't feel cramped. It looked out on to the street so she wouldn't feel shut away.

'I'll take it.'

The woman who'd shown her round beamed. 'Excellent. I'm sure you won't regret it. Shall we go back to the office and complete the paperwork?'

'Yes. I'll have to ring work first to tell them I'll be late.'

'Where do you work?'

'I'm a librarian.'

'Oh, excellent. Nice, steady job, that.'

Helen answered the phone at the library and for a moment Nicole couldn't speak, then she said it out loud. 'It's me. I'm going to be late back, I'm afraid. I'm moving out of home so I've just rented a flat. I've got to sort out the paperwork.'

There was silence, then, 'Your husband and sons haven't started being more co-operative, then?'

'No. Not one of them has lifted a finger for days, not even Sam.'

'I'm so sorry.'

'I am too. See you soon.' Nicole closed her phone and slipped it into her handbag, surprised that she'd managed the call without bursting

54

into tears. Well, she was beyond tears now. Everything felt very unreal, though.

She walked back to the estate agent's office, handed over her credit card with a steady hand and took away a folder of paperwork on what she must and must not do as a tenant.

When she got into work, Helen gave her a sympathetic look. 'You all right?'

'Yes. I feel quite calm now that I've made my decision. Trouble is, I can't move in until Monday.'

'Pity. How shall you cope over the weekend?'

'I'll go out a lot. Can you manage the desk for a few minutes while I organise a day's emergency leave for Monday?'

She marched into the head librarian's office and said, 'Michael, I'm leaving my husband on Monday and I have to move into my new flat. I'll need a day's emergency leave.' She waited for him to grumble.

He looked at her in shock, then said gruffly, 'I'm sorry. Do you . . . um, need any more time off than that?'

'No, I'll be all right with just one day.'

'How are you moving your things?'

'I've not thought about that yet.'

'You could borrow my van if you like. You're licensed to drive a bigger vehicle, aren't you? Or I could nip down and help you carry your stuff.'

Michael usually kept himself to himself and this offer surprised her. She must have shown that.

He added in a rather tight voice, 'I left my wife a couple of years ago. I know what it's like.'

55

'Thanks. I'll not trouble you, though. I'll check out removal firms who do small loads — I'm not taking much — and then get back to you if I need any help. And . . . well, thank you for offering.'

'If you don't mind me saying so, I'd advise you to take everything you can lay your hands on, or you may never see it again.'

It was then she realised she'd been half counting on this being a temporary move — and it might not be. She nodded quickly and went into the ladies till she'd overcome a sudden tendency to weep.

4

Her boss's advice made Nicole start mentally revising the list she'd been making of what she'd take with her. What couldn't she bear to lose? That was the main decider.

As the day passed, however, the white heat of her outrage at her family's behaviour cooled and she began to wonder if she could actually do it, leave home, leave her sons and husband. *Should* she do it, morally?

If she changed her mind about the flat, could she get her deposit money back? Probably not. And anyway, her sons seemed to have rejected her, which made her feel very sad.

She desperately needed a breathing space, time to think what she wanted from life — and from her marriage. Besides, the boys would be leaving home in a year or two. What would she and Sam do with themselves then?

In a sudden resurgence of anger at herself for dithering, she found a removal firm online and rang up to book them for Monday morning at ten o'clock for a small load.

But she felt very apprehensive when she went home that night, worried about what she would find, what she would say to her family, how she would manage to keep her secret.

She needn't have got her knickers in such a twist. The house was empty.

There were signs that the boys had come and

57

gone, but the dirty dishes had only been shuffled around. Presumably they'd been rinsing what they needed for each meal. The overflowing rubbish bin was beginning to smell foul so she decided she'd have to empty that, at least, for her own health's sake.

When she looked into the fridge she found it almost bare, except for a carton of milk and a loaf. She stood with the door open for ages, staring into it, then realised what she was doing and slammed the door shut.

Only then did she see the note on the kitchen table. Paul's writing.

Dad phoned. He's going to be late. Got a meeting.
Me and William have gone for a pizza.
Paul

She wondered briefly where they'd got the money for a pizza, but supposed their father must have given it to them. She felt so hurt and upset by her husband's complete betrayal of her in all her roles — as wife, as mother, as partner — that she had to fold her arms round herself to hold the pain in.

In the end she went out again, buying herself some fruit, salad and cheese, plus a huge roll of rubbish bin liners to pack her things in for the move. When she got back, she cleared a corner of the kitchen table and made a salad sandwich, then washed the rest of the lettuce and tomatoes and bundled them in plastic bags, taking her food up to the spare bedroom. If she turned off

58

the radiator in there, they'd last the weekend. She wasn't very hungry anyway.

Then she went into the master bedroom, which already felt like Sam's territory, not hers, and began her preparations by going through her clothes in the walk-in wardrobe. She hung the ones she wanted to take at one side and moved her underwear out of the lower drawers into the spare bedroom.

After that, since the others still hadn't come home, she walked round the house, looking at the smaller pieces of furniture, deciding what to take with her. The laptop, of course. Just let Sam complain about that! The second television from the conservatory, which the boys used as their den and where she was no longer welcome. How had that happened when she'd been the one who'd wanted a conservatory from which to enjoy the garden she tended so lovingly?

By the time the boys got home she'd finished her lists and was making herself another cup of tea.

They took one look at the mess in the kitchen, exchanged glances and edged towards the door.

'Just a minute, you two. I want to know who broke my ornament.'

More glances, then Paul said, 'Dad did it. He's been behaving a bit weirdly, actually, ever since . . . ' He hesitated.

'Since *you* opted out of doing your job,' William finished for him.

'I've opted out of being the only one to do any housework,' she corrected. 'I'm quite prepared to do my share of it.'

'Well, don't look at me. I'm definitely not domesticated.' He pushed past his brother and clumped up the stairs.

Paul hesitated. 'Mum — can't we . . . sort this out?'

'You mean go back to how it was, with me doing more and more of the housework and you three doing less and less? No. Definitely not. If you mean everyone taking a share, then I'm very open to that.'

He shifted uncomfortably. 'I can't get the others to talk about it. I'm not doing William's share, though. Mum . . . did you know he's in serious trouble at school, been suspended?'

'What?'

'They called Dad in yesterday to see the school principal and counsellor. Dad said not to bother you about it and he'd sort it, but I think you ought to know.'

'What's William been doing?'

'Bullying.'

She felt sick to think of a son of hers behaving like that. 'Does he bully you, too?'

'He tries to. I usually manage to keep him away. Mum . . . can't you talk to him?'

'He doesn't listen to me any more. Now I come to think of it, he's been trying to bully me as well. I thought he was going to hit me the other day.'

Paul gasped and looked at her in dismay. Then he shook his head helplessly and slouched off. He didn't offer to help clear up the kitchen, though. He might be talking to her, but he wasn't prepared to make that gesture — and he was probably right in one sense. It wouldn't make any difference to William. Her elder son had not only grown a lot physically during the past year, he'd changed, turned into a bully, at home as well as at school.

It upset her to leave the mess, but she did.

She had no idea where Sam was or when he'd be back. She couldn't imagine a meeting at work going on so long. In the end she went to bed and lay down, waking with a start some time later.

What had woken her? Glancing at the bedside clock, she saw it was just after midnight. A car door banged outside and there was the sound of a key in the front door. Whoever it was had trouble fitting the key in the lock and that didn't sound like Sam. She tiptoed out on to the landing and looked down, ready to call the boys if it was an intruder.

But it was Sam. He reeled into the hall, weaving to and fro, bumping into the wall, clearly very drunk. Had he driven home like that? He must have done. And yet he'd been strongly against drink-driving ever since she'd known him.

Feeling as if nothing else was left to unravel in her life, she went back to bed, placing a chair under the door handle in case he tried to come in. Wine had always made him amorous in the past.

But this time he made no attempt to find her. The only explanation she could think of was that he was being unfaithful and had already made love that evening.

That thought stiffened her resolution, which

had been wavering. She was definitely doing the right thing in moving out. There was no reason for her to stay here any longer.

Only why did it feel so wrong? Why did it hurt so much?

★ ★ ★

Going for walks not only helped pass the time but the baby loved being out and about. Saturday afternoon was sunny, so mild that Janey lingered in the park and then strolled on to the allotments. She stopped once again to stare enviously over the gate. Come spring, she would enjoy looking at the vegetables, seeing them ripen.

In fact . . . she might put her name down for an allotment and grow her own vegetables. It'd not only save money but give her something to do which she enjoyed. There was probably a huge waiting list, though. A lot of people wanted to grow their own food these days.

She saw the same old man come out of his hut on one of the big central plots and when he waved to her, she waved back without hesitation.

As he began walking towards her, she stiffened then told herself not to be silly. She and her daughter were quite safe here in the open. If you got paranoid about safety, you'd never do anything interesting. He was probably lonely.

So was she.

He stayed on the other side of the big gate, hands thrust deep into the baggy pockets of a well-worn casual jacket. He was close enough to look into the pram and smile at Millie, who gurgled at him and waved her hands around. 'What a bonny baby! Must be a girl. What's her name?'

'Millie.'

'Short for Millicent?'

'Yes. It was my grandma's name.'

'I had a cousin called Millie once. I'm Dan Shackleton, by the way.'

'Janey.' She didn't give him her surname and he didn't comment on that, thank goodness.

'Not much for you to see here at this time of year.'

'How soon will you be doing the spring planting? I'm looking forward to seeing what everyone grows.'

'I don't start my first plantings till early March, whatever the seed packets say. Like gardening, do you?'

'I used to help my granddad in his garden. I loved it. I still miss him.' Her mother had complained about her getting dirty, putting up with it only because her granddad insisted and because he gave her vegetables.

Janey realised Mr Shackleton was waiting patiently for her to say something. 'Um, is there a long waiting list for allotments, do you know? I was wondering if I could get one. It'd be fun to look after and it might save money to grow my own food.'

'I'm afraid there's a long waiting list, because these are statutory allotments and the council can't use the land for anything else. Some allotments are temporary, just there for a few years till the land is needed. These have been here since the year dot, so we can plant trees and shrubs and know it won't be wasted effort.'

'I didn't know about the different sorts of allotments.'

'Not many people do. People lost interest in gardening for a while, but they're coming back to it, my goodness they are. Nothing tastes as good as your own vegetables. I've had my plot for nearly twenty years, got two fruit trees on it. If you're still here in the autumn, I'll give you a bag of apples. They won't look pretty but they'll taste better than the ones you get in the shops.'

'That'd be great.'

'Still, you might as well put your name down for an allotment. That costs nothing and you'll come to the top of the list one day, if you stay around long enough.'

At that moment a pair of police officers came strolling along the street towards them. Janey tensed as she did every time she saw a policeman now, but these two were fresh-faced, pleasant-looking. She couldn't imagine them bullying anyone.

They stopped beside her and looked at her companion, which made her feel anxious. Did they not trust Mr Shackleton? Had she put herself and Millie in danger by talking to someone the police kept an eye on?

The female officer smiled at them both in turn, then turned back to the old man. 'All set for the spring planting, Mr S?'

'I certainly am. I've been studying the seed catalogues and I'm about to send off my orders.

Meet Janey and Millie. They're new to the area.'

'Settled in Sexton Bassett, have you?'

'Yes. Me and Millie have moved into a flat on Peppercorn Street.'

'In that building that's just been renovated?'

'Yes.'

'That'll be convenient for town, with a baby. She's a pretty one. Well, must get on. I'll see you around. Community policing means a lot of walking. I've lost pounds since it came in.'

As they walked off, Mr Shackleton said, 'I knew Katie when she was a little lass coming to the allotments with her grandpop. He's dead now, poor fellow, didn't make old bones, and she's a woman grown. Look . . . do you trust me enough to stop and have a cup of tea with me? I'm quite harmless, I promise you, even though I am known to the police.'

He laughed at his own mild joke and Janey smiled with him, but was grateful that he understood her wariness.

'We can sit outside on my bench — it's on the sunny, sheltered side of the hut — and Phil's working down the bottom end of the allotments, so you'll be quite safe.'

Still she hesitated. Stopping for a quick word was one thing, sitting drinking tea was a much bigger step — for her anyway. She wasn't sure she fully trusted any man after what had happened to her, but surely she'd be quite safe sitting outside on the bench? 'Thank you. I'd love a cup of tea.'

'Good.' He beamed at her and opened the gate, then led the way across to his hut. 'It won't take long to boil the kettle on my gas ring. Would the little 'un like a biscuit? Is she old enough for them?'

'Not quite. I've got some rusks. She's teething and loves to gum them. It'll keep her busy for ages.'

Millie remained in a sunny mood, charming Mr Shackleton with her smiles, chewing the rusk happily. She only smeared it over the bottom half of her face, which was tidy eating for her, and she managed to get quite a bit of it down. Janey pulled out a sippy cup to give her a drink of water.

Mr Shackleton brought out a folding table on which he placed a teapot and two mugs next to the packet of biscuits. Then he brought out a milk carton and sugar in a plastic container. 'I'd rather do things properly when I have a guest. My wife always used to have very high standards when she set a table for guests. Only I don't keep china sugar bowls and milk jugs here. No room to store them, you see.'

'The tea will taste just as good.' He'd spoken of his wife in the past tense, she noticed. 'I hope you don't mind me asking, but is your wife dead?' His face grew so sad she wished she hadn't spoken.

'Peggy's in a home. Dementia. The poor love doesn't even recognise me now.'

'I'm sorry.'

'Yeah. Me too. I miss her something shocking. Fifty years we'll have been married next month. We'd such plans for celebrating it.'

'Do you have children?'

He nodded. 'Two sons, but one lives in Reading,

so I don't see much of him and his family. The other lives here in Sexton Bassett so I see him more often. Both of them are doing well: fancy houses, wives working, holidays abroad, children at private schools. But they never seem to have time to stop and chat.'

She nodded, but she didn't really know how it was for people who had money, lived in fancy houses and had big four-wheel drives. She saw them sometimes as she walked along the posh end of the street, but they didn't even notice her. Her mother worked in a shop and her father worked on an assembly line. They'd always had to be careful with money in order to buy their own house and have enough left for her father's beer.

They weren't loving people and had shouted at her all through her childhood for the slightest thing. She wasn't going to become a misery like them with her daughter, she'd promised herself that.

Taking a sip of tea, she changed the subject. 'What are you going to plant this year, Mr Shackleton?'

'The usual. Carrots always do well, peas, beans, cabbages, lettuce — and a few flowers, just because they look pretty. My Peggy used to love flowers. See that rose bush? It might look like a few thorny sticks now but it'll be a mass of pink flowers come the warmer weather.'

Janey let him talk, enjoying sitting in the sun which had no warmth but was bright and cheerful. She was always happy to learn more about gardening.

Millie dozed for a while, then woke up

squirming uncomfortably. Janey knew the signs. 'I'd better go now. She needs changing. Thanks for the tea. You make a good cup.'

'Stop by any time you're passing. I've always got a cuppa for a friend. Oh, just a minute.' He vanished inside the hut then came back with a cabbage, which he gave her. 'One of my own. Still good eating once you take the outer leaves off.'

'I wasn't hinting for you to give me food.'

He grinned. 'I know that. I can tell a cadger a mile off. I only give my stuff away to people I like. You take it, love.'

The cabbage was huge. Janey didn't particularly like cabbage but free vegetables were a big help when you had to watch every penny and she'd read somewhere that you could use cabbage in stir fries and salads. She'd have to borrow a cookery book from the library or buy one in a charity shop. 'Thanks.'

She felt quite optimistic as she walked back. Perhaps it wouldn't be bad living here if the locals were so friendly. Perhaps she might even make some friends her own age. She'd go to the next meeting at *Just Girls*, see what the others were like, at least.

★ ★ ★

On Sunday, Janey got up early, did all the housework and washing then found it was still only nine o'clock. She heard church bells pealing and stopped to listen. Should she go to church? Why not? She'd been brought up to attend regularly, but hadn't gone for a while, not after

68

her oh-so-Christian parents had abandoned her in her time of need.

She wasn't quite sure what she believed these days but suddenly there seemed something very comforting about a church service. And anyway, it'd get her out of the flat and somewhere with other people.

She'd noticed a small church just off High Street in the other direction from the library. It didn't seem quite as threatening as the ancient parish church, which sat squarely in the heart of the town and had a leaflet all to itself in the pile from the library.

The small church had a plain board outside that said in red letters on white, 'All are welcome in God's house'.

Would she and Millie be welcome? Would anyone even notice their presence?

She wasn't sure about doing this, but the thought of spending the whole day on her own decided her. She desperately needed to be among people. If going to church didn't work out, she'd only lose an hour or so. But you had to try everything you could till you made a new life for yourself, they'd emphasised that all the time in the discussion groups at the hostel.

She decided to get there a little early and suss the place out, see where she could sit with the buggy, ready to make a quick escape if Millie started to cry.

But as she walked through the gate and up the path, a woman minister opened the double entrance doors and smiled at her as she fastened them back.

'I've not seen you here before, have I?'

'No. We've . . . um, just moved into town.' She gestured towards the buggy.

'Then I'm happy to welcome you and your baby to our church.' She looked down at Millie who was drowsy, ready for a nap. 'We have a crèche for the morning service. Would you be happy to leave your baby in it?'

'I didn't realise.'

The minister leant closer, still smiling, and said in a low voice, 'It's probably sexist to say so, but I've children of my own, so I do understand from experience how hard it is for a mother to get time to worship in peace.'

Janey let out a sigh of relief. 'That'd be great.'

'I'm Louise, by the way.' She turned and beckoned to someone. 'A new customer for the crèche, Barbara.'

An older woman with a grandmotherly air beamed at Janey. 'How lovely! Oh, what a pretty baby! What's her name? Millie. I love that name. And you're . . . Janey. Well, come and see our facilities, dear. They aren't fancy but they're bright and clean.'

There was a little side room, with a tiny baby lying fast asleep in a buggy, its face pink and peaceful.

'He belongs to Marcie, who does the flowers,' Louise said.

Barbara came closer, touching Janey on the arm, which made her realise how rarely anyone touched her now, except for Millie, of course.

'I used to be a children's nurse, so your baby will be quite safe with me, dear.'

'That's wonderful.' Janey explained about Millie's needs then went back into the church. Just to sit on her own was wonderful. She could feel herself relaxing and enjoyed watching others file in. There were more people attending than she'd expected, which suggested that the church was quite popular. And everyone who sat nearby smiled and nodded at her.

She really did feel welcome here. That realisation brought tears to her eyes.

When the service started she joined in the first hymn, mumbling awkwardly at first, then getting used to singing aloud again. She'd once wanted to be in the school choir, but her parents hadn't liked the thought of her staying late at school and 'getting up to mischief'.

At the end of the service she slipped out to get Millie and thank Barbara for looking after her daughter.

'She was no trouble, slept most of the time. You could get a coffee before you leave, chat to a few people. I'll still be here.'

But she didn't feel confident enough to do that in a group of complete strangers, so smiled and said, 'Another time, perhaps.'

Another woman came in just then and picked up the tiny baby. 'Has he been good?'

'As good as gold.'

'They always are for you. Thanks, Barbara. My husband's useless if Thomas starts crying, so it's blissful to be free for an hour. I've changed all the flowers and I'll be in on Tuesday to see to them.' She smiled and nodded to Janey. 'You're new here, aren't you? I hope you enjoyed the

71

service. We're a friendly lot, so do come back.'

Janey walked home feeling happy. Perhaps she wouldn't be so lonely after all? Perhaps she could find a few friends here and there. That'd make so much difference to her life.

★ ★ ★

On Sunday morning, Winifred's nephew rang. 'I'm back in England a bit earlier than I'd expected. How are you keeping, Auntie Win?'

'I'm fine, Bradley.'

'I thought you might like a little trip out to the garden centre this morning.'

'I'd love that.'

'I'll pick you up in about half an hour, then. And afterwards you can tell me if you've anything that needs fixing. Think about it.'

Pleased at the thought of an outing, she went to get ready and waited in the front room so that she could see his car arrive and not keep him waiting. He was a busy person but he did make an effort to see her every time he came back to England.

But it was two hours before he arrived and when she asked him what had delayed him, he looked at her in puzzlement. 'I told you two hours.'

'No, you said half an hour.'

'You're getting a bit forgetful. Doesn't matter. I won't tell anyone. You're looking better than last time. You've stopped trying to do the gardening now, I hope?'

'Yes.' She waved a hand at the front of the

house. 'Can't you tell?'

'The house is too much for you.'

'Please don't start that again. I shan't change my mind about moving.'

As he started his car, he hesitated then said, 'I've met someone new.'

'Oh? You mean a woman?'

'Yes. We're going to move in together.'

She didn't approve of the way young people lived together without being married, but she didn't say that. Who cared what old people thought about the world anyway?

'Can I bring my new lady round to introduce you? I think you'll like her.'

'Of course you can.'

They had a pleasant half-hour at the garden centre and she bought herself a new house plant, but she could see that Bradley was getting a bit impatient by then. Well, he had no real interest in gardening. Suppressing a sigh, she suggested they go home. 'I'm sure you'll be ready for a piece of cake now.'

He brightened. 'I'm always ready for a piece of your cake, Auntie Win. What sort is it this time?'

She wished he wouldn't talk to her in that tone, jollying her along sometimes as if she was a child. She didn't say that. At least he came to see her.

Bradley ate a huge piece of her walnut cake but Winifred wasn't hungry. She was still thinking about all the beautiful plants she'd seen so briefly and wishing there had been time to see more.

When he'd finished eating, he looked out at

the garden and shook his head. 'I'm not going to have time to do anything this break, but next time I'm in England I'll find someone to sort out your garden. Maybe we should have some of it paved, or covered with gravel. What do you think?'

She hated gravel and searched her mind for a reason not to have it. 'Not gravel. It's a bit chancy to walk on. I don't want to risk a fall at my age.'

He repaired a drawer handle that was loose, frowned at her fridge and suggested buying a new one.

'Oh, I think that one will do me for a while yet.'

'You don't want to risk it shorting out and starting a fire. Old appliances can be dangerous.'

'This one's never given me any trouble.'

He wasn't fooled. 'Not got enough money to spare for a new one?'

'Stocks and shares haven't been doing very well lately, so I have to be a bit careful. What do they call it? Asset rich and cash poor?'

'Your stocks will rise again. Don't rush to sell them, give them a year or two. I'm sitting on mine, keeping a careful eye on the stock market. And the offer's still there. I'll manage your stocks for you if you want.'

'Oh, I think I'm doing all right. I enjoy keeping an eye on the prices in the newspaper.' She didn't say the other obvious thing: she might not have a year or two left. She tried always to stay cheerful and positive, especially when Bradley was around. So many old people

74

moaned and complained.

That was one of the reasons she didn't enjoy going to meetings for the elderly. She didn't like being called 'aged' or 'elderly' either. People talked about *care of the aged* as if no older people could look after themselves, and *the burden of the elderly* as if they were all a cost to the taxpayer. She could care for herself, thank you very much.

She waved Bradley goodbye with a smile on her face, but leaned against the door when she went inside, feeling suddenly very much alone. Still, she might make a new friend. Oh, she did hope it would work out with Dawn's mother!

She had a lot to be thankful for, really. Her health, most of all. Without that you couldn't do much with your life.

She frowned, quite certain Bradley had said half an hour. He was the one who'd forgotten, not her. This had happened before and he'd insisted she'd forgotten what he said, but she knew she hadn't.

In fact, she didn't look forward to his visits nearly as much these days. They always seemed to leave her doubting herself.

5

On Monday Nicole waited impatiently for Sam to leave for work. She was up by six, but he didn't go till half past seven, which seemed a long time to wait. He gave Nicole a reproachful look when he met her on the landing, but didn't say anything. If he'd just spoken . . . tried to communicate . . . But he'd left it to her to make the first overture, as usual. She wasn't going to do that this time.

Once he'd driven away, she had a quick shower in the en suite, which further strengthened her resolve. Did Sam never put anything away these days? He hadn't even rinsed away the toothpaste he'd spat out.

She packed everything from the spare bedroom, but didn't dare start elsewhere until she was alone.

A short time later the boys went clattering downstairs and she could smell toast. Sam had bought a loaf, butter and jam yesterday. He and the boys seemed to be living off bread and jam, plus takeaway pizzas. She refused to feel guilty about that.

''Bye, Mum.'

Tears came into her eyes as Paul yelled goodbye — the only one to do so. She'd always been closer to her younger son, try as she might to love them both equally. He'd been such a sunny-natured baby, while William had been

76

a colicky infant, crying a lot.

As soon as they'd gone, Nicole went into the master bedroom and began to pack frenziedly, praying her lists were well enough thought out. She'd already written a note to Sam, telling him she was going away for a few weeks to think about things. It had taken her several attempts to write it. One note had been spoilt by tears. She hadn't even realised she was crying until the paper blistered. Her final effort was the best she could manage but still didn't express all she wanted to say.

She debated jotting down her mobile phone number at the bottom, but didn't. He should know it well enough by now! He used to call her on it quite often during the day, but hadn't done that for months.

She was terrified William would come home while she was packing, because he'd skipped school a few times. No, why should he do that so soon after getting into trouble? Even he would have more sense. She stuffed clothes and other items into rubbish bags any old how. If they needed ironing she could do that later. She was taking the iron because she was the only one who used it.

The pile of bags mounted up in the sitting room, where the fragments of broken ornament were still scattered across the hearth, a reminder to her and, she hoped, to them of why she was leaving.

She moved the smaller pieces of furniture she was taking into the hall and dining room, making sure she had the list handy for the bigger things she couldn't manage on her own. She was taking the computer desk and bookcases, as well as her favourite armchair and all her books. No one else in her family seemed to do much reading and she didn't want to lose her collection of favourite books.

When the doorbell rang at quarter to ten she jerked round in shock. Had one of the boys come home? Or Sam? What would she say to them?

But when she opened the door, she found two young guys in jeans and thigh-length overalls with 'Mini-Movers' written in big red letters against the beige twill.

'Mrs Gainsford? We're a bit early. Is that all right?'

'Fine with me.'

They moved her things into the van more quickly than she'd expected and she had to rush out of the house to go and let them into the flat. She'd have to come back to the house to finish off.

The whole move took less than two hours. How could an earth-shattering change happen so quickly?

After the men had gone, she stood in the living room of her new flat, surrounded by piles of bulging bin-liner bags and a jumble of furniture, tears rolling down her cheeks.

When she was a little calmer, she went back to the family house to make a final check, gathering together more of her little treasures, in case those got smashed as well. She tiptoed round, feeling like an intruder in the place that had been her home for nearly twenty years, jumping at every noise.

Working quickly, she went into each room, taking extra small items now, a cushion, another pillow, a Persian rug that had been her grandmother's. She raided the kitchen cupboards systematically, taking spices, herbs, a few of her special jars and tins. It wasn't as if the others were going to be doing any fancy cooking, after all.

As an afterthought she went into the garage and took a few tools: a hammer, screwdriver and some bits and pieces for cleaning the car. She was shocked at how dusty things were there. Sam couldn't have touched his workbench for months, though he'd still been coming out here. What had he been doing? Why had he changed so much?

Carrying the final few things in a bucket, itching now to be away and done with what felt like pillaging, she walked out of the house, nearly jumping out of her skin when she saw her neighbour of ten years looking over the fence.

'Oh, it's you, Nicole. I was just checking. I didn't see your car in the drive and thought you'd be at work. You can't be too careful these days, the number of burglaries there are.'

'I took my car round the side to load things, because . . . I'm leaving.'

Her neighbour's mouth dropped open. 'No! Oh, my goodness, I — '

Nicole didn't linger to explain or discuss it. They weren't close friends, after all. As she put the bucket into the car boot and slammed the lid down, it occurred to her that the reason she wasn't better friends with any of their current neighbours was because Sam didn't like getting too close to them. And lately he'd been avoiding social events altogether, saying he was tired, even with their long-time friends.

He'd not looked well, but had refused point-blank to go and see the doctor so she was helpless to do anything.

Getting into the car, she backed out down the drive. When she hit the gatepost, she yelped in shock and jumped out to inspect the damage. Fortunately she'd been going so slowly there was only a small dent and a scratch. Sam would have gone mad at that. His car was his most treasured possession, a glossy, well-polished beast. She wouldn't bother to get this tiny bit of damage to her car repaired.

She was thoughtful as she drove to her new home. And sad, so very sad. It was as if leaving Sam had opened the lid to problems she'd been avoiding dealing with for a long time. She hadn't stood up for herself as she should have done. Compromise was one thing, giving in to your partner was another thing altogether.

★ ★ ★

Sam was late home that evening. He was sick of meetings and yet more meetings, and beyond reason tired. His head was aching again. It seemed to have been aching on and off for weeks. Perhaps Nicole was right and he should see the doctor, or start taking vitamins . . . or something.

It had been a hell of a day and he'd had to stay behind after the meeting to catch up with an important project that simply couldn't wait because he'd had to go to William's school yet again. Couldn't his damned son stay out of mischief even for one day? That had robbed him of most of the afternoon.

He hadn't passed on the job to Nicole because she'd not been getting on with William lately. His older son seemed to be deliberately looking for trouble, challenging the boundaries in every direction.

And William hadn't been at all repentant after the interview, had offered him only a mouthful of cheek and had been highly reluctant to see the counsellor! Only the threat of a complete withdrawal of his allowance had got him to agree to that. Sam had to make an appointment to see the counsellor, too, but he couldn't do that without his work diary so he'd told them he'd ring later.

For two pins, Sam thought wearily, he'd take off into the wide blue yonder, go somewhere he could be peaceful and quiet, and only spend time with people he really cared about. Families seemed to sap your energy, especially teenagers. And Nicole was too bossy. William was right about that. It wasn't an attractive trait. She'd been much softer when she was young. She'd changed a lot. And why she hadn't done something about the kitchen, he couldn't understand. *She* didn't have to work such long hours.

Paul was in the kitchen, eating a sandwich.

'Is your mother home?' Sam realised he'd not

even noticed whether her car was in the drive.

'No, she's not. Um, Dad — there's an envelope on the mantelpiece.' He pointed.

Sam turned round and saw his name scrawled across it in Nicole's oversized writing. Why would she be writing to him?

He picked it up, staring at it, making no attempt to open it for a few seconds then, suddenly apprehensive, tearing it open.

Sam, I'm leaving. I meant what I said. I've had it with being treated as an unpaid servant by you and the boys.

We seem to have fallen apart as a family and I can't put the pieces together on my own. You don't even seem interested in trying. Perhaps now you're responsible for the boys, you'll make more effort to keep them in order. William doesn't listen to me at all.

I've rented a flat. Get in touch with me when you've decided what you want to do about things.

Nicole

He reread the note with a sick feeling of shock, collapsing on to the nearest chair because his legs had suddenly gone wobbly and his vision had blurred. It had done that a couple of times lately. Stress, he supposed. Well, there couldn't be much that was more stressful than your elder son going off the rails and your wife leaving you.

'Dad?'

He became aware of Paul leaning over him. 'Dad, are you all right?'

'Not really.' He thrust the letter at his son. 'Read that.'

Paul scanned the letter quickly, then read it again more slowly, wishing suddenly that he'd been more supportive of his mother. He didn't want her to go.

He looked at his father for guidance. 'Did you have any idea she was thinking of leaving, Dad? Had you discussed it, splitting up, I mean?'

'No. We've not talked much at all recently. I've been a bit . . . um, busy. Where's William?'

'In his room.'

'Fetch him.'

Paul hesitated then went upstairs and poked his head round the door of William's room.

'Get out!' his brother yelled.

'Something's happened. It's bad. Dad wants to see you.'

'It's probably that thing from school. They've suspended me again, just because I wasn't taking shit from anyone, and they couldn't get Dad to answer his phone.'

'What the hell have you done now?'

William shrugged. 'Refused to listen to that sports teacher who thinks she's a man.'

Paul rather liked the sports teacher, but he knew better than to say that. 'Well, this isn't about you at all. Dad hasn't even looked at the letter from school yet. It's Mum. She's left us.'

William gaped at him then scowled. 'That's all I bloody need.'

Paul didn't wait, but went back down, worried about his father. He felt even more anxious when he saw that his dad's face was chalky white. He hadn't moved, was just sitting in the same place, staring at the floor. He'd been doing a lot of that lately, looking dopey and spaced out. Was he on drugs? No, of course he wasn't. Not Dad. But he didn't look well.

Something was wrong with the whole family. Mum was right about that.

William shoved Paul roughly out of the doorway and he didn't try to shove back because his brother was a lot bigger than he was, and getting more muscular with it. That was because he was taking steroids. Paul had seen them. Stupid twit!

'Dad?'

Paul watched. His dad didn't seem to have heard William, didn't stir, let alone respond.

In the end Paul took the letter out of his dad's hand and passed it to his brother. 'She left a note.' It was eerie that his dad still didn't move.

William read it and threw it on to the table. 'Shit!'

'Is that all you can say?'

'What else is there to say? The bitch has bailed out on us.'

Paul waited for his father to tell William not to speak of their mother like that and when he didn't, found he couldn't let it pass. 'She's not a bitch. And I don't blame her, actually. We've left everything to her. You don't even pick up after yourself.'

'Well, I blame her. She got a family, and it's her job to look after it.' He kicked a chair to one side and it fell over with a clatter.

Paul glanced at his father, but he still didn't move.

'These damned feminists have changed the whole world,' William went on. 'And for the worse. It's up to us men to take charge again.'

'You're just saying what those weirdos tell you. And you're not a man yet. You're still at school.'

His brother looked at himself in the mirror and smirked. He'd been doing that a lot lately, as if pleased with what he saw. 'I'm a man physically. I'm bigger than Dad now. And my friends aren't weirdos. They're *real* men. What they say makes sense.'

'They're thugs — and worse. That's where you've been buying your stuff, isn't it?'

William shot a quick glance at their dad and muttered, 'You keep your big mouth shut about what I do.'

'I have.'

His brother left and Paul wondered what to do next. His dad stood up, but he didn't say anything, just pushed his chair back so violently it fell over on top of the other one. He went upstairs, slamming the bedroom door behind him.

Was that all Dad could do? Hide in his bedroom?

Suddenly Paul wished desperately that Mum was here. This was way too heavy for him to deal with.

He picked up the letter, but it didn't say where she was going. She'd still be working at the library, though. Surely she would? He'd go there and talk to her tomorrow, promise to help more in the house, even if he had to do some of William's share, beg her to come back.

He definitely didn't want to be left alone with his brother, who had that angry look on his face again. As William usually took that out on someone, Paul went upstairs to his bedroom, shooting the bolts he'd fitted inside the door.

But he didn't feel safe there, didn't feel safe anywhere at the moment. His world was falling apart and at fifteen he couldn't manage without at least one parent around. The last few days had shown him that.

What was going to happen to them now? Would his dad snap out of it? Or would his mum come back if he begged her, promised to do more?

★ ★ ★

Nicole felt embarrassed as she went into the library on Tuesday morning. She'd slept badly, unable to settle in a strange place and it had felt weird to wake on her own and get her breakfast without interruptions. She'd put a lot of her possessions away, but there were still a few things to sort out.

Her boss cocked one eyebrow as she walked through the staff room to hang up her coat. 'You all right?'

'I'm fine. I must give you my new address. I'm getting a landline connection but they can't fix that till tomorrow.'

'Good, good.'

Helen demanded much more information and in between customers Nicole gave her a blow-by-blow account of the weekend and the move.

'Want to go out for a meal tonight?' Helen

asked in a lull between customers.

Nicole hesitated. 'Another time, if you don't mind. I'm still getting the flat straight.' And she didn't want to risk meeting anyone she knew and having to tell them. Or worse still, running into Sam.

She went to work at the returns and issuing desk near the entrance and as they were busy, the morning passed quite quickly.

Just before noon she looked up to see William come through the door.

'Isn't that your elder son?' Helen asked.

'Yes.'

'Phew! Storm brewing!'

He stood for a moment, looking big and surly, then cut rudely across the path of an older woman to reach the counter. He glared at his mother. 'I need some money for food — for me and Paul. Twenty pounds will keep us going for a day or two.'

She was so shocked she couldn't speak for a moment or two, then she shook her head. 'Ask your father. He's in charge of household matters now.'

'He was gone by the time I woke up this morning.'

'Well, ask him tonight, then.'

He thumped one clenched fist on the desk, making her jump. 'I'm hungry now and I'm not leaving till you bloody well give me the money!'

She nearly did it, nearly went to fetch money from her purse in the staff area, then she pulled herself together, mentally running over the food supplies she'd left behind. 'There are some beans, tins of fruit, packets of biscuits, enough to keep you going till tonight.'

'I want some proper food. Meat. Eggs. Bacon.' He leant forward. 'And I'm quite prepared to create a scene if you don't give me the money.'

He'd said the wrong thing. She might have fetched him a couple of pounds, but she wasn't going to be bullied. And she certainly wasn't giving him twenty. 'Why aren't you at school?'

'Suspended for a week.'

'But you've only just gone back! What did you do now?'

He shrugged. 'Refused to listen to rubbish from one of the feminist lezzos on the staff.'

'Don't use that word,' she said automatically. 'What did your dad say about that?'

'He didn't even open the letter. And if he had, he'd not have done anything. He hardly says a word about anything these days. I think he's losing it.' William pointed to his head and made a circular motion with his forefinger. Then he thumped the desk again. 'I *need* some money! Give me some!'

'No.'

He swept a pile of books off the desk with such force they scattered across the floor. Customers scattered too, taking refuge behind the book-shelves, since he was between them and the entrance.

When she didn't move, William gave her a nasty grin and reached out for the computer screen, grabbing that.

Instinctively she held on to it to stop him moving it, horrified that her son would behave like this.

He continued to smile, with the sneering confidence of a bully confronting a smaller, weaker person. 'If you don't give me the money, I can easily bust this.'

'And if you do, we'll call in the police,' a voice said near her.

She turned in relief to see her boss standing next to William.

'Your older son? No wonder you left home.'

With a roar of fury, William punched him in the face, knocking him to the ground, glared at his mother and said, 'You've not heard the last of this.' He turned and ran out, shoving another woman aside.

People came rushing up as Michael struggled to his feet.

'Call the police,' he said, holding a tissue someone had given him to his bleeding lip.

Nicole hesitated.

'I know he's your son, but he's big and violent, and he needs bringing up short.'

She realised he was right and made the call.

Two police officers came within minutes. They looked round outside but there was no sign of William, which didn't surprise her. Then they took over Michael's office and interviewed every-one involved in turn.

Nicole felt utterly humiliated by what had happened, but didn't try to minimise what her son had done.

'I should definitely watch your step,' the officer told her. 'He sounds like a very angry young man. Do you think he's — on something?'

'Drugs?' She looked at him in shock.

'Violent mood swings, always needing money, that sort of thing?'

'Yes. He's changed. But I don't see how he could afford drugs. I mean, they're quite expensive, aren't they? I thought it was just, you know, hormones going wild. He's grown so much lately. He's a man physically now.'

'Anything else going wrong?'

'Yes. He's been suspended from school for bullying. Twice. And he was trying to bully me into giving him money today. That's not how we brought him up.'

His voice softened. 'Kids go off the rails sometimes, we don't know why. You could be right. It could just be too much testosterone. But it might be drugs, so bear that in mind. Look, we'll drop by your house a couple of times during the day and see if we can catch him.'

'Um — I'm not there any more. I left home yesterday.'

'Ah. That'll have upset him.'

'Only because he's lost a cook-housekeeper!'

'Do you have your husband's work phone number?'

When she went for her lunch break, she sat numbly in the chair, still unable to believe what had happened. She took out a sandwich and put it away again, bit into an apple, but only ate half before putting that back into her bag as well.

Was William's behaviour her fault for leaving home? No, she didn't think so. He'd been belligerent and rude for a while now, in trouble at school several times during the past year, mixing with a group older than himself outside school, people he never brought home. She'd seen him with them, though.

Should she ring Sam? No, the police were going to do that. She'd just — get on with her own life. Dealing with William was out of her hands now she'd left home, especially now that the police had been called in.

Surely William wouldn't risk coming here again after the police had cautioned him? They were bound to find him soon. He'd have to go home to eat and sleep, after all.

She remembered William's threat suddenly. *You've not heard the last of this.* And shivered.

⋆　⋆　⋆

Janey decided to go to the *Just Girls* group that afternoon. She wouldn't know anyone there because the hostel where she'd stayed at had been on the other side of her hometown, Swindon, but she didn't usually have trouble making friends.

She felt very cut off from her former friends now, though. Having the baby had broken the links. She couldn't get together with them because there were no convenient bus routes and anyway, getting on a bus with a baby and all its gear was not something to be lightly undertaken. She couldn't even email them unless she went into the library or an Internet café. And phone calls from a pay phone cost money, something she didn't have much of.

So she was going to make a huge effort to find new friends.

It was colder today and looked as if it was

going to rain but she still preferred to be out and about so she went for a short walk. Staying in one room all day with not even a television or computer was very depressing.

As she got ready to go out again in the afternoon, she began to feel a bit nervous, wondering what the other girls would be like. How many would there be? Would some of them be intelligent? That sounded snobbish. Was she snobbish? She hoped not. At the hostel several of the girls had spent most of their time goggling at the television and gossiping. They'd talked only of their babies and fashions, the guys they'd known and the television programmes they watched. She'd found that boring.

Outside the shabby shop front with the *Just Girls* sign above it she hesitated, then forced herself to go inside.

Dawn poked her head out of the back. 'Ah, there you are, Janey! I was hoping you'd come today. We have another new girl joining us — well, I hope we do. Come through. Bring the buggy, but there's a step down, so mind how you go.'

She led the way and Janey followed, suddenly remembering a poem she'd once studied:

Into the Valley of Death
Rode the six hundred

Now which poet was that? Oh yes, Tennyson. Only there weren't six hundred here today, just five other girls, three babies of assorted sizes and two toddlers. But she still felt as if she was moving into dangerous territory.

Oh, don't be such a fool! She told herself. *They're only girls like you. Just get on with it.* She forced a smile and moved forward to where Dawn was waiting to introduce her.

The others seemed rather quiet as Dawn tried to get a discussion going, but when she was called away, they talked more freely — about their babies and the way their families were treating them.

'What's it like at your home?' one asked Janey.

'My parents threw me out before Millie was born, so I'm on my own. The council found me a flat.'

'You lucky thing! My mother's driving me mad. She won't let me go out at night unless she approves of where I'm going and who with, and she'll only babysit once a week.'

'It can be lonely living on your own and it's a struggle to make ends meet. I've not got anyone to babysit.'

But she couldn't convince them that her life wasn't a bed of roses.

The other new girl didn't turn up at all.

Janey felt disappointed as she got ready to leave, saw Dawn looking at her thoughtfully and tried to hurry up. But Millie started crying just then and by the time she'd settled her down, Janey was left alone with the older woman.

'You need something to occupy your mind,' Dawn said abruptly.

'I read quite a lot.'

'Not the same. You were doing your A levels when you got pregnant, weren't you? Why didn't you finish the course and take the exams?'

'My parents threw me out and I was too upset to think straight for a while.'

'If I have a word with the local college, will you go back to studying? You ought to be able to get at least one A level this year, perhaps even two.'

Janey stared at her, then surprised herself by bursting into tears, which made Millie start howling again.

Dawn settled her down with a cup of tea. 'What made you cry?'

'There's nothing I'd like more than to go on studying, only what do I do with Millie while I'm at classes and how do I afford the books? My parents wouldn't let me take my computer, so I won't even be able to do assignments properly.'

Dawn patted her shoulder. 'They have a crèche at the college. And we'll look into getting you a computer, perhaps even an Internet connection. Would that make a difference?'

'All the difference in the world.' She chased another of those tears with her crumpled tissue.

'Don't quote me, but those girls today, nice as they are, aren't the most intelligent creatures on this planet. And you're quite bright. Coming here won't be enough for you.'

'They were friendly.'

'Yes, but you're a bird of a different feather. Look, leave it with me. It'll take a week or two to sort it all out, but I'm sure I can manage something.'

'Thanks. It'd mean a lot.' It'd give her hope for a better future, a decent job one day.

So of course she cried her eyes out when she got home. She'd never cried as much in her whole life as she had since she found she was pregnant.

He hadn't had to pay for the mischief he'd caused, but she'd paid dearly. She hated even to think of him. He'd got away scot-free.

6

As three o'clock approached, Winifred became more and more nervous. She looked at the cake, sitting on the fancy glass cake stand with its own lid that had belonged to her grandmother. The cake had turned out well. What was she worrying about? She adjusted one of the teaspoons so that it aligned perfectly with the others.

The doorbell rang at one minute to three o'clock. She nodded approvingly. People should be punctual.

When she opened the door, she found Dawn standing there, together with an older woman very like her daughter, with the same engaging smile.

'Hello, Winifred. Here we are, taking you at your word.'

'It's lovely to see you. Do come in out of that dreadful wind.' She stepped sideways and closed the door quickly. She tried to think what to say next, but to her relief, Dawn took charge of the conversation.

'This is my mother, Hazel Rickard. Mum, this is Winifred Parfitt, who seems to read even more romances than you do.'

As she shook Hazel's hand, Winifred felt it tremble in hers and realised that her guest was also nervous. That made her feel a bit better.

Dawn thrust the bouquet she was carrying into her hostess's hands. 'And this is for you, since it's our first visit to your house.'

Winifred looked at it in delight, feeling tears rising in her eyes. 'Oh, how lovely! I can't remember the last time someone gave me flowers.' And it suddenly occurred to her that her nephew never had, though why she should think about that, she didn't know.

'I love flowers,' Hazel said in a softly musical voice. 'My husband always used to buy me some on the first of the month, to start the month well, he said. Now I have to buy my own and it's not the same.'

'I'd forgotten that,' Dawn said. 'Dad was very romantic.' The two visitors smiled sadly at one another.

Winifred waited till they turned their attention back to her. 'We'd better sit in the kitchen. The house is too big to heat fully, so I only have radiators switched on in the hall and on each landing. That way I can heat the back part of the house properly.'

'Very sensible.'

'Let me take your coats.' The flowers were passed from one to the other as she hung their coats up carefully on the hallstand and led the way into the back room, clutching the bouquet once again.

'Oh, what a lovely view!' Hazel exclaimed. 'Why, you can see right across the park from here. And you have a summer house, too.'

Winifred sighed. 'It used to be white and looked beautiful in the moonlight, but I'm afraid it needs renovating and painting.'

'I don't know how you cope with a big house

like this on your own,' Hazel said.

'I don't cope all that well these days. I've had to let a lot of things go, especially the garden.' She changed the subject. 'Now, let me find a vase for these flowers then I'll put the kettle on.'

But as usual the flowers stood at stiff angles and she looked at them with a sigh. 'I'm not doing them justice. I've never managed to arrange flowers properly. They always defy me.'

'Let me.' Hazel stepped forward and magically the flowers were moved into a soft mass that looked exactly right. 'Change the water every day and don't fill the vase up, just put enough to cover them to an inch above the bottoms of the stems. Flowers don't grow under water, after all.'

'How clever you are! Oh, I shall love having these.'

After that, conversation flourished until Dawn looked at her watch. 'Would you two mind if I leave you now? I've got a meeting to attend then I want to start researching the garden-sharing movement. I don't think you're going to do battle, do you?'

They both smiled at her, then more shyly at each other.

'Mum lives just round the corner, so she'll be all right finding her own way home, Miss Parfitt.'

Winifred saw her younger guest out and returned to the kitchen. 'Shall I make another pot of tea?'

'Oh, yes. I love my cups of tea.' Hazel added hesitantly, 'Do you mind me staying a bit longer? Dawn does like to organise people.'

Winifred didn't pretend to misunderstand the

hidden message. 'I'm very grateful to Dawn for organising this meeting. That is, if *you* don't mind?'

Hazel's lips wobbled for a moment. 'No. I've been very lonely since my best friend died.'

'Me, too.'

'Then let's try each other out.'

Winifred beamed at her. 'What a delightful way to put it!'

Later on, she asked idly, 'What's garden sharing?'

'It's a new thing where people with large gardens let other people use them to grow vegetables and in return they get a share of the produce. I think Dawn said a quarter.'

Winifred stared at her. 'I've never heard of it.'

'Aren't you on the Internet?'

'No. I haven't got a clue about computers.'

'I've watched Dawn use hers, but she's far too busy to teach me properly, so I haven't bought one of my own. She helps a lot of people in this town, but it's a good thing she's got a domesticated husband and her kids have left home. Look, about computers, they're going to run classes for seniors down at the community centre. Why don't we sign up for them?'

Winifred hesitated.

'Go on. We'll attend it together and laugh at each other's mistakes. You have to know about computers these days. They're everywhere.'

'I haven't known how to start. Are they very expensive to buy?'

'Depends what you buy. I think there are cheaper ones. Dawn says she'll help me buy one.

There are funds to get seniors online. She'd help you get one, too, I'm sure.'

Winifred had a lot to think about after Hazel had left, not least that she'd been invited to tea at her new friend's house in two days' time.

To crown her wonderful day, her nephew rang and arranged to come round the following morning to introduce her to his new girlfriend. She would be interested to meet the woman, because he'd never introduced her to any of his girlfriends before. No, he called them 'partners' and he seemed to move rapidly from one to another, rarely spending more than a year with each, if that.

Perhaps she'd been doing him an injustice. Perhaps he really did care how she was. None of her other relatives had kept in touch, that was certain.

She did wish he'd settle down, though. It wasn't right, a man of nearly forty acting like a twenty-year-old and going out with 'chicks' as he called them.

* * *

In the late afternoon Nicole saw her younger son come into the library and stand looking round for her. Not more trouble! She felt like ducking behind the nearest set of shelves but that would be cowardly. She wondered why he'd come. Well, he didn't look aggressive, just uncertain and unhappy, so she waved.

His face brightened immediately.

As he came across to her, Helen mouthed, 'All

right?' from the other side of the room.

Nicole nodded then turned to greet Paul.

'I just wanted to check that you're all right,' he said. 'I mean, you must be really upset to have left Dad.'

'Yes. I am. I worry about you, though. Will you be all right?'

'I suppose so. I thought you should know that after I got back from school today, the police came for William and took him away. They said they'd ring Dad.'

'Yes. I told them Sam was in charge now.'

'What did William do? I knew he'd done something as soon as I got in, because he had that look on his face, but he wouldn't say what.'

'He came in here and demanded money, threatened to make a scene if I didn't give it him.'

'And did you?'

'No. So he started throwing books around, then my boss came across and William punched him.'

Paul whistled. 'Wow! He's really gone OTT lately.'

'He's not hurt you, though?'

Paul shrugged. 'I mostly keep out of his way and I'm a bit careful when he's around. Besides, he knows I've not got any money, so there's no point in him going after me.'

She was upset to hear this dispassionate summary of what use William had for his family, but she suspected it was right. 'What does he need money for?'

Paul wriggled uncomfortably.

'Not . . . drugs?'

'Body-building stuff — but it's still not legal. Don't let on that I told you.'

'Oh, no! How's your father taking this police thing?'

'I don't know because he's not back yet. But he's acting really strange, as if he's living life in slow motion. He's worse than he was before, doesn't answer for ages if you ask him a question. And he does a lot of staring into space.'

'I think he's clinically depressed, but you know he won't go and see the doctor. What about food? Are you coping?'

'We've still got some tins left and I can always get some bread in.'

'If you're hungry, come and see me. I can always give you a meal. Only — if I give you my address, will you promise not to tell the other two? Right then, let me find a bit of paper.'

'Don't write it down, just tell me.' He listened and repeated the address after her. 'I know where Peppercorn Street is.'

'If you feel afraid, for any reason, come to me.'

He gave her another solemn nod. He looked both young and old at the same time, but 'together' as kids called it these days. Paul had always been very self-contained and mature for his age. If anyone could cope with the difficult situation, it'd be him.

'I'm a bit upset still,' she admitted, treating him as an equal, 'but when I've settled down, you must come to tea anyway. Just you.'

'I'd like that.' He glanced up at the library clock. 'I'd better go. Dad was planning to take us out for an Indian meal tonight, but I don't know when he and William will be back from the police station, or if we're still going out.'

'Well, if you go, don't waste the leftovers. Take them home.'

He smiled wryly. 'As if there'll be any leftovers with William. He's eating for England.'

As Paul turned to leave, she had to ask again, 'You're sure you'll be all right?'

'Yes. And Mum — keep an eye on your back. William's furious at you, threatening all sorts of things. He'll calm down, but still — watch your step.'

She stared after him in shock, remembering William's parting threat.

★   ★   ★

Janey picked up Millie and went down to check on her washing. To her dismay, the machine had stopped halfway through the cycle and nothing she did would make it move on or let her open the door to take her washing out.

'Has it finished?'

She turned to see her new neighbour from the ground floor. He looked more friendly today. She reckoned he was about forty, from the grey at his temples. And though he was grumpy, she'd guess that was because he was in pain. She didn't feel at all nervous of him, as she did of some men. 'The washing machine seems to have broken down.'

He limped across to look at it, repeating everything she'd tried to make it react, with as little result.

'Damn! I wanted to get this lot finished today.'

'I can't get our clothes out and my baby doesn't have very many.'

'I'll phone the management people.' He dumped his basket of dirty clothes on the floor and went back into his flat. She could hear him speaking on the phone, but couldn't make out the words.

He came back looking annoyed. 'They don't think they can get anyone out to look at it until tomorrow.'

'Oh, no.' She stared at the clothes behind the glass porthole in the washing machine. So near and yet so far.

'We'd better put a sign on it,' he said. 'Or someone may mess it up further. Who else uses this, do you know?'

'I don't know. I've heard sounds from the other flat on my floor and seen a woman's washing on the lines out at the back, but you're the only person I've met face to face. I'm Janey Dobson, by the way, and this is my daughter Millie. We're in the flat above you.'

'Must be hard looking after her on your own.'

'It's worth it. I love her to pieces.'

Just then someone rang the front doorbell and he went to answer it, calling, 'It's for you.'

She went into the hall to see the door of his flat closing and Dawn standing there. Only then did she realise he still hadn't told her his name.

'Is this a bad time?' Dawn asked.

'Only for the washing. The machine's broken down and I can't even get my clothes out of it. They can't send anyone to look at it till tomorrow.'

104

'What a nuisance!'

'It's more than that. Most of Millie's clothes are in there. She was sick a few times during the night, you see.'

'Are you that short of clothes for her?'

She shrugged. 'I manage with as few as I can because she keeps growing out of them.'

Dawn's face took on a thoughtful look and she didn't speak for a moment or two. 'Can we go up to your flat or are you standing guard on your washing?'

The ground floor tenant came limping back just then with a piece of paper.

MACHINE BROKEN
CLOTHES INSIDE BELONG TO NUMBER 3

'You didn't say what your name was,' Janey prompted him.

'Didn't I? Sorry. I get a bit absent-minded with the painkillers. I'm Kieran Jones. And you're Janey and Millie.' He stuck the note to the machine and turned to leave.

What was he on regular painkillers for? she wondered. Was the limp due to an injury?

⋆   ⋆   ⋆

When the two women got up to the flat, Janey put Millie into the playpen, which had proved a godsend. 'Would you like a cup of tea?'

'I'd love one. I've been too busy to get anything since breakfast.'

Millie rolled around a bit, then settled to sleep

in one corner, looking so peaceful that Janey said quietly, 'I think I'll leave her there. She had a disturbed night.'

'She's a well-cared-for child.'

Janey beamed at this compliment.

'You can usually tell when a child's loved.'

'I love her to pieces. She's all I've got now.'

'You have yourself as well. Never forget that. Now, let me tell you why I came. I've been in touch with the people at the college and they'd like to see you to talk about options. I've made an appointment for tomorrow afternoon and provisionally booked a place for Millie in the crèche there.'

Janey couldn't speak for a moment then her voice came out all choked. 'That's . . . wonderful. Just . . . wonderful.'

'Secondly, I've contacted your mother and explained that you're going back to studying. She was rather hesitant, but in the end she decided to let you have your computer back for as long as you stick with the course. If you mess around or fail, you'll have to give the computer back.'

'How on earth did you persuade them about that? My mother might agree but not my father.'

Dawn grinned. 'Oh, I can be pretty persuasive when I set my mind to something, but actually I left persuading your father to her.'

Janey's heart sank. 'He'll say no. He hates me.'

'Surely not?'

'I've always known he didn't care about me. It was my mother who did everything for me and in the house. He just lorded it over us, tossing out orders and doling out the money to her.'

'That must have been hard. But unless they ring me, I'll arrange to have the computer picked up this evening. I'd better strike while the iron's hot. Unfortunately, I'm going to visit a friend for a couple of days, so I'll have to send a courier to fetch it.'

'Won't that cost too much?'

'There's a really cheap courier service that we've used before. I think it's quite important that you get back into studying, not only to give yourself some way of meeting people but for your future. Your life mustn't revolve only round young madam there.'

Janey beamed at her. 'That's so kind of you. Does that mean I can have my computer back tonight?'

'Yes. I presume you won't need any help setting it up?'

'No, thanks. I'm pretty good with computers. I shall miss being on the Internet but there's still a lot you can do with a computer. I can't thank you enough, Dawn.'

'If you get on well with your studies, I think I'll be able to wangle you an Internet connection in a week or two. It'll be a cheapie, download-limited one. We have to stretch the discretionary money as far as we can. Oh, my dear!' She got up and put an arm round Janey. 'Don't cry.'

'I'm only crying because I'm happy. I seem to cry a lot since I had Millie.'

'Have you mentioned that to the health visitor?'

'No.' She wiped her nose. 'It didn't occur to me. I thought all pregnant women cried a lot.'

'That settles down again after you've had the

baby and it's four months now. Tell Sally. She'll understand and find you help, if necessary.'

'It's not as bad as it was.'

'Tell her anyway. Promise me. You've taken on a lot for someone who's only just turned eighteen. I think you're coping brilliantly. Which reminds me.' She fumbled in her bag. 'I forgot to give you this. We missed your birthday but we always try to give our girls a birthday present.' She handed over an envelope.

Janey opened it to find a voucher for a clothing shop on High Street. 'You couldn't have given me anything I'd like better. I've been trying to save up for a pair of smarter jeans.'

'That's great. I've arranged for Margaret to pick you up tomorrow to take you to the college and look after Millie while you do your interview. Luckily it isn't too far away, so it'll be a nice brisk walk for the pair of you each day that you have classes. Now, I really must go.'

Janey went to the window to watch Dawn get into her shabby car and drive away. What a wonderful woman she was! Always busy helping others. Janey's mother and father did nothing for others, and the minimum for their jobs. All her mother seemed to care about was keeping the house immaculately clean and tidy, and her father spent every evening in front of the television, watching sport on cable TV. It never occurred to him that his family might occasionally like to watch something else.

The day grew even better when someone knocked on her door and she found a workman there.

'Fellow from the ground floor flat said that washing in the machine was yours. I just managed to squeeze your repairs in before the end of the day, and it wasn't hard to sort out. It's working fine now. I set it off for you from where it stopped. I hope that was all right?'

'Thanks for letting me know. I'll go down and see how long there is to go.'

It was a bit late to peg the washing out, so when the cycle was over, she knocked on Kieran's door to let him know the washer was free then carried her wet clothes upstairs. She put them on the clothes airer Dawn had found for her. She couldn't afford to pay for the tumble drier.

She looked round the flat. It was beginning to feel like a home now. Thank goodness there had been people to help her! She didn't think she could have managed without her social worker in the early days and *Just Girls* had been wonderful.

When the doorbell rang and a courier brought up her computer, she could hardly speak for joy.

For the first time in months the evening didn't drag. Millie went to sleep without any hassles and Janey was able to set up the computer without any glitches. Her parents had even sent the printer and a spare cartridge. She didn't remember there being a spare cartridge, but it was so long ago, she couldn't be certain of anything.

She'd been sure her father would override what her mother had said about the computer. But maybe if she worked hard and got good grades, she could prove to them that she wasn't a lost cause. Maybe.

7

Dan looked up to see his son threading his way across the allotments, something so unusual at this time of day that his heart sank and he knew at once what the visit meant. He put down his cup and stood up.

For a minute they stared at one another, then Simon said gently, 'It's Mum. She's gone.'

'I knew it wouldn't be long.' Dan sat down, suddenly feeling his heart pitter-patter. 'Give me a minute. Even when you expect it, it's still a shock.'

'They said it was very peaceful.'

He nodded. Peggy had been nothing but peaceful lately, not even the hint of a response to his remarks.

'Shall I drive you over to see her?'

'No. I'd rather not look at her. Perhaps now I can start to remember her as she used to be, so lively and happy. She meant the world to me. And we didn't quite make our golden wedding anniversary, did we?' His voice wavered on the last words and Simon gave him a quick hug.

'We'll go and see a funeral director, shall we? Matron gave me some names.'

'I know who I want to do it. Lawson's. They made a good fist of my mate Andy's funeral. And I know exactly what Peggy wanted.' He saw the surprise on his son's face and added quietly, 'You have to talk about that sort of thing as you

110

get older, you know, because death is inevitable. I'll arrange my own funeral with them afterwards if they do this one well.'

Simon looked at him in alarm. 'You're not ill?'

'Heavens, no. I'm better than I was when I was trying to look after Peggy on my own, actually. It all got a bit much, especially when she turned on me. My heart was playing up just then, but the doctors have pretty much sorted that out now. No, I just want things to be ready for when I go, to spare you and Terry as much as I can.'

The funeral director was quietly sympathetic but it was still painful to explain what sort of funeral Peggy would have wanted and make all the associated choices.

'What about a clergyman?' the undertaker asked when they'd finished dealing with caskets and timing.

Dan frowned. 'I don't know. I've not attended church for a long time.' Not since Peggy developed dementia. He'd had trouble worshipping a god who did that to such a lovely woman. 'I don't want that chap from the parish church, though. He looks down his nose at you if you're not posh enough.'

'What about Tidmas Street Chapel, then? They've got a woman minister and she does a good job, very sensitive, she is. One of my cousins goes there and he thinks the world of her. Of course, you may prefer a man to officiate, in which case — '

'No. We'll give this woman in Tidmas Street a try. If she'll come. Do you have her name and number?'

The undertaker looked at his watch. 'She's usually there at this time of day. Her name's Louise.'

So Dan and Simon set off again, this time going to the small church, which looked more like a village hall than a place of worship. The minister was there, sitting with bowed head at the side. Dan no longer believed in anything much but he instantly preferred this cheerful, homely place to the dim grandeur and heavy columns of stone inside the Gothic church.

Peggy would have preferred it, too.

When Simon had explained what they were there for, Louise touched Dan's arm for a moment. 'I'm truly sorry for your loss, Mr Shackleton. It always hurts. Why don't you come into my office and we'll go through what you want?'

She was quietly respectful, not trying to impose her wishes on them or to persuade Dan to attend her church, which was a huge relief to him.

He was weary beyond measure, so when they left, he said, 'All I want to do now, son, is go home and be quiet.'

'Would you like me to stay with you?'

'Thank you, but no. If you don't mind, I'd like some time to myself.'

'I'll help you clear Mum's things out after it's all over.'

'There's not much left. I knew she wasn't coming back. I couldn't bear to see her clothes in the wardrobe, so I gave them away. I'm keeping her books. I'm not a big reader but every now and then it's good to have something to read, and at least those romances she used to love have happy endings. I don't need miserable stories. That'd not cheer me up. Eeh, she'd laugh to see *me* reading them, wouldn't she?'

He got another hug from his usually undemonstrative son when Simon dropped him off at the allotments. That warmed his heart. He went to lock up his hut and pick up his sandwiches, then walked slowly home. He didn't bother to bring his car here unless he had stuff to carry because he only lived three streets away. He still had the use of his legs, after all, and they said exercise was good for you.

The house was quiet, folding around him in a comforting way. Because it seemed important to mark the occasion, he got himself a glass of whisky and raised it in a silent toast to Peggy's photo. As he sat sipping it, he looked at his lovely young bride and remembered the good life they'd had together until the past three years.

He was glad it was over. He knew she'd not have wanted to linger in that condition.

But the house felt even lonelier tonight. She wasn't even in the same world as him now. He didn't know where she was or even *if* she was still Peggy. He couldn't quite believe that people would be wiped out when they died. It didn't make sense. He preferred the Buddhist view of a series of lives, striving to improve.

Had he done his best with his own life? He hoped so. He'd tried, anyway.

*   *   *

Bradley used his key to walk into the house without knocking, calling, 'It's only me, Auntie!'

Winifred went to meet him, wishing she'd never given him that key. It had only been meant for emergencies. She didn't like him feeling he could just walk in, even less do it when there was someone else with him.

'This is Ebony.'

Ebony was an extremely thin young woman, at least ten years younger than Bradley, dressed in a collection of clothes, one layer on top of another and with hair in a deliberate tangle. How strange!

She shook hands perfunctorily with Winifred but seemed more interested in the house than in her hostess, staring round openly.

When they went into the kitchen, Winifred asked, 'Would you like some tea — and I made a chocolate cake yesterday?'

'That'd be great. All right if I show Ebony round first? She loves old houses.'

Winifred stared at him in shock. 'Um — '

But before she could say no, she didn't want a stranger poking round her house, he'd put an arm round Ebony and led her from the room, shutting the kitchen door firmly on his aunt.

Both puzzled and annoyed, Winifred walked across and opened the door slightly, listening to them as they stood in the hall, discussing the house. *Her* house.

'Of course it's far too big for her,' Bradley said. 'The silly old biddy can't cope. And the garden's a real mess. I'm sure that'll detract from the value.'

114

'Not if they're going to pull the place down. It'll be block value then. This is the only old house left with its original garden. They've subdivided the gardens of all the other old places. This one is so big, it ought to be worth a fortune to developers. Are you the heir?'

'Yes, of course. She told me so years ago and I make sure to keep in well with her. Why?'

'I was just wondering how you'd deal with winding up her affairs, with you working offshore like you do. My firm could help. We specialise in maximising the profit on big old properties and deceased estates.'

'I'll remember that when the time comes. Let me show you upstairs and the attics. Goodness knows what she's got up there. It's not been cleared out for yonks. Pack rats have nothing on old Win.'

'You should get expert advice when you do clear it. You don't want to overlook any valuable antiques.'

Their voices faded as they went up the stairs and Winifred went back into the kitchen, shutting the door quietly behind her and leaning against it for a moment. She felt shattered by what she'd heard. How could Bradley bring *that woman* here and talk about — what had they called it — maximising the profit of a deceased estate? Was this Ebony creature really his new girlfriend or was she an estate agent come to check the place out? Or was she a gold-digger who'd seen that he might inherit the place one day?

But he wouldn't inherit now. Even a 'silly old

biddy' still got a choice of who she left her possessions to.

Pride gave Winifred the strength to smile at them when they came back down and listen to their comments on her home. The cheek of it! But when Bradley again urged her to buy a smaller retirement home, offering to deal with the money side of things for her, saying she'd probably have a little left over from selling this place, she cut him off short, feeling sick inside at the realisation that he was trying to swindle her as well.

'I've told you before, Bradley. This is my home and I'm staying here till I die.'

Ebony spoke to her gently, in the tones you might use to a halfwit. 'You may not be able to look after yourself one day, Miss Parfitt. Surely it'd be better to plan accordingly?'

The hidden Winifred nearly took over then, the one who'd been kept firmly in check for most of her life but who peeped out occasionally. What she'd have liked to say was: 'Oh, I've planned it all right. I've got a sharp knife and I've studied how to slit my veins.' She'd love to shock them rigid.

But it would be unwise, might give them ammunition to claim that she wasn't competent to manage her own affairs. It was her fallback plan, though. She didn't intend to go into a care home — or even buy a retirement villa. Her mother had lived to ninety-seven, in reasonable health until the last couple of years, so it was not unreasonable to hope Winifred might enjoy a few more years in her own home.

She'd suddenly had enough of them, enough of pretending. 'Well, if you've finished, I'll put the cake away. I don't want it drying out.'

Bradley made a show of looking at his watch. 'And we must be leaving. Sorry to rush, but we've an appointment to see a flat. We're moving in together, you see.' He gave his new love a fond look and she gave him a cool smile as she patted his cheek.

After Winifred had showed them out, she watched through the window as they stood talking outside for several minutes. In a rush, indeed!

Ebony pointed to this and that, doing most of the talking. Bradley kept nodding thoughtfully. She was sure they were still making plans for what they would do with her house. Well, that young woman was going to be disappointed. Very.

And so was Bradley.

She'd heard of relatives trying to con old people out of their life savings, but had never expected to find her nephew doing that to her. His father would have been so ashamed about it. Her brother had been a decent sort.

Winifred put the chain on the front door in case her nephew tried to let himself in again, then walked briskly back to the kitchen and picked up the phone, anger still humming through her. 'Could I make an appointment to see Mrs Farley, please? As soon as possible. I have an emergency.'

She was not yet too old to manage her affairs. And no one — no one in the world — was going to force her out of her home.

There were other members of the family she

might also consider as heirs, even though they weren't as closely related to her. Otherwise her money would go to charity. Plenty of worthwhile charities around.

She'd have to sell something in order to find out about her remaining family, but that was all right. She had several pieces of old jewellery that had belonged to her grandmother, pieces she disliked intensely and would never wear.

She'd been saving them for an emergency. Now it had arrived.

★ ★ ★

Someone rang Janey's doorbell in the morning just as she was about to change Millie. Muttering in annoyance, she picked her daughter up and went across to the intercom.

'Janey Dobson?'

'Yes.'

'Police here. Can we come up?'

'Just a minute.' She ran across to the window to check and saw a police car there. She went back to the intercom and pressed the entry button. 'I was just checking that you really were the police. I've opened the front door. I'm in Flat 3, on the first floor.'

She went to the door, still holding Millie, and saw two police officers and a woman in a grey suit coming up the stairs, looking very solemn. This made her feel nervous. Who were they? What did they want with her?

She didn't invite them in, but stood squarely in the doorway. 'What can I do for you?'

'Can we come in?'

'Could I ask why?'

'Because you've been accused of theft,' the woman officer said.

Janey could only gape at her. '*Theft?* I've never stolen anything in my life.'

'It really would be better if we came in.'

She nudged the door open and closed it after them. 'I'm just changing my daughter's nappy, so I'll have to finish doing that. I can't leave her half dressed.'

'It's not very warm in here,' the woman in grey said.

'I don't keep it like a greenhouse. I read that it's not good for babies to be brought up in a hothouse environment, then go out into the cold winter air.'

The woman looked surprised but didn't give in. 'Where would *you* have read that?'

The scorn in her voice made the female police officer stare at her.

Janey raised her chin defiantly. 'In the book the health visitor gave me about looking after babies and toddlers.'

The woman looked surprised. 'You've seen a health visitor, then?'

'Of course I have. I met her at the practice.' Something made her add, 'When I went to register,' rather than mentioning that Millie had been ill. 'She came round here to see me and said I was doing well.' Deftly she finished changing the nappy, wrapped her daughter up warmly but kept Millie in her arms, because she felt less alone that way.

Perching on the arm of the couch, she waited for them to speak, sure this was some stupid mistake. What a horrible way to start the day, though!

Instead the policeman walked across to her computer. 'How long have you had this?'

'I had it when I lived at home and Dawn from *Just Girls* persuaded my parents to let me have it again, so that I can do my study assignments.'

'What study assignments?' the grey woman asked sharply.

'At the college. I'm going to finish my A levels.' Why did the woman look so surprised?

'What about the printer? And the spare cartridge?' the policeman asked.

'The courier brought them with the computer last night, so presumably my parents sent them.'

'When did you leave home?'

'Eight months ago. My parents threw me out when they found I was pregnant.'

'Why was that?'

Janey was beginning to feel seriously worried now. This was more like an inquisition than a mistake. What did they really want? 'I can't see how that's relevant to your visit. Look, all you have to do is contact my parents and they'll confirm that they gave me my computer back.'

'They've already said that they gave you back the computer, but it's your father who reported the printer and cartridge missing, presumably stolen.'

She was unable to speak, so shocked was she by this.

It was the woman officer who came up to her.

120

'Why don't you sit down properly, Miss Dobson? You've gone white as a sheet.'

She let herself sink into the armchair. 'I can't believe what you're saying. There must be some mistake. The computer and printer were delivered here by a courier last night.'

'Which courier service?'

Her mind went blank, then she admitted, 'I don't know. I was just so pleased to have them back, I signed the piece of paper and the guy went away.'

'There has also been a suggestion that you're not capable of caring for a baby properly,' the woman in grey said. 'Which is why I'm involved today. I'm from the council.'

That was when terror came to sit inside Janey because she knew it was *him*, reaching out to hurt her again. He'd have told her father what to do to get her baby taken away from her. He'd said he didn't want her to keep it and bring it up in the town he lived in. It could cause too many complications if it looked like him or his other children.

What was she going to *do*?

* * *

At about nine-thirty in the morning, Kieran saw the police arrive and with them a woman he'd met before, a council official who had treated him like a criminal for getting injured by one of the council vehicles, even though it'd been driven by a driver who'd forged his large vehicle licence and had a few other accidents. And when

121

Kieran had dared to claim compensation, she'd seemed to take it as a personal affront.

What the hell was she doing here? She was one of the nastiest people he'd ever met.

He went out into the hall and heard the words, 'Because you've been accused of theft' echo down the stairwell from above. *Theft? That nice young lass? Never.*

It was none of his business so he went back inside his flat, but as the minutes passed and the police didn't leave, he began to wonder whether Janey might need help. If it was something that could have been easily cleared up, they'd have left by now. And theft didn't explain why Miss Bossy Britches was there with the police.

Janey seemed so alone and everyone needed help sometimes. He'd seen no one except officials go up to her flat, no people who might be friends or family. If he hadn't had his brother there during the blurred nightmare time after the accident, he didn't know how he'd have stood up for himself, let alone fought for the compensation he richly deserved for the injuries that had ruined his life.

Uncertain whether to get involved, he went out into the hallway again, then gave in to the urge to interfere. If he wasn't wanted, she could always tell him to leave, after all. Limping up the stairs, he cursed under his breath at the stabs of pain this caused.

But it was the pain which carried him forward, reminding him how innocent people could be stamped on — by chance, as he had been, or on purpose by people like Bossy Britches.

He didn't even hesitate but knocked loudly on the door of Flat 3.

The conversation inside stopped but no one came to answer it. Then, just as he was about to knock again, the girl opened it, looking so young and scared his heart went out to her.

'Is something wrong, Janey?' he asked, seeing how white and strained her face was.

'Yes. They're saying I stole something, and I didn't.'

'Do you need a friendly witness to this conversation?'

'Would you really do that? Yes, please.' She held the door open.

Old Bossy Britches sucked in her breath audibly at the sight of him. 'What are *you* doing here?'

He smiled at her and raised one hand, waving his fingertips mockingly. 'Lovely to see you too. I thought my friend Janey could do with a little support. Three against one is pretty poor odds, don't you think?' Was it his imagination or did the policewoman give him a quick, approving nod?

'This matter is no concern of yours, Mr Jones,' Bossy Britches snapped.

'When my friends are upset by bureaucracy, of course it's my concern. What exactly is the problem?'

When they'd explained, he couldn't hold back a disgusted snort. 'I never heard such a specious reason for accusing someone of theft in my whole life. However, as it happens, I can back up some of Miss Dobson's claims. Since I live on the ground floor, I see all the comings and goings in this block of flats. A courier did arrive late yesterday evening and carried up several boxes.'

'Did you see the printer?'

'No, of course not. I saw a courier bring in several boxes.'

'She could still have gone back home and stolen that printer,' Bossy Britches insisted.

He waited for the police to protest this assumption and when they didn't, he said calmly — he could always keep calm when dealing with an issue, however angry he got afterwards, 'Where do her parents live?'

'On the other side of Swindon.'

'Well, there you are. She doesn't have a car. That's got to be at least twenty miles away from here. How would she get there and back with a baby in its buggy? Anyway, I saw her coming and going several times yesterday, so I know she didn't have time to get the bus into Swindon and back.'

'That's as may be, and will be fully investigated, but there is another, much more important complaint, that she's a negligent mother. We shall need to establish how well that child is cared for. Such claims are extremely serious, can be a matter of life or death for an infant of that age.'

'Who has made this claim?'

'Confidential information.' She turned to the male police officer. 'I think for the child's sake, we'd better take it into protective care temporarily till we can make sure of the facts.'

Fury rose in him but the woman police officer

spoke while he was still trying to rein in his anger.

'I've two children of my own and I'd say that this baby is very well cared for, Miss Stevenall. I've been watching carefully how Miss Dobson deals with her daughter and how the child looks. It's quite clear to me that she loves the baby and though she had no warning of our visit, the baby is clean and well clad, and the flat's clean, too.'

'All the same — '

'You can ask the health visitor about what sort of mother I am,' Janey blurted out. 'Her card's on the mantelpiece.'

The woman officer went to get it. 'Sally Makepeace. She was my health visitor too, after I had my second son. I'd trust her word absolutely. I'll phone her straight away. We don't want to upset anyone unnecessarily, do we? And a baby can get very upset when taken away from a loving mother.' She whipped out a mobile phone and dialled the number, waiting impatiently, foot tapping.

Kieran saw tears rolling down Janey's cheeks even though she held her head up defiantly, except when she bent to murmur soothing nonsense to her daughter. If ever a mother loved a child, that one did, he thought angrily. What was it with Bossy Britches? Did she enjoy adding to the misery of people in trouble? Didn't she recognise love when it hit her in the eye . . . or did she have some ulterior motive for getting at Janey? He couldn't think what, but he'd seen far stranger things during his twenty years as a journo.

He'd find out what lay behind this, though. He was good at doing that. And it'd give him an interest, the sort of interest that used to be his *raison d'être*.

After a short conversation, the policewoman snapped her phone shut. 'The health visitor is convinced that even though she's so young, Ms Dobson is a capable and loving mother, but she'll keep an eye on the situation. I'll contact Dawn Potter later about the computer pickup.'

'She's gone away for a few days, but someone else at *Just Girls* may be able to help you,' Janey said.

'Fine. Thank you for your co-operation, Miss Dobson. We'll leave you and your daughter in peace now.'

Kieran watched Bossy Britches hesitate, glare at Janey as if she'd done something wrong and follow the police officers out. He shut the door after them with a bang and said what he'd been thinking, 'Who's got it in for you?'

She closed her eyes for a moment, then said, 'My father made the complaint. And he has a friend in the police force.' She shuddered at the thought of *him*. 'I'd guess they hatched this between them.'

'Why on earth would they do that?'

'My father hates me.'

'There must be more to it than that.'

She shook her head, 'I'd rather not say any more.'

'You know something else, though, don't you?'

She nodded. 'But I daren't tell you. Believe me, sometimes it's better to let sleeping dogs lie.'

'But this particular dog isn't sleeping, is it? It's trying to bite you.'

126

'Nonetheless, I can't say anything.'

'Or you daren't.' When she bent her head avoiding his eyes, he knew he'd hit the bullseye.

For the first time since his accident, Kieran felt fully alive. 'We'll talk about that again. You look like you need a bit of peace and quiet now.' He saw a piece of paper and scribbled his phone number on it. 'If they come back, if anyone at all hassles you, give me a call and I'll come straight up.'

She took the paper from him. 'I'm grateful for your help, really I am, but I can't understand why you're doing it. You hardly know me. And you have your own problems.'

'I used to be an investigative journalist, then a damned stupid accident nearly ended my life. Until tonight I've been stumbling along, thinking my useful life was over. You can see how difficult I find it to get around now. But suddenly, because of this incident, I'm feeling alive again. It might seem strange logic to you, but I'm really grateful to have something to get my teeth into, something to prove that I can still help the underdog.'

'It's very kind, but I don't want you investigating this. *Please.* It's best to ... let things go. It's not worth provoking him.'

'I'll do nothing to hurt you,' he said soothingly, moving towards the door. Who the hell was this person she was so afraid of? Not her father, he felt sure. 'Will you be all right now?'

She nodded.

'Then I'll go back to my flat.'

She went with him to the door, balancing her

baby on her hip as if Millie was part of her. The baby was rosy and happy, reaching out towards him, smiling and showing a couple of half-grown teeth. Bad mother, indeed!

'If you're an investigative journalist, why are you living in subsidised accommodation like this? Have you run out of money?'

He grinned. 'On the contrary. My very capable lawyer brother got me an excellent compensation payout, then helped me invest it carefully, which included buying this block of flats. We didn't know then whether I'd ever be able to walk again, so I kept the largest flat for myself, on the ground floor, and the others provide me with a decent income.' He'd chosen to offer them as subsidised accommodation because he knew how often people in need were given substandard places to live. His brother said he was an idealist and could have got far more in rent, but he'd lived his whole life by a certain set of standards and he wasn't going to stop now. Anyway, he didn't need more money, had plenty put aside from his work before the accident.

'Oh, I see. I'm glad for you.'

'I'd be grateful if you'd keep that information to yourself. I've got the place managed, because I don't want to deal with the day-to-day collecting of rent and that sort of thing. Actually, I don't want the other tenants even knowing I'm the owner, because they'll run to me whenever things go wrong.'

'That's why you knew who to phone about the washing machine — and why they hurried to repair it!'

'Right first time.'

'OK. I won't say anything. And Kieran — thank you. I was panicking when you turned up.'

'Never panic. Keep calm and fight back.'

He found himself whistling as he made his way slowly and carefully down the stairs. Janey reminded him of his little sister, who emailed him more regularly than he emailed her. On that thought, he went to the computer and sent off an email to her.

Then, because he realised he'd not bothered to fix himself a proper breakfast, he made himself some cheese on toast and munched an apple while he waited for it to grill.

Perhaps he might manage on a smaller dose of painkillers today? Maybe adrenaline helped keep pain at bay.

Whatever. The world suddenly looked a brighter place.

8

In the afternoon, when Margaret came to pick her up and take her to the college, Janey immediately asked, 'Did the police contact you about the courier?'

'About the printer? Yes. I gave them the details. You look . . . upset. Are you all right?'

'I don't know. Someone has claimed that I'm a bad mother and a horrible woman from the council wanted to take my baby away.'

Margaret stared at her in shock. 'What?'

Janey explained what had happened and Margaret's expression grew grim. 'That Stevenall woman is a constant thorn in our flesh. She doesn't like amateurs like us doing social work, or council money being spent on people in need. If she tries to take your baby again, you must phone me or Dawn. Here. This is my private mobile number. And this is Dawn's. Call us any time, day or night. Don't give the numbers to anyone else, though. We only hand out these cards in emergency situations.'

'Thanks. I'm grateful, not only for this but for all you're doing.'

'You're doing things, too. You're looking after Millie beautifully. And it's good to see someone taking advantage of the other chances offered to her. What sort of student were you before this happened?'

'I used to get good marks,' she admitted. Well,

she'd not have dared do other than her best with her father ready to jump on her for the slightest thing.

'I'll come into the interview with you, if you don't mind. I won't interfere, but I'll hold Millie and back you up if necessary.'

'With a bit of luck, she might go to sleep in the buggy. She often has a nap at this time of day.'

They had to wait ten minutes at the college, then were shown into an office and a man interviewed Janey. Only it felt more like a friendly chat.

'We've got your records from school and you were doing very well till — this young lady happened.' He smiled at Millie, who was fast asleep. 'Bad timing, eh?'

'Something like that.'

'It's good that you want to go back to studying. What do you plan to do after the A levels?'

'I wanted to go to university to study English before. Now, I'm not so sure. I still want to go to university, but I want to do something more practical that'll help me earn a decent living as Millie gets older.'

'Teaching might fit, especially if you go on the maths or science side. You'd have the school holidays to look after her, then. If you're any good at those subjects, you might consider that. They're always short of maths and science teachers.'

Janey nodded, filing the information away.

After only a few minutes of chatting, he said, 'I don't see any reason why you shouldn't carry on with your studies here, and if your tutor thinks you're on track, you'll be able to take at least one A level this year.'

'That'd be brill! It'll give me something to do in the evenings. I'll work really hard, I promise.'

'We'll go through all the paperwork, then you can go and see them at the crèche while I find out if your tutor can fit you in for a quick chat before you leave. You've only missed a couple of classes this term, so far.'

The crèche was a delightful place and the baby room was supervised by a woman with a soft West Indian accent and the widest smile Janey had ever seen. They had to speak in low voices because other babies were taking a nap. Millie slept through it all, stirring once and mumbling to herself, then snuggling down again.

On the way home Margaret said again, 'Don't forget. If you need help, get straight on to me. Dawn will be back next week, but if something really serious happens, I know she'll want to be told and will come back early if necessary.'

'You people at *Just Girls* are so lovely,' Janey replied in a choked voice. 'I don't know what I'd have done without you.'

'You'd have managed. You're a capable young woman. But maybe we've made it a little easier. We try to.' She drove away with a wave.

But Janey knew she wouldn't have been able to manage on her own, not with *him* pressuring her first to have an abortion, then to have her baby adopted.

★ ★ ★

132

Winifred dressed as smartly as ever because she'd always loved clothes, but her heart was heavy as she walked into town. She'd heard of old people changing their wills at a whim, threatening their heirs with disinheritance. Was this a whim? Was she being foolish?

No. The conversation she'd overheard between Bradley and that sharp-faced female had been all too revealing. There could be no doubt about it. For all his show of caring, he didn't give two hoots about her, just his inheritance. Not only that, but he was planning to swindle her if he could get her to hand over the house to him. That explained why his help was always focused on the house and not her needs.

The callous way he'd spoken of her had upset her greatly. 'The silly old biddy'. What a dreadful thing to call her!

Well, he'd not be walking into her house at will again. She made a mental note to visit a locksmith on her way back, however tired she was.

Her lawyer was as cool and pleasant as ever, but when Winifred explained why she'd come, Mrs Farley frowned.

'Are you sure about this, Miss Parfitt?'

'Yes, I am. I'm not in my dotage yet. I'd rather leave my money to charity than to someone who considers me a gullible old fool.' She was aware of a searching scrutiny and waited, meeting Mrs Farley's gaze without flinching. 'It's not easy being the last of my generation. I try to think very carefully about important things like this, because I no longer have anyone to discuss them with.' She waited and added, 'Do you believe me about what I overheard?'

'I do, actually. There have been some rather pushy property deals in town lately by certain companies.'

She didn't elaborate or name names, and Winifred didn't expect her to. But it was a good bet that Mrs Farley had heard of Ebony's firm in this connection.

'Who exactly do you wish to name as beneficiary?'

'I'm not sure, so as an interim measure, until I can gather more information about my distant relatives, I'd like you to draw up a will leaving everything in equal shares to these charities.' She handed over the list she'd drawn up. 'Make it very simple because if I'm spared long enough, I'll be changing my will again within the next few months, once I've checked the other members of my family out. For the time being, I simply wish to make sure that Bradley doesn't inherit.'

'That will be quite a simple task. And haven't you given him a power of attorney? Do you want to cancel that?'

'Yes, definitely. I'm glad you reminded me.'

Mrs Farley fiddled with the piece of paper, staring down at it as if uncomfortable about what she was going to say. 'If you can drop in tomorrow afternoon — around say, three o'clock — I can have the new will ready to sign. I would, however, advise you to see your doctor before you do sign and get a letter from him confirming that you are of sound mind.'

'*What?* Is that really necessary?'

'Not now, but your nephew may contest the will after you die and your eventual heirs may need proof that you were in your right mind when you changed your will.'

'Oh. I see. Well, in that case, I'll do as you suggest and let you have the doctor's letter.'

'Good. Now, is there anything else I can do for you?'

'Not directly but I wondered if you could suggest the best way of selling this? I find the thought of dealing with a pawnbroker rather distasteful and even if I was prepared to do that, I don't like the looks of the one in the high street.' Winifred got out the brooch she'd chosen for selling, a small, ugly piece, which she'd never liked. Her mother had always insisted the stones were of superb quality and valuable, but she'd never worn it, either.

Mrs Farley took the brooch from her. 'What gorgeous diamonds! See how they sparkle in the light. You can't fake that.'

'I think it's rather vulgar and clumsy-looking, but I'm sure my grandfather wouldn't have bought anything shoddy.'

'I'd suggest you try Doring's on the high street. They're old-fashioned in many ways, but have an excellent reputation as a jeweller. Ask to see Michael Doring and tell him I sent you. I know him socially and he seems a decent fellow.'

'Thank you. I'll go straight there.'

'Do you keep any other jewellery in the house?'

'Only one or two pieces. Most of my jewellery is safely locked up in the bank.'

'If your other pieces are of as good quality as

this, I'd suggest you put them in the bank, too.'

'Perhaps you're right.'

She went straight from the lawyer's to the jeweller's and found it embarrassing to explain what she needed but steeled herself to do it, because she had no other choice. The man with whom she was dealing — she'd not expected Michael Doring to be so young — was very kind and noticed how she was feeling. He showed her into a private room to continue their bargaining, for which she was grateful.

After he'd studied the brooch, he brought in an older man to give him a second opinion.

'You're right, Miss Parfitt. It's a very good-quality piece,' he said in the end. 'You could get more than I'd be able to offer by putting it into a fine jewellery auction.'

'How much are you offering?'

'Two thousand pounds. You might get another thousand on top of that in an auction.'

'Or I might not. In any case, I don't want to wait for the money, so I prefer to sell the brooch to you now. Could you give me a cheque, do you think? I don't like to carry large sums of cash around with me.'

'Certainly. Very wise.'

That transaction completed, she visited the bank to deposit the money. She felt rather tired by now, but since the locksmith's was on the way home, she called in and arranged for a man to come and change her locks, front and back the very next morning. Bradley was never going to walk into her house like that again.

As she passed the newsagent's, she stopped for

a rest, idly gazing at the display of small local advertisements in their window while she got her breath back. It was getting too much to do the heavy shopping herself. Now that she had a little more money, she'd see if she could find someone to do that job for her. She'd write out a postcard and place it in this window the next time she was in town.

She had to sit down when she got back, feeling extremely tired now but satisfied that she'd taken the right steps. Of course she dozed off, something she detested. It seemed so lazy to take naps in the daytime.

She was getting very old in body, had to face that every time she looked in a mirror, though she hoped she wasn't losing her wits, whatever Bradley said. He'd probably lied about that too.

Maybe at her age the odd nap wouldn't hurt? She'd ask the doctor. Her mother hadn't been right about everything.

★   ★   ★

When Nicole left the library that evening, she walked home briskly, shivering as an icy wind speared into her face. She did hope it wouldn't snow. She'd decided to walk to and from the library every day. It was not only good exercise, but it was hardly worth taking her car to work when she lived so close, well, not unless the weather was bad.

As she turned into Peppercorn Street, she thought she saw William's reflection in the shop window on the opposite corner, and spun round.

But there was no sign of him. She'd only seen the person out of the corner of her eye. It must just have been an illusion, someone who looked a bit like him.

She loved her new street, which had real character, and had strolled up and down it a couple of times, studying the other houses. Such a varied group of dwellings. From the information in the library records, she knew a Parfitt still lived at the top end, but she hadn't realised what a magnificent old house this Miss Parfitt owned until she'd gone exploring. The garden was in a sad state, though.

The garden at her block of flats was minimalist — and that was a flattering way to describe it. Almost bare was perhaps more accurate. Maybe she'd ask if she could plant a few annuals once the weather warmed up a little. She missed her garden.

When she turned into the car park of her flats, she stopped in shock. Her car was still parked where she'd left it, but the tyres on this side had been slashed.

As she cried out in shock, a man who was limping slowly past stopped. 'Are you all right?'

She turned to him. 'Look at my car! I can't believe this!' She walked round it. 'The other side's the same.'

He stared at her tyres. 'Better call the police, though I doubt they'll be able to find out who did it. I'll stay with you till they come, just in case whoever did it is still hanging round. I live a few doors down the street at number twelve.'

She made the call. 'The police will be here as

soon as they can.' She held out her hand. 'I'm Nicole Gainsford.'

'I'm Kieran Jones. I've seen you going past, but only recently. I was just out for a bit of exercise.' Exercise! Walking a short way up the street and back, though he made it a little further each day.

'I've only just moved in. Fancy you noticing!'

He looked down at his leg with a grimace. 'I do a lot of staring out of the window since I got injured. It's only recently I've been told to go out for walks, which is a welcome improvement. I'd volunteer to keep an eye on your place but I can't see it from where I live and in any case, I'm in no fit state to tackle vandals. Strange that they should target your car when there were plenty of others closer to High Street. You'd think you'd be safe in the part where our street starts to get posher.'

His grin said he was teasing and she smiled back at him. 'Do you want to wait inside the lobby? That wind must have come straight from the Arctic.'

'Good idea.'

The police didn't get there for another half-hour, by which time she'd decided Kieran was harmless and invited him in for a cup of coffee. She stayed near the window as they chatted to watch out for the police.

Conversation didn't falter because he was an avid reader too. He took one look at her bookshelves and began to study the titles. Soon they were comparing books. Then he broke off abruptly in mid sentence. 'They're here.'

'You've got better hearing than me. Oh yes, it is them.'

They both went outside and the police examined the tyres.

'We'll report this but I doubt we'll find out who did it,' one of them said. 'Unless you have any known enemies?'

His tone said he was joking, but she suddenly remembered how Paul had warned her to watch her back. She hesitated, then said, 'My older son is very angry at me because I've just left home. No, surely it can't be him!'

'Has he done anything else to upset you?'

'Well, he came into the library and made a scene because I wouldn't give him some money. He said it was for food, but he asked for far more than he needed to buy a snack.'

'Ah. Would that be William Gainsford? I thought your surname was familiar. He's the son you're talking about? We're the ones who took him in for questioning.'

She nodded, feeling sick at the thought of her son doing something like slash her tyres. Surely, surely, it couldn't be him!

'We'll keep an eye out for him. In the meantime, is there anywhere else you can leave the car?'

She shook her head. 'There's only this open parking space, though I shall take my car to work from now on during the daytime. We have a fenced car park for staff there. But at night, well, I've no choice but to leave it here.'

Kieran, who'd been standing quietly to one side, took a step forward. 'You can share my garage, if you like. It's a double one and there's only my car in it at the moment. I'm about a hundred metres down the street.'

She was startled. 'Are you sure? You hardly know me.'

He shrugged. 'I happen to believe neighbours should help one another.' He turned to the police. 'I live at number twelve, flat one.'

'Will the owner let a non-resident use the garage?'

'I am the owner.'

They nodded and one of them said to Nicole, 'It sounds like a good offer to me, Ms Gainsford. I can vouch for Mr Jones being an honest citizen. I used to read his column in the newspaper all the time.'

'You're *that* Kieran Jones!' she exclaimed. 'Why, I used to read your column too.' To her surprise, he blushed at her compliment. She hadn't expected that reaction from a man of his reputation, a man who'd won major awards for his journalism, and smiled at that. 'You should be very proud of what you've done to make the world a better place, Kieran.'

He shrugged. 'I do my best. So . . . you'll take the garage?'

'Yes. I'll have to call someone out to fit new tyres first, but if they can do that tonight, I'll put my car into your garage straight away.'

'We'll be leaving, then,' one of the officers said.

Kieran moved towards the door, too, and she felt sorry to see him go, had been enjoying their conversation.

141

'Just ring the doorbell for flat one when you come, Nicole. I don't go to bed till late.' He walked slowly away down the street.

She remembered now reading about his accident and how he'd nearly lost his life. It had certainly left him with a bad limp and he looked as if he was in pain when he moved.

How kind of him to offer to share his garage with her! She'd have to insist on paying him something. It was only right.

But no one could come and replace her tyres till morning so she used the phone number he'd given her to say the car would have to stay where it was until the next day.

* * *

Janey was just coming back down the hill from the park when she met the old lady from the big house, struggling along with a wheeled shopping bag, trying to balance another shopping bag on top of it.

On an impulse she stopped. 'Could I help you with that? I could easily put your second bag on my buggy and that'd make it lighter. I have a tray for my shopping underneath.'

The old lady stopped to look at her in surprise, then nodded. 'Thank you. I must admit I bought too much today. It's these silly two-for-one offers. And I am a bit tired. I had to wait ages at the doctor's.'

Janey turned the buggy round and took the bag of shopping, stowing it in the tray underneath while Millie alternated between blowing bubbles and smiling at the new person.

'She's a very pretty baby and she always looks very well cared for.'

'How do you — '

'How do I know? I watch you sometimes going along the path at the top of the street.'

'And I've seen you going into that lovely old house. I'm Janey, by the way, and this is Millie.'

'I'm Miss Parfitt. And I'm very grateful for your help.'

'It's nice to be able to help someone else. People have been so kind to me since I got pregnant. Except for my parents. They threw me out.'

'That seems rather drastic.'

'Yes. It was hard. They wouldn't believe me when I told them it wasn't my fault, that I'd been forced.'

'Someone attacked you? How dreadful!'

Janey nodded and then looked at her in puzzlement. 'I don't know why I told you that. I don't usually tell people any of the details. But you have a kind face.'

'I do?'

'Yes. I've seen the way you smile at dogs.'

'We always used to have dogs. They're good company if treated properly and taught their manners. I couldn't cope with one now, though.'

'No. And I couldn't have one in an upstairs flat, even if I could afford to feed one, which I can't. The benefits money doesn't stretch very far.'

They arrived at the big house and Janey stopped. 'I'll help you in with the shopping, shall I?'

'Thank you. And perhaps . . . perhaps you'd

143

like a cup of tea and a piece of my chocolate cake?'

'Are you sure? You don't have to. I was glad to help.'

'If you're too busy, I shall understand.'

'I'm not too busy. I have too much time to fill, actually, because Millie still sleeps a lot. She's such a good baby, so easy to look after compared to some. And I'd love a piece of chocolate cake. I haven't had any for ages.'

★ ★ ★

Inside the house, Winifred led the way to the kitchen, explaining about it being the only really warm area.

'My flat's got high ceilings so it's a bit hard to heat properly. I make sure Millie is always dressed warmly because I can't afford to keep the gas fire burning flat out.'

'Do sit down. It won't take long.' She got the cake container out and set the remaining piece of cake on one of her pretty gilt-rimmed plates, taking out two matching tea plates to serve it on then turning to deal with the kettle.

Her visitor watched with great interest. 'What lovely china! And all matching.'

'It was my grandmother's.'

'The cake looks delicious.'

'It's an old family recipe.'

'Did you make it yourself? How clever! My mother used to buy cakes from the local supermarket, the cheapest ones. Not very interesting. Just to fill my father up. He's a big man and eats a lot. They weren't prettily decorated like this one. Look how the icing swirls.'

'I could show you how to do that. It's not hard.'

'Would you? Oh, I'd love to learn to cook properly. Mum would never let me do anything at home. She said I was wasteful.'

Winifred looked at her in wonder. For the second time in a week, she'd made a gesture and it had been richly rewarded. It made up a little for her bitter disappointment with her nephew. 'I'd be happy to show you how to cook. Why don't you come round one afternoon and we'll bake a fruit cake? I have an infallible recipe that's very economical, but delicious. Then we'll have half of it each. I'm always making too much for one person.'

'You must let me provide some of the ingredients, then.'

'Certainly not. But if you could help me up the hill with my shopping occasionally, that'd be a fair return for any cakes we make together.'

'It's a deal.' Janey stuck out one hand and they shook solemnly.

Winifred saw her guest's eyes turning towards the books. 'Do you like reading?'

'I love it. I'd go mad without books. I go to the library two or three times a week.'

'So do I. It's a wonder I haven't seen you there.'

'I've only just moved to Sexton Bassett.'

'That accounts for it.' So the poor girl didn't know anyone here yet. How lonely she must be. She was too young to be on her own. How could any parents treat their daughter like that?

When Janey got up to go, because it was time to feed her baby, Winifred opened her freezer and took out a quarter of a cake. 'Do take this. My freezer is full of portions of cake.'

She was surprised and very touched when Janey gave her a hug. Her nephew had never done that.

Afterwards she went to sit in the kitchen with a book, but spent the first few minutes going over the encounter in her mind.

Maybe . . . just maybe . . . she was learning to reach out to people better. It would be such a pleasure to teach that nice girl to cook.

It was never too late to learn new ways. She must remember that. Why, she was even going to computer classes. She smiled. She was becoming quite modern in her old age.

Well, it couldn't be that hard to use a computer, since nearly everyone had one these days. And no one would shoot her at dawn if she messed things up.

She hummed as she cleared up after her young visitor.

9

Dan got up early on the day of his wife's funeral. He didn't know why, because the funeral wasn't until midday and he wasn't going to his allotment beforehand, but he couldn't bear to lie in bed, had to be moving, doing things.

With a mug of tea in his hand, he walked slowly round the house, once again looking at the photos of his life with Peggy. They'd been a great comfort since the real Peggy had faded away. Some of the later ones brought tears to his eyes because the changes in her were starting to show, a slight bewilderment as if she wasn't quite sure what was going on, a distant look instead of her former loving gaze.

His son Terry and his wife were coming over from Reading for the funeral, but their children were at university in the north and they'd decided it wasn't worth coming down just for the one day.

He thought that wrong, but you couldn't tell this generation anything. He'd have liked to have them all gathered round him out of respect to Peggy and to show that something of her lived on in them and the generations to follow. That was such a comforting thought.

Simon and his wife were bringing their two daughters, though. He didn't see much of the girls, but they were a nice enough pair of lasses. Today's teenagers seemed to care much more about friends than family. It wasn't just him they steered clear of. They didn't 'hang out', as they called it, with their parents, either.

When the doorbell rang, he found he had a mug half full of cold tea in one hand. How long had he been holding that?

Putting it down on the nearest surface he opened the door to Terry and Karen, glancing at the wall clock. 'Is it that time already? Come in, come in. Why don't you make yourselves a cup of something while I change into my suit?'

He joined them in the kitchen, where they were sipping cups of coffee. Terry gave him a searching scrutiny. 'You all right, Dad?'

'Yes, son.'

'What will you do with yourself now?'

'What I've been doing for the past year or so: spend my days at the allotment, there's always something going on there, someone to talk to. In the evenings I watch TV or read a book.'

'Might it not be better if you found yourself a retirement unit, so that you could be with people, somewhere that's monitored in case you have trouble?'

Dan shook his head. 'No! I like my own home.'

'But the rest of us worry about you and — '

His irritation with their insistence that he should move overflowed, because this day of all days was not the time to nag him. 'Why does your generation always want to hide us oldies away in little compounds? Does the sight of wrinkled faces upset you? When I was growing up, everyone lived together, young and old, and it was a far more interesting way of life for everyone.

'My family lived in Peppercorn Street then, but it was a rented house and when the owner wanted to live there himself, we had to move. The street's changed but it's still a nice place to live. They knocked that house down years ago and built some big new houses, the sort yuppies live in. That part of the street is not only deserted in the daytime now, but people shut themselves up indoors in the evenings. I walk along it sometimes on sunny summer evenings and you never see the owners chatting over the garden fences or out in the street. What would someone there do if they needed help? You could scream yourself hoarse and no one would hear you behind all that double glazing.'

He realised his son wasn't really listening, had that glazed look in his eyes that said he was bored. You could never talk to Terry about the past, only about money and his job. He waited and his son realised he'd stopped speaking.

'Dad, if people in those houses were living on their own, they'd get one of those pendants that's a security alarm, then they could easily call for help.' Terry's voice grew a little sharper as he added, 'As I've begged you to do. At least you could do that to set my mind at rest.'

'Gadgets! You're always on about gadgets. Electronic thingamajigs don't pick you up when you fall over on an icy day, or help you with your shopping or comfort you when you're sad. Give me real people any day. I can call on my neighbours round here, day or night. Look out of

149

the window. In every single house you can see, there's someone who'd come over and help me if I asked.'

He saw Terry open his mouth again and wondered why he was bothering. 'Leave it be, son. You've said your piece and I've said mine. I'm an adult, not a child to be looked after and told what to do. I'll make my own decisions.'

Karen nudged her husband and made a shushing noise, then moved forward. 'Let me straighten your tie, Dad.'

'Thanks.' He couldn't resist adding, 'You'd not get a machine to do this, either. Peggy always used to do it for me. I've never been good at ties. I hate wearing the damned things. She used to laugh at me for that.' His voice broke on the last words and he had to swallow hard or he'd have disgraced himself.

Terry sighed loudly and looked at his watch. 'Well, shall we be going?'

As he went to lock the back door Dan paused for a moment, bracing himself for the ordeal to come, then followed his son out the front way. This time he'd go in someone else's car, because he was more upset than he was letting on and knew he wasn't fit to drive. It was his Peggy he was saying goodbye to today, his lovely darling Peggy, and it hurt like hell. He'd always hoped he'd be the one to go first.

At the crematorium Simon and his family were waiting. The girls came forward to give him a hug, looking so apprehensive he pulled them back and said in a low voice, 'It's only saying goodbye to your Gran, you know. Nothing to be

150

afraid of.' But it was their first funeral and they still looked wide-eyed and nervous.

After that everyone stood in silence in the reception area and waited for the hearse to arrive.

It seemed a long time to Dan, but when it came into sight he glanced at his watch and saw that they'd only been there for a few minutes and the hearse was spot on time. He'd always said time was as stretchable as elastic. It pulled out a long way when you were bored and pinged quickly past when you were enjoying yourself.

He studied the fancy flower arrangements from his sons perched on each end of the coffin. His own offering was in the middle, a bunch of scented narcissi, just a simple bunch not a tortured arrangement. His local florist said they came from the Scilly Isles. Peggy had loved their beauty and perfume at this time of year when no flowers were in bloom at his allotment.

'You always used to buy Mum narcissi like those around now, didn't you?' Simon whispered.

Dan nodded because he didn't trust his voice.

The men from the funeral directors slid out the coffin and wheeled it slowly into the crematorium. Dan moved forward to follow it, but stumbled. His granddaughters were nearest and they grabbed him, then held on to his arms from either side. He didn't know if they were helping him or he was helping them, but it felt so much better to have them beside him. Today, at least, they were hanging around with their family.

Terry's children should have come. He was still upset about that.

The service was very simple. He wished there hadn't been any words, just a chance to sit beside the coffin and be with her for a final time, but you had to do what people expected on these formal occasions. He let his mind wander, stood up when the others did and sat there quietly as the minister made a little speech, a tactful, gentle consignment of Peggy's soul to God. He was glad this woman was taking the service, not that snob from the other church.

To his surprise Simon moved forward after that.

'I'd just like to say goodbye to Mum on behalf of myself, Cath and the girls. We hope you're at rest now, Mum.'

Terry shook his head when the minister looked at him enquiringly. She turned to look at Dan, who moved forward, feeling he had to do this.

'As you all know, in one sense we said goodbye to the real Peggy a while ago, but today we're letting the rest of her go, too. I'm sure she'll be at peace in a better place now. She was a wonderful woman. I couldn't have asked for a better, more loving wife and I know how deeply she cared about all of you.' He turned towards the coffin and added, 'Goodbye, my darling.' His voice broke on the last words and he fumbled for his handkerchief.

As he moved back to his place, he wiped away the tears and settled his glasses back on his nose. Simon nodded at him, also with over-bright eyes, and his granddaughters were clutching tissues.

And then it was over. *Thank goodness!* He didn't know whether he'd said that aloud or not, hoped he hadn't. The curtains drew slowly round the coffin — too slowly for him! — soft music played and they were free to leave.

As he'd planned, he went to wait in the area where they set out the flowers afterwards. There were wilting bouquets lying around on a low wall that formed a sort of shelf. When he picked up his own bouquet again, his family looked surprised but he didn't care. He'd press one of the flowers to remind him of her, and he'd keep the others until they were completely dead. It'd be the last contact he had with her.

Till they met again.

He spoke to friends, thanked them for attending and invited them to come to the pub, where Simon had helped him book a buffet meal and drinks.

As they got into the car it began to rain. That felt right, somehow.

He leant his head back with a sigh, grateful when none of his family said anything. He didn't really want to go to the pub, but it was another of the rituals you had to go through.

It went better than he'd expected, though. People came up to speak to him. He was pleased at how many of Peggy's old friends had come, those still alive. They spoke of her as she used to be and he found that easier to cope with than enquiries about her progress.

In the end, however, he was so exhausted he had to ask Simon to take him home.

'I've had enough, son,' he said simply.

'You look dreadful.'

'Well, I doubt I'll get any better by staying here.'

When they got to his house, Simon insisted on coming inside. 'Dad, we're all worried about you, so just to make us feel better, would you please use this?' He fumbled in his pocket and pulled out a mobile phone.

It was the last thing Dan had expected. He stared at it then at his son's anxious face. 'For you, then, but I'm not leaving it switched on all the time.'

'It's for the opposite reason, really. In case you need to call for help.' He grinned. 'We know you'll not leave it switched on.' The smile faded. 'And we'll be very glad if you never need to use it.'

'All right, then. Show me how it works.'

'You're tired. Now isn't a good time.'

'We can make a start, go through the basics. It'll take my mind off . . . things.'

So he had a lesson in using one of the damned contraptions he hated. But if he didn't have to leave it on, if it was just for emergencies, well, he wasn't getting any younger. You have to be sensible about these things.

And if nothing else, it was a symbol of how much Simon cared about him. That felt good.

★ ★ ★

Janey went for a walk past the allotments, but though she stood by the gate and stared, there was no sign at all of Mr Shackleton. A man

154

working on a plot further down looked across at her and came close enough to yell, 'If you're looking for Dan, his wife's died. The funeral's today.'

'Thanks for letting me know.' She turned and wheeled Millie slowly round the park. Poor Mr Shackleton! How awful to lose your lifelong partner like that. But at least he'd had a partner. She'd never even had a steady boyfriend, thanks to her parents' restrictions on her comings and goings, only a brutal rapist.

When she got home she saw Kieran staring blindly out of the window and waved to him. But he didn't see her, let alone wave back. He seemed lost in thought. His life must have changed terribly, poor man. She knew how that felt.

As she climbed the stairs, the door to the flat opposite hers opened and a woman came out. Janey stopped to introduce herself, but with the briefest of nods the woman hurried down the stairs before she could get a word out. So much for having pleasant neighbours.

As she went inside, it began to rain, a few drops pattering against the window panes at first, then more until rain was beating hard against the glass. It wasn't warm enough inside the room and she kept feeling Millie's hands and cheeks to see if she was cold, but Millie never seemed to feel the cold. She played for a few minutes, glugged down a bottle of milk then fell abruptly asleep.

Janey wrapped an old shawl round her shoulders. She'd found it in a charity shop for a

155

pound and it had been so useful. She loved the comforting warmth round her neck. As she stared out of the window, she wondered if Kieran was staring out too.

When a police car pulled up outside, her heart began to pound with anxiety. What now?

★ ★ ★

Kieran saw the police car draw up. What the hell did they want now? Without coming to a conscious decision, he left the flat and went upstairs as quickly as he could manage, knocking on Janey's door.

'If they're here for you again, I thought you might welcome some company.'

'Thanks. I'm grateful.' She turned to answer the intercom.

When the officers came up, she saw it was two different ones and wished suddenly that the female officer was there. She'd seemed to be on Janey's side, or at least on the side of truth and fairness.

Bracing herself for more questions, more accusations, Janey waited for them to start the ball rolling.

'We've come about the computer. I gather someone came to speak to you about it yesterday?'

She nodded, but didn't say anything, just continued to wait.

'Your father says your mother only agreed to let you have the computer and you shouldn't have taken the printer. If you give it back and the spare cartridge, he'll let the matter drop.'

It annoyed her that they were acting as if she was being forgiven for stealing something. 'They must have given the printer to the courier or he wouldn't have brought it here. And I don't have any way of getting it back. I haven't got a car and I'm living on benefits, so I can't afford a courier.'

'It must be returned, he says.'

'I'll take it back for you,' Kieran promised rashly, though he'd not yet started driving again. But how hard could it be to go twenty miles and back? He wanted to make sure her parents couldn't pretend anything went wrong with the return of the printer. He'd seen every dirty trick in the book during his time as a journo.

'Do you have a car, Kieran?' Janey asked. 'I've not seen you driving one.'

'I'm only just starting to drive again. My car's in that double garage to the side.' Which wasn't quite the truth. He'd not actually driven his replacement car at all. But surely he could manage such a short trip, or find a friend to help out if necessary?

'Thank you. You're very kind.'

He looked at the police officers. 'Would I be in order to ask Janey's father for a receipt for the items?'

They shrugged and took their leave.

Janey looked at him, her mouth wobbling. 'I keep worrying what he's going to do next.'

'Your father?'

'Him and his policeman friend. My dad does just what *he* tells him to.'

He noticed how she almost spat out the word 'policeman' and didn't name him, and wondered who this fellow was, why she hated him so much. 'Whatever it is, we'll cope.'

'I'm not your responsibility, though I'm grateful for your help.'

'I have a lot of time on my hands at present and it's good to do something to help others. Leave it to me. Consider me your older brother.' He saw by her quick nod that she'd understood the implications of this image, that he wasn't interested in her sexually. She was smart and very mature for her age, had probably had to grow up fast in the past year and that must have been hard. But he'd never been attracted to much younger women.

Well, he'd had a hard year too, so he could sympathise. His freedom had vanished, and with it his whole way of life, the career he loved. His brother said he'd had a prolonged adolescence doing a job like that. Kieran smiled as he went back down the stairs. If so, he'd enjoyed every minute of it.

★   ★   ★

Soon after he returned to his own flat, Kieran saw Nicole arrive. He unlocked her half of the garage and stood watching as she drove her car inside. It had four new tyres and they gave off that new rubber smell. He lingered to chat to her.

'I must pay you rent for this garage,' she said. 'I can't take advantage of your kindness.'

He suddenly had an idea. 'I'd rather you paid me in kind.'

158

She became instantly wary.

He tutted at her and twirled an imaginary moustache. 'Aha, my proud beauty!' But he couldn't keep it up and when he laughed, she joined in.

'Don't jump to conclusions, Nicole. I'm no danger to any woman at the moment, can hardly get around let alone play the seducer.'

She blushed a vivid red. 'Sorry.'

He gestured towards the flats. 'What I meant was, one of my tenants is a single mother, only eighteen, and she needs to return a printer to her father. They're pretending she stole it. The poor girl can't afford to pay a courier and she has no car of her own, so how they can claim she got there to steal it, I don't know. I said I'd see to returning it, but if truth be told, I'm not quite fit to drive yet — though I'm getting there. It's only twenty miles away in Swindon . . . ?' He left the question hanging in the air and waited.

'I'm happy to do that.' She frowned at him. 'It seems a strange thing for parents to do. Can't the father come and pick it up himself if he needs it?'

'I'll explain as we drive. When would be convenient for you? I can go anytime.'

'How about tomorrow morning, about eleven?'

'I'll check that someone will be in — no, on second thoughts, I think it might be better to take them by surprise. People are usually in on Sundays, after all.'

'Whatever.' She glanced down at her watch. 'I have to go. I'll pick you up on Sunday, then.'

'Great. I'll be waiting.'

He watched her walk up the street towards her flat, trim and neat, moving briskly. Nice woman.

159

He found her wholesome appearance attractive. He'd never gone for glamorous women, who often spent more time thinking about their appearance than living a life. Even when he was quite well known and meeting celebrities galore, he'd cared more about intelligence and a caring attitude, the mental equipment of a decent person.

Yes, he really liked Nicole. Funny how quickly you could tell. Pity she was only just separated. Too soon to ask her out for a proper date. That thought made him pause, then smile slowly. He must be getting better. It was the first time he'd been attracted to a woman since the accident.

Still, he could perhaps become her friend, as a start. It'd be good to make a few friends. His brother was always so damned busy making money that Kieran didn't like to trouble him. And the journalists Kieran had hung out with in London rarely had the time to come down to Wiltshire to see him, though one or two emailed him now and then.

10

Winifred walked across to her new friend Hazel's house, wrapping a woollen scarf tightly round her neck and taking her umbrella because it looked like rain. The house was only three streets away, on the other side of the park, and she enjoyed the stroll. Usually she only went out to the shops. She really should do more walking for pleasure. No wonder she tired so easily these days. Use it or lose it, they said.

She felt a bit nervous as she knocked on the door, because they'd had to postpone the meeting. What if Hazel didn't really want to see her again? But she needn't have worried. Hazel was as warm and friendly as before and they spent a pleasant couple of hours getting to know one another better.

'I found out about the computer classes,' Hazel said after a while, 'and booked us two places. They're specially for oldies, as I thought, and are going to be held at the library, in that big side room.'

'I shall look forward to them. Though I'm a bit nervous about computers, I must admit.'

'So am I.'

It began to rain as Winifred walked home, getting steadily heavier, with a wind blowing it sideways, so that she had to hold on tightly to her umbrella.

To her dismay, her nephew was just arriving at

her house. He didn't see her and she ducked quickly back into the little path between the two houses, watching as he took out his key and tried to fit it in the lock.

She enjoyed his surprise when he found it didn't fit. He bent to look closely at the new lock, muttering something that could only be a curse from the expression on his face.

He went to peer into a window, but she always kept the curtains drawn in the front room. When he went round to the rear of the house, she moved further back down the path till she could see him again through the slats of the trellis. He was feeling around for a spare key — as if she was stupid enough to leave one under a flowerpot!

In the end he got into his car and drove away, scowling.

By that time she was soaking wet, so she hurried into the house and changed her clothes, making herself a cup of drinking chocolate and soon feeling warm again.

She wondered if Bradley would try to see her once more before he went away. Or send that whip-thin caricature of a woman round to speak to her. Either way, he wasn't coming inside her house again. She loathed disloyalty and cheating.

But she felt a bit nervous at the prospect of telling him to his face that he no longer held power of attorney on her behalf, let alone that she'd changed her will. She was afraid he might try to bully her or trick her in some way. He'd spoken so scornfully about her to his girlfriend.

★ ★ ★

162

That evening Paul turned up to see his mother.

'Are you all right?' he asked as Nicole let him in. 'Only your car isn't there. If I hadn't seen your light on, I'd have thought you were out.'

'Of course I'm all right. Why do you ask?'

He hesitated.

'It's something to do with William, isn't it?'

'Yes. He's been boasting that he's got his own back on you and saying that if you don't do what he wants next time, he'll give you another demonstration of why you should.'

She closed her eyes and prayed to say the right thing, because she didn't want to lose this son as well. She decided on the simple truth. 'Someone slashed all my tyres yesterday.'

Paul's shoulders sagged and he looked at her in dismay. 'Is that why your car isn't here? Is it being repaired?'

'No. I've got the new tyres on it but I've found myself a garage, so I keep it locked up now. I'd guessed it was William, though.'

'He's very chancy lately. I try to keep out of his way.'

'Was that why you stayed in your room so much? I thought you were avoiding me.'

He looked startled. 'No! It's just — if he doesn't see me, then he doesn't do things on the spur of the moment.'

'He used to hit you?'

Paul shrugged.

'I'm sorry. I should have realised, helped you more. Why didn't you *tell* me?'

'What could you have done? He's been body building and weight training, so he's stronger

163

than Dad now, could wipe the floor with any of us — and he knows it.'

She sighed, feeling guilty, but Paul was right. She'd found out for herself that she couldn't do anything with William now. 'Have you had some tea?'

'Sandwiches.'

'I've got some of my hearty soup, if you'd like a bowl.'

'I love your soup. And have you some grated cheese to put on it?'

'Of course. Is there any other way to eat my soup? Take your coat off. It's soaking.'

'It's waterproof so I'm dry underneath.'

Paul seemed to enjoy having her fuss over him and ate up the rest of the soup, which she'd intended to have for her tea the next day. But she didn't mind that. She'd always felt closer to her younger son than to William, who'd been a surly child, and maybe she was building bridges with Paul now, at least.

★   ★   ★

There was a knock on the front door and when his father didn't seem to notice, William got up to answer it. He saw the police and tried to slam the door in their faces, but the burly officer standing nearest to him thrust it back with one meaty hand while grabbing him with the other.

'Dad!' William yelled at the top of his voice. 'The police are hurting me.'

'Don't tell lies!' The policeman shook him hard and shoved him down the hall towards the room where the light was on and the television blaring.

By that time Sam had got to his feet and was looking at them with a bewildered expression on his face, like a man half lost in a dream.

'Mr Gainsford?'

'Er . . . yes. Could you let go of my son, please?'

'If I do, I'm afraid he'll try to run away.'

'I won't, Dad.'

'Let him go, please. He won't — '

As soon as the hand left his shoulder William took off for the French windows and would have got out if the window hadn't been locked. The policeman followed him across the room, sending his father staggering back as he passed.

'They attacked you as well, Dad!' William yelled. 'Tell them to stop.'

But his father was now fully alert and shook his head. 'They didn't attack either of us, William. Stop pretending. Why did you try to run away?'

'The police keep telling lies about me. I'm frightened.' He tried to look frightened but when the second policeman grinned openly at that, he guessed he'd not succeeded.

'Sit down, please, lad.'

When he didn't move, the officer thrust him on to the sofa next to his father and went to stand behind him. His father looked at the other man, who was standing in front of them, but didn't say anything.

'We're here tonight, Mr Gainsford, because your wife's car had its tyres slashed. It happened yesterday evening and a lad answering to your son's description was seen running away.'

'Was he identified as my son?'

'It was too dark to be sure.'

'I don't know why you think William would slash his own mother's tyres. It's a ridiculous idea.'

'Because he threatened at the library to get back at her.'

Sam looked at William in shock. 'Did you go to the library? You know you're not to disturb her when she's working.'

'I needed some money.'

'I gave you some.'

'I spent it. Besides, I wanted her to come home again. The place is a mess without her. It's her *job* to look after us.'

'That's an outdated idea for a lad of your age,' one of the officers said. 'Anyway, sir, we'd like to question your son about the incident and we'd prefer to do it at the station, so perhaps you could accompany him there?'

'Now?'

'Yes.'

William watched angrily as his dad meekly stood up, scribbled a note for Paul and got ready to go out. He wasn't going to be weak like his father when *he* left school. And he wasn't going to stay around in this house once he had money of his own, either. No wonder England was going down the tube. Softies like his dad were *giving away* their masculinity as well as their country. His new friends had explained it all to him.

Well, the police would get nothing out of him.

166

Let them prove he slashed the tyres if they could, which he doubted. He'd made certain there was no one around to see him when he did it.

He wasn't stupid like his dad and brother.

And his mother was going to regret a few things. What sort of woman dobbed in her own son to the police without proof?

★ ★ ★

When Paul got home, he found the lights on but no one there. He didn't see the note on the kitchen table at first, but when he did, he read it with a sinking heart. William was going to be even harder to deal with now.

After thinking about it for a few minutes, he rang his mother and told her what had happened.

'You should be double careful now, Mum.'

'I'll be all right.'

But he heard the doubt in her voice.

The next day after school he bought himself a pair of much sturdier bolts and fitted them to the inside of his bedroom door. It made him feel a bit safer — but not totally safe, not as long as William was going feral.

★ ★ ★

Late on Sunday morning, Nicole drove Kieran over to Swindon to leave the printer at Janey's parents' house. No one was home the first time, so they went for a coffee then tried again. This time there was a car parked in the drive.

'In view of what I've told you, will you come to the door with me?' he asked. 'I'd prefer to have a witness to this. In fact, could you take a photo of me handing over the printer? And if you could bear it, would you pretend to be my girlfriend, then he can't accuse me of being involved with Janey?'

'Good thinking. Of course I will.'

He got out the camera, showed her how to work it and then led the way to the front door.

A very overweight man answered it. 'Yes?'

'Mr Dobson?'

'Go away. I'm not buying anything.'

'I'm not selling anything,' Kieran began.

'I don't care why you're here. Go and pester someone else.' He tried to close the door on them.

Kieran tried to hold it open but the other man was stronger. As it began to close, he yelled, 'I've brought back the printer.'

The door stopped moving but the man scowled at him as if this was unwelcome news, so Kieran said, 'You asked for it to be returned, didn't you?'

'Where's Janey? Why hasn't *she* brought it back?'

'She's not got a car and she has a baby to look after.'

'Are you Janey's new fancy man, running errands for her like this?'

Kieran was glaring at him so furiously that Nicole took over. 'What an insulting thing to say! You don't know your own daughter if you think she's like that. Darling, just give him the printer and let's go.'

Dobson ignored her. 'She's the sort who

managed to get a bastard into her belly, isn't she? There's only one way to do that that I know of and you don't manage it by yourself.'

'She was forced,' Kieran said.

'My friend's a high-level policeman and he said they all claim that.'

'Well, we believe her. And as she lives in the flat above me — us — I can assure you she's not getting up to any mischief now,' Kieran told him.

A disbelieving snort was his only answer.

'You go and get the printer, darling,' Nicole said. As he moved away, she turned back to Dobson. 'Not only do my partner and I think very highly of your daughter, so do her social worker and health visitor.'

'She always was a good liar. I never managed to beat that out of her.'

Nicole felt sickened by the relish in his voice as he said this. Janey was a slender girl and he was a large man. She'd have had no chance against him.

Kieran limped back from the car with the printer and cartridge, dumped them on the step and took out a piece of paper. 'Could you sign this, please?'

'What is it?'

'It says you've received the printer and cartridge.'

Dobson took the piece of paper, screwed it up and threw it away. 'Stuff your piece of paper! And this is what I think of computers.' Grinning he kicked the box containing the printer and cartridge off the doorstep, then stamped on the contents hard several times.

Even though she was disgusted by this act of spite, Nicole raised the camera and took a couple of photos of Dobson in the very act of destruction.

With a growl of anger the man turned on her, arm outstretched to grab the camera. Nicole knocked the arm away and Kieran pulled her behind him just as another large man turned in at the gate.

'Afternoon, Lionel. Something wrong?'

Dobson stopped trying to snatch the phone. 'They're photographing me without my permission.' He turned to Kieran. 'This is the friend I told you about. He's a policeman.'

The newcomer looked at them, eyes narrowed, then stared down at the mess of broken printer. 'What's this about?'

Kieran answered him. 'We brought back the printer and cartridge Dobson claimed Janey stole — though she couldn't possibly have done that because she hasn't got a car and wasn't out of town on the day the computer was picked up. He not only refused to sign a paper saying he'd received them from us, but deliberately smashed them. I took a photo of him doing it in case he ever suggests I did that.'

Dobson's friend looked down at the box with the smashed printer in it and said mildly, 'Bit of a waste that, Lionel. Just because you're mad at the little bitch, no need to waste a good printer. I could have used that for my son.'

'Sorry, Gary. I never thought. I'd have got the computer back too, only the wife had promised some interfering social worker to let Janey have a

170

chance at studying and she didn't want to go back on her word. But she never promised her the printer. As if the little bitch will ever make good of herself, anyway! She was born a lying slut, that one was, and lazy with it.'

The two men turned and went into the house, completely ignoring Kieran and Nicole, who exchanged disgusted glances as they walked back to the car.

Kieran let out a sigh of relief as he eased himself into the passenger seat, lifting his bad leg up with his left hand because it was less painful that way. 'I'm going to find out who the other guy is. I've got his car number and his name's Gary. I've still got friends who'll help me find out. I doubt he's a high-ranking policeman, though, because I know most of the local hierarchy. He can't be more than a sergeant or I'd have run into him before.' He winced as he moved to fasten the seatbelt.

'Are you in pain?'

He gave her a wry smile. 'A bit. I've not been as active as this for a while. I'm sure it'll be good for me in the long run. My physio said to increase my activity level bit by bit, as soon as I felt up to it.'

'It must be hard to be so restricted in what you can do after being active.'

He couldn't hold back a sigh. 'They tell me I'll continue to get better, but it's been a year now and I'm still on regular painkillers.'

When they were nearly back at Sexton Bassett, he said, 'Why don't we turn right at the next crossroads? There's a pub in the village that does

171

great Sunday roasts. I used to pop in there sometimes. Unless you're in a hurry to get back?'

She looked at him uncertainly then switched on her indicator and made the turn.

He felt a little uncertain too. It wasn't a date, but it felt like one suddenly.

And she hadn't said no. In fact, she'd blushed.

★ ★ ★

The next day Kieran popped upstairs to see Janey and tell her he'd taken back the printer and cartridge.

'What did Dad say?'

He hesitated.

'I'd rather know.'

'He smashed the printer, stamped on it. Then a friend of his called Gary turned up and they went inside the house.'

Her face turned white and she looked suddenly terrified. 'Did his friend say anything about me?'

'Gary?'

She nodded.

'No, not a word, and he calmed your father down a bit.'

'You didn't tell him where I live, did you?'

No use giving her false hope. 'He'll be able to find out easily enough. He's what — a police sergeant?'

As she nodded and pressed one hand against her mouth, he could see tears welling in her eyes. 'Why are you afraid of him?'

There was a long silence, then she said, 'I

can't talk about that.'

He didn't press the point. But he was pretty sure now that this Gary was somehow involved in what had happened to her. Surely a police sergeant wouldn't go round raping young girls? If such a thing ever came out, the man would lose everything, not only his job, but his freedom and his early retirement.

'If you ever need help, whoever it is that's troubling you, call me,' he said quietly, patting her on the shoulder then going back to his flat.

11

When someone banged the door knocker hard Winifred went into the front room to peep, sighing to see her nephew standing there. She let him knock again, hoping he'd think she was out.

But he didn't go away. He called through the letter box, 'I know you're in there, Auntie. Let me in. I shan't go away until you do. We need to talk and we can't do it like this.'

She felt suddenly nervous and on an impulse rang her friend Hazel, grateful when the phone was picked up straight away. 'My nephew's banging on the front door, insisting on being let in, and I don't know what to do. I'm afraid of him.'

'I'll ring Dawn. She'll come straight across, I'm sure.'

Winifred put down the phone and told herself not to be such a coward. She walked to the front door, not opening it but calling out, 'Go away, Bradley. I don't want to see you.'

'I'm worried about you, Auntie. Why have you had the locks changed?'

The way he said that made her feel even more nervous, his voice was so loud and harsh. And he was a tall man, towering over her. They'd joked about that now and then, but today, she felt threatened by it. She was too frail now to risk dealing with a furiously angry man, so she wasn't letting him in.

'I'll give you two minutes, then I'm coming round the back and breaking in,' he yelled.

'Don't you dare!'

'Something's wrong and I'm worried about you. No one will blame me for checking for myself that you're all right.'

She could guess what that would lead to, calls to social services. She hoped Dawn would get here soon. She didn't want Bradley breaking her windows.

* * *

Janey decided to take advantage of a fine spell and go out for a walk. It'd perhaps clear her head a little, take her mind off worrying about what her father might do next.

She'd just turned down the narrow path between the houses when she heard someone yelling. It was unusual even to see anyone at this end of the street in the daytime, so she slowed down to listen. She heard a man threatening to break into Miss Parfitt's house and stopped walking in shock, standing on tiptoe to peep over the hedge.

The man had his left wrist raised and was looking at his watch. 'One and a half minutes to go, Auntie. Open this door or I'll break in.'

For all he was calling Miss Parfitt 'Auntie', he sounded as if he intended to harm her. Janey didn't want to put Millie at risk but she couldn't leave that nice old lady on her own, just couldn't.

Bracing herself, she turned back on to

Peppercorn Street and walked briskly along to the gate of the big house, opening it with a loud clang of the old-fashioned catch.

'Thirty sec — ' The man spun round. 'Who the hell are you?'

'A friend of Miss Parfitt. Is something wrong?'

'Nothing you need concern yourself about. She's not well enough to see anyone today.'

'Janey!'

She looked up to see Miss Parfitt standing at an open bedroom window above them. 'Are you all right?'

'I will be if my nephew will go away. I don't want to see him and he's threatening to break in.'

'Shall I call the police?' The last thing Janey wanted to do was get entangled with the police again, but she couldn't leave Miss Parfitt to face this tall, angry man on her own, just couldn't, so she got out her mobile.

'Don't you dare!' he growled. 'Or it'll be the last call you ever make on that phone.'

She gaped at him in shock, taking an involuntary step backwards.

He looked back at his watch. 'Ten — nine — eight — '

A car came up the street fast and screeched to a halt outside the house. Dawn jumped out of it and ran to join them on the path.

'Thank goodness you could come,' Miss Parfitt called down. 'Tell my nephew to go away.'

'She's my aunt. And she's not well.' He tapped his forehead to indicate a mental problem.

Even though he was taller than her, Dawn walked right up to him so that he had to step

176

back. 'Don't you dare even hint at that! Miss Parfitt's mind is in excellent working order and if she doesn't want to see you, then she doesn't have to.'

His face went even redder. He scowled up at the window and then at Dawn. 'Someone's poisoned her mind against me. Perhaps it's you. I don't know what you're after, but I'm not letting you take advantage of her like this. I'll be back with help — *official* help. She needs looking after for her own sake and as her only remaining relative with power of attorney, I'm going to make sure that happens.'

There was silence. When Janey would have spoken, Dawn shook her head to warn her not to and pointed towards the gate. 'I think you'd better go, Mr Parfitt.'

He pushed past them with a muttered curse and strode back down the garden path, slamming the door of his car hard.

Dawn waited till he'd driven away before calling up, 'You can come down now, Miss Parfitt.' She turned to Janey. 'Are you a friend of hers, too?'

'I met her coming back from the shops and helped her carry back her groceries. She gave me some lovely cake and she's going to teach me to bake. I was passing by today, taking my baby for a walk, when I heard him threatening her.'

They both turned as the front door was unlocked. Winifred stood there, tears streaming down her cheeks.

'Oh, Dawn, what am I going to do? He'll try to get me locked away, I know he will.'

Dawn moved forward to put an arm round Winifred. 'First of all, let's all go inside. I think a nice cup of tea is called for, don't you?'

The old lady sagged against her for a minute then straightened up with a visible effort. 'I felt terrified of him,' she confessed.

'I felt a bit nervous myself. He's a big man,' Janey said, 'and he was very angry. Um — perhaps you'd like me to leave you two alone now you're all right, Miss Parfitt?'

'No, dear. You come and have a cup of tea too. Don't say you wouldn't like a piece of cake?'

'Well, if you're sure.'

'Dawn, I can't thank you enough for coming so quickly. I don't know what I'd have done without you today.'

'I was just sorting stuff out at the charity shop, so I was nearby. It's lucky I answered my mobile. I don't always. I'll give Mum a ring to let her know you're all right. She'll be worried.'

Winifred was feeling better by the minute, but was already wondering what she'd do if Bradley came back again. Dawn seemed to be reading her mind.

'Does he really have power of attorney?'

'Not now. I've just changed it. But I was afraid to tell him.'

'I'm not surprised. Look, I think you should tell the police about this, and also ask the authorities for a security pendant so that you can call for help if necessary. They issue them to older people living alone for that very reason.'

Winifred frowned. 'I've always tried to avoid getting into the hands of the authorities. Before you know it, they put you in one of those dreadful old people's homes.'

'I think things are a bit different these days. They're more keen to keep people in their own homes, because it saves them a lot of money. I have a friend I could speak to. She's already set Mum up with a pendant. I'm sure she'd make you a priority.'

'I — don't know.'

'It wouldn't hurt to see what they say,' Janey said. 'I've had a lot of help from Social Security people with Millie. They've nearly all been lovely with me — except for one woman from the council, Miss Stevenall. Don't have anything to do with her.'

'I've met her, but she's more admin than social care these days just because she's not good with people.' Dawn looked at Janey in surprise. 'Is she the one who tried to take your baby away?'

'Yes. She came with the police to answer my father's complaint. If a neighbour hadn't helped me, she'd have taken Millie away from me there and then.'

'Even if she was a field worker, she has no right to do that on such flimsy evidence! What on earth is going on?'

'If she'd taken Millie, I bet I'd have found it hard to get her back.' Janey leant forward to kiss her daughter's soft cheek, even though it was smeared with rusk.

'You're right. Look, Miss Parfitt, I'll speak to a

friend,' Dawn said. 'And we'll make sure that Stevenall woman doesn't come anywhere near you. And I'll mention her coming to see you, too, Janey.'

'Would you . . . be with me when they come to see me?' Winifred asked. 'I know I'm being a coward, but I've been keeping away from the authorities for years.'

'I'd be happy to be with you. I was there for Mum only recently, so I know what sort of questions they'll ask.'

'Thank you.' Perhaps it was a good idea, Winifred thought. She had felt so helpless today. Hazel had shown her the security pendant and said how much better it made her feel to be able to call for help.

She was so glad she'd changed her will. And got that letter from her doctor to say that she was in full possession of her mental capacities.

Surely Bradley wouldn't continue to pester her once she made everything clear to him? But she remembered the gloating look in his eyes as he'd stood outside with that Ebony creature, evaluating the house, planning to get her out of it and knock it down.

'Let's call in at the police station tomorrow and report this,' Dawn said. 'I can drive you there. Ten o'clock in the morning suit you?'

'Yes. Thank you so much, dear.'

★ ★ ★

As she left Miss Parfitt's, it began to rain again and Janey had no alternative but to take Millie

180

home. She'd wanted to go to the allotments to see if Mr Shackleton was all right and to say how sorry she was to hear about his wife. She shivered. It was not only wet but bone-chillingly cold today and she didn't like to keep her baby out in it.

Whatever the weather was like, she was going to her college classes, if she had to push Millie's buggy through snowdrifts to get there. She was really looking forward to it, determined to make the most of this unexpected chance to start working for a better life.

She'd managed to get copies of the books she needed for English really cheaply by scouring all the charity shops in town, which seemed like a sign that this was meant to be. She'd started to read them again, trying to remember what her teacher at school had said about them.

How long ago that seemed now! How young and naïve she'd been! And how terrified of what was happening to her. She had learnt a lot since, to look after herself, to be totally responsible for another human being's life, to budget — but she hadn't managed to lose the fear that one day *he* would come after her again.

★   ★   ★

To Janey's relief, the next day was fine and warmer too. She got ready to go for a walk, smiling to see how excited Millie became as she was wrapped in her warm outer clothes. She carried the buggy downstairs first then went back to scoop Millie out of the playpen and carry her down too.

Kieran came out of his flat to open the front door and help her with the buggy. 'Have a good walk!' he called, standing on the steps to wave her goodbye.

Perhaps when she first met him, he'd been feeling ill and that was why he'd been so grumpy and stand-offish. All she knew was he'd been a good friend to her when she needed one and he looked quite cheerful this morning.

She walked up past the big house, but there was no sign of anyone today. She hoped Miss Parfitt was all right but didn't like to knock on her door to find out.

She went on through the park, heading for the allotments. She wanted to see if Mr Shackleton was all right and tell him how sorry she was about his wife.

★ ★ ★

Dan woke up early, lying there for a few moments, trying to pull himself together. He felt washed out today, but lying in bed never did you any good, so he got up and made his breakfast. He could only eat half of it, didn't have much of an appetite lately.

He'd cried last night after he went to bed, when there was no one to see or hear him. This morning he was determined to make a new start. Or rather, to get back into his old habits. At least he wouldn't have to go and visit Peggy in that horrible place any more. He'd dreaded it each time, not only seeing her like that, but even going into the building, which seemed heavy with despair, for all the efforts of the kind people working there.

To his delight the post brought some packets of seeds and that cheered him up a bit. He riffled through them quickly, smiling at the photos of perfect specimens shown on the packets. As if they always grew like that! Afterwards he put the package into the backpack, which he always took to the allotment, and as an afterthought the mobile phone. He'd promised his sons to keep it with him and he always kept his promises.

He'd walk there today, as usual. He didn't need to go fast, just take it easy. The fresh air would do him good. There was nothing like sun on your face, even the watery sun of late February.

He got there by nine, greeted a couple of people he knew and accepted their condolences about the loss of his wife with as much dignity as he could manage. He had to get used to that, he knew, and people meant it kindly, but it seemed to rub salt into his wound each time.

At ten o'clock he put on the kettle for his morning cup of tea and got out his tin of biscuits. The water was boiling merrily when someone tapped on the half-open door. He turned round to see the young lass with the baby.

'Hello, Janey love. You're just in time for a cuppa.'

'Are you sure? I didn't mean to intrude. I just wanted to say how sorry I was about your wife.'

'Thank you, dear. And you wouldn't be

intruding because this young miss is just what I need to cheer me up today.' He bent to tickle Millie and soon had her giving some of her fat, happy chuckles, which always made those watching laugh with her.

'She's a happy baby, that one, knows she's loved.'

'What a nice compliment.'

They sat together in companionable silence, then Janey started telling him about college.

He smiled indulgently. 'You sound excited.'

'I am. I can't wait to do something that uses my brain. I never thought I'd miss school so much.' She sipped the tea, then noticed the pile of packets. 'Oh! The new seeds have arrived. When are you going to start planting them?'

That led them into a lively discussion about the pros and cons of early planting, greenhouses and cloches.

'You remind me of my granddad,' she said wistfully as the discussion eventually flagged. 'He loved his gardening and he made me love it too. I do miss having a garden. Even my dad used to let me grow vegetables for them.' She glanced at her watch. 'Well, I'd better go now. I've got to get us both ready for tomorrow. It'll be Millie's first day in the crèche.'

'I wish you well at college — both of you.'

'Thank you, Mr Shackleton.' She hesitated. 'Is it all right if I come and see you again? I'd enjoy watching your plants grow.'

'I'd love to see you. It gets a bit lonely sometimes.'

He watched her go, thinking what a brave lass

she was, taking on the burden of rearing a child at such a young age. It was youngsters like her who gave you hope for the future — as well as brightening your day.

12

Nothing seemed to go well that day: customers were grumpy, library books fell apart and the officials at the council wanted yet more forms filling in. They were probably responsible for whole forests being destroyed, with their repetitive forms.

Nicole was exhausted by the time she finished a late shift at eight o'clock in the evening. She'd walked to work today because it was fine and sunny, leaving her car in the garage, but as she left the library, she wished she'd driven here. It was dark and even though there were people around, she felt uneasy walking through the streets on her own.

Thanks, William! she thought. *This is down to you. I never used to be afraid after dark.*

As she turned into Peppercorn Street, she thought she could hear the echo of footsteps behind her. She stopped, turning quickly, but could see no one except a group of youngsters laughing and shoving one another as they moved in the other direction.

When she set off again, she tried to walk more quietly, listening carefully for footsteps. But it was how she felt that made her suspect someone was following her, rather than what she heard. It was as if she could sense a hostile presence behind her. She'd read a book once that said you should trust your instincts and pay heed to such feelings.

186

She was still a hundred yards from her block of flats and the street ahead was much darker than the part near the shopping area. Worse, there was no one else around. Should she run the rest of the way? No, that showed fear.

She almost turned to go back to the high street, but if she did that she'd be heading towards whoever was following her.

It could only be William. This was a small town, with a low crime rate.

As she reached Kieran's building, she almost sobbed with the sheer relief of finding a solution. He'd help her, she knew. Turning abruptly, she hurried across the car park to the front door, ringing the bell. Someone laughed in the darkness behind her and she rang the bell again before Kieran had had time to answer, made even more desperate to get inside by that laugh.

The intercom crackled. 'Yes?'

'It's me. Nicole. I think I'm being followed.'

There was a loud click. 'Come in. I've slipped the catch on the door.'

As she pushed it open, something hit her on the back of the head and pain exploded in her skull. At the same time she heard a yell of triumph. She recognised that yell. Definitely William! The force of the missile made her stumble forward, but she managed to yank the door shut behind her even as she was falling.

Something hit the glass panel in the door and shattered it, sending shards of broken glass scattering all over her as she lay on the wooden floor. The second missile landed beside her, a half-brick with jagged edges. She waited, feeling too dizzy to get up, but nothing else followed.

'Don't move!'

She looked up to see Kieran standing at the edge of the glass-littered area. He looked blurred, almost like a double image.

Janey called from the landing. 'Are you all right?'

'I'll look after her,' Kieran called back. 'You go back inside and lock your door.'

He turned back to Nicole. 'We don't want you cutting yourself. Wait there. I'll get some newspaper for you to walk on.' He kept glancing outside. 'I've put the outside lights on, but I can't see anyone, so I think whoever attacked you has gone. Stay where you are unless he comes back. I'm going to call the police.'

She didn't protest at that because she still didn't feel up to moving. The hall kept blurring around her. No more bricks came through the glass as she lay there, waiting for Kieran to return.

It was hard to think clearly. Was her son really doing this to her? Was he attacking other people as well? If so, had he gone mad?

Or perhaps she had? Perhaps she was imagining she'd heard his voice?

No. He had a nasty, testosterone-filled way of yelling, like triumphant footballers sometimes did. You couldn't mistake that yell. And like the sportsmen, he'd had an ugly mask of triumph on his face whenever he yelled like that and pumped his fists in the air.

Kieran's voice made her jump because she hadn't heard him return. 'Are you all right to get up now, Nicole? Let's get you inside my flat.'

He helped her across the thick layer of newspapers that formed a path across the hall. Beneath their feet glass crunched and crackled, and if it hadn't been for him holding her she'd have staggered all over the place.

When they went inside his flat, he took her into the kitchen area. 'We don't look out on to the street here and I've pulled the blinds down, so I think we'll be safe.'

Even as he spoke there was the sound of more glass smashing from the hall, then silence fell for a moment, to be broken by the sound of voices from the street and footsteps going across the floor above them.

'I was wrong,' Kieran said flatly. 'He was still out there, watching us. I'd better tell Janey and the other tenants to stay away from their windows.' He slipped out of the flat again.

Without the comfort of his arm round her shoulders, Nicole began shaking and when she felt the back of her head, it hurt and her hand came away covered in blood. The room still looked blurred.

The door of the flat clicked shut quietly as Kieran returned. 'It's only me.'

She felt him bend over her and a gentle touch on her head.

'That looks nasty. It was a half-brick, I think. There are three on the hall floor now, one with blood on it. It must have been thrown really hard and from quite close to have made a cut like that.'

'William was a good bowler, on the school

team until he got into a fight.'

'William? Your son? Surely he didn't do this?'

'Yes. I recognised his voice.'

Kieran grasped her hand, seeming to understand that she was more upset by it being her son than by the injury itself. 'I'm sorry,' he said softly. 'So very sorry.'

She started to nod, but pain jabbed through her so she said, 'Thanks.'

'Look, I think we're going to have to take you to the hospital to get that cut stitched.'

As she looked at him, she felt warmth on her cheeks. It was a moment or two before she realised it was tears.

'Oh, my dear! Don't cry.'

Once again his arms went round her and she leaned against him, sobbing.

'Do you know why he attacked you?'

'Because he's out of control. Because I won't do what he says and give him money. He's been threatening to make me sorry for leaving them and when he came into the library he looked so wild-eyed and aggressive, I hardly recognised him.'

Flashing lights heralded the arrival of a police car and Kieran went to let the officers in and explain what had happened.

When they came into the flat, one checked her head and said at once, 'Let's get you to hospital before we do anything else. That's a bad cut and I think you've got concussion.'

She couldn't seem to think straight, so let them do what they wanted, comforted by Kieran's arm round her shoulder.

'We'll call for an ambulance. Is there someone

who can come and pick you up after you've been attended to, Mrs Gainsford?' one officer asked.

★ ★ ★

Kieran watched her struggling to think clearly. 'I'll come and pick you up, Nicole. I'll get things secured here first, then drive over to the hospital for you.'

'Thank you.' Her voice was little more than a whisper and her face was chalk white, but her hand clung to his.

He turned to the officers. 'I have some pieces of particle board in the garage which were used when the place was being remodelled. If you can help me carry them into the house, they should fit the hall windows and front door exactly. I kept them in case one of the windows got broken. Good thing, isn't it?'

'Don't you want to call someone in to do the job for you, sir? You're hurt yourself, limping. Do you need checking out as well?'

'No. It's an old injury. I want to make the building safe as quickly as I can, then go to the hospital to be with Nicole.'

The ambulance arrived ten minutes later and he watched bleakly as it drove her away. The paramedics had promised to ensure she was kept safe in case whoever it was pursued her.

'Let's get your wood panels, sir,' one of the two officers said quietly. 'It's not strictly speaking our duty, but it'll mean we can get away more quickly. We don't want to leave this place open to further attacks.'

As they worked Kieran explained in more detail what had happened and who Nicole thought had done it. He promised to go into the police station the next day to make a statement and bring Nicole, if she was up to it.

'Do *you* think it's her son? Did you hear anything?'

'I did hear a yell — she's right about that — but I've never met her son, so I wouldn't recognise him. She was quite sure it was him.'

'She had her tyres slashed too. We took the son into the station, but he denied doing it and we had no proof. Once we've finished here, we'll go and find out where he was tonight.'

Only after the police had left did Kieran wonder how he was going to get to the hospital. He hesitated. Should he call a taxi or . . . No, he'd drive. He could do it. About time, too.

He went to find the car keys. It wasn't all that far to drive and the physio had told him he could try driving when he felt ready. And if it hurt, well, he was used to pain by now.

He had to make sure Nicole was all right and see that she got back safely.

★ ★ ★

The two officers pulled up at the Gainsfords' house. 'Wonder what the husband thinks of her fancy man?' one said.

'If he even knows. He seemed a bit dopey when we came to ask him about his son. Do you think he's using?'

'I don't know. We'll keep our eyes open.'

Sam stared at them even more dopily tonight as they explained why they were there.

'Is your son William here?' one of them repeated.

A lad came into the room to join them. 'He's not been home tonight.'

'And you are?'

Sam stirred. 'This is my younger son, Paul.'

'Did you say Mum's been injured?'

'I'm afraid so. Someone threw a brick at her and it not only stunned her but a sharp edge made a bad cut on the back of her head. It probably needed stitching, so we called an ambulance.' He saw Mr Gainsford blink and lean forward at that, suddenly looking more alert.

'You say Nicole is in hospital? I must go to her.'

'Let's talk about your son William, first. Could he have done it?'

'I can't believe he'd hurt his own mother.'

'He would, Dad. He's been threatening all sorts of things. I told her to be careful.'

'When was the last time *you* saw William, Mr Gainsford?' the officer persisted.

'This morning, before I left for work. He was complaining there was no milk, so I gave him a fiver to get some.'

'He didn't get any, though,' Paul said. 'I had to use my bus money to buy a loaf and some milk for tea.'

Sam jerked to his feet and stood there for a moment before saying, 'I've got to go to the hospital and fetch Nicole back here. She'll need looking after.'

'Doesn't William live here? Will she be safe?'

He stared at the officer in horror. 'I'll — make sure she is, chuck him out if necessary.'

'I don't think she'll come back, Dad. Not with William around.'

'She'll have to. She'll be in no state to look after herself.'

★ ★ ★

Kieran unlocked the new car, which he'd never driven before. It was quite small, one of the more upright models, to cope with his injuries. It was ridiculous to feel so nervous, because he'd been driving for years until the accident, and that had definitely been somebody else's fault, not his. Still, this would be the first time he'd driven in a year and nerves were natural.

He started the car, listening to it purr like a kitten because his brother took it out for a drive every week or two and made sure it was running smoothly. Hagen had been nagging him to try it out on a short drive.

After sitting staring at Nicole's car for a moment, neatly parked beside his in the garage, he pressed the remote to lift the door and slowly backed out. Given the troubles of the night, he zapped the remote again and waited till the door had finished rolling downwards before he moved off.

Thank heavens the car was an automatic and he could manage with only his right foot on the pedals! Even so, it hurt to drive, especially when he had to brake suddenly.

As he went along, he gained in confidence and

nodded approval of himself as he got to the hospital safely. Once there, he was grateful to his brother yet again, this time for making him apply for a disabled sticker. They'd argued about that at the time, and he'd hated the thought of it, but if he hadn't had the sticker, he'd have had to park a long way away from Casualty.

His bad leg and hip were aching ferociously now, so he had to use his walking stick. He looked down, remembering what his leg had looked like after the accident. The leg and hip had had to be rebuilt and would never function properly again. But at least he still had a leg, could still walk if not run.

When he went into Casualty he had to wait in a queue, but someone noticed him leaning on his walking stick and someone else said he looked pale, so a nurse came out to see him.

'Is it yourself you're here for?' she asked, scanning his body as if looking for an injury.

'No, no. I'm here for Nicole Gainsford, who was brought in by ambulance. She'd been hit on the back of the head by a rock.'

'Just a minute.' She went and consulted the computer, beckoning to him to approach the desk. 'Close friend, is she?'

He suddenly wondered if they'd let a mere friend see her or take her home, so said, 'I'm her husband.'

'I'll take you along to see her, then. Doctor's checked her and stitched the cut. It was a nasty one. Don't upset her. She needs to rest for a while before she goes home.'

He found Nicole lying on a high, narrow bed

in a cubicle and she shaded her eyes as light shone into it through the open curtains. He closed the curtains quickly.

'Thank you for coming.' She frowned. 'How did you get here?'

'I drove.'

'I thought you hadn't driven since the accident?'

'Well, the physio said I could start when I felt up to it and tonight seemed a good time to get my hand in again. You'll need a lift home, after all.' He fumbled his way into a chair and groaned in relief. 'Ah. That's better.'

Somehow he found he was holding her hand again and she was clutching his very tightly. It felt so right.

'I want to get out of here as quickly as I can,' she said in a low voice. 'What if Sam comes and tries to take me home? I'd be totally in William's power then.'

'You might have problems if you went back to your own flat tonight, though. Your son clearly knows where you live and you're on the ground floor, so it'd be easy for him to break your windows. Look, don't take this the wrong way, but how about coming to me? I've got a couple of spare bedrooms and I think you'll be much safer there.'

Relief showed on her face. 'Would you mind?'

'On the contrary. I'd enjoy the company.'

'Yes, please, then. I do feel safe with you.'

He couldn't help chuckling. 'Fine Sir Galahad I am! Can't even walk properly.'

She squeezed his hand and smiled. 'We're a bit

past the age of sword fights. Offering a spare bedroom and picking me up from hospital seem very chivalrous actions to me.' She stared at their hands and added softly, 'And there's a connection between us. Don't you feel it?'

'Of course I do, only I was worried it was too soon. You've only just left your husband.'

'My marriage ended years ago. I just — didn't realise it. When he got his new job, he said he had to work longer hours. He simply wasn't there. Then lately — I'm sure he's been seeing someone else.'

'I'm sorry. That must hurt.' He raised her hand to his lips and she let go briefly to caress his cheek. 'I'd better confess. I told them at reception that I was your husband. They'd not have let me see you otherwise.'

'That's fine by me,' she said softly.

They smiled at one another, then didn't say anything, just sat quietly, holding hands again.

Someone screamed suddenly nearby and she jumped in shock. A young child had been crying somewhere close by ever since he arrived, on and on. Amazing how irritating a child's crying could be.

'How are you? Really.'

'My head's thumping and what I'd really like to do is lie down somewhere dark and peaceful, then sleep for a million years.'

'In other words, you want to leave.'

'Please.'

'I'll go and see what they say.'

Her anxious expression returned. 'No, just *tell* them I'm leaving. I won't stay here, whatever they — or you — say. I was planning to go to a hotel if you didn't come. Only somehow I felt you would come for me — and you did.'

It took him nearly quarter of an hour to get her out of there. They took her to the entrance in a wheelchair, then she settled in the car beside him with a sigh of relief.

He eased himself in next to her, not allowing himself to groan.

After a couple of miles, he asked, 'You all right?'

'My head aches.'

'They've given me some more painkillers for you, but you're not to have another one for an hour yet.'

He'd been secretly dreading the journey back, but in fact, it was better than the journey to the hospital. He felt more confident about driving now and having Nicole beside him cheered him up, so that he didn't seem to notice the pain as much. If he could drive again, even if he couldn't go very far, it'd make a huge difference to his daily life.

He'd needed shaking out of his depression, he realised, and thinking of others, helping them, was a very good medicine for doing that.

As they turned into Peppercorn Street, she roused. 'Could we go to my flat first? If no one's around, I'll nip inside and grab a few clothes. These are bloodstained and dirty and I need my night things. I can be in and out within five minutes.'

'Are you sure you're up to that?'

'Yes. Honestly.'

His father drove to the hospital more slowly than usual, too slowly for the traffic conditions on the M4 motorway. Paul glanced sideways at Sam a couple of times but didn't comment on this. 'Where do you think William is?' This was worrying him considerably.

'I don't know. Do you think he did it, attacked your mother?'

'Yes, I do.'

'I can't believe it!'

'Well, he slashed her tyres the other night.'

'Slashed her tyres? Oh, yes, I remember you said so. But they couldn't prove it was him, could they?'

The car slewed to the left suddenly and Paul grabbed the steering wheel to stop them running off the road. 'Watch it, Dad.'

'Sorry. I was distracted for a minute.' He fell silent, then said, 'He's out of control, isn't he? William, I mean.'

'I think it's more than that, Dad. I think he's gone crazy. Maybe it's the steroids he's taking.'

'He's taking steroids?'

'Haven't you noticed how he's beefed up?'

'I thought he was just — growing into a man. No, you must be mistaken.'

Dead silence. Paul didn't break it because you couldn't convince someone who didn't want to believe what you said. His dad looked unhappy. The whole family was in a mess. He didn't blame his mum for bailing out. She was safer away from William. Paul wished he could bail out too.

199

He had wondered about going to see the school counsellor, only it seemed like such a disloyal thing to do. If his dad didn't pull himself together soon, though, he'd have to do it. He wasn't going to hassle his mother about it. She had enough to deal with.

When they got to the hospital, his dad seemed to have difficulty deciding where to park. In the end Paul had to point out a place and just about order him to park there. This was getting weirder and weirder.

In Casualty they waited for ages, then the woman behind the counter told them Mrs Gainsford had already gone home.

'Is she all right, then?' Sam asked.

'And you are?'

'Her husband.'

She looked at him suspiciously. 'Her husband picked her up already and she went with him willingly. I don't know who you are, but — '

Sam got out his wallet and showed them some identification.

The woman went a bit red. 'Well, I'm sorry, but they both said he was her husband.'

'Have you any idea where they've gone?'

'Back home, I suppose. I can find you the address she gave us, but I can't guarantee it's the right one.'

Paul interrupted. He couldn't take much more of this. 'I know where she lives, Dad. We'll go there, shall we?' He had to tug his dad's arm to get him moving and guide him through the car park.

He wished his mum was there, or any adult.

This was too heavy for him.

And he still had William to face when they got back. Would his brother turn on him next?

★ ★ ★

There seemed to be no one lurking near Nicole's flat. Kieran wanted to go in with her, but she insisted she'd be all right. There was a security number pad on the door and she didn't think William was good enough technically to bypass that.

Kieran rolled the car window down so that he'd hear if she called and watched her as she went inside. She seemed to be walking steadily now, thank goodness.

He kept an eye on the street, but nothing moved and no one passed by on foot. It wasn't as well lit here as near his house, because there was no reflected glow from the brightly lit shop windows in the main street.

In a very short time Nicole came out again, her face a pale blur as she moved towards the car.

'You all right?' he asked.

She nodded and winced. 'I must remember not to nod. It hurts.'

He drove back down the street, relieved when he got the car safely into the garage without them being attacked, though he didn't tell her that. He was glad of the back door that led from the garage into his flat.

Once inside, he showed her the spare bedrooms. 'Choose whichever you prefer and I'll help you make up the bed.' While she was looking, he went into the kitchen to find his own painkillers.

She came in just as he was swallowing a tablet. 'Is your leg hurting a lot?'

'A bit. It's not used to so much activity. But I feel good about driving again. Um — I may get a bit dopey when this kicks in. It's quite a strong painkiller and I only take them at night to help me get comfortable enough to sleep. Just help yourself to anything in the kitchen or fridge if I fall asleep on you.'

'Let's both sit down. My head's thumping and I'm having that other painkiller as soon as I'm allowed. I'm sorry you got caught up in my troubles, Kieran. I hope your insurance will cover the damage to the hall windows.'

'It should do. And it's not your fault. You've nothing to apologise for.' He let the silence flow for a few seconds then added, 'Your son is seriously disturbed.'

'Yes. I realise that. I've been trying to think where I went wrong with him.'

'I doubt it was your fault. Mental illness can happen in the best of families.'

'Mental illness.' She couldn't speak for a moment or two, shocked at that label being put on a lad of almost eighteen, a lad whose life should just be moving into a rich and happy phase. 'That sounds so terrible.' She couldn't help it. Tears overflowed again and she mopped her eyes with a crumpled tissue.

He picked up a box of tissues and dumped it on the coffee table, hesitated then sat next to her

202

on the couch. As she tried desperately to stop weeping, his heart went out to her and he put one arm round her. With a sigh, she leant against him and they stayed there for some time without speaking.

Once again, it felt right.

13

On Wednesday morning Paul woke slightly later than usual and got out of bed hurriedly, not wanting to be late for school. He peered cautiously out of his room, listening intently. The house was absolutely silent. His dad must have gone to work already, but his brother was normally still around at this time so he had to tread carefully.

He went to listen at William's door, but there was no sound from inside. His heart thumping nervously, he cracked open the door just a little, then pushed it wide open with a sigh of relief. No one there!

The bed was a mess — well, it hadn't been made since their mum left — but there was no sign of the owner of the room. He looked round and noted that William's backpack was missing. That went everywhere with his brother so he must be out.

Greatly relieved Paul went along the landing towards the stairs. He'd better get a move on.

But as he was passing his parents' room, he stopped in shock. The door was half open and his father was still lying in bed. He was going to be very late for work because now he'd catch the heavy morning traffic. He went across to the bed. 'Dad?'

His father didn't stir.

'Dad? Wake up.' He shook his father's shoulder. Very slowly, as if he was still more asleep than awake, his father opened his eyes. But he still made no attempt to get up.

'Dad? Are you all right?'

Sam frowned and rubbed his forehead. ''S worse today.'

'What's worse?'

'Headache. Weeks now. Won't go 'way. Can't think straight.'

'Have you seen a doctor?'

'Don't go to doctors for headaches.'

Paul sat down on the bed. There was only him left to say it. 'Dad, I think it's more than a headache — you've been acting a bit strange as well. I think Mum was right. You really should see a doctor. Shall I ring up and make an appointment?'

'No.' He tried to stand up and winced, lying back, both hands clasping his head. 'Can't get up. Feel dizzy.'

'Shall I get you an appointment?'

His father just groaned and closed his eyes.

'Dad, speak to me.'

But his father didn't even groan this time. His eyes were closed and he looked dreadful.

Paul ran downstairs and found the number for the medical centre, impatiently waiting for a human being to answer. 'My father's not well. He's acting strangely. I don't know what to do.'

'Can he come in to see one of the doctors?'

'No. He just tried to get up and fell back on the bed. He said before he felt dizzy. Now he won't answer me.'

'Isn't there anyone who can drive him here?'

'No. There's only me and I'm fifteen.'

205

'You're sure he spoke to you before?'

'Yes.'

'Did he make sense?'

'Sort of.'

'Perhaps it's just a migraine. Still, we'd better check. Where do you live? Oh, Eastwick Street. Good. Our health visitor's about to leave to visit another house nearby. I'll get her to pop into your place first and see what she thinks.'

'How long will she be?'

There was a mutter of voices, then, 'About ten minutes. She's setting off straight away.'

After he'd put the phone down Paul hesitated. He should probably have called an ambulance straight away. But how did you know? Anyway, if this nurse was coming, she'd know better than him.

It seemed more like ten hours till she arrived. Paul could get no sense from his father, who occasionally groaned but mostly just lay there.

When the doorbell at last rang, he bounded downstairs to answer it.

'I'm Sally Makepeace, the health visitor. You rang our medical centre.'

'I'm Paul Gainsford. Come in.'

'Is your father still feeling unwell?'

'He's lying in bed and he keeps groaning. He hasn't said a word since I rang the centre.' Paul was hugely embarrassed to find himself near tears and blinked his eyes furiously.

She laid one hand on his forearm. 'It's all right to get upset when someone you love is ill. Where's your mother?'

'She left home a couple of weeks ago. I can't

get her to answer the phone in her new flat. She was attacked last night and had to go to hospital, so I don't know if she's gone back there. And if she hasn't, I don't know where she is.'

'I see. Well, first things first. Let's go and look at your father.'

The back door banged open and William came in. He stopped dead when he saw the health visitor, then looked at his brother. 'Who's she?'

Paul explained quickly.

'Oh, hell, that's all we need. Well, don't expect me to look after him. I only came back for some clean clothes.' He pushed in front of Mrs Makepeace and went up the stairs two at a time.

She frowned and looked at Paul.

He shook his head to warn her not to tackle William about this rudeness, then led the way up to his parents' bedroom.

She couldn't get his father to respond, either. 'We need to get him to hospital. I'll call an ambulance.'

William came to lean in the doorway. 'What's wrong with him?'

'I don't know, but he's not fully conscious.'

He came into the room and picked up his father's wallet from the side of the bed. 'I need some money for going to school.'

'You've been suspended!' Paul protested. 'You don't even need to go out of the house.'

William gave him a backhander that made his head ring and sent him staggering back against the wall. He took all the notes out of the wallet and shoved them in his pocket.

The health visitor stood defensively in front of

Paul, glaring at William. 'You can't need all that much! Put it back.'

Paul held his breath, ashamed that he was sheltering behind her.

William grinned. 'Oh? And who's going to make me? You? I don't think so. Him? He's a weakling like my father. They deserve one another.'

He threw the empty wallet down on the bed and went out again into his bedroom. Drawers opened and shut, then they heard him laughing as he ran down the stairs.

Only when the back door banged shut did Paul let out his breath in a whoosh.

'The police are looking for him,' he said in a shaky voice. 'He attacked Mum last night, threw a brick at her. That's why she had to go to hospital.'

The health visitor sucked in her breath in shock, then shook her head helplessly and turned back to the man on the bed, saying, 'You'd better pick up that wallet and any other money or valuables in the house. I'll take you to hospital and we'll keep trying to get in touch with your mother. You definitely can't deal with this on your own.'

He nodded. He felt about ten years old and scared, so very scared. What if his dad died? What if William hurt their mother again?

And what was going to happen to him?

* * *

Janey got up feeling excited and a bit apprehensive. When she and Millie were ready, she set off for college, arriving much too early for her class because she'd been so afraid of being late.

She took Millie to the crèche and saw her settled, liking the way the staff there dealt with her daughter and asked quite a lot of questions about her needs and habits. The littlies were playing happily in the next room, there were a couple of other babies in this one, and in the bigger kids' room, everyone was sitting round on the floor listening to a story.

'Don't worry,' the woman in charge said. 'We'll take good care of your baby. You just concentrate on your studies.'

'What time do I have to pick her up?'

'Whenever you like, as long as it's before six o'clock. You may want to do some studying in the library on your days here. You're never really free to concentrate if you're caring for a baby, are you?'

Janey walked away feeling astonished. She hadn't realised they'd look after Millie all day. It'd be great to go to the library. Suddenly she felt younger and less burdened. She loved Millie to pieces but it was wonderful to have some time for herself. Straightening her shoulders, she went to find the room where her class was.

The tutor was already there, so she introduced herself and he told her where they were up to, offering to give her an hour or two of personal tuition to help her catch up, if necessary.

'That's very kind of you!'

He gave her an understanding smile. 'My older daughter's a single mother, too, though she's older than you and she's got me and my wife to help her. I know what it's like, how hard it's been for her at times, even with our support, so if I can help you to catch up, it'll be my pleasure. Ah, here they come.'

People came in, one or two at a time. When everyone was settled, he introduced her to the others then started the lesson. She listened intently, relieved when she found her recent reading had given her the information she needed to follow what they were discussing.

It wasn't at all like the classes at school. There were students of all ages, some quite old, and after the lesson was over, a group of them said they were going for coffee and invited her to go too.

Rashly she said she would, but began to worry about the cost of the coffee.

'Something wrong?' the girl walking next to her asked.

She hesitated but it was no use pretending. 'I've — not got much money.'

'If you can't afford to buy a coffee, just get a cup of water from the dispenser. It's what I do when my money's running low.' She grimaced. 'I've been unemployed for over a year now.'

It was wonderful to sit and chat, though the group went silent when she told them she had a baby and lived on her own.

'Phew! That must be hard work,' one of them said.

Janey shrugged. 'It's worth it.'

After the group broke up, she had time before her next class, so went to the library to start finding her way around it. She was tempted to nip over to the crèche to check on Millie, but didn't really have time to do that. She worried though, kept thinking of her baby and hoping she wasn't upset. They'd not been separated for so long since she brought Millie home from hospital.

The next class was run by a woman totally without a sense of humour, but at least she knew her stuff. It wasn't half as interesting, though, because the woman talked at them and didn't give them much opportunity to discuss anything.

As they were leaving, one of the younger guys started walking alongside her. 'She's an old tight-knickers, isn't she? Want to come for a coffee?'

It took Janey a minute to realise he was chatting her up. She hadn't expected that somehow and wasn't sure how to deal with it. In the end, she said, 'Thanks, but I want to go and check on my daughter. It's her first day at the crèche.'

He gaped at her. *'Daughter!'*

She held her head high. 'Yes. I'm a single mother.'

'You don't look old enough to have a child.'

She shrugged and was turning away when he said mildly, 'I was only inviting you for a coffee. I'd still like you to come.'

He had a nice smile. She was tempted. It was so long since a guy had even looked at her with interest. You became sort of invisible when you were behind a baby buggy. 'Another time, maybe. I really do have to check up on Millie.'

'Cool name.' With a wave of his hand he slouched off.

She stood there motionless, gobsmacked that anyone had wanted to chat her up. As she walked away, she smiled. It was nice to feel attractive again. Maybe one day . . .

She went to the crèche and they showed her a sleeping Millie who looked rosy and serene. 'Thanks. I was just a bit, you know, worried.'

'First-day syndrome. You go and enjoy yourself. We have looked after one or two babies before.'

She ate her sandwiches sitting in a sheltered corner, finding it a bit cold, but not knowing where else to go. People were hurrying here and there. Some were standing chatting in groups. There were only one or two others on their own and they were older than her.

Afterwards she went back to the library and began to make notes for an essay they'd been set, able to work so much more quickly without any interruptions.

Even when she'd lived at home, she'd not been able to work so steadily, because her father had interrupted her regularly, shouting at her to make him a cup of tea if her mother was out, or even to fetch his newspaper from the next room. He was a bully and a slob, always insisting on his womenfolk waiting on him hand and foot, and once he got home he sat on the couch and only stirred to get his tea or visit the toilet.

Sometimes she'd felt he asked her to do things on purpose to interrupt her studies. When the subject of her going to university came up, he often said that he'd never got any qualifications and it hadn't stopped him finding a job and keeping it. Women only got married so university was a waste of time. But for some reason her mother had always stuck up for her, saying she wanted her daughter to go to uni. Her mother didn't often stand up to him, but when she did, he backed off.

His opposition had only made Janey more determined to do well at school, but he'd never praised her for getting straight As on her reports, just grunted and tossed it aside.

At three o'clock she gathered her papers and books together and went to pick Millie up, feeling rested and happy in spite of a hard day's work. She had a lot of catching up to do if she was to build on her good results so far. If she could get through more than one subject a year, that'd be great.

And she'd meet people her own age, too. Maybe even make a friend or two.

Was that too much to ask? Surely nothing else would go wrong?

★ ★ ★

Winifred felt nervous all morning. Someone was coming today to check out her need for a security pendant and anything else they thought might help her. There were apparently all sorts of services to support the elderly in their own homes. She wasn't at all sure she wanted to be beholden to the authorities, but she was at a stage in life where she had to get some protection and help.

Dawn arrived at the appointed time, bright

and smiling as usual. What a lovely woman she was!

'I'm so grateful to you for coming, dear.'

'My pleasure. I hope one day, when I'm old, someone will help me if I need it. And besides, you're Mum's friend, so that makes it even more of a pleasure. She's cheered up so much since she got to know you.'

Winifred could feel herself flushing with pleasure and was glad when the doorbell gave her a chance to turn away.

A man was standing on the doorstep and behind him was her nephew.

'Dawn!' she called in a panic.

Dawn came running, saw Bradley giving them a triumphant smile and turned to the official. 'I don't know why you've brought this man here, but he's been asked to stay away from Miss Parfitt.'

'He's her nephew and he's worried about her.'

Winifred felt ashamed of herself for being so weak-willed and stepped forward. 'Well, he's not coming into my house, not now and not at any time in the future, if I have to take out a restraining order to stop him.' She wasn't sure how you did that but it seemed to hit home to Bradley, who glared at her for a moment then forced a false smile on to his face.

'It really would be best if your sole surviving relative joins us,' the official said.

She looked at him in surprise. 'He's not my sole surviving relative. Whatever gave you that idea?'

'The others don't count,' Bradley said. 'They

haven't been near you for years, Auntie. I'm the only one who cares about you and I'm sure this is all a mix-up. You do get confused sometimes.'

'I do not get confused. And it's my fault that I've not kept in touch with my other relatives but I've already taken steps to remedy the matter. In the meantime I have good friends like Dawn here who keep an eye on me.'

'Couldn't you just let him come in and talk, to set his mind at rest?' The official's tone was again that of someone talking to a rather stupid person.

'No. He's not setting foot inside my house again.' But she was beginning to get worried about the way the two men kept looking at one another meaningfully.

Dawn looked at the official. 'Who are you, anyway? We haven't seen your identity card nor do we know your name.'

'My name's Hersen.' He fumbled in his pocket. 'I must have — um, forgotten my ID card. Ring the council offices and ask them if they know a Hersen.'

'I certainly shall. In the meantime, you'd better come back another time when you do have ID with you. And this time, make an appointment first.' She started to shut the door and he put out one hand to stop her. She looked at him in amazement. 'Excuse me!'

'Please go away, Mr Hersen,' Winifred said. 'This is my house and I say who comes in.'

From the look her previously loving nephew gave her, Bradley was getting very angry indeed.

Dawn took the opportunity to shut the door.

215

'Shall we ring up the council and ask if they know a Mr Hersen? It's strange, but I've never known an official try to get into someone's house without an ID card.'

'I'll check the letter I received first. It'll have the phone number on it.' Winifred led the way into the kitchen and took out the letter from the council. As she read it, she looked at Dawn in shock. 'This says a Ms Mary Hersen will be coming to see me today. Ms not Mr.'

'Ring the number they give for enquiries. Do you want me to speak to them for you?'

'No. I can do that myself, but I may need you to corroborate what I say.' It took her a long time to get through to the correct department — did they think ratepayers had unlimited time to wait around while they played idiotic music in their ears? — but she didn't hang up. This was too important.

When she explained why she was calling, there was silence, then the woman at the other end of the line said, 'But you wrote to cancel the appointment.'

'I most certainly did not.'

'I have your letter here. It has your signature on it. Perhaps you've forgotten.'

'And perhaps someone else wrote that letter. Excuse me for a moment.' She explained to Dawn what had happened.

'Can I speak to her?'

'Dawn Potter here. I'm a friend of Miss Parfitt and I can assure you that she is in complete possession of her faculties. If she said she didn't write to you, I believe her. She's currently having

216

trouble with her nephew and is about to see her lawyer about him. If your letter has what looks like her signature on it, she'll need to change the way she signs her name, as well.'

She listened, nodding. 'Yes, terrible. So we'll be down to see you in ten minutes. Thank you so much for sparing us the time. It's much appreciated.'

She turned to Winifred. 'I'm sorry to have taken over and made arrangements without consulting you, but I've had a lot of practice at dealing with bureaucracies. Now, we'd better go there and check this letter that supposedly has your signature on it. I'll drive you there and back.'

'I'm very grateful for your help.'

'It's my pleasure. I can't bear the way some people treat the elderly.' She smiled wryly. 'Various older celebrities are trying to do something about that and I hope the Dignity in Care Campaign makes a difference. Sometimes systems and carers don't allow old people any dignity or choice. It's rather a thing of mine, after seeing the way some officials have tried to treat Mum. And now you. Is the house locked up at the back? Right. Get your coat and handbag and we'll go and see this Ms Hersen.'

★　★　★

At the council offices, Dawn parked the car, winked at Winifred and led the way inside. She was known by one or two people and greeted cordially. Within two minutes they were being shown into an office.

After they'd introduced themselves, Dawn sat back. 'I'll let Miss Parfitt speak for herself, which she's well able to do.'

Winifred explained what had happened, answered questions about why she had turned against her nephew, then asked to see the letter cancelling the appointment. She studied it then showed it to Dawn.

'This is very like my signature, but I definitely didn't write this letter.'

'Would you do me a signature now?' Mary asked.

She did so and they compared them.

'It is very alike,' Mary said. 'What worries me is how they knew you had an appointment in the first place, or that it was with me. Did you tell your nephew about it?'

'Definitely not.'

She pursed her lips. 'Then either someone has been intercepting your mail or we have a person in the office prepared to sell information — which is not unknown in local bureaucracies, unfortunately.'

Winifred sighed. 'Either way, I'd better go to the bank and change my signature. I've already cancelled the enduring power of attorney vested in my nephew.'

'Indeed yes, and the quicker the better. Have you any idea what signature you'll use? Ah. Good idea. And if it's all right, I'll come and see you at home this afternoon, Miss Parfitt, with a pendant. I can see that it's urgent for you to be able to summon help.'

'Thank you.' Winifred looked at them both and they were two women of such obvious goodwill that she confided, 'I can't believe this is happening. My life was boring and uneventful for years, then suddenly it's one thing after another, most of them good, but now this!'

Dawn smiled at her as they walked out. 'You did well there. She didn't need convincing that you're in full possession of your faculties. No one would have doubted you, listening to you explain things so succinctly. Which bank are you with? Oh, good. We can walk there from here.'

'I'm taking too much of your time.'

'I'm giving my time willingly. I believe what goes around, comes around.'

Winifred had to blink her eyes again and sniff rather inelegantly to clear the tears that threatened.

After explaining to the bank manager what was happening and registering a new signature, they went on to the lawyer's office, where Winifred also changed her signature and then created a new power of attorney naming her lawyer, whom she trusted absolutely.

As they came out, Dawn smiled at her. 'A good morning's work, don't you think? This calls for a cup of tea and a piece of cake to celebrate. Let's go round to Mum's. She loves visitors to drop in.'

14

Paul sat beside Mrs Makepeace in the hospital waiting area. They'd taken his father away and he felt very much alone, in spite of the kindness of the woman sitting beside him.

'I'm sorry for taking up your time,' he said.

She smiled at him. 'It's an emergency. No one's fault. And call me Sally. I always think it's my mother-in-law if someone says 'Mrs Make- peace'.'

'Sally.' He stared at the floor, kicking the heel of his trainer against it. 'Dad should have gone to a doctor sooner, you know. He and Mum kept having rows about that. They were always arguing towards the end, except when they weren't speaking to one another.'

'That must have been hard for you.'

He nodded, his throat suddenly feeling too full to force any more words out.

'And your brother? How long has he been acting up?'

That was easier to talk about. 'Years. But when I was little, he mostly ignored me and hung out with older boys. He only started being really gross last summer after he got in with a new crowd, grown-ups mostly. He looks like a grown-up too, he's so big, but he hasn't grown up inside his head. I don't think his friends know he's not eighteen yet. And . . . I think they're dealing in steroids or body-building drugs of some sort. He always needs money and it doesn't last.'

Paul looked at a poster on the wall opposite, which was just a blur because of the tears brimming in his eyes. 'Those guys seem to hate women, from the rubbish William's been spouting ever since he joined them. He's been really rude to Mum and he won't help in the house. He won't even pick up his own clothes.'

When Sally made an encouraging noise and continued to look interested, Paul went on talking, feeling relieved to be telling someone.

'William's been punching me sometimes, not where it'd show. He used to take my lunch money till I started hiding it in my shoe. He's way out of control. My parents argued about him as well, because Dad wouldn't even try to sort him out and Mum couldn't. And then — '

'I'm sorry to interrupt but I think they want us,' she said gently. 'We'll go on talking later.' She led the way to the desk.

The woman there asked him all sorts of questions about his father, most of which he couldn't answer, then she turned to Sally. 'We need an adult member of the family to deal with this.'

'Do you know where your mother is?' Sally asked.

Paul hesitated, then nodded. 'I've got her mobile number. Should I ring her?'

'I think you'd better.'

'If she's at work, she may not answer.'

'In that case, we'll ring the library.'

But his mother did pick up the call. The sound

of her voice made him want to weep in relief. 'Mum, it's me and I — ' It was a moment before he could continue, then he said in a rush, 'Dad's in hospital and they need to speak to an adult about him.'

'*What?*'

He lost it then and as tears started rolling down his cheeks, he handed the phone to Sally, wiping away the tears with his sleeve and trying in vain to stop more leaking out.

★　★　★

Nicole listened in horror to what Sally told her. 'I'll come straight away.'

She switched off the phone and looked at Kieran, wondering if she dared ask him to go with her. 'It's Sam. He's in hospital and he's not fully conscious. There's only Paul there, so I have to go.'

'I'll drive you. You've still got a blinding head-ache, haven't you?'

She'd learnt by now not to nod. 'Yes. And those painkillers make me muzzy-headed. Are you sure you're all right to drive? I could get a taxi.'

'Of course I'll drive you there.'

They travelled in silence. She had a pillow be-hind her head to soften the impact of any jolting around, but the movement of the car as it stopped and started, turned corners and slowed down still hurt. When they got there, she was relieved to find they could park close to the entrance, in a disabled bay.

As they walked into the hospital, Kieran looked

at her in concern. 'You've not got a vestige of colour in your cheeks. You're not going to keel over on me, are you?'

'No.'

They were ushered into a little side room and Paul jerked to his feet at the sight of his mother.

As he was about to rush over to her, Kieran put out one hand to stop him. 'Don't jolt her. She's got a bad cut on her head and any sudden movement hurts.'

Nicole tried to smile reassuringly at her son, clasping his hand and giving it a squeeze. 'Sorry, Paul. Consider yourself hugged.'

'I didn't realise he'd hurt you so badly. Me and Dad heard about William attacking you and we came to the hospital, but you'd left, so I thought you must be all right. Only you weren't at your flat. Where were you?'

'In a spare bedroom at my place,' Kieran said. 'She was afraid to go back to the flat in case your brother turned up again. Sit down, Nicole, before you keel over.'

She sank down on the seat next to her son and reached out for his hand to give it a quick squeeze. Paul introduced Sally, who then took over and explained the situation.

'Now that you're here, Mrs Gainsford, the doctor wants to talk to you about your husband.'

'Thank you for your help,' Nicole said automatically.

Even as she spoke there was a tap on the door and a tired-looking man in a crumpled white coat came in. He looked at Nicole, frowning slightly.

'I'm Mrs Gainsford.'

'Didn't I attend to you last night?'

'Yes.'

'How's the head?'

'A bit better but still throbbing.'

'You really should have stayed in hospital overnight.'

'I was afraid to.'

He picked up her wrist, took her pulse then shone a light into each eye in turn. 'The concussion seems to have cleared up at any rate. I was going to suggest you continue to take it easy, but with your husband here and in such a serious condition we need you around.'

'Shall I wait outside?' Sally stood up. 'You may want to be private for this.'

'Don't go!' Paul said. 'Please.'

Sally looked at Nicole, head cocked in a question.

'Yes, do stay.' She turned back to the doctor. 'Have you found out what's wrong with my husband, doctor? He's been having these headaches for a long time and lately he's started acting strangely. I've been trying to get him to see a doctor since last year, when it first began. I left him a couple of weeks ago, so I've not seen him since then. He sounds to have got worse rapidly.'

The doctor hesitated then said quietly, 'It might have been better if he'd seen a doctor a while ago, but the outcome would probably have been the same in the long term. We think he's got a brain tumour, a glioma this sort is called, and I'm afraid they're inoperable.'

224

There was dead silence in the room, then Paul reached for his mother's hand again.

She sat there numbly, feeling sick with horror. And guilt. She'd left him — and he'd been ill. What sort of woman did that? 'I thought he was having an affair.' She burst into tears.

Paul hugged her, Sally thrust a tissue into her hand and the doctor glanced at his watch.

Nicole forced herself to calm down. 'Sorry. It was the shock. Go on, Doctor.'

'We'd like to make sure our diagnosis is correct. We've done a CT scan and we'd like to do an MRI scan tomorrow.'

'How is he?'

He sighed and seemed to be bracing himself to speak, so she knew it wasn't good news.

'Only semi-conscious, I'm afraid. We suspect the cancer has metastasised and is now affecting both mental and physical functions.'

'Can I see him?'

'Yes, of course. But I'd better warn you that he probably won't recognise you. He's drifting in and out of consciousness at the moment. If you wait here, one of the nurses will let you know when we've got him settled in the ward. And perhaps you can bring him some things from home tomorrow? If he regains consciousness, he'll be happier with something familiar to hand. We . . . um, are never quite sure how people will be affected when we get to this stage.'

She stared at him in horror at this further shock. *If* Sam regained consciousness? *If?*

When the doctor had left, Sally asked, 'Is there anything I can do to help?'

'I don't know. I can't seem to think straight. Give me a minute or two to get my head round it.'

They left her in peace but she couldn't seem to focus. She looked up and it was Kieran she turned to instinctively. 'What am I going to do?'

'Take one step at a time,' he said gently. 'It was the best advice I received after my accident, when I didn't know if I'd walk again.'

'Yes. You're right. First I have to see him. I can't do anything till I've seen for myself how he is. And then — ' She shook her head and winced at the jolt of pain.

'Then you need to rest. Shall you be going back to live in your house now?'

Nicole shuddered. 'No. I'm still afraid of William.' She turned to Paul. 'I have a spare bedroom in my flat. It's not very big, but you could stay there with me until — until we see our way clear.'

He gulped and nodded. 'Thanks, Mum. I was terrified of going back home. I've put extra bolts on the inside of my bedroom door, but William could easily kick it in.'

'Why didn't you tell me he was bullying you?' Nicole burst out. 'I'd have taken you with me when I left.'

'It's not the sort of thing you talk about. What a wimp I'd sound, afraid of my own brother. And really, he mostly left me alone. I didn't have any money, you see. He used to take it out of your purse sometimes, boasted about that.'

She stared at him open-mouthed. 'I just thought prices were going up quickly.' After a moment she added, 'I was afraid of him too.'

'A difficult situation,' Sally said. 'There is help available, you know. Grown-up children do bully parents, and if they have mental health problems it's even harder for families to deal with this on their own. One of your next steps might be to seek professional help.'

'Mental health problems!' That phrase again. She was finding it hard to come to terms with it. 'The trouble is, William knows where I live. He followed me to the flat from the library last night.'

'I'm sure the police will keep an eye on the flat.'

'But by the time they get there, he could have . . . done anything.'

'Why don't you and Paul both stay with me, for tonight at least?' Kieran suggested. I have two spare bedrooms and you'll rarely be on your own there, because I don't go out much.'

'We can't impose,' she said automatically.

'You need help.' He looked at Paul. 'Tell your mother it's a done deal. We'll make your flat more secure tomorrow, then you can go back if you want.'

'He's right, Mum. We can't be on our own just now. William could beat up the pair of us with no trouble. You should have seen him today. He took the money out of Dad's wallet while Dad was lying on the bed. Sally was standing there. She'll tell you.'

'I didn't like to confront him, either,' she said. 'He's — frightening. There's a wild look in his eyes.'

Kieran nodded. 'That's settled, then. You're both coming to stay with me. So that's another step planned. After you've had a rest, you'll be able to see your way more clearly.'

It was surprising how often she wanted to nod. She stopped herself and said, 'Yes.'

A nurse poked her head into the room. 'Mrs Gainsford? You can see your husband now. Only five minutes, though.'

Paul and Kieran stood up, too.

The nurse shook her head. 'Only one visitor, I'm afraid.'

'We'll wait outside his room,' Kieran said. 'Mrs Gainsford is in some danger at the moment from a — a stalker, and she can't be left on her own.'

The nurse goggled at them. 'What about Mr Gainsford?'

'I think he'll be safe, but don't let his son William in to see him.'

'Tell me that name again when we get up to the ward. I'll write it down and warn the others.'

★ ★ ★

Nicole went into the room reluctantly, wishing Kieran was with her. It was all too easy to rely on him.

She stood by the bed looking down at her husband, only at the moment he didn't look much like Sam. He looked years older, more like her father-in-law. Which reminded her, she'd have to get in touch with Sam's parents and let them know their son was terminally ill. And tell

228

them about William. She did hope the police would have caught him by then.

Tears welled in her eyes. The estrangement between her and Sam wasn't only because of the changes associated with the tumour, but those changes in behaviour had certainly weighed heavily on her decision to leave. And she'd been so mistaken about him having an affair. Guilt sat like a heavy stone inside her chest.

And yet, how could she have known he had a brain tumour?

She bent over to kiss his cheek and he muttered something indistinguishable without opening his eyes.

Someone came to join her, another nurse. 'He's not in any pain, Mrs Gainsford,' he said quietly.

'How can we be sure?'

'We're pretty sure.' He glanced at Nicole's bandage. 'Now, you look like you've been in the wars too and need your rest. Go home and take it easy.'

'If my other son comes here — William — he's dangerous. You should call the police. They're looking for him. But I don't think he will come.'

'That's partly what I came in to see you about. My colleague told me. What does your son look like?'

'He's about six foot tall, muscular, with dark hair and eyes, and a — a fierce expression, that's the only way to describe it. The police are looking for him.'

'Very well. I'll put that in your husband's notes.'

With a final glance back at Sam, Nicole left the room. She found Paul and Kieran outside, chatting in lowered voices. They both broke off, then Paul came forward.

'How is he, Mum?'

'Not really conscious. Shall I ask if you can see him, just for a minute?'

'No. I don't want to see him again, not like that.'

'We'll go to my place, then,' Kieran said. 'Do you want to go home first to pick up some clothes, Paul?'

He shook his head. 'I'd rather do that with the police nearby.'

'You're that scared of William?' Nicole was aghast.

'I am now. You didn't see him today. He was, like, Aggro-Man.'

★ ★ ★

Janey was sitting quietly, playing card games on her computer and thinking of going to bed. When she heard a car, she went to the window. Living alone made you nosy, she'd found.

The garage door began to roll up and the light inside showed her that it was Kieran. He had the kind librarian with him, as well as a lad. They drove into the garage and the door rolled down on them. There must be another way inside the building from the garage because they didn't come out.

Were the woman and boy staying here? As far as Janey was concerned, the more people there were around her, the better. She'd been feeling jittery this evening, worrying about her father and Gary, worrying that either or both of them might come after her.

Her parents had never believed her when she said she'd been forced. They'd think she'd gone crazy if she told them it was Gary. She hadn't said a word about him to anyone because he'd threatened to kill her if she revealed who'd raped her. And she'd believed him.

If he'd thumped her about, it'd have been easier to prove, but by the time she realised what he was doing that night, he'd had handcuffs on her and she'd been helpless.

She felt fairly safe here, but if Gary came near her again, she was going to tell the world who'd raped her. If he tried to hurt her again, she'd make sure he got in trouble about it. But surely a man in his position had too much to lose to mess around with her again?

She'd always hated him. He was as chauvinistic as her father. No wonder he'd not got promoted. She'd heard him complaining to her father about that more than once, saying they only wanted toffee-nosed, squeaky-clean policemen these days, some of them trained at university. If they listened to men like him, men who knew what the world was really like, they'd solve a lot more crimes.

With a sigh she went to bed, not forgetting to slide the bolt on the outer door and jam the chair under the handle. She always kept the door locked, even in the daytime, but one little lock never felt quite enough to keep her safe.

Kieran led the way inside. He was in considerable pain now, but it didn't seem to matter as much as before. What was much more important was making sure Nicole got a good night's sleep.

'Drinking chocolate?' he asked. 'Old-fashioned, but so comforting.'

'Yes, please.'

Paul looked at him doubtfully.

'If you're hungry, there's plenty to eat.'

'I am a bit hungry.'

'I'll get him something,' Nicole said automatically.

'You're to go to bed and get the rest you need or you'll not be fit to face tomorrow. I'll look after Paul.' He smiled at her, wanting to give her a hug, she looked so forlorn, but knowing she'd not want him to do that in front of her son. Would she want him to do that if they were on their own? He hoped so.

'Well, if you're sure,' she said, rubbing her forehead.

'Go to bed, Mum.'

In the kitchen Kieran asked, 'Toasted cheese sandwiches or a bowl of cereal?'

'Um — could I have both? I've not had much to eat lately and I feel empty.'

'Of course. Here, take your choice of cereal and I'll make some toasties. I'm a bit peckish myself.'

There was silence but from the way Paul shovelled the muesli down, he hadn't been exaggerating his hunger.

'Here you are.' Kieran shoved the cheese toasties across and watched the lad demolish those as well. He ate his own more slowly. 'There's plenty of fruit. Just help yourself.'

'Are you sure? Mum'll pay you back.'

'I don't need paying back. If I can't help a friend, I'm not much of a person.'

Paul picked out a banana and started to peel it. 'Have you known Mum for long?'

'No. Only since she moved into the flat. But sometimes you get on with people straight away. And she was a big help to me.'

'Oh?'

'Yes. I'd been recovering from an accident for nearly a year and I was stuck in a rut. Your mother needed help and that made me feel useful again. I was able to start driving and oh, feel more optimistic about the future.'

'I don't know what's going to happen to me.'

'You have your mother. Whatever happens, you'll not be alone.' He was glad to see the lad's face brighten and judged it time to end the confidences for now. 'Right, then, let's make up your bed.'

'If you give me the sheets and stuff, I can do that. I'm never going to be like William and expect everyone to do things for me.'

Kieran was touched by this, and by Paul's earnest expression, neither child nor man. How could a woman have two sons so different? It must upset her. 'OK. Thanks. I'll lend you some shorts and a tee shirt to sleep in, if you like.'

He went to bed, lying there for a few minutes while another half dose of painkiller kicked in, thinking what a nice lad Paul was and how lucky Nicole was to have him.

He wished suddenly that he had a son to carry on his name and genes.

15

It was a fine day and since she didn't have any classes to attend, Janey decided to go for a walk. As she was carrying Millie down the stairs, Kieran came out of his flat and waited for her to strap the baby into the buggy before holding the door open.

'Going for a walk?'

'Yes. It's quite a nice day, isn't it?'

'It is. Nearly March now. Spring is in the air.'

Whistling cheerfully, something she'd never heard him do before, he went back into the flat. It was such a happy sound, that whistle. It made her smile. And he was right. There was a feel of spring in the air, just a hint, enough to make your blood stir and your spirits rise.

As she was walking up the road, she heard a car come out of the flats behind her and glanced sideways to see three people sitting in it. The librarian and her son were with Kieran again. Was it their presence that was cheering him up? If so, she hoped they'd stay.

Oh, to have a car! It'd make her life so much easier. But she'd still go for walks because she loved being out in the fresh air.

Of course she headed for the allotments first, because she liked chatting to Mr Shackleton and knew he enjoyed company. He was there as usual, this time turning over the soil at one end of his plot. As soon as he saw her, he beckoned.

'You're just in time for a cuppa!'

She'd had a cup of tea before she left the flat but accepted his offer anyway. 'It looks like good soil, nice and dark.'

'Yes. Best Wiltshire, that is. You can grow anything in soil like that. Wait till you taste my runner beans.'

As they were waiting for the tea to brew, Dawn came into the allotments and walked briskly across to join them.

'Hello, Dawn,' he called. 'Haven't seen you for a while.'

'I've been even busier than usual. Have you got a spare cuppa, Mr S? And a spare minute, too? I'd like to talk to you about something and ask your advice.'

'I can leave if it's private,' Janey offered at once.

'No, don't do that,' Dawn said. 'It's not at all private and another opinion is always helpful. How are things going, Janey? I can see your Millie is thriving. Just look at that smile.' She turned back to Dan and said in a gentler tone, 'I was sorry to hear about Peggy.'

'Thank you.' He busied himself with the tea, then passed the mugs to them. 'Right then, what can I do for you, Dawn?'

'I'm thinking of starting a shared gardens scheme.'

'What's that?' Janey asked.

'It's when people who have too much garden to cope with let other people use it to grow vegetables, in return for a share of the produce. It's usually the gardens of older people who can't

236

do the heavy work any longer or else people who're too busy or are simply not interested in gardening. And there are people in flats who'd love a bit of garden, or mad-keen gardeners who'd like more land.'

'I'm one of the ones in a flat,' Janey said at once. 'I love getting my hands into the soil, and you can't beat home-grown fruit and vegetables. Nothing you buy at the shops tastes half as good.'

'It's a great idea!' Dan said. 'People can wait years to get allotments in this town. What can I do to help?'

'Well — and you must say no if it's too much to ask — I'd be happy if you'd help generally, but specifically I'd love you to advise people who aren't used to gardening. You know, be our resident expert. You've not only got green fingers, you always seem to know the science behind what you're doing.'

He beamed at her. 'What a nice compliment! And I'd love to do that. Just what I need to keep me busy . . . now.' Then he nodded towards Janey. 'And this lass can be the first on our list to garden share.'

Dawn looked at her doubtfully. 'People your age don't usually want to be responsible for a garden.'

'I love gardening. I used to help my granddad, and after he died, I grew vegetables for my parents. My father didn't enjoy gardening and he didn't like me going out with friends, but he approved of that because it saved us money. And it got me out of the house.'

237

'Then you can be our guinea pig.'

An idea started growing in Janey's head as she listened to them talking about how they could organise it. When there was a break in the conversation, she said, 'Um — I think I know someone who'd love to share her garden, if you want to try it out before you go public. It upsets her that she can't look after it and it's a really big garden. You know her, too, Miss Parfitt who lives in the big house at the end of Peppercorn Street.'

'I should have thought of Winifred myself. Good idea, Janey. Let's go and see her today.' Dawn looked at her watch. 'Oh no, is that really the time?' She drained her cup. 'I can't fit her in today. I'll have to try to find time tomorrow.'

'I could call and see her, if you like,' Janey said. 'Give her a rough idea of what you want to do, so she can think about it.'

She knew Dan was lonely and guessed that Miss Parfitt was too. Suddenly her idea expanded. 'Though it might be better if Mr Shackleton came with me. He could check out the garden and think how to divide it up. We could practise on it, couldn't we, Mr Shackleton? If you don't think I'm too young to take part, that is.'

'Of course you're not too young!' he said at once. 'And do call me Mr S. Most people do. Shackleton's such a mouthful of a name.'

Dawn beamed at them both. 'Great to see you making friends. I don't at all approve of the way people from different generations stay so separate.' She looked thoughtful for a moment. 'Perhaps we could get my mum and Winifred to do the paperwork for the scheme. I don't really have time to run it, but when I heard about the idea, I knew it was *needed* in our town.'

She stood up. 'Could you go and see Miss Parfitt today, do you think? I don't believe in letting the grass grow under my feet.'

After she'd gone, Dan grinned at Janey. 'She sweeps everyone along in her plans, Dawn does. She's a treasure, that lass is. Does a lot of good in this town. Her husband's quieter, but he helps behind the scenes and he's very proud of her.' He started gathering the mugs together. 'Shall we go and see this Miss Parfitt now?'

'Yes. We've just got time before lunch. Millie plays up if her food is late.'

It felt strange but nice to have someone walking along beside her, chatting, as she pushed the buggy. She'd grown so used to being on her own with Millie, didn't ever again want to feel as utterly alone as she had the day she moved into the flat.

*   *   *

When Winifred heard the doorbell, her heart started to beat a little faster. Bradley's fault. He'd made her nervous of answering her own front door. She went into the sitting room and peered out of the window, breathing a sigh of relief when she saw Janey there, with her baby in the buggy, and an elderly man standing beside her, smiling down at the baby. Such a nice smile, the man had, kindly and tolerant.

She hurried to open the door.

'Is this a convenient time to call?' Janey asked.

'Yes, of course. I don't get many visitors so it's nearly always convenient. Call any time you feel like some company or a piece of cake.' She wondered if she'd said too much but Janey's smile didn't falter as she nodded acceptance of this ongoing invitation. At least, Winifred hoped that was what the nod meant.

'This is Mr Shackleton. He has one of the Grove Allotments and he's a friend of Dawn's. She sent us over to ask you something.'

'Then you'd better come in. Would you like a cup of tea?'

They both laughed.

'We've just had one,' Janey explained. 'Mr S has a little gas ring at his shed on the allotment and he's always making me tea.'

'Come and visit me sometime and I'll make you one too, Miss Parfitt,' he offered. 'And my name's Dan.'

Winifred blinked, surprised at such an immediate gesture of friendship. 'I'd like that. And do call me Winifred. Come and sit down.'

But he went to the kitchen window first, staring out at the garden and giving a soft whistle. 'I didn't realise how big your place was. The wall and hedge hide it.'

'Far too big for me now, but I don't want to leave my home.' Winifred couldn't hold back a sigh.

He came back to join them at the table. 'That's what we've come about. Dawn wants to start a garden sharing scheme in the town. Do

240

you know what that is?'

'She mentioned it one day, so I have a rough general idea.'

'It's a great concept, isn't it? There's such a long waiting list for allotments, people lose heart, yet more of them are wanting to grow their own food, *if* they can find somewhere to grow it.'

'But what has it got to do with me?'

He gave her another of his gentle smiles. 'We thought you might like to be our guinea pig and be the first person to share a garden.'

Winifred stared at him as this idea sank in. She'd not thought about the scheme in relation to herself. She looked out of the window thoughtfully. 'I wouldn't know where to start, how to find people, but I would definitely be interested in sharing my garden. It looks such a mess these days, it upsets me to see it. I used to love gardening, but I can't do the bending and kneeling now. Arthritis.'

'It's a curse, arthritis is,' Dan said. 'I've got it in my hands and knees but it's not too bad yet.' He spread out his gnarled old fingers, looked at them with a grimace, then shrugged. 'Anno domini. I try to ignore my age and carry on anyway.' He leant forward. 'I thought you could help us start the scheme together. And Dawn suggested her mother might help too. It'll take some organising if we're going to involve the whole town.'

'The whole town?'

'Oh, yes. Dawn never does things by halves.'

'I don't think her mother is very fond of

241

gardening and as I said before, I can't bend or — '

'No, but there's going to be a lot of paperwork, so Dawn thought you and Hazel could take charge of that. What do you think?'

Winifred took another chance, excitement rising in her. 'I think it's an excellent idea and I'd love to help out in any way I can. I'm sure Hazel will too.'

* * *

Nicole and Paul had decided to go to the hospital before they went back to visit their old house, and this time both were allowed in to see Sam. He was still lying there, not seeming aware of what was going on around him.

'He had a disturbed night, I'm afraid,' the nurse said. 'Is he worrying about something?'

'Could be. Our older son has gone off the rails and the police are looking for him.'

'Did your husband know about that before he collapsed? What a terrible thing for you all! Anyway, stay as long as you like. There are no restrictions on visiting times.'

That sounded ominous to Nicole but she could see that Paul hadn't picked up the implications, so she didn't comment.

They stayed for ten minutes, sitting by the bed, finding it hard to chat to a man who didn't respond in any way. In the end Nicole could bear it no longer. 'Shall we go now?'

Paul nodded, looking relieved.

'I don't like to see Dad looking like that,' he

242

whispered once they got outside.

'Neither do I.' She led the way down to the foyer, where Kieran was sitting at a table drinking something from the refreshments kiosk.

He stood up as soon as he saw them. 'Would you like a drink?'

'Not really. I think perhaps we should go home now and get Paul's clothes and the other stuff he needs for school.'

'I've been thinking — it might be better to ring the police first and check that it's all right to go back. We don't know what William's been up to overnight, after all. Do you have the card they gave you?'

The person at the other end of the line seemed to know about the case and said she'd ask a car to drop round to the house, just to make sure everything was all right.

When they pulled up outside her old home, Nicole shivered.

'Is something wrong?' Kieran asked.

'I'm just . . . a bit nervous.'

'What if William's here?' Paul asked. 'He has to hide somewhere, after all.'

'If he is, we'll run outside again.' She tried to joke but her voice wavered on the final words. Paul made no attempt to go rushing ahead of her as he usually would have done and Kieran stayed firmly by her side.

She got out the front door key, but fumbled and dropped it on the path.

Paul picked it up and put it in the lock for her, turning it and stepping forward.

She dragged him back by his jacket. 'I'll go

first.' Taking a deep breath she pushed the door fully open and took two steps into the hall, stopping to wrinkle her nose because the place smelt of sweat and rotten food. She looked into the front room, where the pieces of her broken figurine were still scattered across the hearth. It didn't look as if anything had been touched in here since she left.

Kieran and Paul waited near the door, still taking their cue from her. She went across to the dining room and gasped. Gouged into the polished tabletop was the word: BITCH.

Kieran came and put his arm round her shoulders. Paul pressed against her other side.

'He's a sicko, Mum. Let's go outside again and wait for the police.'

She stiffened. 'No. Let's continue exploring.'

'What if he's here?' he whispered. 'He's already hurt you once.'

She put her hand up to the back of her head instinctively as he said that.

'Paul's right,' Kieran urged. 'Better to be cautious.'

As they moved into the hall again, there was a sound from the kitchen.

Without asking permission, Kieran pushed her and Paul outside again and moved to stand in front of her.

As Nicole looked into the house, she saw someone come out of the kitchen and stand at the end of the hall: her son — and yet, not her son, somehow. William's face was so full of anger, he didn't look like the lad she knew. Though why he was so angry all the time, she couldn't work out. He stood there glaring at her, then took a step forward, one fist raised as if he was about to attack them. She couldn't help it — she took another quick step backwards.

William smiled and took another step forward, taunting her with that brandished fist. 'Keep away from here, bitch!'

'Get in the car,' Kieran muttered.

But just then another car drew up behind hers in the drive, a police car.

'Thank goodness!' Paul said.

William made a rude sign with one finger and vanished into the kitchen.

One of the police officers came hurrying towards her. 'Everything all right, Mrs Gainsford?'

'No. My son William is here. I think he was about to attack us when you arrived. He went into the back of the house.'

The officers looked at one another then one pointed and ran through the front door while the other ran round the side towards the rear.

Kieran watched them intently, keeping an eye on the other side of the house. 'I wish this were a semi-detached house,' he murmured. 'If he comes round the other side, don't try to stop him, either of you.'

But there was no sign of William coming round the side and after a while the police officers returned.

'I reckon he went over the back fence,' one said. 'The plants were freshly trampled in one corner. Do you want to check the house now?'

Nicole nodded, guessing there would be further nasty surprises waiting for her. Best get it over with. 'Paul, when we're sure it's safe, sort out your clothes and anything else you want to take with you. Work as fast as you can. Pile the clothes on the bed and we'll wrap them in the sheet.'

'Right.'

It hurt her to see him looking so upset. Well, she was upset too — very — but she didn't dare give in to her feelings. She went back into the house, ignoring the two rooms at the front. The kitchen was even messier than before. A can of baked beans had been overturned recently and the sauce was still slipping out into a glutinous puddle on the table. There was a carton of milk on the draining board, with splashes where it had been dumped in a hurry.

In one corner was a pile of broken crockery. It looked as if someone had simply lobbed pieces there on purpose. She moved closer and gasped. 'That's my best dinner set,' she told the police. 'He must have brought it in from the dining room to break like this. Why does he hate me so much? What have I ever done to deserve it?'

'From what your younger son and husband told us before, he's on anabolic steroids, and they can do terrible things to young men, especially if he's on the designer version. Rage and mindless aggression are among the common side effects.'

'I don't understand why young men do this to themselves.'

'The medical gurus say they want to be more powerful. Others because they think drugs are where it's at. Anything for kicks.'

'William was never an easy child to rear. He

wasn't very good at school, right from the start. We had to hire tutors to get him reading properly. Paul was different, a good student all along. I suppose this is William's way of making up for it.'

He gave her a sympathetic look, waited a moment then asked, 'Shall we go and check upstairs now, Ms Gainsford?'

She nodded and turned to Kieran. 'Will you come with me as well?'

'Of course I will.' He took her hand for a moment, sure they'd find something unpleasant upstairs. 'Let's do it.'

She turned to her son. 'Paul, you follow us. Keep a few steps back and if I say you're to go downstairs again, do it.'

Upstairs it looked as if a hurricane had swept through. William must have been searching for something, because all the drawers had been emptied out and half the clothes dragged from the wardrobes and left in tangled heaps.

'Looking for something valuable to sell, probably,' the male officer said.

She looked at him anxiously. 'I took my jewellery to my new flat. You don't think — he won't have gone there, surely? Not with the police looking for him?'

The officer was already pulling out his mobile phone. He walked out on to the landing to make the call, suggesting they send someone to her flat immediately. He turned. 'Address?'

She gave it with a sinking heart. 'I don't know whether to hurry back or stay here,' she told Kieran.

'Stay here. Retrieve what you can now, because it's my guess he'll be back.'

Paul's room had also been ransacked and the computer monitor lay smashed in one corner. He stood for a moment fists clenched, expression anguished, then said, 'I think the computer itself's OK, but I'll need to get a new monitor, Mum, if you can afford one.'

'You can take your father's. In fact, take your father's computer as well. It's in the study downstairs. We don't want it getting smashed.' It didn't sound as if Sam would need it again. Her throat clogged with guilt which was weighing her down so heavily she didn't know how to bear it. She should have tried harder to persuade him to go to the doctor's.

Paul touched her arm briefly, as if he sensed her distress. 'You all right, Mum?'

She pulled herself together. 'Yes. Work as quickly as you can.'

When they left an hour later, they took as much as they could with them, odd-shaped bundles, boxes. Paul had to sit squashed into one corner of the car's back seat, on top of some bundles of clothes and with head-height bundles beside him, and even on his lap.

The police escorted them to Nicole's flat, where their colleagues were now keeping watch.

★ ★ ★

Janey walked down Peppercorn Street from Miss Parfitt's house, pleased with how her life was turning out. She'd left Mr S pacing out the

248

garden and she hoped this project would help cement his friendship with his hostess. They were both lonely, she could see that. There ought to be introduction agencies for old people, not for them to find new marriage partners, but just for finding friends.

She felt happiness well up inside her like a warm fountain as she counted her blessings. She was starting to make friends, finding activities to occupy her time, not to mention coping with looking after her daughter, something which had terrified her at first.

Lost in her thoughts and plans, she didn't notice the car until it slowed right down next to her. She looked sideways at it, expecting someone to be asking directions. But it wasn't. It was *him*, giving her that confident gloating smile which made her shiver.

She stopped, unable to move for sheer terror. Her heart started to pound and she would have screamed, only she couldn't make a sound, except for a soft whimper of protest. *He'd come back looking for her! He was going to spoil her lovely new life!*

As he waved one hand in greeting, a police car with its light flashing drove past and *he* drove off at once, not stopping to ask what the police were doing there. Well, he was stationed on the other side of Swindon so they couldn't be members of his team.

It was a while before she could move on and then she walked slowly and heavily like an old person, couldn't help it because fear was still weighing her down. She'd known he could find her easily enough, but she hadn't seen any reason why he would bother.

But he had bothered. Why? And why had he made his presence known to her today? What did he want from her? Hadn't he done enough to ruin her life?

She gasped. He surely didn't expect her to let him near her again willingly?

But he didn't want a willing woman. He'd really enjoyed hurting her. That had terrified her most of all, because she'd thought at one stage he was going to kill her.

If only she'd gone for help straight away, shown people her bruises. But she hadn't known she was pregnant. She'd thought she could just forget it and take care never to be alone with him again.

She looked down at Millie, amazed as she always was, that she could love *his* child so much. Maternal instinct, she supposed.

But she wasn't going to let him force her again. She didn't know how she'd stop him, but she would. She couldn't prove that she'd been unwilling to have sex with him but she'd already decided she didn't want to have a DNA test done on Millie, because she didn't want *him* to have any rights of access to her daughter. He might hurt her too.

So it had to be stopped.

But how?

* * *

One of the police officers keeping watch on Mrs Gainsford's flat from a little way down the street

250

turned to the other. 'Wasn't that Gary Yarford?'

'Yeah. Same old surveillance vehicle. Everyone in the force for fifty miles around knows it by now. You'd think that lot would have the wit to replace it, because if we know it by sight, you can be sure others will too.'

'I wonder who he was keeping watch on?'

'He drew up beside that girl who was walking with her baby. I saw him wave to her. She didn't look happy to see him, though. Did you see her face? Hey, she's turning into those flats just down the road! Pull forward a minute. There's nothing parked on the road outside them.'

They moved further down the street and watched as Janey hauled the buggy up the step and into the entrance hall. She unfastened the baby and carried it upstairs, then came back down for the buggy.

'She doesn't look like a crim or a hooker to me.'

'Me neither. But she knew him and she was definitely scared of him. Did you see her face?'

'You never know who that bugger's watching. He's a law unto himself. Glad he's not my sergeant.'

'Me, too. A couple of my pals work under him and they hate his guts. Ah, here are the others. We can hand over to them now. This Gainsford lad is causing a lot of trouble. 'Bout time he was picked up.'

Nicole followed the police officer into her flat, relieved to see that it hadn't been touched. Then everyone helped lug in the things they'd brought from home. She wanted to tell Kieran to leave it to the others, because he was looking tired and his limp was worse, but she bit back the words. What he needed most at the moment was to feel useful and normal.

And she felt better when he was around. Much better.

'I don't know if I'll ever feel safe in that house again,' she murmured as she set down the last bundle. She didn't realise she'd spoken her thoughts aloud until one of the officers answered.

'You'll probably be safer here, Mrs Gainsford. This is a fairly secure building, but nowhere's completely safe because windows can always be broken and you're on the ground floor. So . . . you're not going to go back to the house?'

She couldn't help shuddering. 'No way.'

'We'll keep an eye on it, then.'

'You and Paul can stay on with me, if you like,' Kieran offered.

'We can't trespass on your goodwill.'

'It's been nice to have company.' He lowered his voice as he added for her ears only, 'It's doing me good to make friends again. We are friends now, aren't we? Perhaps . . . more than friends?'

She smiled. 'Oh, yes. You're very kind, Kieran, but I think we'd better stay in my flat. I don't want William thinking he can walk all over me.'

'Why not get a cheap security system?' one officer suggested. 'One with a siren that screams loudly if anyone tries to break in while you're out. There are plenty of neighbours within earshot.'

'Are they expensive?' She was already starting

to worry about money, because Sam hadn't been with that company for long and she didn't know how much sickness entitlement he'd have accrued or how his superannuation stood. He'd refused to discuss that with her when he changed jobs, saying by the time he retired, they'd be rich.

'Security systems aren't that expensive if you get a do-it-yourself kit. Are you at all handy? They come with full instructions.'

'I could have a go,' Paul offered. 'I like fiddling with computers and electronic stuff.'

'I could help him,' Kieran volunteered. 'I've got a system fitted at my flat and I watched how they installed it. Paul can climb up and down ladders, and I'll play foreman.'

Paul grinned at him and Nicole felt pleased at how well the two of them got on.

The police left her to sort out her possessions and Kieran sagged against the door frame. 'Look, I need to get something to eat so that I can take a painkiller. I'm only taking halves now, so it's even more important that I take them on time. I can come back and help after that.' He didn't tell her that he'd reduced his dosage so that he'd be more alert to help her. But the doctors had told him to start doing that when he felt he could cope.

'Why don't you have a rest and we'll come down about two o'clock, then you can help us buy a security system?'

'If you're sure you'll be all right till then?'

'I'm sure.' Pretty sure. She hoped.

'I'll program our phone for the police so you

253

only have to hit one button to get that number they gave us,' Paul said. He watched Kieran leave and drive off down the street. 'He's a nice guy, isn't he?'

'Very.' She saw her son looking at her speculatively. 'Hey, watch what you're thinking. I only met him a few days ago.'

Paul gave his mother a very solemn look. 'But there might be . . . possibilities. He looks at you as if he's attracted.'

'And what do you know about that?'

'I've got eyes, and I have my moments, too, you know. You may not realise it, but geeks are cool these days and I'm a bit of a babe magnet.'

'You are?' She tried not to hide her surprise.

He shrugged. 'Yeah. Not many girls go for dumb beefy types. And William's acne was a big turn-off. Besides, Dad's been treating you like shit for a good while now. I think you deserve better, so you should go for it. Get a life.'

'It was the tumour that made him so lazy.'

'Mum, he was lazy long before he got the tumour. You've had to nag him to help in the house for as long as I can remember.'

'That tumour could have been developing for years.'

'Don't fool yourself, Mum. Just because he's ill doesn't mean he was a saint.'

'You don't sound very — upset.'

'I am, but not as much as I could have been. He's not been a very hands-on father, has he? He always put his best effort into his job. He just — wasn't there for me.'

'But that was to earn money for us.'

254

He rolled his eyes. 'Mum! Get real. You've always had to earn money too. If his job was as hot as he boasted, you wouldn't have needed to work.'

She gave up protesting. How could you argue against the truth?

Paul came and gave her a quick hug, something he did so rarely she'd not got over her surprise before he moved away.

'It's all right, Mum. I always knew you were there for us, even if I didn't show it.'

'You've not talked to me like this for a long time.'

He bit his lip, shrugging. 'I've been keeping out of everyone's way since William went aggro, hiding out in my room a lot. He could have beaten me into a pulp if I'd upset him.'

Thrusting his hands into his pockets he went to stare out of the window with his back to her and she guessed the confidences were at an end for the moment. 'I'll go and do some unpacking, then make lunch.'

'When's lunch?'

'About half an hour. I want to unpack the things that will crease first. There are some apples in a bowl in the kitchen if you're feeling hungry.'

He loped off to get one, then hoisted up two large bundles of clothes and disappeared into the smaller bedroom.

She carried some things into her own bedroom, feeling sad that Paul felt like that about his father, especially now, and also a bit flustered by his far too perceptive comments about their new friend. She did like Kieran . . . and trust him . . . and was attracted to him. It had happened quickly. But it was good that Paul also seemed very much at ease with their new friend.

And her son was right. Although Sam had reluctantly done his share of household chores he'd always acted as if they were her responsibility and waited for her to tell him what to do. It was years since he'd talked to her properly. He'd not only worked long hours, but had always been the active sort, going out playing sports at weekends ('networking'), working extra hours (she hoped that's what he'd been doing), leaving her to look after the children.

She hadn't minded at first, because she'd been thrilled to be a mother and too busy to think straight. But later, she'd started to resent Sam's attitude, wanted a more willing partner in raising their family.

Had Sam's attitude influenced William? Was his behaviour the result of taking anabolic steroids or was he mentally ill? Who knew?

She got angry with herself. Why was she going over all this old stuff about Sam and the family? She had unpacking to do, then food to provide.

But before she started, she rang work and explained what was going on, asking for emergency leave. Michael was once again very understanding.

A short time after she'd got off the phone to him, Helen rang to find out exactly what was going on and the two friends had a short chat.

'We'll go to the hospital first, then buy a security alarm,' she said later, as she and her son ate lunch. 'I'm sure Kieran won't mind.'

'I'm sure he won't.' Paul gave her another smug smile and she could feel herself blushing. Honestly! At her age!

'Anything you need for your computer while we're at it?'

'Well, I do need a new connecting cable, if that's OK. William cut mine into several pieces.'

'I think my budget could stretch to that.'

'Thanks, Mum. You're the best.'

Warmth filled her. At least one of her sons was normal, and loving.

★ ★ ★

Once Janey had left, Dan smiled at Winifred. 'Is it all right if I go over the garden. I can pace it out and start thinking how many plots we can make — if you're all right about sharing it? Don't let anyone dragoon you into this if you're not.'

'I think it's an excellent idea. Shall I get some paper? You can call out the number of paces and I'll put them on to a diagram. That at least I can do.'

'Good. It'll speed things up.'

They worked together for an hour, then she realised she was hungry. 'Would you like something to eat?'

He stopped, head on one side. 'Are you sure? After all, I've been dumped on you. I do have some sandwiches back at my allotment.'

'It's nice to share a meal. It'll just be ham and lettuce sandwiches and cake. I need to go and do

257

some shopping later.'

'Sandwiches will be great. Can I help?'

'No, thanks. It won't take me a minute.'

He sat down at the table, watching her. 'I hope you don't mind me asking, but you've never been married?'

'No. And you? Are you on your own?'

'My wife died recently. Alzheimer's, poor love. In the end, it's a relief when they go.'

'My mother suffered from dementia for the last few months of her life. Then she had a heart attack. I looked after her as best I could, but oh dear, she could be very difficult at times. In the end, they took her into hospital.'

'I had to put my Peggy into care in the later stages. Eh, we never know what'll happen to us, do we? I try to enjoy each and every day. A friend of mine used to say, 'As long as you're on the right side of the grass.' Now he isn't, poor chap. But I still am.'

'My friends have all died and I've been doing most of my living through books. Recently, thanks to Dawn, I've met Hazel and I bumped into that nice young girl one day in the street, or rather she came to my rescue when I was trying to bring back too much shopping.'

'Janey's a lovely lass.' He smiled. 'And that's a cracking baby. Widest smile I've ever seen, little Millie has.'

'I'm going to teach Janey to bake cakes.'

'You couldn't teach me at the same time, could you?'

She looked at him in surprise.

'I miss home cooking.' He gestured to the

piece of cake on his plate. 'This is delicious.'

'I'd be happy to.'

Somehow she found herself telling him about her nephew and he grew upset. 'How can he try to rob you like that? Family, too. Have people like him no consciences?'

'They don't understand how deeply we care about our homes, do they? And they think any place is good enough for the elderly, as long as there's no obvious cruelty and the inmates have enough to eat. They don't even allow room for people to take many of their possessions with them. I've visited friends in such places. One wasn't too bad, and the staff were lovely, though she'd still had to get rid of most of her treasures, but the other place was awful, three people to a room.'

When Dan had gone, taking his rough plan of the garden with him, she sat for a while thinking. Her life was opening up in so many ways. She must go to church and say thank you properly for that.

And surely Bradley would leave her alone from now on? He had nothing whatsoever to gain from pestering her now. She'd made sure of that. It occurred to her suddenly that he didn't know that. Well, if he came near her again, she'd tell him straight out that he'd get nothing under her new will.

But she didn't want to be alone with him when she said it.

16

Janey went off happily to college. Was it only a few days since her first visit here? So much seemed to have happened in the meantime.

Today she felt more confident about leaving Millie in the crèche and found her way to the first class easily. She recognised some of the people from last time and smiled at them, though she couldn't remember their names.

At lunchtime she again went and sat in a quiet corner of the gardens, thankful it was fine, not wanting to spend money in the canteen.

'Mind if I join you?'

She looked up to see the lad who'd asked her out for coffee, and suddenly her mouth felt as if it was made of wood and unable to form words. She still wasn't emotionally used to the idea that she could sit and chat to anyone she wanted without getting into trouble. She managed a nod and he sat down beside her, pulling a plastic box of food out of a bulging backpack.

'I bring my own lunches. It's much cheaper. I'm Al Bevan, by the way, short for Alexander not Alan.'

'I'm Janey Dobson and I'm doing the same thing as you: saving money.'

They were both holding sandwiches so he mimed shaking hands.

'How's your baby? Millie, isn't it?'

She was amazed he'd remembered that.

'Millie's fine. She's in the crèche at the moment. It's such a help being able to go and study in the library as well as come to classes.'

'Must be hard sometimes.'

She shrugged. 'Worth it.'

'My mum brought me up on her own. My dad ran off soon after I was born.'

'Do you wish now that you'd had a father?' It was one of the things that concerned her for the future. Would Millie resent not having a father, not even knowing who he was? Janey hoped she'd never have to tell her how she'd been conceived.

'I don't know. I never had one, so I'm used to being with Mum. We get on really well these days, though I gave her a few hassles when I was younger. She's only thirty-nine so I keep telling her to start dating, but she says she's too set in her ways to put up with another man.'

Maybe being with his mother had made him more communicative than other lads she'd listened to. And he certainly had a good appetite. She watched in amazement as he started on another round of doorstep sandwiches. How could someone so thin eat so much?

He swallowed his mouthful and grinned as if he understood what she was thinking. 'I get hungry.'

She picked up the piece of the cake Miss Parfitt had given her and started telling him about the cookery lessons and the garden sharing. After that they chatted more easily, though he knew nothing about gardens. It seemed natural to walk to the next class together and sit next

261

to one another, but she was glad when he left after the class.

She didn't want to get involved with anyone. Involved! As if! He was just being friendly because his mum was a single mother. No guy of her age would be interested in dating a single mother with a child to bring up.

In the library she settled down to some serious study and was amazed when it was time to collect Millie and leave.

She kept a careful watch as she walked home, but she didn't see *him*. She felt better immediately she got into her flat, because there were people all round her there, especially Kieran. She was so lucky in her landlord.

Perhaps Gary had just been looking at where she lived or wanting a glimpse of his daughter. Perhaps now his curiosity was satisfied he'd leave her alone.

And pigs would fly! He liked causing trouble, laughed with her father about nasty things he'd done.

The worry of it all niggled at her and in the end she wrote a letter in case anything happened to her. She'd ask Kieran to keep it safe and open it if anything went wrong.

That settled her mind enough for her to fall asleep and to her relief, Millie slept right through until five o'clock.

★ ★ ★

Several pieces of mail fell through the letter box that day. As Winifred picked them up, she saw that one was from her friend Molly's solicitor. No doubt it'd be a reminder to make an appointment to see them. She'd completely forgotten that she was supposed to get in touch about a bequest.

Another letter was from an estate agent, offering to sell her house for her. She was about to rip it to shreds when she saw that it was the same company for which Ebony worked. Was Bradley still trying to get her to sell? Or was Ebony working on her own? Whichever it was, they'd get nowhere with her. She tore it into tiny pieces, taking out her annoyance with her nephew on it.

A third letter was from a social care officer, not the one who'd provided her with the pendant. She frowned and reread it. Following her phone call to ask for help, they would be happy to come and assess her home, and were sure they'd be able to help her to cope. Would she please ring to make an appointment?

She rang up, all right, but it was to ask why they thought she'd contacted them.

She was passed from one to the other, then a woman with a soft, cooing voice said gently, 'Perhaps you've forgotten, dear. We have a record of a call from you on Monday and we responded quickly, since you sounded distressed. There was no answer when we rang and you don't seem to have an answering service.'

'I didn't phone anyone on Monday.'

Silence, then, 'Perhaps you've forgotten.'

'No. I've not forgotten anything. I'm old but not losing my wits, thank you very much. Please make a note in your records that I did not make that call, and in future, you should check back with me. This is the second time someone has tried to contact the council, pretending to be me.'

'There's nothing to be ashamed of in forgetting things, and — '

'If you won't do as I asked, I'll get my lawyer to contact you on my behalf.' She put the phone down, furiously angry at the way that woman had talked down to her.

She might check with Dawn later about what she could do. For the moment, she had some shopping to do, just a few bits and pieces, then she was going to walk over to Hazel's house for coffee.

Smiling, she went to get ready, dismissing the woman at the council from her mind. It was some silly mix-up, but that was still no excuse for treating her as if she'd lost her wits.

★ ★ ★

A couple of days later Nicole decided to go back to work and suggested Paul go back to school.

'I can't! Kieran's coming round to help me fit the security system.'

She hesitated — and was lost. 'Very well. Just this once. But from now on, you'll be going to school regularly, whether we stay here or move back home. You're an intelligent lad and you could go to university or anything you liked.' She glanced at her watch. 'I haven't got time to discuss that now, but we should have a serious talk about your future at some stage, don't you think?'

'I've got a few ideas about what I want to do,

but Dad said they were rubbish and he wanted me to study business.'

'It's your life and in the end, your choice, but I do hope you'll listen to advice before you make up your mind. There's just one thing: would you mind if we stay here at the flat for the moment? I know it's quite small, but I wouldn't feel safe going back to the house.'

'I'd rather stay here. This street is quite busy, so I'll feel safe walking back from school.'

He kept shocking her with such revelations. 'Have you been feeling that unsafe? Is it William or someone else?'

He hesitated, then said, 'William and some friends of his. And Mum — take your car to work this time.'

'I will. And don't open the door to anyone except Kieran.'

She walked down the street. The garage door opened smoothly, and as she backed her car out, Kieran came across from the flats to see her, so she rolled her window down.

He bent over. 'Going to work today? Are you sure you should?'

'I can't keep taking time off. But I'll take things easy physically. They'll understand. Paul's staying home to help you with the security system.'

'He's a great kid.'

'Not such a kid any more. He's growing up fast.'

'Will your car be somewhere safe?'

'Yes, we have a locked basement car park for staff.'

'Good. Are you going to the hospital today as well?'

'Yes, of course. I thought I'd nip across in my lunch hour. I don't see the need to make Paul go through that every day. It's hard seeing someone who was walking and talking normally a month ago lying comatose.'

'How about I pick you up at the library and drive you to the hospital? It'll be safer.'

She went very still, then had to ask, 'Do you think William's that dangerous?'

'No one knows exactly how far he'd go. Some drugs have unpredictable effects and we don't know exactly what he's been taking. Those car parks at the hospital are very big. Better safe than sorry, don't you think?' He waited then asked gently, 'So . . . what time shall I pick you up?'

'One o'clock. At the main entrance to the library. I'll ring if there's any difficulty with that.'

As she drove off, she could see him in her rear-view mirror, a lean man with a thin, intelligent face. A kind man, helping strangers like her.

And a very attractive one, too.

Guiltily she tried to suppress this train of thought, but it wouldn't be suppressed. It was a long time since she'd felt that stirring in the blood which came from sheer physical attraction. It made her realise how long that had been missing from her relationship with her husband.

Had Sam stopped finding her attractive? No, she kept forgetting. He'd not been unfaithful, he'd been ill.

Only . . . what *had* he been doing all those times when he'd come home late? He said he'd been working late, but she'd rung once or twice and the security guy said there was no one in the building.

Maybe he'd been having a drink with friends.

Oh, hell, why was she obsessing about this? Done was done. You had to move on.

* ★ ★

Janey rang up Miss Parfitt to see if she was going shopping and needed any help.

'No, dear. Dawn's going to drive her mother and me out to one of those big shopping centres to get our heavy stuff. It'll be a wonderful help. But how kind of you to remember me! I hope you're still coming for some cookery lessons?'

'I'd love to. Just tell me when it's convenient, only not Wednesdays and another day. I'm not sure which yet because I'm changing to another class to avoid a boring lecturer. One of my friends told me you could do that.'

'How about coming tomorrow? I can get the ingredients today. We said we'd make a fruit cake, didn't we?'

'That'd be great. Only you must let me buy my share of the ingredients.'

'No, dear. You've enough on your plate. And we may have another student. Mr Sh — Dan wants to learn how to make cakes, too. I'll give him a ring. Will one o'clock suit you? I'd like to go to church in the morning.'

'One o'clock would be fine. I'm going to church too. Tidmas Street Church have a crèche for littlies and the people there are so friendly.'

267

'I've always gone to the parish church. But I don't know anyone in the congregation there any more. My mother would be horrified at me offering that as an excuse, but it does make a difference.' She chuckled. 'Especially on rainy days.'

Poor Miss Parfitt, Janey thought. She'd been under her mother's thumb all her life, from the sounds of it, and she still felt guilty if she went against her mother's rules. Janey's mother always did what her father told her to. She was as unnoticeable as a piece of wallpaper.

Janey felt very pleased with the progress she'd made in the last few weeks in getting her life together. Surely *he* would leave her alone if she made it obvious she wasn't going to cave in to him?

She picked up her baby and forgot her worries in giving her a tickle and a cuddle, which made them both laugh. Millie was growing so fast. Soon she'd be too big for this. Soon she'd be sitting unsupported, feeding herself, walking, talking. How wonderful to watch all those milestones!

They had an appointment next week at the child health clinic, so that Millie could be weighed and checked generally.

As she was going out, she knocked on Kieran's door, hoping to catch him in so that she could leave the letter with him. The more she thought about the letter, the more certain she became that it would be a wise precaution. But no one answered the door.

She was walking slowly home from the supermarket, pushing a heavily laden buggy when a voice said, 'You'll need some help getting that up the stairs.'

And when she looked, *he* was there, standing right beside her, smiling.

She couldn't move, could hardly breathe.

He wasn't going to leave her alone!

★　★　★

Kieran grinned at Paul. 'Here goes!' He switched on the security system they'd just installed, waited a minute or two outside on the landing, then gestured to Paul. 'You christen it.'

Paul walked inside. There was a thirty-second delay then it began to scream a warning. The noise was ear-piercing. No one could ignore that. 'You should warn the other owners about this, and the neighbours, so that they can ring the police if it goes off while you're out.' He switched the alarm off. 'Right, I'd better get back now. I'm taking your mother to the hospital. Will you be all right?'

'Yes. I want to set up my computer properly and change our Internet connection to this phone number.'

'Don't go out on your own.'

Paul looked sharply at him. 'You told Mum to be careful, too. Do you think William would really hurt us?'

'Yes, I do. I haven't been able to forget his expression when we were at your house. He looked wild and menacing. I'd not have liked to face him on my own, even before my accident.'

Paul shivered. 'You don't have to persuade me to be careful. It's Mum you have to persuade. I'm worried sick about her. She doesn't really believe he'd hurt her.'

'That's why I'm taking her to hospital, and she didn't refuse, did she? I can park really close in a disabled bay.' He grimaced at the thought. 'See you.'

Kieran got into the car and drove the hundred yards or so to his flat. He wanted to change into something smarter before he met Nicole.

When he got near the flats, he slowed to a sudden stop and parked by the side of the road because a man was standing over Janey and she looked terrified. They didn't seem to have noticed him, so he got out of the car and moved closer to them, staying behind a tree. Because he was wearing sneakers he could move silently.

As he stopped to watch, the man laid one hand on Janey's arm, gripping it tightly. That was not a polite hold.

She wrenched away from him, standing defensively between him and the buggy.

He laughed at her and grabbed her arm again, throwing her aside so hard she staggered a few steps. Taking hold of the buggy handle, he began shaking it hard, making Millie cry in fear.

Janey didn't move, staring at the man like a mouse trapped by a cat.

Kieran waited to see if he could learn anything more about this bully, who fortunately had his back to the street. The two others were so engrossed in their confrontation that neither of them noticed him and he was able to hear part of what they were saying.

'Either you take me up to your flat and be a good little girl, or there will be an accident. It's not hard to hurt a baby, and these buggies tip over so easily.' He feigned tipping the buggy over and Janey shrieked in terror.

'Don't! Don't! Why are you doing this? Haven't you hurt me enough?'

The man laughed softly. 'No. Not nearly enough. Now, move inside! I'll bring her.'

This was clearly the man who'd raped Janey, the man she was so terrified of that she didn't dare tell anyone who he was. He thought the fellow was taking a risk, coming after her in the daytime, but the street was very quiet, so he might have got away with it.

Kieran got out his mobile phone and took a photo, then the damn thing began warbling at him, and the man jerked round.

Kieran feigned answering the call, pretending not to be interested in them.

Janey grabbed the buggy and yanked it away from the man, who said loudly, 'There, it's working again. Told you I could fix it.' He turned and walked away.

Kieran watched him move out of sight round the corner of High Street then moved across to Janey, who was standing weeping, near hysterics now.

'Let's go inside,' he said gently.

'I shan't be safe even there. He'll be back. I know he will. It's only a matter of time before he catches me on my own.'

Kieran didn't at first know what to say to that, then caught a glimpse of his watch. 'Look, I have to go somewhere. Let's get you and Millie inside first. If it'll make you feel safer, you can stay in my flat till I get back.'

'Can I? Really? I just have to nip up to get some food and nappies for Millie.'

He didn't know whether he was doing the right thing leaving her in this upset state, but he needed to pick Nicole up and surely Janey would be safe in his flat?

He went in and studied the windows. He'd thought of getting sheer curtains to guard his privacy during the daytime but hadn't bothered. Now he would. For the time being, he drew the curtains.

'Don't switch the lights on,' she said. 'I can see well enough. I don't want the flat to look occupied.'

He hesitated by the door. 'Janey, who was that man?'

'Better if I don't tell you.'

'Better for me or better for you?'

'Both.'

'You're that frightened of him?'

She nodded.

What was the world coming to? he thought as he drove off. How could this be happening in a sleepy little town like Sexton Bassett?

But he had enough contacts to find out who the brute was — and he would. He already knew his first name, Gary.

Energy surged through him, the same energy that had once carried him through investigations into companies and millionaires and criminal bosses.

He smiled, thinking, *Welcome back.*

Nicole stood on the steps outside the library, waiting for Kieran, who was a little late. She shivered in the cool air but that didn't stop her enjoying its freshness after the rather stale air inside.

When his car drew up, she ran down the library steps, happy to see him, but his expression was so grim her happiness evaporated abruptly. 'What's wrong?'

'When I got back to the flats, a man was there, bullying Janey. She looked terrified. He had hold of the buggy and was shaking it hard.'

'Oh, no! Poor Millie. Did he run off when he saw you?'

'No, he brazened it out, pretended he'd been fixing the buggy. I've seen him somewhere before, but I can't place him. It'll come to me, though. She refuses to tell me who he is, though she's given me a letter revealing all, to be opened in case of trouble.'

'Will she be safe on her own?'

'I left her in my flat, as a temporary measure.'

She shook her head. 'What's wrong with the world? It's getting so violent.'

'I'm not sure it is, on average. The statistics don't say so. I think it's just that we hear about it more these days because we're living in an age of information flow — and of course, violence is affecting both of us and our friends at the moment.' He reached out to give her hand a squeeze. 'I know William's gone off the rails, but you'll get past this into calmer waters.'

'That time can't come soon enough for me.'

When they got to the hospital she made no effort to leave the car. 'I'm not looking forward to this.'

'It must be hard.'

'It's not knowing what's going to happen. Is he going to recover at all or . . . just get worse until he dies? If he recovers, I'll have to look after him. And if he doesn't, what am I going to do, with William running wild? I daren't even go back to my own home.'

Kieran got out of the car and went round to open her door. When she got out, he pulled her into his arms and gave her a hug. It wasn't a sexual gesture, just a comforting hug from a friend and she accepted it as such, leaning against him for a moment or two, drawing strength from him.

The warmth of that hug helped her walk into the hospital and up to the ward.

Sam wasn't in his room. She hurried along to the nurses' station and they showed her into a private room and fetched the ward sister.

'I'm afraid the news isn't good, Mrs Gainsford. Your husband is going downhill rapidly.'

Nicole stared at her incredulously. 'You mean — he's dying?'

'Yes.'

'How long does he have?'

'You'll need to ask the doctor that. He'll be here in — ' she looked at her fob watch 'about half an hour. In the meantime I'll show you where your husband is. Perhaps you'd like to sit

274

with him? I'll bring the doctor to you there.'

Sam was lying flat on his back in a tiny, window-less room to one side. It was a room for patients who didn't see or care about their surroundings. He looked like a wax effigy of her husband, no expression on his face, no movement.

'I can't believe it's ending like this,' she said aloud. 'We didn't even have time to make up our quarrel. Can you hear me, Sam? Or am I talking to myself?' It felt as if she was and she didn't speak again.

Time passed very slowly. She kept looking at her watch and finding that two or three minutes only had passed. She wondered if she should go and tell Kieran what she was waiting for, but if she did, she might miss the doctor. So she sat there, fretting internally, numb and motionless externally.

When the door opened, she looked round to see Kieran.

'I came up to see how things were going. They told me. I'm so sorry.'

She nodded. 'Would you stay with me? The doctor's coming in a minute. I'm frightened I won't remember what he says.'

'Of course.'

The door opened a few minutes later and a man came in, introduced himself and looked at Kieran.

'I'm a family friend, here to support Nicole.'

He nodded and turned back to her. 'I'm afraid it's not good news.'

'No. So I gathered. But the nurses wouldn't tell me any details.'

'The tumour is affecting just about every function now. He's not able to speak or move.'

'Can he hear?'

'We don't think so. We can't be sure, though, so it wouldn't hurt for you to speak to him as if he can.'

'What's going to happen next?'

'We look after him, make sure he's in no pain. And we can either try to prolong his life or let nature take its course. Your choice. Do you want him put on a ventilator, if necessary?'

She shuddered, but there was no doubt in her mind. 'No. I'm sure he wouldn't want to linger in this state. He was — is a firm believer in euthanasia.'

The doctor made a note on his pad and moved towards the door. 'You can visit him at any time, day or night.'

She sat very still, waiting for the door to close behind him, then turned towards the bed, feeling she had to say something — in case he could still hear. 'I'll be back later, Sam. I'll bring Paul to see you. William has run away. If I can find him, I'll send him too.'

It made her shiver that he didn't respond by so much as the blink of an eyelid. She'd had as much as she could take, so turned towards the door, reaching out for it blindly, her vision blurred by tears. She was aware of Kieran's arm round her shoulders, aware of the cool air hitting her cheeks as they went out of the hospital, then remembered nothing till they arrived back at her flat.

Paul opened the door and stood aside to let

her in. She wanted to reassure him, but couldn't.

Time seemed to be moving jerkily. She found that she was sitting on the couch. How had she got there? Paul and Kieran were sitting nearby, watching her anxiously.

'Sorry. I was just — a bit overwhelmed. Thank you for bringing me home, Kieran. I can't go back to work. Not now.'

'If you give me your car key, I'll go to the library and drive your car back. Can you ring them and let them know I'm coming, then I'll call a taxi?'

'Yes.' After a moment she remembered to say, 'Thank you.' But he'd gone by then.

★　★　★

Paul watched his mother and when she seemed a bit better, asked quietly, 'How was Dad?'

'Not good. They think — he's only got a few days.'

He stared at her in shock. 'How can it happen so quickly?'

'I don't know. I think it depends on where the tumour spreads and how quickly, I suppose.'

'William doesn't even know Dad's dying.'

'No. I can't do much about that, though, because I don't know where he is. I thought you might like to come and visit your father with me this evening. We don't have to bother about visiting hours. We can go and see him any time.'

He sat, head bent, staring down at the ground, then took a deep breath and stood up. 'I'll come with you if I'm back in time. I need to go out.'

'Where to?'

'To find William. I've got a few ideas where to look. He has to be told about Dad.'

'He might attack you.'

'I'll risk it. He *has to* know.'

She wanted to stop him, but didn't think Paul would forgive her if she even tried. He wasn't a child now, seemed to have grown up very fast during the last few days. As people did in times of crisis. 'Be careful,' was all she dared say.

'I will. But I think I'll be all right because he'll want to know. Can you phone the hospital and tell them it's all right now for William to visit Dad? Don't call the police. I need to promise him he's not walking into a trap.'

'All right. I'll do that right away. Take care.'

*   *   *

When Kieran got home, he was in pain and had forgotten about Janey. She was still in his flat and looked wan and upset.

He ate a biscuit then took another half tablet. He was not going back on to full tablets. 'Everything all right?'

'Yes. No one rang the doorbell and I didn't see him outside. Sorry for being so wimpy about this, but he frightens me.'

'He's a big man.'

'Yes. And very strong.' She shivered.

'I'll help you upstairs with your things, shall I?'

'Yes. Thank you. I've got my head together now, and besides, there are other people in the building, so I'm pretty safe here. The woman on

278

my floor hardly ever goes out. The last thing he'll want to do is be seen publicly harassing me.'

'He was willing to risk approaching you in daytime.'

'He thought I'd be a pushover. I didn't really fight back last time, you see. I was so scared I just froze.'

'Some people do. I gather it's hard-wired into you how you react to sudden danger.'

At her door he said, 'If you need help, don't hesitate to ask.'

'Thank you. You're so kind.'

When she'd closed the door he went across the landing to ring her neighbour's doorbell. A quiet and reclusive woman, Miss Fairbie. He explained quickly that Janey was being stalked, describing Gary.

'I don't want to get involved.'

'You'd ring the police, though, if you thought she was in danger?'

She thought for. a moment, then nodded, already shutting the door.

He sighed. Miss Fairbie had her own problems, but he thought she'd help if the worst came to the worst.

Once in his own flat, he went to lie down. The next thing he knew it was the middle of the night, so he used the bathroom and crawled under the covers, fully dressed.

His last thought before he drifted off to sleep again was that he was certainly sleeping better since he'd got involved with Nicole.

17

Paul went to the headquarters of the group
William spent a lot of time with, which looked
more like a small, shabby house than the
headquarters of anything. He knocked on the
door and when a bearded man opened it and
scowled at him, said quickly, 'I'm William
Gainsford's brother. I need to speak to him
urgently.'

'He isn't here.'

'Can I leave a message for him?'

The man shrugged.

'Look, our father's dying. I need to tell
William what's going on. He'll want to go and
see Dad — while he still can.'

'And this could be a neat little police trap.'

'I wish it were. It's real. Dad's dying.' He
sniffed, feeling his eyes filling with tears.

'You're as soft as William said.'

'It doesn't matter whether I'm soft or not.
He'll want to know about Dad. Tell him I'll be
waiting at our old home to explain and I've not
told the police I'm doing this.'

He turned and walked away, wondering i
William was inside the headquarters, wondering
whether his brother would come to see him.

He saw the neighbour as he went into his old
home, raised one hand but didn't let her star
talking to him. Inside he stopped in shock. I
looked as if a bomb had hit the place. Surely

280

they hadn't left it in this bad a state? Had William been back?

The heating wasn't on, but he found a blanket and went to sit in the kitchen with it wrapped round his shoulders, waiting. He didn't switch on the lights as that might bring the police to check things out.

It seemed a long time before he heard a sound outside, but when he squinted at his watch in the moonlight, it was only just over an hour. He turned to see a dim outline of a face at the window. William. It must be.

The door opened but no one came in.

'It's not a trap,' he said in a low voice.

The door banged fully open and William stood on the step but still didn't come inside.

'What's the matter with Dad? Tell me quickly. I'm not staying long.'

'He's got a brain tumour and . . .' When he'd finished his explanation, Paul said only, 'I thought you'd want to know.'

His brother looked at him. 'If you're telling me lies, setting up a trap, I'll kill you.'

'I'm not. Dad's dying. He only has a few days left. You can visit him any time. Mum's told the hospital to let you in.'

'I'll think about it. Maybe tomorrow.'

And he was gone, just like that. He didn't say thank you. He didn't ask about Mum. Well, that sod didn't care about anyone except himself. He probably wouldn't go to the hospital, either.

But Paul felt good about what he'd done, which was what mattered most.

His mother was waiting for him at the flat. She

281

looked as if she'd been crying.

'Did you find your brother?'

'Yes.'

'Is he going to see his father?'

'I don't know. Who can tell what William's going to do? Did you ask the people at the hospital to let him in, Mum? You didn't tell the police, did you? Not about this.'

'No.' She came across to hug him. 'I rang the hospital and said it was all right for him to see his father, told them we'd resolved our differences, given the circumstances, and he was a shift worker.' She moved towards the kitchen area. 'Are you hungry? Good. I've got some food ready, then we'll grab a bit of sleep. Kieran's offered to take us to hospital in the morning. I've to ring him. I thought you'd want to come and say goodbye to your dad.'

She paused and looked at him. 'You don't have to, if you don't want.'

'Yes, I'll come with you tomorrow.'

★ ★ ★

Just after one o'clock in the morning, William slipped into the ward, alert in case *they* were waiting for him. The nurse at the reception desk was yawning over some papers and there was no one else around.

When he introduced himself, she said, 'Ah, yes. Your mother said you might be in quite late. Just come off your shift, have you?'

He stared at her, then nodded.

'I'll show you where your father is.'

'How is he?'

She gave him a pitying look. 'Going downhill fast, as I expect your mother told you.'

'Can he — like, hear me if I talk to him?'

'We don't know. He isn't reacting to stimuli at all now, but you should treat him as if he can hear you. I always do. It seems more respectful.'

William followed her into a small room set apart from the others. It made him feel like a rat in a trap. If they tried to capture him here, he'd create mayhem. He flexed his muscles and looked down at his arm admiringly. You could see the biceps even through his clothes now. He needed some more stuff to keep up this progress. When was the stupid nurse going to leave?

She went up to the bed first, to check out the still figure, then turned to beckon him forward. 'I'll leave you alone with your father. Would you like a cup of tea?'

It might be drugged. 'No, thanks. I just had one.' He kept himself very alert, ready to act. Man the hunter, just as it was meant to be.

After she'd gone, leaving the door slightly ajar, he went to close it, and only then did he move closer to the bed to study his father's face carefully. He was shocked rigid at what he saw.

This wasn't his father!

But it was. He shivered. His father seemed more dead than alive. For once, Paul the Softie had been right. William had needed to come here.

Bending forward, he said in a low voice, 'I don't know whether you can hear me, Dad, but I wanted to say goodbye. That's all, really. I'm sorry you're dying.' He stood there for a moment or two, then said, 'Can't think of anything else to say. 'Bye now.' He shrugged off the feeling of helplessness and went out, on the alert for traps.

That fat nurse didn't even see him go out the back way, towards the fire stairs, because she was talking to someone hidden by the corner of the wall.

It was so easy to do what he wanted. Most people were mugs, doormats, fit only for treading on. He wasn't.

Outside the hospital, however, the cold bit in and William began to shiver. He did *not* like living on the streets and he damned well wasn't going to sleep out on a night like this. The only place he could think of going was home. He'd slept up in the roof space last night, on a platform his dad had built across the joists for storing their camping gear. They'd got rid of it years ago, but there were still a couple of tatty old sleeping bags and a few other bits and pieces left up there.

He'd got up into the roof by standing on the banisters and pulling himself up. He woke up when the police came in to check out the house and smiled as he heard them moving round. They'd not catch him.

They came back again just as it was starting to get light, without suspecting that he was overhead. He was a lot smarter than them, as well as a lot stronger.

He yawned and stretched. Probably be best to get out of here once they'd gone, before the neighbours started stirring. He'd change his clothes whilst he was at it, and get something to eat.

He did a careful check before leaving, but couldn't see any police or other watchers near the house. He gave a scornful sniff. It was as his friends said: the police relied on most people acting like meek bloody sheep. They didn't have resources to follow up on everything.

But he had to get hold of some money, if he was to stay ahead of the game. He'd soon be needing some more stuff. And he'd have to find somewhere to exercise. When he was inducted into the group, it'd be a lot easier, but until then he had to fend for himself. Those were the rules. All they'd do for the first few months was sell him the stuff.

* * *

Dan went to the allotment as usual on Sunday morning, looking forward to his lesson on cake making later in the day. He could probably have found instructions for doing it in Peggy's cookery books, but in practical matters, being shown was often more useful.

Same with gardening. Books didn't give you a *feel* for it, or tell you the local soil conditions, weren't able to look up at the sky and figure out what the weather was going to be like.

If the cake he'd tasted at Winifred's last time was anything to go by, she was a top cook.

Besides, this was a way of cementing a new friendship. At his age, new friends were few and far between, and mostly women, because men

died sooner. Thank goodness he'd never smoked
The friends who'd smoked had died first, i
seemed to him.

Humming under his breath, he checked his
trays of seedlings in the little lean-to greenhouse
he'd built from scrap wood and old windows
bought cheaply from the salvage yard. He was
pleased to see several more seedlings standing up
and testing the world around them by opening
two little leaves on a delicate stalk. Soon he'd be
starting his first plantings, pricking them out. He
loved doing that. There was so much promise in
a row of young plants. They stood up so bravely
out in the big world and responded so well to a
little care.

Still humming, he began to potter around
bending over to clear up some wind-blown
debris. From that position he noticed a burly
young fellow coming out of Martin's hut and
something about him looked menacing. Dar
stayed where he was, not even standing up. Still
crouching, he moved closer to his hut, not liking
the looks of the fellow at all.

Some instinct made him slip inside. He'd have
locked the door, only it had no locks on the
inside. He'd never even considered that before
but now it seemed a stupid omission.

He continued to peer out of the window and
to his horror, saw the young fellow trampling on
some seedlings Martin had just set out, doing it
deliberately. Dan's heart began to pound and he
took out his mobile phone. Was he in enough
danger to ring the police? He switched it on, in
case.

The young vandal wandered over to another of the makeshift huts and kicked the door in, vanishing inside for a moment or two, then coming out, clenched fists hanging by his side, looking annoyed. Hadn't found anything valuable, probably.

He kicked again, smashing the flimsy wooden door panels and then chucking a stone through the little window.

That settled it. Dan dialled 999 and said in a voice breathless with fear, 'There's a young guy kicking in the hut doors and trampling plants at the Grove Allotments. I think he's looking for things to steal. I'm alone in my hut and I'm frightened. I'm an old chap. I can't defend myself against a brute like that.'

There were some fuzzy crackling sounds then a voice said, 'Car on its way.'

'Thank you.'

But would it come fast enough?

He tried to jam the chair under the latch, but the chair back wasn't high enough. They might do that sort of thing in novels, but it didn't work in real life. He thought of the padlock, hanging uselessly on the outside, but didn't dare open the door to get it, in case he drew attention to himself. If he survived this, he'd fit good strong bolts inside.

Keeping out of direct sight — he hoped — he continued to watch through the little window.

Oh, no! The fellow was coming this way now.

★   ★   ★

Janey woke on Sunday morning feeling apprehensive. For a moment she couldn't think why, then she remembered Gary turning up yesterday, the way he'd grabbed the pram and threatened her baby. He hadn't really looked at Millie, even though she was his child.

But at least she'd given Kieran the letter now. If anything happened to her, they'd know who'd done it. And the letter meant she'd have something to threaten Gary with.

She hesitated about going to church, then got angry. Why should she stop doing the things she wanted to? She'd be careful, very careful, but she wasn't going to hide in her flat all the time.

She got ready, dressing as smartly as she could, put Millie in the playpen and pushed the buggy out on to the landing, moving it carefully down the stairs. It was irritating the way she had to juggle Millie and the buggy to get them both down safely.

As often happened, Kieran's door opened before she reached the bottom and he smiled at her. 'Need some help?'

'No, thanks. I've just got to fetch Millie down then we're off to church.'

'I'd offer to walk with you, but I'd slow you down.'

'That's all right. There'll be plenty of people around at this hour.'

'I'll come and watch you walk down the street and if you give me a ring when you're nearly back, I'll come out and make sure you get home safely.'

Tears filled her eyes as she looked at him. 'You

are so kind, Kieran. I can't tell you how grateful I am.'

He went a bit red. 'People have helped me a lot this past year. When you're more settled, perhaps you can help someone else in your turn.'

'I will. You know, you're walking a lot better than when I first moved in.'

He beamed at her. 'Do you really think so?'

She nodded, happy to have pleased him. But it was true: he was limping less — and smiling a lot more, too.

When she got down to High Street, she turned and waved to him, then set off for church. There were enough people around for her to feel safe.

This time she knew to take Millie to the crèche and when she sat on one of the hard wooden chairs, waiting for the service to begin, a couple of people nearby said good morning to her, which made her feel welcome.

To her surprise, Al from college came in with a woman who didn't look old enough to be his mother, but who looked so like a female version of him that she must be.

He nudged his mother and they came over to join Janey. After introductions, they sat down beside her.

'I enjoy Louise's sermons,' his mother said. 'She's got her feet on the ground, unlike some.'

After the service, people stayed around chatting, and to Janey's surprise, Al offered to get her a cup of coffee.

She looked in the direction of the side room. 'I need to fetch Millie.'

'The crèche doesn't shut till an hour after the

service,' his mother said. 'Louise thinks people should enjoy their outing and do some talking of their own, instead of leaving it all to her.'

Al grinned. 'And she provides decent coffee too. It's only 20p a cup, so I can afford to treat you.'

'She must be making a loss.'

He shrugged. 'She gets things wholesale and sometimes people give her stuff.' He looked round at the groups of people, chatting and smiling. 'Bit different from the parish church, eh?'

It was half an hour before Janey left and she really enjoyed chatting to Al and his mother, who introduced her to a few other people. Afterwards they offered to walk her to the end of her street.

It was his mother who noticed her relief and asked, 'Is there a problem? Are you afraid to walk the streets?'

She hesitated, then said, 'When they're quiet like this, I am a bit. I'm being stalked, you see.'

'Who by?'

'I . . . daren't name him.'

Al frowned at that. 'It's the only way to stop him.'

She shook her head, not daring to let any more information out.

His mother shushed him when he would have said something else and took Janey's arm. 'We'll walk you right to your house, then. It's not much out of our way.'

'Thank you. I was going to ring my landlord before I turned off High Street. He offered to watch me up the street.'

But Al wouldn't be stopped. 'Can't the police do *anything*?'

'I have no proof, so I daren't complain. He's . . . um, quite well known in the town.'

His eyes went to Millie and then back to her. Had he guessed it was her baby's father she was talking about?

When they got back, she thanked them, but they refused to come in for a cup of tea as they were going on to some friends. She went to knock on Kieran's door to let him know she was back.

It had spoilt the pleasure of the morning to feel so scared of walking back. And how long could she keep Gary at bay, anyway?

In an hour or so, she had to walk up the street to Miss Parfitt's for her cookery lesson. Another risk. Was it worth it?

She stiffened. Yes, it was. If she let fear take over, she'd never do anything and he'd have won. But she would be very careful. Very careful indeed.

★　★　★

Dan crouched on the floor underneath his little table so that anyone looking into the hut through the small window wouldn't easily see him. It hurt his knees to get down and it hurt his back to crouch for long, but he'd seen that fellow going wild, destroying things for no reason, and being a witness could put him in serious danger.

He heard trampling sounds outside, coming closer, and pressed one hand against his chest, where his heart was alternately pounding and stuttering. Was he going to have a heart attack? He didn't want to die, especially not like this.

Where were the police?

The sound of footsteps on the gravel path grew louder and then he heard glass smashing on the other side of the thin wooden wall. His little greenhouse was being smashed! Why? His heart hiccupped again.

There was muttering as someone tried the door of his hut. It was flung open and the young fellow came inside. He laughed when he saw Dan hiding under the table and hauled him out without a word, jerking him upright and slamming him against the wall with enough force to rattle all the bottles, jars and seed trays on the shelves.

But just as Dan had given up hope of avoiding violence, was waiting for that huge bunched fist to smash him into oblivion, there was the sound of a police siren in the distance coming closer. Realising he had a faint chance of escape, Dan seized it. 'I called the police. That's why they're here. They know me and they know which hut I'm in.'

For a few seconds the young fellow stared him straight in the eyes. 'Are you scared of me, old man?'

'Yes.'

'Good. They should all be scared of me.' Then he threw Dan aside and took off running.

Dan steadied himself against the wall, then tottered to the door, feeling as if his legs would hardly hold him. He watched his attacker trample across the plots and scramble over the fence at the far side. Once Dan wouldn't have been vanquished so easily. Once he'd have chased after that fellow, yelling for help. And other people would have come running, because there was always someone nearby when he was younger.

These days, even when they saw something bad happening, people didn't always pitch in and help. Some folk just stood by, letting thugs take over the world.

The car with its flashing blue light drew up. Clinging to the doorpost, Dan waved and two figures in blue came pounding across the bare earth towards him. Like the vandal, they ignored the paths and took the most direct route. He pointed in the direction his attacker had taken. 'He went over the fence.' Then he sank down on the outside bench, shaking from head to toe.

The police ran to the far edge of the allotments, going a good deal more nimbly than the heavy-footed young fellow. One officer boosted himself up to peer over the wall but shook his head. The other called in the information. Then they came back to Dan. He knew them by sight. He knew all the local police and they knew him.

'Are you all right, Mr S?'

'Shaken up a bit,' he admitted.

'We'd better get you to hospital.'

'No need.'

'Just a quick check-up, eh, to be sure?'

He glanced down at his watch and pulled himself together. 'No. I've arranged to visit someone and I don't want to let her down.'

'She'll understand.'

'I *want* to go and see her. I don't *need* to go to hospital.'

They exchanged glances and one rolled his eyes. Did they think he wouldn't notice?

'Can't see your car here today, Mr S, and you're in no fit state to walk anywhere.'

'Take me to her house in the police car, then. You can do that, get me to a place of safety, can't you? My friend lives at the top of Peppercorn Street. It's not far. I can catch a taxi home afterwards.' He held his breath, wondering if he'd gone too far by asking this.

'OK, Mr S. If you're sure you're all right. Do you want to lock up here first? Shame about your greenhouse.'

He looked sadly at his smashed lean-to. He'd been so pleased to build that for practically nothing, making it out of recycled bits and pieces that he'd picked up here and there. You had to be ingenious when you were on an old age pension. Now he'd have it all to do again, just when he needed to use it. 'I'll have to put the trays of seedlings inside the hut first, to stop the frost getting them. They're not ready to face the world yet.'

'We'll pass them in to you.'

It didn't take long and it cheered him up a bit, because most of the seedlings were still intact, only a few having been damaged by shards of glass.

Dan glanced at his watch again. They'd arrive a bit early, but he didn't think Winifred would mind. She'd understand that he needed to be with people his own age, people who understood his frustration at not being able to fight back — though even in his younger days he'd not have been able to hold his own against such a large opponent.

He picked up his backpack. Tomorrow he'd go and buy a couple of bolts for the inside of the door, top and bottom. It was a good solid door, another recycled piece, built to last. It'd hold an intruder for a while and he'd keep bringing his mobile phone.

Thank goodness Simon had insisted on getting him one. Dan would never criticise those things again, even though he still didn't want to leave his switched on all the time.

*   *   *

Winifred went to peer through the front room window and saw Dan standing there, flanked by two policemen.

She hurried to the front door. 'Sorry to keep you waiting. I was just checking who you were.' Then she noticed how white and shaken Dan was. 'What's happened?'

'There was an intruder at the allotments, he was smashing things up and if the police hadn't answered my call quickly, he'd have smashed me up, too.'

'Have you been to the doctor's?'

'No. I'm not hurt, just upset. I wanted to come here and have a quiet sit down. I'm a bit early, I know.' He looked at her pleadingly. 'Do you mind?'

'Of course I don't. Go and sit in the kitchen. You know the way. I'll see these officers out.'

When Dan had gone, one of the men said quietly, 'If he shows any signs of being affected, call an ambulance. But he's a tough old bug — er, devil. I think he'll be all right with a little TLC.'

Winifred nodded. 'I'll keep an eye on him.'

She went back into the kitchen and saw Dan sagging in a chair by the table. She remembered how she'd felt when her nephew threatened to break in. Helpless and upset. She moved the kettle on to the Aga. 'Hot, sweet tea — or would you rather have drinking chocolate?'

He brightened a little. 'Drinking chocolate. Peggy used to love it. I haven't had it for ages.'

She soon had a mug of it steaming gently in front of him.

He put his hands round the mug and relaxed a little more as if the warmth comforted him. 'It smells wonderful.'

'Do you want to tell me what happened?'

He had a think, head on one side. 'Just the short version.' He explained quickly then looked at her. 'What upset me most was how helpless I was, how I had to hide. If I hadn't had that mobile phone, I'd probably be lying on the ground bleeding now. Or dead even. My son had to persuade me to have one, but by hell, he was right. Do you have one?'

'No. I don't go out much.' She pointed to the pendant hanging on the wall. 'The social care people gave me that, though, in case I need to call for help. I hate having it. I hate being so old and feeble. I'm supposed to wear it all the time, but it drives me mad.'

'I'm not so fond of being old, either. But look on the bright side. We're both still on the right side of the grass *and* we have all our marbles.'

She smiled reluctantly. 'That's one way to put it. Janey will be here in a few minutes. Should I put her off?'

'No. We both want to learn to cook cakes. And I want — no I *need*, to do something normal.'

Winifred could understand that, so stopped talking about the attack. 'That girl's mother doesn't seem to have taught her about cooking, does she?'

'No. And she didn't sound to have stuck up for her against the father, either. What a bully he is! But *we* could keep an eye on that lass, couldn't we? Hazel could do that as well, if she wants. You can't have too many fairy godmothers.'

Winifred looked at him, a scrawny old man with sparse silver hair and rather big ears, then glanced at herself in the mirror, an equally scrawny old woman, with iron-grey hair, though she still had plenty of it, thank goodness. 'Fairy godmothers! Look at us!'

They both laughed and suddenly Dan's smile was back to normal. 'You're doing me good, Winifred. Better than a doctor.'

'Oh. Well, I'm glad about that.'

She felt flustered by this compliment, hadn't had enough of them in her life to get used to them. Her mother had always found fault. Nothing had ever been good enough.

She wished things had been different. Her life

297

might have been — more enjoyable. She'd done her duty, always, but that was cold comfort now

★ ★ ★

As the police car drove off down Peppercorn Street, one officer said to the other, 'There's old Yarford again and outside the same house. That's in our area. If he suspects someone there, he should have passed the information on to us.'

'He always goes his own sweet way. It's probably someone he's got a grudge against.'

'Hmm. I'm taking down the number and address. I'll see if anyone in our office knows about that house.'

His companion grinned. 'Tell Sergeant McNaught. She's got issues with Yarford from way back, though no one knows exactly what. She'd love to be able to complain about him. Fearsome woman, that. I'd not like to get on the wrong side of her.'

'I hope he puts a foot wrong.'

They both grinned.

★ ★ ★

Janey saw to Millie's needs and grabbed a quick sandwich for herself before getting ready to walk up the street to Miss Parfitt's. It wasn't far, just a couple of hundred yards. Surely she'd be safe for that short distance? There was no sign of Kieran, so she waited till someone else was walking up the street and set off, staying behind them, even though they were walking slowly, lost in conversation.

298

Was *he* watching her from somewhere? How would she ever know? She might be imagining she saw him so often. But if she wasn't . . . There was too much at stake. She wasn't going to let him do that — no, she said the word to herself — *rape*, that was what he'd done, raped her. And if she made him aware how determined she was, well, surely he'd lose interest after a while?

If he didn't, if he continued to pursue her — she swallowed hard, upset at the mere thought — then she'd have to ask to go into a women's refuge. She'd been thinking about that during the night. It would be the very last resort, though, because if she had to move to another town, she wouldn't be able to take her exams this year and she'd lose her lovely new friends.

It wasn't fair!

She blinked away the tears. She didn't want to arrive crying.

The people she'd been following turned into one of the houses, but there wasn't far to go then to Miss Parfitt's house, so she walked along briskly, shivering with relief not cold as she went through the gate.

She was safe here, surely?

18

Nicole felt tired and the cut on her head was still painful. She watched Paul pick at his lunch and thought he looked as washed out as her mirror said she did. They'd both spent half the morning lying in bed, reading. 'You all right?'

He shrugged. 'How can any of us be all right when Dad's lying there unconscious?'

'It's horrible, isn't it? Are you coming to the hospital with me this afternoon?'

'I suppose.'

'Don't come if you don't feel up to it. He won't know.'

'I have to come, don't I? In case . . . ' His voice wobbled for a moment, then he finished his sentence. 'In case Dad dies. You're going there every day for the same reason.'

'Yes. It's . . . well, what you do.'

'So I'm coming.'

The phone rang and she let Paul pick it up because he was nearest.

'She's here.' He held out the phone to her. 'It's the hospital.'

'Mrs Gainsford? I have bad news for you, I'm afraid. Your husband's condition has deteriorated suddenly and it might be wise if you came to see him today.'

'I was coming later on.'

'It might be wiser to come now. He seems to be failing quite rapidly.'

'I'll come straight away.'

'It's a good thing your older son came in to see him last night, isn't it?'

'*What?*'

'Your son William came in just after one o'clock. He didn't stay long.'

'I wasn't sure he'd make it. I'm . . . glad.'

She put the phone down and turned to Paul. 'William went in to see your father last night.'

He closed his eyes, shaking his head helplessly, unable to speak.

'You did well contacting him,' she said softly, rubbing his arm for comfort.

He scrubbed at his eyes, then asked, 'Are you going to ask Kieran to take us there?'

'We can't keep turning to him. He's done more than anyone could have expected already.'

'If you don't ring him, I will. He'd want to be there with you. And anyway, you need him. You're still wincing when you touch that cut on your head and you're very pale. You shouldn't be driving.'

'Nor should I be using Kieran like this.'

'That's what friends are for, isn't it? I feel as if we've known him for years. Look, I'll do it. No hassle.' He picked up the phone and dialled the number without needing to check it. 'Kieran? Paul here. No, things aren't all right. We've just had a call from the hospital. They think Dad's . . . failing. I agree. Mum definitely shouldn't drive there on her own. Thanks.' He put the phone down. 'He'll be round in five minutes.'

He came across and gave her a quick pat on the shoulder, but she needed more, so she grabbed him and hugged him tightly, rocking slightly. 'Thanks, darling.'

'I'm coming with you. I didn't see him yesterday. It's, like, the last chance today, isn't it? Something I'd always regret if I didn't do it?'

She nodded.

'Even William went in to see him. I'm glad about that. It means he's not quite a total shit.'

She could only nod again. How her life had changed in the past few weeks! No, it had been changing for a while, but the rate of change had suddenly accelerated. Sometimes she couldn't believe this was happening at all, kept thinking she'd wake up in her old bed and find it had all been a nightmare.

But it hadn't and wishing wouldn't change things, especially the way she'd treated him.

If only she hadn't left him. If she'd still been at home, she might have made his last weeks easier. She'd never forgive herself for jumping to conclusions about him having an affair. Never.

By the time Kieran drew up, they were waiting in the entrance hall. An icy wind whistled round them as they hurried out to the car. But even with the car heater on full blast, she still felt cold.

★ ★ ★

Winifred went to answer the door, feeling more secure about doing that with Dan in the house. 'Janey, dear! I'm so glad you could come. Let me take your jacket.' She hung it up and beamed down at Millie. 'Isn't she gorgeous? Bring her through to the kitchen before you take her out-door things off.'

302

Mr S was already there, smiling at her but not looking his usual self.

Winifred explained briefly what had happened and Janey stared at him open-mouthed. 'You mean, this man, a complete stranger, attacked you for nothing?'

'He was looking for something to steal. Must be stupid if he thinks people keep anything valuable at the allotments. I don't even take my credit card down there.'

'You shouldn't stay there on your own again, Mr S.'

'I'll be all right. He won't come back. He's found out now that there's nothing to steal.'

Winifred judged enough had been said, made sure the baby was all right, then put the ingredients on the table. She'd wondered if she'd be any good as a teacher, but the words seemed to flow and since the recipe was an easy one, the cake was soon finished and in the oven.

'I've written out the recipe for you.' She gave them each a piece of paper, handwritten in a beautiful sloping script.

'I'll start a new file on my computer for recipes,' Janey said. 'I love the way you write. It's so pretty.'

Winifred smiled. 'We all learnt to write like that when I was at school, and we got into trouble if we didn't get it perfect each time.'

'I think you were a decade or so before me,' Mr S said. 'Funny how such differences blur when you get older. My generation didn't have to do copperplate handwriting, but we had to write neatly or we were forced to do it all over again.'

'I sometimes feel I'm the last person of my generation left,' Winifred said with a sigh. 'All my friends have died.'

'But you're making new ones,' he reminded her with a smile.

Millie chose that moment to yawn loudly and rub her eyes, so Janey pulled up her soft checked blanket and wheeled the buggy out into the hall. She waited to see her settle down, but to her relief Millie didn't need much persuading to go to sleep. What a happy child she was when she wasn't teething!

When she went back inside, Janey heard Miss Parfitt say, 'Hazel and I are going to classes to learn about computers, but I'm not at all sure how I'll cope with that.'

'I don't think I'll ever understand the damned things,' Dan said. 'I'd rather be out in the fresh air than sitting indoors goggling at a screen.'

'I love my computer,' Janey said. 'And if you don't mind me saying so, Mr S, you'd find a computer very helpful for keeping records for your allotment. And you could go online and find out all sorts of things about gardening, join a group and discuss gardening by email, order seeds online. There's nothing like a computer when you're on your own. I just wish I could afford to go on the Internet.'

They were staring at her rather disbelievingly so she explained a few of the things you could do with a computer, answering their questions patiently because they clearly knew nothing. 'Look, it's hard to explain without being able to show you. If you'd like to come round to my flat one day, I'll show you some of what you can do on a computer.'

She watched them exchange glances, uncertain, hesitant, and realised in amazement that they were afraid of computers. 'It's not hard, you know, it's just fiddly.'

It was Mr S who spoke first. 'Well, why not? My Terry's always nagging me to get a computer and go on email, so that it's easier for him to keep in touch.'

'You should go to the classes with Miss Parfitt and Dawn's mother, then.'

'We-ell, I might just do that if you'll help me in between classes. I'm going to have some extra time on my hands . . . now.'

Janey had noticed before how he tacked on 'now' and it upset her because she knew he was speaking about his wife being dead. She realised he was speaking, asking her about college, so dropped the subject of computers and told them about her classes and meeting Al and his mother at church.

Before they knew it the cake was ready and Winifred was pulling it out of the oven.

'That smells delicious!' he said.

'Don't you need to test it?' Janey asked. 'You know, poke it with a skewer or something. My mother always did.'

'Goodness no. I've baked this one so many times in this oven I know to the minute how long it takes, and anyway, you can see that it's coming away from the sides of the tin, plus the top is firm in the middle. I'll just let it cool for a bit, then put the kettle on and we'll test a piece and have a cup of tea.'

Mr S was looking better now, Janey thought. She felt better here too, safe and relaxed. 'This is almost like having grandparents again,' she said without thinking. 'Well, I only ever had one granddad really, but I still miss him a lot.'

'Then perhaps you could adopt us as your honorary grandparents,' Mr S said at once. 'My grandchildren don't come and see me very often, even the ones who live nearby.'

He was looking at her anxiously as if afraid of rejection, but she didn't hesitate. 'I'd love that!' Then she realised Miss Parfitt hadn't spoken and looked at her. The old lady was looking as nervous as Mr S had about computers. 'Do I get an adopted grandmother too?'

'That'd be very . . . nice. I've got plenty of time on my hands and no close relatives at all.' She blew her nose firmly and added, 'Let's have a piece of cake to celebrate.'

It was surprising, Janey thought as she got ready to leave, how comfortable she felt with the two of them. As if they really were her grandparents.

But as she stepped out of the gate, she saw a familiar car parked down the street. In a panic she dragged the buggy back up the steps and hammered on the front door.

When Miss Parfitt opened it, she nearly fell through it, so upset was she.

★ ★ ★

Dan put an arm round her as Winifred locked the door. 'Calm down and tell us what's wrong, Janey. No, take a deep breath and don't star speaking till you've got control of yourself.'

So it all came tumbling out and this time she didn't hold back on saying his name.

As he listened, Dan exchanged shocked glances with Winifred. 'You can't go back to that flat.'

'She can stay here,' Winifred said at once.

'But all my things, all the baby's things, are in the flat. I have to go back and he knows it.'

'I'm going to ring Dawn.' Winifred was picking up the phone even as she spoke. 'She'll know what to do.'

As she listened to a quick summary of her story being repeated by Winifred, Janey thought how far-fetched it sounded. Since Gary had turned up again, everything felt unreal, like a nightmare that never ended.

Winifred put the phone down. 'She says to stay here, not to go back to the flat on your own under any circumstances.'

'I don't want to cause you any trouble, Miss Parfitt.' And she couldn't help crying again, feeling so helpless.

It was a while before she calmed down enough to realise she was sitting next to Miss Parfitt, who had an arm round her shoulders and was clasping her hand.

Dan had picked up Millie and was joggling her about next to the window, talking softly to her and pointing out some birds.

'I can't believe how kind you're being to me!' Janey said, blowing her nose in a futile effort to stop weeping.

The doorbell rang. 'Ah, that'll be Dawn.' Miss Parfitt went to let her in.

307

The hospital looked huge and grey, more like a prison in the dull light of an overcast afternoon. Nicole shivered as she walked towards it, Kieran on one side of her, Paul on the other. Her steps faltered just before the entrance, and she had to force herself to go inside.

At the ward, a nurse she'd seen before greeted them, then he took them along to Sam's room though they knew the way by now.

'We have screens round the foot of the bed, so that even when the door is open, no one can stare in,' he said quietly. 'They'll be round with the tea trolley in a minute. I'll get them to give you a cup.' He hesitated, then asked, 'Do you want a minister to come and see him?'

Nicole's mind seemed blank and she couldn't think what to say.

'Dad didn't go to church,' Paul said. 'Does that matter?'

'Not many people go to church these days, but a lot of them want a clergyman at the end.'

'We don't know any.'

'We have a chaplain at the hospital.'

Nicole saw Paul nodding at her. 'Yes. All right. I do think it'd be good for him to see Sam.' She wanted to do everything properly, to make up for the huge mistake she'd made. As if that would wipe out her guilt.

She turned towards the bed, dreading what she'd see, but there seemed no change visible at first, not until she looked more closely and saw a complete lack of colour in his face. It was a look, more than anything specific she could put her finger on. He lay so still, she wondered for a moment if he'd died already, then she saw his chest rise and fall very slightly.

She sat down beside the bed and clasped his hand for a moment. There was no response. The fingers lay limply in hers. The flesh was warm, but Sam no longer seemed to be inhabiting it. Guilt seared through her yet again.

Suddenly noise erupted outside, raised voices, a woman shouting, sounds of a scuffle. As she looked up in shock, Kieran slipped outside so she left it to him to find out what was happening. Bending her head again, she tried to pray and ignore whoever was shouting. But the words wouldn't come, so all she could do was sit there and wait, feeling sad and bewildered.

From time to time she looked at her son, who was sitting on the other side of the bed. When she caught his eye, she mouthed, 'All right?' and he nodded. She winced as someone outside let out a piercing yell.

You couldn't help listening when someone outside was making such a fuss. Nicole stood up as the shouting became screaming, a woman's voice, shrill and full of pain. Why hadn't they moved the person somewhere else?

Kieran hadn't come back. Perhaps they needed his help to control this person.

★   ★   ★

Outside Kieran found a plump, blonde-haired woman struggling with two nurses. She was

309

putting up a hell of a fight and screeching at the top of her voice. He suddenly jerked to attention as what she was saying sank in.

'Let me in to see him! I'm the only one who cares about Sam. The only one.' She paused, panting, and slapped away a hand as one of the nurses tried to move her away from the door. 'I'm *not* — going away. I'm not! And if you throw me out of the hospital, I'll camp on the doorstep and go on screaming and shouting there.'

'But only the family is allowed in at a time like this,' the male nurse said, letting go for a moment as she stopped struggling.

'I'm as good as family. Better than *his* family.' She wiped her eyes, but more tears rolled down her cheeks.

The other nurse glanced at him meaningfully and mouthed, 'Stay here,' then slipped away. Kieran guessed she was going to summon assistance. Well, he'd do what he could to help if the woman tried to go into the room and disturb Nicole.

'Let me see Sam,' the woman said, and her shrieks subsided into loud sobbing. '*Please.* Just let me say goodbye to him. We're lovers. *She* doesn't love him any more, but I do.'

Kieran wondered how much of this was penetrating into the small room beyond the door. He felt sorry for this woman, who was clearly in great anguish, but didn't know what to do about that.

How could they keep her away from the man she loved when he was dying? Only, how could they let her go inside and upset Nicole and Paul?

Dawn arrived at Miss Parfitt's on her usual wave of energy. When they all tried to tell her at once what the matter was, she quietened them with a gesture, then suggested they sit down.

'Now, I think Janey should be the one to tell me what the problem is. Don't hurry, dear. I've got as long as it takes. Margaret is keeping an eye on the shop.'

She listened intently as Janey told her about Gary and the way he was pursuing her.

'Stalking,' Dawn corrected. 'He's stalking you. It's a pity you didn't take a photo of his car.'

'What with?' Janey asked bitterly. 'I've got a cheapie old mobile phone and it doesn't take photos. Oh, I remember, Kieran who owns the flats took a photo on his mobile phone of him harassing me.'

'Good. It's always useful to have evidence. But one thing's clear: if this goes on, you'll have to move into the women's refuge.'

'Couldn't she stay here?' Winifred asked.

Dawn frowned, tapping her forefinger on her lips as she thought this through. 'We'd need more than you to make her safe, Miss Parfitt, with all due respect.'

'I could stay here too,' Dan offered. 'I've got a sleeping bag, just find me a sofa. I'd be really happy to help. We've both grown very fond of Janey.'

'You're so kind, but I think I'm safe once I'm inside my flat,' Janey said. 'It's when I go out I feel threatened.'

'I'll get in touch with Kieran and ask him about the photo,' Dawn said. 'And I can take you home now. Just let anyone try to mess with you when I'm around.'

'Have a cup of tea first,' Winifred offered. 'You look tired.'

'Been a busy few weeks, but someone else is starting at the charity shop tomorrow, so I should have a bit more free time. Now, let's talk about something more cheerful. Have you had any chance to think about advertising this garden scheme?'

'Not really.'

'Let me know how I can help you get started.'

★   ★   ★

Nicole suddenly realised exactly what the woman was shouting and reached out to clutch Paul's shoulder. Still listening, she exchanged startled glances with her son then looked at the figure on the bed. If anything would have made Sam respond, surely the woman's cries would? But it hadn't: his expression hadn't changed at all, not even when there was all that passion and fury so close.

The woman outside had it right, though. Nicole didn't love him, hadn't done for quite a while. It was guilt that had brought her here and that was a poor substitute for love.

The stranger renewed her sobbing and pleading. 'Let me in. Please let me see my Sam before he dies. How can you keep me from him at a time like this?'

312

Paul shifted uneasily from beneath his mother's grasp. 'You shouldn't have to listen to this, Mum. And Dad shouldn't have been unfaithful. How could he?'

'People fall out of love — and into love. It happens. Though Sam should have been more open, left me. I can't think why he didn't. That woman's right about one thing, though. She should be allowed to see him.' Nicole took a deep breath. 'Say goodbye to your father, Paul, then we'll give her the chance to say her own goodbye.'

He gaped at her. 'Are you OK with that?'

'I'm not OK with anything very much at the moment, but she definitely needs to see him.' Nicole walked to the bottom of the bed, turned to take one last look at the effigy-like figure lying there, well tended, neatly arranged, but somehow not really Sam any longer. She opened the door in time to hear the woman's next words all too clearly and see the instinctive gesture that went with them.

'You're heartless, that's what you are, heartless. Shouldn't call yourselves nurses.' She cradled her belly in a gesture known through the ages. 'I'm carrying his child! If anyone should be sitting with him now, it's me.'

Nicole couldn't move for a moment at this second shock. She heard her son's gasp behind her and saw Kieran gape at the woman, then pride stiffened her spine and she moved forward. 'I'm Nicole. I don't know your name but I agree with what you're saying. You do have a right to be with him, to say farewell.'

313

The woman looked at her for a moment, face working as she fought not to sob. 'I'm sorry if I've hurt you, Nicole. I didn't mean to. Sam didn't mean to, either. But I love him so much.'

'Tell me your name and address. I'll make sure you know when the funeral is so that you can attend.'

'You'd let me — do that?'

'Yes.'

She nodded, wordlessly, fumbling in her handbag. 'Here. My business card. I'm Tracey.'

The two women stood for a moment, studying one another, not with anger, but with intense curiosity, then Nicole stepped aside and gestured with one hand. 'We've all finished saying goodbye. Go to him.'

'You're as nice as he said you were. Thank you.' Tracey pushed past the nurse, waited for Paul to step out of her way, then went into the room, making no attempt to stem her sobs now.

'Are you sure about this, Mrs Gainsford?' the nurse asked in a low voice.

'Letting her see him is the only thing I am sure about at the moment. Let her stay with him for as long as . . . is necessary. I won't be coming back.'

She felt Kieran move closer on her right side and Paul on her left, and each took one of her hands. With their support, she got herself out of the hospital and into the car.

Only then did she break down and start sobbing, vaguely aware of the car starting up and moving off. But through all the pain and tears about Sam, one thought consoled her and

314

gradually helped her to stop crying. She had no need to feel guilty about leaving him, because he really had been having an affair. She hadn't done anything wrong; he had.

And though she felt dreadfully sad about him dying, it was as if a huge burden had been lifted from her shoulders.

Another thought crept into her mind. Tracey had said, 'You're as nice as he said you were.' It was as if Sam himself had reached out from the mists of death to comfort her.

She hoped the baby would comfort Tracey.

19

Even before Dawn turned into the car park,
Janey stiffened. 'That car in the visitor's bay. It's
him!'

'The gall of the fellow!'

'He's not inside it. Where do you think he is?'

'I'm about to find out. Let's go up to your flat
and check that out first. I'll just write down his
car number.'

As Janey got out of the car, she caught a
glimpse of someone standing round the side of
the building. It was him. As he started walking
towards her, she froze.

'Can I help you carry the baby up, Janey?' He
smiled and reached out as if to open the back
door and unfasten Millie from the baby seat.

'No.' Janey moved between him and the car
pushing him away.

Dawn came running round to join her.

'I can see them up,' he told her, as calmly as if
he was a friend.

Janey found her voice. 'No, you can't. I don't
want you near me. Why won't you leave me
alone? I don't want to see you ever again.'

'That's going to be a bit difficult because your
father's so worried about you, he's asked me to
keep an eye on you. As he's a good friend, I'm
going to do just that.'

'What I do is no concern of his now. And
anyway, I don't believe you.'

He pulled a piece of paper out of his pocket. 'Read this.'

Dawn twitched it out of his hand and shared it with Janey. 'Is that your father's handwriting?'

'Yes. But it doesn't matter. He's weak and lazy, always does what Gary wants and believes the lies Gary tells about me.'

'Tch! Tch! Not a nice way to talk about your father.' He turned to Dawn. 'So you see, my dear, I'm *in loco parentis*.'

'Don't you "my dear" me,' Dawn said. 'You're not acting as a parent, either. Janey's eighteen. She's an adult now.'

He sighed. 'I didn't want to go into this but there are some official concerns about what sort of mother she is. We're as concerned about the baby as about Janey. That's why I'm here.'

Janey couldn't speak for shock and fear at this implied threat.

Dawn was silent for a moment or two. 'What official concerns?'

'Ask Ms Stevenall, who's in charge of the case.'

'I will,' Dawn said, 'and in the meantime, I'm telling you to stay away from Janey, who has made her wishes very plain where you're concerned.'

As the two locked glances, another car pulled into the car park and since they were standing in front of the garage, the driver sounded his horn.

'It's the owner.' Janey thrust the pushchair handle into Dawn's hands and ran across to the car.

Kieran wound down the window, but before he could speak, he saw Gary. '*What?* Don't tell me he's come back to bother you again.'

317

'Yes. He says there are concerns about me being a good mother and — '

'Don't say anything else now. You don't know how he'll twist your words. Save your talking until we're inside. Who's the woman?'

'Dawn. She's from *Just Girls*. She's a good friend.'

'I'll wait here till you and she have gone into the house.'

She hurried back to Dawn, who was holding the pushchair, watching. 'Let's go inside. It's no use talking to *him*.'

'You're going to regret it if you're not co-operative, Janey,' Gary said. 'Your father will be angry.'

'No, you'll regret it. You've a lot to lose as well.'

He just smiled. Confident. Menacing.

She grabbed the pushchair and moved towards the front door, followed closely by Dawn.

Gary looked towards Kieran with a frown, as if trying to work out who he was. He didn't attempt to follow them, but stood and watched and somehow that too was threatening.

Janey hoped he hadn't seen how she was shaking.

★ ★ ★

When the front door had closed behind Janey and Dawn, Kieran shouted across to the man still standing there, 'Please remove yourself and your car from my property and don't come here again.'

318

Gary made a rude sign with one finger and got into his car. But he didn't drive away; he parked in the street outside, in full view of the flats. Switching off the engine, he leaned back, as if making himself comfortable.

Kieran got out his mobile phone and took a photo of the car and driver, then eased his own vehicle into the garage.

'What was all that about?' Nicole asked.

'That fellow is stalking Janey. And as he's a policeman, it's a bit harder to accuse him without proof than it would be to accuse someone else. I've been keeping an eye on her but I can see I'm going to have to do more.'

She smiled warmly at him. 'If anyone can, it's you.'

There was a moment's silence as he smiled back at her. 'Sorry. I didn't ask if you wanted driving home. I should have done.'

'We'll walk. It's only just up the street and William isn't going to be attacking us in broad daylight, I'm sure. A bit of fresh air will do my headache good.'

'It's still aching?'

'A bit.' She turned to Paul. 'Coming?'

'Yeah.' As they walked, he said, 'I can't believe that fellow was doing it so openly. That poor girl looked scared stiff.'

'Some men think they rule the world.'

'Who is he?'

'He's a policeman. I remember him coming to give a talk at the library once, a few years ago. He didn't do it very well, kept ordering them to do this or not do that and the audience got very

319

restless. He's put on a lot of weight since then and he looks — I don't know, sour. I don't remember his name, but it'll come back to me if I don't obsess about it.'

'There's a lot of shit happening, isn't there? Not just to us.'

'Yes.' She opened the front door and they went inside, switching off the security system.

'Do you want to talk about Dad and what's-her-name . . . Tracey?' Paul asked.

'I don't know. I'm still getting used to the idea of this woman — and the baby.' She let out a mirthless laugh and shared one thought with her son. 'The thing that's been upsetting me most was that I'd wrongly suspected Sam of being unfaithful. I felt so *guilty*. And now — does it sound crazy to say I'm glad she exists, glad I don't have to feel guilty any more?'

'Nah. I get that.'

'Do you realise the baby will be your brother or sister?'

He gaped at her, then rolled his eyes. 'Well, I'm not volunteering to babysit.'

'You'll probably not see the woman again once the funeral is over. Want a cup of tea or a can of something?'

'I'd really like something to eat. How about we get a takeaway? We can walk down to the end of the street and pick something up.'

'Good idea. I don't have much food in because of not being able to go shopping lately. What do you fancy? Indian, Chinese, pizza?'

'Pizza.'

'Right then, pizza it is.'

'And can we buy some fruit? And make sure there's something in for breakfast? I get a bit hungry.'

'A *bit?* You're a stomach on wheels.' She smiled and ruffled his hair. 'You can go and order the pizza while I'll nip into that little supermarket.'

They walked down the street, passing Kieran's flats again. 'Don't look now,' Paul said, 'but that fellow's not moved. He's still watching the flats. I wonder if they know he's there?'

'I'm sure Kieran has everything in hand.'

'He's a great guy, isn't he? Pity about the accident. He says he'll never get full movement back. But we'd not have met him otherwise because he used to be travelling around the country all the time. He called it 'tilting at windmills' but I think he was a lot more successful than Don Quixote. Even I'd heard of Kieran Jones. He's won a couple of awards for his work, you know. I saw him on TV collecting one. He wasn't as thin then.'

She loved the way Paul had started talking to her, hoped he'd never feel a need to withdraw from the world again.

As they walked back up the street half an hour later, Paul said, 'What is that guy like? Look at that comb-over. As if you can hide baldness. And he's stalking a girl old enough to be his daughter. He's a real sicko, that one. I think I'll ring Kieran and make sure he knows the guy's not gone away.'

'Do it quickly. We don't want the pizza to go cold.'

Kieran joined them upstairs. He chatted to Dawn while Janey fed Millie.

'I really need to give her a bath and put her to bed now.'

'You do that,' he said with a smile. 'Take all the time you need. I'm in no hurry to go anywhere. After you've finished we'll do some serious planning.'

'Do you know what to do?'

'Oh, yes. I've not been an investigative journalist for nothing. I'm about to call in a few favours and if I don't manage to stop that fellow once and for all, then you've still got the women's refuge to go to.'

'Thanks. Only I'd rather not. I'd still be looking over my shoulder, wherever I went.' She picked Millie up and went into the bedroom.

'She's very near tears,' Dawn said to Kieran in a low voice. 'She froze for a moment or two when she saw him. I hated to see the fear on her face.'

'Poor kid. But that fellow's lost touch with reality if he thinks he can get away with this. He must be obsessed by her or he'd not have come out openly. I can't believe her father would support him.'

'I'm worried that this man has got the Stevenall woman on his side as well. She seems to hate her clients. She and I have tangled a few times. I'd never let her handle one of my girls.' She frowned. 'Stevenall wasn't dealing with Janey's case, so why is he threatening us with her?'

'I'm beginning to think it's part of a bigger

322

;cam. Major local corruption. It'll take a bit of unpinning, but I'm sure we'll get there in the end.'

'And in the meantime, Janey suffers.'

'She's made a few friends. If we draw up a roster to keep an eye on her, I'm sure we can guard her for long enough to catch him.'

'I hope you're right. But don't underestimate Stevenall. If she's helping him you can expect some nasty tricks.'

'Why would she do that?'

'I've heard that she's been passed over for promotion several times and is furious about it. And Janey's defied her once. Stevenall's known for getting back at people who upset her, and of course, she goes for the powerless ones.'

'Well, Janey isn't powerless. She's got us. Ah, here you are.'

She came out of the bedroom just then. Millie's asleep already. She was tired out.'

'So are you. Sit down. Can I get you a cup of tea, or perhaps something to eat?'

'I'm not hungry. I had some cake at Miss Parfitt's.' With a sigh she sat on the couch, shoulders drooping, staring at the floor.

Dawn moved to sit beside her.

'Right then,' said Kieran. 'This is what we need to do. The most important thing is that we all keep a diary, noting sightings of Yarford and what happens each time. You as well, Dawn. And then . . . '

* * *

323

The phone rang at three o'clock in the morning. Nicole rolled over, stared at it bleary-eyed, then suddenly jerked wide awake. She knew what it'd be, even before she heard a hushed voice say 'I'm so sorry, Mrs Gainsford, but your husband died a few minutes ago.'

She swallowed hard. 'Was it — peaceful?'

'Yes. His — um, friend was with him. She's very upset.'

'Yes.'

'You'll need to make arrangements for a funeral. If you or your funeral director can let us know the arrangements later today, that'd be very helpful.'

Nicole put the phone down and turned to see Paul standing in the doorway. 'Your father's dead.'

'I thought it'd be that.' He wiped his eyes. 'He was only forty-two.' His voice cracked on the last words.

'I know.' She moved closer and hugged him but he pulled away, and walked into the sitting room, so she followed.

'Was that woman with him when he died?'

'Yes.'

'Mum? I went online about the baby.'

'What about it?'

'Won't it be entitled to a share of Dad's estate? Has he made a will?'

She hadn't even thought of that. 'I — don't know. I don't think he did. I haven't.'

He went to the fridge. 'All right if I grab a drink of milk?'

'Yes, of course.' She watched him pour it into

324

a glass and raise it with a questioning look.

'No, thanks. I'm not a big milk drinker. We should go back to bed. There's nothing we can do now.'

He yawned. 'All right.'

But the thought of what the baby might mean kept her awake for the rest of the night. Why hadn't she thought of that? She wanted to sell the house, she already knew that, but she'd need the money it brought to buy another one for herself and Paul. She knew Sam's insurance was up to date because she'd paid the bill herself a few months ago at the same time as the house insurance, but was a big chunk of it to go elsewhere?

It wasn't *fair*. Why should she have to pay money to Tracey when she'd worked so hard to pay off that mortgage? All her wages had gone into that until recently. And she was the one who'd kept up the insurance payments.

It seemed as if every time she turned round another worry raised its head.

And they'd heard nothing from or about William today. What was he doing? More important, what was he intending to do?

And . . . how mentally unstable was he? He'd already hurt her. She put up a hand to touch the cut on the back of her head, though it was starting to heal now. She didn't want him to hurt other people.

★   ★   ★

In the end, Gary took the surveillance vehicle back to base, then drove to his friend Lionel's,

325

stopping en route to buy a carton of six bottles of beer — only the owner of the off licence owed him a favour, so never took any money. As was only right. Gary wasn't greedy, just took a little present from people every now and then.

He found Lionel watching soccer on the television with his mouse of a wife sitting in a corner, knitting. She was always knitting, stupid bitch. How a woman as plain and colourless as Dorothy could produce a daughter as lovely as Janey, he didn't know. Janey's youthful beauty haunted his dreams.

'Getting tired, are you?' he asked Dorothy pointedly.

She looked at her husband.

Lionel jerked one thumb towards the door. 'Go up to bed now, Dot. Us men like to chat in private. Oh, wait! Just see if there's anything to nibble with the beer.'

Without a word, she went to fetch some peanuts and crisps.

That was how a wife ought to behave, Gary thought as he sat down in the armchair he always occupied when he came here. He passed a beer across and waited till the mouse had gone upstairs before he started talking. 'I saw her, your Janey.'

'Bloody tart!'

Gary stared down at the rug, as if reluctant to speak.

'What's she doing with herself?'

He sighed.

Lionel thumped the arm of the sofa. 'She's giving it out again, isn't she?'

326

'Yes. Sorry to be the one who tells you.'

'What if she gets herself up the duff again? What if she starts walking the streets? How do you think I'll look then, with a daughter on the game?'

Gary shook his head and took a pull of beer.

'You have to stop her.'

'I've tried to talk to her a couple of times.'

'And?'

'This guy who lives in the same block of flats is acting as her protector. I reckon the only way to get her under control is to hit her through the baby, get it taken away from her for a while, to frighten her into behaving. She may not be a good mother, but she loves it.'

'How can we do that?'

'I've got a friend in the council offices.' Gary tapped his nose. 'Leave it to me. Only it'll cost you. My friend doesn't do anything out of love. She's risking her job, after all. But she feels sorry for people sometimes, knows the law can be stupid.'

'How much does she want?'

'A thousand.'

Lionel yelped.

'She wanted more. I bargained her down for you.'

'You're a good friend.'

$$\star \quad \star \quad \star$$

At the top of the stairs, Dorothy pressed one hand to her mouth, tears leaking out of her eyes.

Janey wasn't a bad girl, she'd always known

327

that, and known how the child was conceived too. But Lionel could be violent and it wasn' wise to go against his wishes.

But this was going too far. To take the baby away! Only, what could she do? What had she ever been able to do against a heavy-handed man like Lionel?

She sat there, listening carefully, even though they were talking about football now. Then she heard Gary saying goodbye and crept into the bed room before the two men came out into the hall slipping quickly out of her clothes and getting into her nightie.

By the time Lionel came up to bed, she was pretending to be asleep, something she was very good at.

But he didn't try to touch her tonight, thank goodness. And he was soon snoring.

It was well after midnight before she got to sleep. Guilt sat heavily in her chest. But so did fear.

She didn't dare go against Lionel — especially when he was plotting something with Gary.

20

William rang the hospital to ask about his dad. When they put him on hold, he nearly dumped the phone and left, but then looked at his watch. He'd give them three minutes to put him through to whoever could tell him about his dad. No one could trace him that quickly from a public phone.

'Mr Gainsford? How may I help you?'

'I'm calling to ask about my father, Sam Gainsford. Are you one of his nurses?'

'Um, no. Haven't you seen your mother this morning?'

'I don't live with her. We don't get on.'

'Oh. Well, I'm the chaplain at the hospital and it's my sad duty to tell you that your father passed away during the night.'

'Oh . . . ' For a moment he didn't know what to say, wanted to cry, but strong men didn't cry so he fought the weakness back. Then something occurred to him. 'Was my mother with him?'

'No. Look, if you want to come and see him, say farewell properly — '

William slammed the phone down and leant against the wall beside it for a minute, glaring at a woman who was hovering, waiting to make a call. He'd known his father was going to die, but still, it was a shock that it had happened so quickly. And it surprised him how much it hurt. He hadn't had much hope of his father finding

329

his manhood again, as William had, but he'd been fond of him, remembered childhood outings.

And that unfaithful bitch hadn't even stayed with him!

He thrust his hands in his pockets and walked out of town, taking a country path he'd followed a few times before. You had to exercise to build up muscle, even with the help of that stuff, so he walked and he did some of his other exercises where no one could see. He hadn't missed a day's workout, even now.

He tried to figure out what his mother would do next. Sell the house, of course, and then live off the profits of his father's hard work.

First there would be a funeral, though, and William wouldn't dare go to that. His father had always said he wanted to be cremated. The oldest son should be there to see his father's coffin go down to the fiery furnace, but doing that would mean giving himself up to the police. No, thank you.

He had to mark the day of the funeral somehow. He'd mugged some old guy last night in a car park and scored plenty of cash, so he was OK for a few days. He'd buy some more stuff, then he'd make a gesture of his own, a warrior's gesture, in his father's honour. He stopped and smiled at the thought. *Yes!* A warrior's farewell.

He turned on to a side path, bumping into someone.

'Watch where you're going, lad.'

He swung round. 'No, *you* watch where you're going, fattie.'

'Don't you talk to me like that, you young — '

William punched him in the face and watched him fall, then roll to one side, cringing away, expecting another blow. But he didn't hit him again. It was enough to show who was master. You didn't need to beat someone senseless.

He ran off, laughing quietly at the memory of the fat bloke tumbling backwards. Not until he got further out into the country did he let his laughter loose, a great belly laugh of triumph.

As he laughed, he saw some hikers, all togged up in fancy gear. They stopped as he strode towards them, then scattered like a flock of pigeons when he didn't slow down. He walked through the gap they left, still laughing.

They were frightened of him. And so they should be. He was a real, old-fashioned man, powerful.

She would learn to fear him, too. He was going to teach her to respect the stronger sex. That would be his farewell gift to his father. She was going to regret baling out on her family and leaving his father to die alone.

William walked on, climbing over a fence on to private property and ending up down by a lake. He did some upper-body exercises, then sat down on the ground, with his back against the trunk of a big tree that was just coming into leaf. It'd been a long winter! March now. Spring coming. Before summer he'd become a full member of the group, then he'd have friends to watch his back and could stay in the clubhouse.

He looked up at the grey sky, working out what to do with himself until the day of the funeral. Time passed slowly when you didn't have a telly to watch. He'd have to see if he could snatch an iPod from someone younger.

Once it was dark, he'd go back into town and buy some food, then he'd sleep at home, as usual. No one had even thought to look in the roof and though they'd locked the doors, he had the keys.

★　★　★

The morning was fine, with a feel of spring in the air. Winifred hummed as she prepared breakfast, then ate it while reading her newspaper, sitting in a patch of sunlight near the rear kitchen window.

When the phone rang, she picked it up, expecting to hear Hazel or Dawn. Instead, a woman said, 'Miss Parfitt?'

'Yes. Who is this?'

'I'm from the council.'

'Could I have your name, please?'

Silence, then the phone was put down.

Now, what did that mean? Was it someone playing tricks on her? Her nephew came to mind straight away, only he'd gone back overseas again, so it couldn't be him.

She didn't want to stay in and fret about the call, so decided to call the lawyer who was handling her friend Molly's will. Luckily, they could fit her in that morning, so an hour later, dressed smartly, she called a taxi. She was a regular customer of the taxi company, so they didn't usually keep her waiting long.

The lawyer's practice was quite large, with several names on the gleaming brass plaque

332

outside. She was shown into a comfortable waiting room and picked up a magazine to read. Magazines were something she didn't buy these days. Too expensive. There was more to read in a book. Anyway, who wanted to read about the doings of celebrities? She had better things to think of. But still, she'd just have a glance through this one while she waited.

'Miss Parfitt? Would you please come through to the interview room? Ms Rosher is free now.'

She put the magazine down and followed the clerk into a bare room, containing only an oval table and matching chairs, with a small sideboard against one wall containing a carafe of water and some glasses.

A woman in a smart navy suit held out one hand. 'Dale Rosher. I'm so glad to see you. We were beginning to think you were avoiding us. Do sit down. Would you like a glass of water or a cup of tea or coffee?'

'Nothing, thank you.'

'Now, as you know, this is about Molly Hooper's will — were you aware she'd be leaving you something?'

'She said she'd leave me her books and bookcases, which I'd very much enjoy having, both in memory of her and because I love reading. Is that what she's left me?'

The lawyer smiled at her. 'She left you a little more than that — her whole estate, in fact.'

Winifred couldn't form a single word, so surprised was she.

'It's quite a valuable legacy because her house is in a good suburb and there are some pieces of antique furniture plus some rather fine china.'

Winifred found her voice, but her words came out breathless and scratchy. 'Didn't she have a cousin she was going to leave it to?'

'Molly changed her will in your favour last year because the cousin upset her. Clearly, she didn't tell you.'

'No.'

'You know the house?'

'Yes. I've been there many times. We were such good friends. I still miss her.' She blinked to dispel the tears in her eyes at the thought of Molly.

'We have to get probate first. I'm the executor so I'll deal with all that and keep you up to date on what's happening, if that's all right? Good. Do you have a lawyer? Do you want him involved?'

'Yes.' She gave the name. When she stood up, she felt dizzy for a few seconds.

'Are you all right?'

Winifred managed a smile. 'Oh, yes. I stood up too abruptly, that's all. I'm still — in shock. Could someone call me a taxi, do you think?'

'Of course.'

She gave the driver Hazel's address and fortunately caught her friend in. As Hazel oohed and aahed over her news, it gradually began to seem real. The relief was tremendous. Winifred wasn't going to be scratching for money now, scrimping to pay her council taxes so that she could stay in her home. She could enjoy her life, maybe take a holiday abroad — she'd always wanted to see Paris.

334

She smiled at her friend. 'When this is all finalised, I'd like to take you and Dan out for a special meal to celebrate. Will you come?'

'Of course I will. Now, about the computer classes. I've rung them up and got Dan a place. We start this week.'

'Oh, my!'

'Don't lose your courage now. We all need to learn about computers.'

It was suddenly clear to Winifred that Dawn had got her pushy ways from her mother. Pushy in a nice sense, though.

'Look, Janey said she was willing to help us if we're struggling. But I think we'll manage just fine. We're not stupid, are we?'

'No.' Winifred knew she wasn't at all stupid, but she was absolutely terrified of making a fool of herself, always had been.

*   *   *

Janey was woken by Millie whimpering in the cot nearby. She looked at the clock and gasped. Nearly nine o'clock. She'd slept late. Well, she'd been awake worrying till well past midnight and been up at two with Millie, cuddling her back to sleep.

She got up and soon had everything organised for breakfast, then gave her baby a bath. It was fine today, so she'd go for a walk. Tomorrow she'd go to the *Just Girls* meeting. She hadn't clicked instantly with any of the other young mothers, who were all living at home or with their boyfriends, and were getting a lot of help. But it was somewhere to go.

Then there was college, which she was looking forward to. She had her homework to do, mostly reading at this stage, but one short essay had been set as well. If only she had a printer! It still hurt that her father would smash up a perfectly good printer just to stop her having it. She'd wait till Millie went down for her nap to start on her homework.

By ten-thirty she was outside, striding along happily, breathing deeply. Gary couldn't be watching her all the time and she'd looked up and down the street, but seen only empty, parked cars. She'd have liked to walk round the little park, but for security, she kept to the streets where there were other people. When she got fed up of that, she went across to the allotments, following two women carrying bags of shopping.

There were several cars parked outside the gates, one with a woman inside, reading a newspaper. No threat there.

Mr S was kneeling on his plot. It looked as if he was putting in seedlings. There was another guy working down at the far end and a woman digging at one side. Good. People around.

She waved and went across to greet him. 'What are you planting today?'

'I'm taking a risk with the weather and putting in a few early onions and shallots. I'm also going to set out some cloches to warm up the soil. I'm going to have to buy seedlings till I get my little greenhouse set up again.' He looked regretfully towards his hut and the debris to one side. 'I shall have to look at salvage and recycling places, see what I can pick up cheaply.'

She'd guessed from other chance remarks that he didn't have a lot of money to spare, so didn't comment on that. 'Anything I can do to help, Mr S?'

'Put the kettle on.' He grinned. 'I'm a devil for my cups of tea.'

She parked the buggy outside the hut, setting on the brake carefully as always, then got the kettle going and took down the mugs and tea bags. Outside the window at the end of the hut, she could see the jagged remains of the greenhouse, and that made her feel sad. Mr S didn't have much and why someone would want to destroy even that, she couldn't understand.

An hour passed pleasantly as they chatted together like old friends, then Millie started showing signs of sleepiness.

'I'd better be getting back. She needs changing and it's time for her nap.'

'I'll walk with you.'

'No need. There are people around at this time of day.'

'There's every need, lass. You shouldn't really have come here on your own.'

'I was very careful, stuck to busy streets, followed two women along the last bit.'

'And we'll be even more careful as we walk you back. I could do with stretching my legs, anyway. I've been on my knees all morning.'

'You're a fine one to talk about security. I bet you were the first here.'

He gave her a wry smile. 'I don't think I'm at risk. That fellow was wanting money. He'll have realised now that there's none to be found here.'

'Well, you still need to be careful.'

At the end of the path between the houses, she said firmly, 'I'll be all right from now on.'

'I'll stand here and watch you down to your flat.'

She was touched by his concern and felt really good as she went into her flat. She just had to be careful for a while. Gary would get tired of pestering her. Surely he would?

As she was about to change Millie, the doorbell rang.

'Sally here.'

'Come up.'

The health visitor came in, smiling at Millie, who was kicking and squirming on her changing mat on the floor. 'She looks in fine fettle.'

'She is.'

Sally hesitated. 'There's been a query about you. Apparently your parents are worrying about you not looking after the baby properly.'

Janey knew *he* was behind this. She just knew. 'Even if it was true, which it isn't, what's it got to do with them?'

'They say they're concerned grandparents. What I don't understand is why people at the council have latched on to it. So . . . I thought I'd drop in regularly. I'll be able to give you better support if I can say I've seen how carefully you look after Millie.'

'That's fine by me. You can come any time. Um, who is this social worker? Surely it can't be Pam, who was my case worker till I moved in here?'

'It's someone called Stevenall, and she isn't

338

exactly a social worker.'

Janey gasped. 'She came here once when my father accused me of stealing a printer — which I didn't. She tried to take Millie away from me then.'

'Did she now? Tell me exactly what happened.'

When Janey had finished her tale, Sally said grimly, 'She didn't have the right to do that. It's even more important that we keep my visits secret. I know it sounds melodramatic, but I left my car at the practice today and didn't tell anyone where exactly I was going. I even walked here along the alley behind the house and came in via the back door to the lobby. I'll record the visit in my notes, though.' She patted her companion on the shoulder. 'Don't let it get you down, dear. I'm on your side and they can't prove what doesn't exist.'

Janey nodded but all these hassles were getting her down. And she wasn't at all sure what Gary could do. Look what he'd got away with already. 'I know you're on my side, Sally, and I'm grateful. What I can't understand is why my parents are causing trouble. They disowned me months ago, as the *Just Girls* people can tell you.'

'I don't understand it, either. There's something fishy going on and — oh, look at that expression. Unless I'm mistaken, that little girl of yours has just filled her nappy again. I'll change her and you put the kettle on. I'm dying for a cup of tea.'

Janey knew this would give Sally a chance to check that she was keeping Millie clean. She didn't mind. The more evidence on her side, the better. But still — why should she have to keep proving herself?

When she was alone again, she hesitated then picked Millie up and went downstairs to knock on Kieran's door. As he opened it, she couldn't hold herself together and blurted out, 'I thought you should know what they're doing now.' And felt hot tears run down her cheeks.

'Come in.' He held the door open and gestured to a chair. 'Tell me.'

When she'd finished, he nodded thoughtfully and didn't speak for a moment or two. 'It's good that the nurse is on your side.'

'Yes. Sally's lovely, ever so helpful. But Gary's fooled everyone before. And why's this person at the council getting involved? I never had anything to do with her.'

He smiled at her. 'Chin up. You've done nothing wrong. And this time you're not on your own. In fact, you seem to have gathered quite a few allies, for someone who's only been in the town for a few weeks.'

'I have, haven't I? People have been lovely. Especially you. I can't thank you enough.'

The baby murmured and burrowed into her neck. Janey dropped a kiss on her head. 'Well, Millie needs her nap and I have some homework to do. Thanks for listening, Kieran.'

★ ★ ★

When she'd gone, Kieran said grimly, 'I'm going to do a lot more than listen.' He picked up the phone. 'Jim?'

'Kieran! How are you? It's been what? A year now?'

'Give or take. I'm a lot better, getting around now without crutches. Look, I've got a friend who's in trouble. I'm too close to those involved to report it credibly, but I'm happy to point you in the right direction. Could be a great story, police corruption and all sorts of nasties, though we'll need to do some digging first to nail them.'

'You don't usually give away your leads.'

'I'm not working at the moment, thinking of taking up another sort of job, actually . . . now that I'm not as mobile.'

'Bummer, that accident. Well, I'm grateful. You've never given me a bad tip yet. I'll come straight round.'

'No, don't come here. The friend who's involved lives in one of my flats and certain people are watching the house on and off. How about we meet at the pub, in that back room? Say, one o'clock?'

He didn't put the phone down, but rang another guy he knew, a guy who could find out almost anything as long as you didn't ask questions about how he did it. All this man needed was the assurance that it was to help someone who was genuinely in trouble. And he didn't say no if you slipped him a few quid for his efforts afterwards.

What worried Kieran, though, was the time this might take. Unless he much mistook the situation, Gary was moving in for the kill. He must be very confident to do it so openly.

Kieran wondered whether to go round and see Nicole in the evening. In the end, he decided he would and set off, limping slowly up the street. Do him good to walk, he decided.

When he was halfway there, he admitted to himself that he was pushing it, and although he'd make it there, he didn't like the thought of coming back again on foot. Better go back now and get his car. Cursing under his breath, hating the infirmity that restricted what he could do, he turned round and made his way slowly back, stopping dead at the sight of a man in a car parked near another block of flats. He recognised that head, even though this was a different car from last time. Even as he watched, the man got out and began to stroll towards the house.

Had he deliberately waited until Kieran went out? What was he intending to do now? Surely he wasn't going to attack Janey so blatantly?

Kieran pulled out his mobile phone and dialled Nicole's number. Paul answered and in a few words Kieran explained what was going on and asked him to come down the street as a witness. 'Bring your mobile phone and take photos if you can, but stay back. Do not, under any circumstances, get involved. You were just passing by, right?'

He began to follow Gary. It was hard to walk quietly with a limp, but willpower and determination helped.

At the flats, Kieran remained behind the big tree he'd insisted the builders leave in place. He could see Gary looking round, checking that no one was near before pulling something out of his pocket and fiddling with the door. To Kieran's disgust, it opened quite quickly. He'd paid good money for a lock that was supposed to be tamper-proof.

He moved quietly across the car park, standing behind a car as Gary shut the door behind him and peered through it to make sure once again that he hadn't been followed.

Kieran got out his mobile phone and set it to take photos, then moved round to the side door to his own flat and entered that way, coming out of his inside front door into the hall just as Gary tried to open Janey's flat. She'd be all right. Bolts were better than fancy locks if you were inside and he'd fitted two good ones to her door.

Gary knocked on the door and his voice floated down the stairs quite clearly. 'Open up, Janey. If you're nice to me, it'll all be a lot easier, for you *and* the baby.'

She must have said something, but Kieran couldn't hear what. He watched Gary shake the door, testing its strength.

Then, to Kieran's relief, the tenant from next door came out. No light had been showing at her windows or under the door. They rarely did. Miss Fairbie said she was recovering from an eye operation and found the darkness more soothing.

'Who are you? What are you doing here?' she asked sharply.

Gary turned and snapped, 'I'm trying to visit my friend's daughter. He's worried about her.'

'She's just told you to go away. I heard her

343

clearly. If you don't do that, I'll call the police.'

'Mind your own bloody business.'

She held up a can. 'I will. And you mind yours. I've seen you here before. If you come one step nearer I'll use this spray.'

Kieran stayed out of sight, delighted that someone else had seen Gary pestering Janey. The man must be utterly obsessed to do it so brazenly. Well, she was a lovely girl, but that's what she was really — a girl. And Gary must be all of fifty, his waistline heavy and his face plump and jowly. Kieran hadn't realised that quiet Miss Fairbie was quite so courageous.

He could see from the reflections in the tall windows of the lobby that Gary was staring across at the small woman, who was still holding up the can with one finger on the trigger. He shouted through the door to Janey. 'I'll be back. Your father's worried sick about you and that poor little baby. It's shocking the way you treat it.'

As the man clumped down the stairs, Kieran moved back into the shadows of the passage that led only to his own flat.

Gary went outside and a moment later there was the sound of a car starting up in the street.

After it had driven away, two people moved out from behind the tree and crossed the car park.

Kieran went to open the front door. 'Hi, Paul, Nicole. I didn't mean to drag you out as well. Let's go up and talk to Janey.'

Miss Fairbie's door was shut again, with no light showing. He knocked on Janey's door and

344

called, 'He's gone. It's only me, Kieran.'

Behind him, Miss Fairbie's door opened. 'Ah, Mr Jones. I was going to come and see you in the morning about this incident. I thought we had a good lock on that front door. If intruders can get in so easily, I think it needs improving.'

'You're right. I'll be complaining to the manufacturers and getting something better fitted: a key lock *and* a number pad, perhaps. And I'm going to get CCTV fitted, too. Thanks for sticking up for Janey tonight. That fellow's been stalking her.'

'I've seen him round here before.'

'Yes. So have I.'

'I'll make sure I keep my pepper spray handy from now on.'

He held up one hand, palm flattened in a stop signal. 'Don't tell me about that. Pepper spray is illegal.'

She smiled, not a nice smile. 'It's not real pepper spray, just looks like it. All that comes out if you spray is a green dye that's hard to remove. The mere sight of it makes people think twice about attacking usually, as it did tonight.'

'I must find some for Janey.'

She looked at him, then shrugged. 'I've got a spare. Wait a minute.' She went back into her room and came out with a small spray can, labelled 'pepper spray' in large letters. 'Us women have to stick together.' She closed the door again, and he heard bolts being shot on the other side. He'd not put them on her door, but he wasn't going to complain about her doing it. She clearly had security fears.

When he turned round, Janey had opened her door and was standing there, looking white and terrified.

He walked across the landing. 'I think you know Nicole and her son Paul. Can we come in?'

She nodded.

When they were all seated, he said, 'First, I'll get a better lock fixed to the front door tomorrow, plus CCTV. And that back door to the washing area isn't going to be left open any more. He won't get in again easily.'

She nodded, but she didn't look cheered by it, so he gave her the spray can and told her what it contained. 'Carry it everywhere from now on.'

She looked down at it and sighed.

'Thirdly, when I'm going out at night, I'll tell you and we'll ask Miss Fairbie if she's going to be in. She's one tough woman. Gary backed off when he saw her pointing the pepper spray at him.'

'He might come back and try to charge her with something, knowing him, or send someone else to do it.'

'If he does, he'll be admitting to pestering you tonight.' He paused. 'The man's gone beyond reason. It's an obsession now.' He waited and saw her relax a little. 'You look tired. We'll leave you in peace. I'll be in for the rest of the evening so you'll be quite safe tonight. And we'll be getting that new door lock fixed tomorrow.'

'Thank you.'

As they walked down the stairs, Paul said 'She's in trouble, isn't she? What's with that old perv? Fellows of his age who pester girls should be locked up.'

346

Kieran nodded, feeling very sad that a young woman who had enough problems should be facing stalking and sexual harassment on top of it all. 'I'm working on the problem.' He looked at Nicole. 'I was coming up to your place to ask when the funeral is. Do you two want to come in for a quick drink with me instead?'

'That'd be nice.'

When she was seated with a glass of white wine in her hand, she said abruptly, 'The funeral's in two days.'

'I'll come with you, if you don't mind.'

'I'd welcome your support.' She turned to her son. 'Do you want to leave a message for William again?'

He shook his head. 'Waste of time. He won't dare come because of the police.'

Kieran didn't walk them home, but he stood at the entrance to his car park and watched them up the street, angry that he should have to do this in a small, normally peaceful town like Sexton Bassett.

When he got inside, a message light was blinking on his email system and he smiled as he read it.

Interesting.

He typed back, 'Do it. Whatever it costs. The quicker the better.'

*   *   *

It took Janey a long time the following morning to nerve herself up to go out to the shops. She hated feeling like this, but last night she'd been

347

terrified, and the feeling hadn't gone away. She hoped they'd come and fit a new lock quickly. The thought that someone could get in made her feel nervous even to go down and put her washing on.

She made a quick round trip to the shops and the library, not seeing anyone following her, but what did she know? Gary had been trained to shadow people and he was in charge of other people he could assign to watch her.

For the rest of the morning she stayed in her flat, not daring to go out.

When someone rang her doorbell, she nearly didn't answer, then told herself not to be stupid. She was letting this get her down. 'Yes?'

'Janey? It's Dan and Miss Parfitt. We were passing by and thought we'd drop in to see how you were.'

'That's wonderful! I'll press the buzzer and unlock the door. I'm upstairs on the right.'

She opened the door of her flat and smiled as they made their way creakily up the stairs. 'Come and sit down. Let me make you a cup of tea.'

He held out a pot plant. 'House-warming present. It'll have lovely flowers on in a month or so.'

'How kind of you!'

As they took seats, he said, 'Don't bother with the tea. We can't stay for long. We're on our way to a computer class at the library, but we set off a bit early so that we could call in and check you were all right.'

Miss Parfitt reached inside her shopping bag and held out a parcel. 'A house-warming present from me as well. It's only a cake, one of my almond delights. It'll freeze beautifully.'

'Thank you.' She felt tears rise in her eyes at their kindness.

'Has something happened?' Miss Parfitt asked. 'You look upset and tired.'

'*He* came here last night. He got into the flats through the front door, we don't know how. The lock is supposed to be tamper-proof. And he started banging on my door, threatening me if I didn't let him in. I'm so glad Kieran had put bolts on the inside of the door, or he might have picked my lock too.'

'That must have been terrifying.'

'Yes. But the lady opposite came out with pepper spray and he backed off.'

There was a knock on her door and because she had people with her, she didn't hesitate to open it. Kieran was standing there. 'Come in and meet Miss Parfitt and Mr Shackleton, who've brought me house-warming presents.'

'I gather you've been helping protect this lass,' Dan said. 'It's a scandal what that fellow is doing.'

'He'll make a mistake. So far he can claim he's acting on behalf of her parents, but we're building up evidence. There's someone at the council involved, a so-called social worker.'

'Not Miss Stevenall?' Miss Parfitt said.

'Yes. How do you know her?'

'She's trying to have me moved to an old folks' facility, claiming I'm not in possession of my wits. It can only be because my nephew wants to get his hands on my house. He can't, though, because I've changed my will.'

'Did you tell him that?'

'Not yet. I was a bit nervous of doing it while I was alone with him, to be honest.'

'Would you mind giving me details about what's been happening to you?'

She looked at her watch. 'Another time I'd be delighted to, but Dan and I have to go to a computer class now.'

'And she's nervous,' Dan said with a smile.

When they'd gone Kieran said quietly, 'That was a very fortunate meeting. It'll help me build up a picture of what's going on. What I really came to tell you is that someone is coming this afternoon to put the new lock in. You'll have both a key and a pin number. And that's for front and back doors, I'm afraid, so you'll have to take your key with you when you peg out your washing.'

'It'll be worth it to feel safe.'

He looked at her with complete understanding. 'But you still won't, will you?'

'No. I know what he's like. He boasts that he never lets anyone get the better of him.'

'Give me a few days. We'll either nab him or drive him away.'

'If he isn't caught, I'll have to leave, because I'll never feel safe while he's around in such a powerful position.'

'That's one of the reasons I went into investigative journalism: people who abuse power.'

'And because you like helping people,' she said softly. 'Me, Nicole and Paul — anyone you meet who needs help.'

He nodded. She was very perceptive for

350

someone so young. 'Yep. And my second piece of information is that I'll be out tomorrow. It's Nicole's husband's funeral.'

'I'll be at college.'

'How do you get there?'

'Walk.'

'Get a taxi there and back tomorrow.'

'I can't afford it.'

'Let me pay.' He fumbled in his pocket.

'I can't let you do that.'

'You can. You must. I've plenty of money and I don't want to lose my best tenant.'

She hesitated, then took the money. 'I'll pay you back one day.'

'I'm sure you will, but in the meantime, you're right about one thing. I am enjoying being able to help people again. Makes me feel more — normal, gives me a purpose in life.' His smile wasn't in evidence as he shrugged and limped back downstairs.

She could see pain engraved in the lines of his face, not only physical pain when he moved unwisely, but also emotional pain. Well, his whole life had been taken from him for a while. She knew about that, had had counselling about it at *Just Girls*. But she'd also heard him lately whistling and humming as he pottered around the place — and seen the way he looked at Nicole. No hiding that look. He really fancied her, might even be in love.

But Nicole had only just lost a husband, hadn't even buried him yet.

Life was so much more complicated than Janey had believed a year ago — and yet, that

351

year had not only brought her pain but deep satisfaction at coping on her own, joy at having a baby to love, and since she'd moved to Pepper corn Street, the pleasure of making new friends. She smiled, as she added mentally, *friends of all ages*. Before Millie she'd not have been capable of that, wouldn't have thought of older people as friends.

She felt as if something was growing inside her, something warm and strong and hopeful. If she could just hang on to that, perhaps she could move on to better things.

★　★　★

Sitting in front of a computer, Winifred listened to the tutor explaining what happened when you switched it on. He'd already shown them a motherboard, the mouse and other bits and pieces, and talked about memory and RAM. She repeated the new words again to be sure of remembering them.

It seemed clear enough so far. She could feel herself relaxing just a little.

'Now,' he said, 'before we do anything else you need to understand and *believe* that you can't break a computer by pressing the wrong button or clicking on the wrong part of the screen.' He smiled round at them. 'Do you honestly think the college would let you near these computers if you could break them?'

Winifred relaxed still further.

By the end of the class, she had lost her fear and was eager to learn more. They'd played cards on the computer to learn how to handle the mouse. She hadn't played patience for years, only they called it solitaire now. It was more pleasant to play on the screen than have pieces of card slipping and sliding when you tried to put them in piles.

Hazel linked arms with her as they walked out. 'There. That wasn't bad, was it?'

'It was fascinating.'

From behind them Dan said, 'Not too bad at all. It's the Internet I want to know how to use. Janey says you can join groups discussing gardening, rare-seed societies, all sorts of things.'

'I came here by taxi.' Hazel pulled out her mobile phone.

'If you don't mind a walk, why don't we go to my house?' Winifred suggested. 'Maybe we could buy something for lunch? I've got plenty of cake for afters but not much for starters.'

21

On Wednesday morning Nicole woke early, lying in bed listening. What had woken her? Birdsong she realised. Some birds were sitting in the tree outside the flats, making a cheerful noise. I was too early for the hum of traffic from High Street, too early to get up really, but she was wide awake, so she went into the kitchen and pu the kettle on. Inevitably her thoughts turned to the funeral and she sighed. Hearing someone approach, she turned to smile at her son.

'Couldn't you sleep, either?' Paul asked.

'No. Did you hear the birds?'

'Yes. And it's starting to get light earlier, isn' it?' He sat down at the table, legs stretched out soft brown hair tumbling every which way.

As she set a mug of tea in front of him, he sighed. 'I'm not looking forward to this after-noon, Mum.'

'No. I'm absolutely dreading it.'

'Do you think William will do something to upset it?'

'Why should he? He got on quite well with your father until recently, when he seemed to hate everyone.'

He shrugged. 'I just feel — uneasy. I reckon he will do something, and probably something stupid. He's lost the plot.'

She shivered because she too felt apprehen-sive. It was sad to feel that your son wasn' behaving rationally. She kept going over and over her own part in his life. Was it her fault he'd gone off the rails? Had she been a bad mother? She'd tried so hard to be a good one.

Paul took a drink of tea, then set the mug down and stared into it. 'I wish the funeral was in the morning. I hate hanging around, waiting for it to begin.'

'Me, too. Do you want a cooked breakfast?'

He shook his head. 'I'm not really hungry, thanks. I'll just grab a piece of toast, then I'll go on my computer.'

That lack of appetite showed how upset he was. Paul usually had an amazing capacity for eating, though he was still thin and leggy, looking as if his hands and feet belonged to someone bigger. He reminded her sometimes of her father, who'd been a gentle giant.

Paul didn't eat much lunch, either. Nor did she. 'Time to get ready,' she said at two o'clock, feeling as if the day had been twenty hours long already.

She hadn't bought new clothes, wasn't even dressing in black, just a dark-grey suit with a white blouse. Black didn't suit her and she wasn't buying something she'd never wear again for a man who hadn't been faithful to her. She tied her hair back neatly, put on some lipstick and wiped it off again, because it looked too bright against her pale face. There, that'd have to do.

When they were both ready, she gave Paul a hug, then held him at arm's length and smoothed his hair back. 'We should have got you a haircut.'

'No one will care.' He hesitated. 'Do you think *she* will come?'

'Bound to. She loved him.'

'How are you going to introduce her to the rellies?'

Nicole shrugged. 'I don't know. I'm not even sure how many of your father's relatives will be coming. A couple of cousins and that old aunt maybe. I didn't ask my family. They didn't like him, anyway.'

He looked at her sideways. 'Not even when you first married?'

'No. And he didn't like them, either.'

'Didn't that worry you?'

'It should have, but I was madly in love with him then.' Disillusionment had come later.

She was relieved when the luxury car drew up outside the house and they could leave. 'Let's do it!' Taking a deep breath, she led the way towards the door the driver was holding open for them.

'We'll need to stop just down the street to pick up someone else,' she told him.

Kieran was waiting for them on the pavement outside his building. As he got into the car, Paul moved to sit on one of the fold-down facing seats and Kieran sat beside her. When he took hold of her hand quite openly, she didn't protest. She shot a quick glance at Paul, who gave her a nod and half-smile, as if to say *Go for it!*

Kieran's hand was warm in hers. A visible sign of support. She needed all the comfort she could get today. She saw Paul watching them, still with that half-smile and could feel herself blushing. When she looked to the side, Kieran gave her hand a little squeeze and she returned the gesture.

Heaven help her, she was going to her husband's funeral and thinking about another man. Fate seemed to be giving her a gift, for once, a man who cared about her, was there for her in her time of need, and who got on well with her son.

As the driver opened the door, she moved out into a grey, overcast world, which was in tune with her spirits, just right for the closing scene of a major part of her life.

Kieran wasn't holding her hand now, but it felt as if he'd left a warm, loving touch behind.

At the crematorium she and Paul greeted the other mourners, not many, just Aunt Megan, two cousins and a man from Sam's former workplace. Nicole spoke to them briefly, accepting their condolences and introducing Kieran as 'a friend of the family'. Then there was nothing to do but stand with Paul by her side, waiting for the hearse to arrive.

Then a taxi drew up, from which Tracey descended, covered in black from head to toe, with a veil hanging from a small hat and covering her face to her chin. Kieran moved forward to stand beside Nicole, his expression grimly determined.

The other mourners stared at her, and turned puzzled faces towards Nicole.

'This is — um, a close friend of Sam's.' She stared at them defiantly, daring them to probe further as she saw comprehension dawn in everyone's eyes, except for Aunt Megan's.

'You'd think *she* was the wife, parading in black like that,' Paul muttered. 'She's pushing her luck. Mum, if you want me to get rid of her — '

'If I'm all right about her attending, no one else should care.'

'But are you all right?' Kieran asked quietly from her other side.

Nicole couldn't lie to him. 'No. Not really. But I do see that she needs to be here, to say her final farewell. I just wish she was less — ostentatious about her grief.' She glanced at her watch. 'Why don't they get on with it? I hate all this hanging around.'

'There aren't many people, are there?' Paul murmured.

'No.'

'Dad didn't have a lot of friends. It was you who made friends easily.'

What did you reply to that? He was right. Sam had said he didn't invite people back because he didn't dare let his guard down with his business colleagues and she'd accepted that. But she wondered now if it had been true. He'd not kept up with his old university friends who weren't business colleagues either, and if she hadn't invited his cousins round occasionally he'd never have made the effort to see them. Unlike her, he hadn't come from a close, loving family.

She vowed suddenly to get in touch with her own cousins. Strangely, she hadn't even thought of inviting them today. She'd spent a lot of time with them when she was young, because they all lived near one another, but contacts had dwindled in the last few years. Well, she'd been juggling a full-time job, raising a family and doing the lion's share of the housework.

358

More fool her. She'd let Sam get away with murder.

The hearse arrived and the men wheeled the coffin inside. She and Paul followed it, with the relatives behind them. Tracey, thank goodness, didn't push forward but walked behind the relatives, weeping noisily into a lace-edged handkerchief.

Kieran came last and Nicole glanced round to see him sitting at the rear of the chapel. He gave her a quick nod. She wished he could have sat beside her, but that would have outraged everyone.

Then the minister began the service. It was short but it brought home to her how final this was and she found herself weeping again. She'd loved Sam so much when they first married and even though they'd been estranged for a long time, the thought of him dying so young made her feel desperately sad.

This time it was her son who held her hand and she clutched it like a lifeline.

★   ★   ★

William scrounged breakfast from the tins of food his mother had left in the pantry, pulling a face at the sweetness of the tinned pineapple, then slipped out of the house. He went for a walk because there was nothing else he could do at this early hour, but he kept a careful eye on his watch. He'd decided to do it at the exact time the funeral started, but he had an hour or two to go yet.

He wound up by the lake again, because it was

359

as good as anywhere to hang out. But it was a damp, chill sort of day and he kept shivering. And another spot had popped out on his chin. He fingered it, then forced himself to leave it alone. Spots made you look like a child and he was furious about having so many of them. He didn't even dare go into the chemist for some stuff to put on this one, not with the police looking for him. He had some old stuff in his bedroom. He'd find it later, before he took care of his grand farewell to his father.

He heard voices in the distance and stood up, wishing it were summer with lots of foliage to hide behind. Two people were coming towards him, so he decided it'd look better to walk along briskly, but when he got to the fence round the edge of this private park, he was back in public territory with the problem of finding somewhere else to hide.

The allotments? Nothing to eat there, no money either, and the old guy had been pretty quick to call the police. In the end William risked going home and hiding in the roof.

But as he was about to climb over the fence he had to duck back again because the neighbour was working in her garden, the stupid bitch. She was always fiddling around with plants. Had she nothing better to do?

In the end he went to the clubhouse and hammered on the door. 'I need somewhere to hide for an hour or two.'

'You're supposed to be able to look after yourself.' Baz stared at him then shrugged. 'Oh come in, then. You look frozen. Want a coffee?'

360

'Yeah. Thanks.' He slumped in the main room. No one was around and he'd not really seen it by daylight before. It was shabbier than he remembered. But what did a room matter? It was the men who counted, men like Baz, who was really well built. William wanted to be exactly like him one day.

'Need some more stuff?'

William shook his head. 'Not yet. Thanks.'

Baz looked at his watch. 'You can stay for two hours, then we have a meeting.'

'That's cool. I've got something to do this afternoon, anyway.'

'You'll go out the back way when you leave?'

'Yeah. I know.'

Then he was alone. Of all things, he could hear a washing machine running. Surely Baz didn't do women's stuff like that? But women weren't allowed in here, so he supposed someone had to do the washing.

The time passed slowly and Baz didn't come out to talk to him again till it was time to leave.

Why didn't he feel more excited about what he was going to do?

★   ★   ★

Dan and Hazel took Winifred for a short walk because they'd all decided to get a bit fitter.

When they saw the police car parked outside, Winifred hurried forward. 'Is something wrong?'

'We're just checking on the old lady who lives here,' a female officer said. 'Her nephew is very worried about her. We haven't been able to get a reply to our phone calls or to the doorbell, so my colleague has gone round the back to break in.'

'What?' Winifred pressed one hand to her chest. 'Stop him at once! This is *my* house.'

'I'll get him.' The officer ran off round the side of the house.

'Are you all right, Winifred?' Dan asked.

'No, I'm not all right. I'm very angry. What does my nephew think he's doing?'

'I'm phoning my daughter.' Hazel pulled out her phone.

The officers came to join them.

'The back door was open already,' the young man said. 'You should be more careful about locking up, Miss Parfitt.' He looked at Winifred who was clutching Hazel's arm, then at Dan.

'Hello, Mr S.' He lowered his voice. 'Did you find her wandering and bring her home?'

The three older people looked at one another in puzzlement.

'It's she who brought us back to lunch,' Dan said. 'We've been for a walk together.'

Hazel put her mobile away. 'Dawn's coming round. She says this has to stop.' She looked severely at the officers. 'Someone is harassing my friend. This isn't the first time there's been some stupid misunderstanding.'

Winifred pulled herself together. 'Let's go inside. It looks bad standing outside here with the police.'

In the hall she stopped in shock. 'What's happened here? Someone's changed all my furniture round.'

She went into the kitchen and found it in chaos

362

with half-eaten food on plates and a rubbish bin overflowing. She couldn't speak for shock.

'You're not keeping it very tidy, Miss Parfitt,' the female officer said. 'Are you finding it too much for you? Your nephew has apparently been very worried about you for a while now.'

Dan moved forward to stand protectively by her side. 'That's rubbish. And as for this — ' he gestured to the messy kitchen, 'I called for Miss Parfitt this morning at nine o'clock and the kitchen was in apple pie order, not a thing out of place. I saw her lock the back door myself and she's been with me ever since. We have about twenty other witnesses to prove that, which means someone must have broken in and dumped this stuff here.'

There was dead silence, then, 'You sure of that, Mr S?'

'I'd stake my life on it,' he said grimly. 'Are you accusing me of not knowing what I saw?'

'No, of course not. Only . . . well, it was a council official who called us in.'

Winifred reached out to the table, wanting something to lean on, but it was so dirty she didn't like to touch it. 'Who would have made this disgusting mess?'

'Have you looked upstairs?' the female officer said.

She shivered. 'I suppose I'd better.'

'Wait till my daughter arrives.' Hazel turned to the officers. 'Miss Parfitt was right about the rooms near the front door too. I come here to visit her regularly and they aren't normally set out like that.'

She went to put an arm round Winifred. 'I don't think we should say anything more or touch a single thing till Dawn arrives. She's bringing a friend of hers to help.'

'Well, in view of what you've told me, no one ought to touch anything,' the female officer said. 'We don't want to destroy any evidence.'

'Let's go and sit outside on the garden bench,' Dan said.

Winifred sat down there with a sigh. 'It's getting me down having to fend off these — these *happenings* all the time.'

'Well, you're not alone today,' Hazel said. 'I can — ' She stopped. 'Sounds like Dawn's car. Let's go round to meet her, catch her before she sees the police.'

Dawn had a man with her, balding, wearing thick glasses and very casually dressed. They both turned as the three rounded the corner of the house.

And Winifred shamed herself by bursting into tears.

Dawn was by her side in an instant, but her companion wasn't far behind her.

He interrupted to say, 'Look, Miss Parfitt, I know it's embarrassing but will you please let me take a photo of you now, while you're in tears. It'll be brilliant evidence against those who're harassing you.'

'Why not?' She couldn't stop weeping anyway. She'd never, ever let go of her emotions like this, not since she was a tiny child, not even when her mother died.

The two police officers came to stand at the front door, looking embarrassed.

Just then a car drew up and Ms Stevenall got

out. She spoke to the police as if Winifred couldn't understand her. 'Poor old dear. She definitely needs looking after.'

That was all it needed for Winifred to pull herself upright and glare at her. 'How dare you patronise me like that? I don't know what you're doing here, but believe me, you're neither wanted *nor* needed.'

'Who sent you?' Dawn asked as her companion moved back a little to take a photo of the newcomer.

Ms Stevenall rounded on him. 'Don't you dare take photos of me. Stop that this minute.'

'I was photographing the whole scene, not just you.' He looked at Winifred. 'You did want me to make a record of this, did you not, Miss Parfitt? For the court case?'

She hadn't a clue what he was talking about but if he'd come with Dawn, she trusted him. 'I certainly did.'

'I'm only trying to look after her,' Ms Stevenall told everyone.

'Why?' Dawn asked.

'Because she's not capable of looking after herself. Her house is in a mess, she's forgetful and her nephew has an enduring power of attorney, so he's worried that he might have to exercise it.'

Winifred glared at her. 'Bradley does not have an enduring power of attorney any longer. *If* that's any business of yours, which it isn't.'

Ms Stevenall gaped at her. 'But . . . he showed me a copy of it.'

'I had it cancelled last month.'

Stevenall pulled herself together and said scornfully, 'A cancellation might be invalid i you're not in a stable state of mind.'

As Dawn began to speak, Winifred raised one hand to stop her and forced herself to speal calmly. It seemed important that she stand u for herself. 'That's why my lawyer suggested i might be wise to see my doctor and get a lette from him stating that I was in full possession o my faculties before I cancelled it.'

There was silence, then Dan chuckled. 'And yes terday, she was the star of the beginners' compute class. There's nothing wrong with our Winifred'. mind, young woman. It's her nephew who need help. He sounds like a conniving devil, out t snatch his inheritance before it's due.'

'He should know her better than strangers do, Ms Stevenall insisted, but less forcefully.

'I'm no stranger. I'm a close friend,' he said a once. 'And so is Hazel.'

Winifred could have hugged him. It made he feel warm inside to have such loyal friends.

Dawn offered her a mobile phone. 'Let's rin your lawyer now and ask him — '

'Her!' Winifred said.

' . . . her to send someone along to show M Stevenall the relevant documentation.'

The social worker glared at them and turnec to the journalist. 'I hope you'll go and look inside her house before you write up your story.'

'I shall. I'll do some very careful research into all aspects of it. Just one thing. You haven't beer inside yet. How did you know about the mess?'

'Her nephew told me what it's like all the

ime. But I'll leave you to manage this, if you can, and we'll see where that leads you. You'll be calling me back in to help, mark my words.' Ms Stevenall marched back to her car.

'Let's go and photograph the mess,' Dawn said. 'Oh, and by the way, this is Jim. He's a friend of Kieran Jones down the street, and he's an investigative journalist too. It seems there are a few suspicious things happening in our town.'

'Well, someone's definitely broken into my house. I'll have to have the locks changed again.' Winifred sighed.

One of the police officers said, 'If you can just wait until someone comes to check things out before you touch anything, Miss Parfitt. We don't want to destroy any evidence, do we?'

And for the first time in her life, she corrected that to, 'Ms Parfitt, if you don't mind.'

To one side she saw Dan clapping his hands silently and grinning; to the other, Hazel and Dawn were standing close, as if on guard.

She'd get through this. No one was going to drive her from her home.

* * *

aney had been looking forward to going to college again. She went by taxi, because she'd promised Kieran. She kept a careful eye out as they drove along the streets, but there was no sign of Gary. Well, he was like her father, not a morning person. She'd often heard the two of them cursing early morning starts at work.

When she got to the crèche she breathed a

sigh of relief, feeling safe now.

Al was waiting for her outside the classroom and as they ate lunch together, she asked him rather hesitantly if he would walk her home afterwards.

'That fellow still stalking you?'

She nodded.

'Of course I will.'

She enjoyed his company. They never seemed to run out of conversation.

When they got back, she asked shyly, 'Would you like to come in for a cup of tea?'

He glanced at his watch. 'Another time I'd love it, but I've got a part-time job at the supermarket, so I can't today.'

'All right.' She waved him goodbye and pressed the combination on the new lock before using her key. That lock made her feel so much safer.

But when she unlocked the door of her flat, it suddenly swung inwards and Gary grabbed her. He said in a very low voice, 'If you value your daughter's life, you won't say a word about who I am. Now, tell your neighbour you've changed your mind about seeing me and send her home.'

Only then did she see Miss Fairbie sitting hunched on the sofa, looking terrified. 'Has he hurt you?'

'A bruise or two. I can't believe he's come back. Everyone knows who he is.'

Janey tried to decide what to do, but couldn't seem to think clearly. She only knew she didn't want anyone else hurting. 'I — think you'd better go home.'

Gary smiled. 'I apologise for troubling you.'

368

She looked at Janey, not him. 'Will you be all right? I think we should call the police.'

She saw Gary shaking the buggy suggestively and added hastily, 'I'll make sure he buys you some flowers as an apology. He can be a bit rough at times, doesn't know his own strength. I'm still angry at my father, you see. But I . . . um, don't want him to worry.'

'Well, if you're sure . . . ?' She moved towards the door.

When the door had closed behind her, Janey said, 'You'll never get away with this.'

'I have done already. I know her sort. She won't talk. She has her own secrets.'

Millie chose that moment to start crying, picking up her mother's fear.

Gary looked at the infant sourly. 'Got a good pair of lungs on her, I'll give her that.'

'She needs changing and feeding. If I don't, she'll keep on crying.'

'Do it quickly, then. You and me have some unfinished business and we don't want her interrupting us. I like to take my time.'

Feeling terrified and helpless, she went to get Millie's food and he followed her into the kitchen area.

'Don't get any knives out. I'll do any cutting that's needed.'

As if she'd let him touch Millie's food!

She tried desperately to think how to get rid of him but he stuck so close to her, she had no chance to find any sort of weapon. The thought of him touching her in that way again made her feel physically sick.

William went to the end of the street and looked along it. No one around and next-doors' car was gone now. Good. He hurried down to his own house and slipped round the back.

Inside, he went up to his room and packed a bag of clothes and another of things he wanted to keep, then he went out to the garage through the kitchen entrance. His father's car was there. Maybe he should take it and ride around in comfort for a while? No, it had an anti-theft device, and even if he got round that, they had ways of identifying cars from the number plate. It'd lead the police straight to him, that car would.

The spare can of petrol was empty, which made him curse. His father had certainly let things slip recently.

He had to find a tube and siphon some petrol out of the car's tank, so his preparations took longer than he'd expected.

Excitement rising in him now, he splashed petrol on the car upholstery, set his packed bags outside the back door and took the can of petrol upstairs. He went into the master bedroom and began to splash petrol around there. It was only right that the fire should start in his father's room.

He splashed petrol in each bedroom to ensure that the fire would spread quickly, then looked at his watch. He was only five minutes late. His dad would forgive him that.

He took out the box of matches and struck

one. It went out. Annoyed he struck another, waited till it was burning steadily then tossed it on to the petrol-soaked bed.

The bedding burst into flame with a loud whoosh and he laughed aloud, standing watching it for a minute or two, then raising one hand in a salute. 'Vikings! Warrior's funeral! This is for you, Dad.'

He laughed as he walked to each of the other bedrooms, flinging matches inside, pleased when they too caught alight easily. The flames were burning brightly now, crackling and roaring as they jumped from one piece of furniture to another. He stopped halfway down the stairs to watch a door frame burst into flame, relishing the sight, swelling with pride at his handiwork.

He paused in the kitchen to stuff the last few cans and packets of food into a shopping bag. The fire was roaring nicely upstairs now, though there was hardly anyone around to see it at this time of day.

He opened the back door, intending to go and set the car alight, and walked straight into two policemen. Cursing, he struggled but they were ready for him and soon had him cuffed so tightly he couldn't get away.

'Where's that damned fire engine?' one said.

Just then the window of the master bedroom burst outwards and flames shot everywhere.

William laughed. 'It's too late. Too bloody late!' He laughed as they stuffed him into the back of their car and continued to laugh as they waited for the fire brigade. He'd done a good job.

'See how you like that, you stupid bitch!' he yelled as they moved the car to make room for the fire engine.

22

Nicole thanked people for attending the funeral and invited them to join her at a local pub for a drink and nibbles, but everyone said they had to get off. Only Tracey lingered, heaven knew why.

As Nicole stood watching the relatives go, a police car drove up and a female officer got out, straightening her hat and uniform top before walking across to Tracey.

'Mrs Gainsford?'

Tracey promptly burst into tears and the officer shot a harassed glance at Nicole.

Reluctantly she moved forward. 'I'm Nicole Gainsford,' she told the officer quietly. 'Just a moment.'

She turned to Sam's mistress. 'It's time for you to go. If you have anything else to say to me, you can do it through my lawyer. I've written his name down.' She offered a piece of card.

'You'll definitely be hearing from me!' Tracey said. 'My baby's not being done out of his inheritance.'

'It's a boy?'

'Yes. And I'm going to call him Sam for his father. And I'm not going till I'm ready to leave.'

Paul moved forward. 'You've bothered my mother enough. Go away now.'

She looked at him, pressed a handkerchief to her mouth and tottered away on her ridiculously high heels, pulling out some car keys, dropping them and letting the male police officer pick them up for her.

Nicole watched her for a moment, wondering yet again what Sam had seen in a woman like that, then turned back to the officer. 'What did you want to see me about?' It'd be William, of course. What else could it be? Perhaps they'd caught him. She hoped so. Maybe if he got treatment . . .

'It's bad news, I'm afraid. Your house is on fire. It was well alight before anyone notified the fire brigade and there's nothing they can do to save it — though they did manage to push the car out of the garage, if that's any consolation.'

She couldn't take it in for a moment or two.

Kieran asked, 'How did it catch fire? Does anyone know?'

The officer sighed. 'Your son William started it. He was caught leaving the house just as the flames really got hold upstairs. He's being held at the police station but he's refusing to say anything. Do you want to come and see him? He's — um, apparently been a bit violent, but he's not eighteen yet so we need a responsible adult.'

'My brother's been taking designer steroids,' Paul said. 'I think he's gone mad.' He hugged his mother. 'Don't cry. Please don't cry, Mum. We've got somewhere to live and we've saved some of our things. We'll be all right.'

'I'm crying for William, for what he's turned into.' She felt Kieran's arm go round her and leaned against him. 'I don't want to go to the police station yet. I don't want to see William

374

I've just cremated my husband. All I want is to go back to my new flat and sit quietly.'

'I'll come with you, Mum,' Paul said. 'You shouldn't be on your own.'

'I can take you both home,' Kieran offered, 'then I'll go and see what's happening at your house, if you like.'

She felt too tired to say anything but, 'Thank you. I don't know what I'd do without you.' For a moment their eyes met and they didn't need words to communicate their feelings. But it wasn't the time to bring them out into the open.

Kieran turned to the officers. 'All right if I call a taxi and take her home?'

They looked at one another.

'We'll take you home, Mrs Gainsford. It'll be quicker.'

Nicole got into the car, closed her eyes and leant back, surprised when someone told her they'd arrived.

Kieran came to the front door with her, but she stopped in the doorway. 'I need to be on my own for a while, if you don't mind. I'll be all right. I promise.'

'OK. I'll call back later.' Outside Kieran said to the officers, 'I'd better get my car. I can't walk very far yet and you won't want to be ferrying me home from the fire afterwards. I live just down the street.'

'We'll take you to see the fire and bring you back, Mr Jones.'

They didn't stay long. Even though the worst of the fire was out, the house was a lost cause — blackened, stinking, dripping with water.

375

There was a car parked in the street, with the doors open, but it reeked of petrol.

'Needs cleaning professionally before you can use it again, sir,' one of the firemen said to him

'Do you know where I can get that done?'

'Darby's, in Swindon. Give them a ring and they'll come and fetch it.'

'Thanks. Mrs Gainsford is too upset to come here at the moment. She's just had her husband's funeral.'

'She's copping it hard, isn't she? The neighbour said she doesn't live here any more Do you have her phone number and address?'

Kieran took out a card and crossed his own details off, scribbling Nicole's address and phone number on the back.

On the way back, he used his mobile to arrange for the car to be picked up.

* * *

As they turned into Peppercorn Street, Kieran shouted, 'Stop!'

'What's the matter?'

'That car. It belongs to a man who's been stalking one of my tenants.'

The driver braked sharply. 'Are you sure?'

'Very sure. Why?'

'That's a police car, a surveillance vehicle from the next district. It's a bit of a joke because everyone knows it by sight.'

'The guy who's stalking her is a policeman Could you go forward slowly but stop before you get to my block of flats? I think he'll be there.

376

Kieran stared up and down the street, but could see no sign of Gary, which worried him even more.

'Um — you wouldn't happen to know this stalker's name, would you?'

'Gary Yarford.'

Both his companions sucked in air sharply.

'You know him?'

'Well, he's the sergeant of a neighbouring district. This isn't his patch, strictly speaking, but we work with other teams quite often. Why are you so sure he'll be at your place, Mr Jones?'

'He's been stalking one of my tenants. I've seen him doing it.' He thought rapidly. 'You don't have any plain clothes with you, do you?' he asked the female officer. 'A jacket or something. Only I'm not much use in a fight these days, so I thought you could walk to the flats with me, pretending you're my girlfriend, and then we can check things out quietly.'

'Can do.'

'Yarford will cause trouble if he finds out you've been getting involved,' the male officer warned her. 'He's not the sort you mess with unless you've got absolute proof and we only have Mr Jones's word for this.'

'How the hell are you going to get proof if no one will confront him?' Kieran demanded.

The female officer had a determined look on her face. 'I haven't said anything at work but Yarford sexually harassed a friend of mine, so I believe it of him. I will walk into the flats with you, Mr Jones, and have a quick look round, at least.'

As the two of them walked from the street into the car park, arm in arm, his companion suddenly swung him round and said, 'Pretend to kiss me and move so that you can see the upstairs windows.' Surprised, he did as she asked and saw Miss Fairbie standing at her window signalling to him and pointing to the next flat.

He saw the outline of a man briefly in the window of Janey's flat. 'Something's wrong. Take a look.' He turned slightly so that his companion could see the building.

'I'd say there's trouble,' she agreed.

'Did you see the man in the other window? No? Well, I did. Yarford must be inside. How the hell did he get in? I had all the locks changed.'

'Walk on past or he'll get suspicious. Act like a guy in love.'

So they walked across the car park, stopping for another brief fake kiss, then going round to the side door of his flat, where she immediately let go of him and became very businesslike.

'Show me where to go, then ring this number on your landline. He may be tuned into the police network so I don't want to call in directly. Tell them Sandra Collins needs backup and give them this address. Then leave it to me unless I shout to you to fetch Harry from the car.'

Kieran handed her a master key. 'This'll get you into Janey's flat.'

'Good.' She took off her bright pink jacket and pulled out her police hat, jamming it firmly on her head.

Kieran left her climbing quietly up the stairs and went to ring the number she'd given him

378

The minute he mentioned Sandra's then Yarford's name, the person at the other end became very attentive. After he'd explained what was going on, he was told a car was on its way. He went into the hall, not liking to leave Sandra on her own confronting a senior officer. Voices floated down to him.

He crept upstairs, hoping there wasn't a stalemate, hoping desperately that Yarford didn't have an excuse for being there and that Janey would have the courage to accuse him.

* * *

Janey ran out of ways to prolong Millie's meal and nappy change. She was nearly sick with fear by now. Then someone knocked on the door of her flat and hope flared.

Gary stiffened. 'Expecting someone?'

She hitched her shoulders. 'Friends pop in all the time.'

'Well, tell them to go away.' His eyes fell on the infant. 'Say the baby's sick.' He pulled Millie out of her arms. 'I'll hold her for you. A bit of insurance, shall we say?'

She gasped. 'Don't hurt her.'

The knock came again.

'Go and answer it, damn you.' He moved into the bedroom with the baby.

She went to the door, opening it to see a police officer there. She mouthed 'Help!' before she spoke. 'Yes?'

'We're checking all the flats. There's a dangerous intruder on the loose in the district, an arsonist. He's broken into several flats.'

'Well, he's not here.' She pulled a face and tried to show that someone was there and the other woman nodded. 'I need to come in and check.'

'My baby's not well. She's in the bedroom. I don't want to disturb her.'

'Oh, I'll be very quick. Will you stand aside please?'

The door to the bedroom opened and Gary came out, carrying Millie. 'There's no intruder here, Officer. But I commend your care.'

'Sergeant Yarford!'

'I'm a friend of the family, aren't I, Janey?'

She didn't dare contradict him, but couldn't bring herself to say yes.

'Even so, sir, I have to check. You know what my sergeant is like, a stickler for doing everything by the book.'

He smiled. 'Go ahead and check.' He sat down in an armchair, still holding the baby.

Janey stood near the door, terrified he'd hurt Millie if she said anything, terrified of not speaking out, too.

Outside in the hall, Kieran had been eavesdropping. It sounded as if the fellow was holding Millie. If he hurt that child . . .

He rapped on the door and entered the flat without waiting, seeing the terror on his tenant's face at once. 'Janey, I've come for — Oh, sorry. Didn't realise you had visitors. Look, we're due at my friends' house in quarter of an hour. I'd expected you to be ready.'

'She can't go with you,' Gary said at once

380

'She's promised to ring her parents and that's much more important than a social event.'

Kieran moved across the room, exaggerating his limp. 'It's not a social outing. It's a part-time job offer and if she mucks them around, they'll give the job to the next person on the list. Hand me the baby and I'll hold her while Janey gets ready. You'll have to come back another time.'

Even as he spoke, he reached out for the baby and for a minute there was a tussle, then the police officer came across to them and Gary let go.

Kieran moved quickly back, holding Millie carefully, but he wasn't going to let it go at that. 'I know this is difficult, but if you *don't* take Yarford in for questioning, I'll be complaining to my friend the Commissioner.' He gave Janey the baby.

With Millie safe in her arms, she blurted out, 'Gary came and threatened me, said I had to . . . to let him . . . It's rape when you don't want to do it and he's done it to me before.' She burst into tears.

'Only her word against mine,' Yarford smiled, not looking in the least upset.

Janey cried even harder.

'There's my word, too,' said a voice by the door and Miss Fairbie came in. 'He made me let him into her flat earlier, Constable, threatened me if I didn't do as he said. I should think my washing is still lying on the ground at the back, where I dropped it when he grabbed me.'

Yarford's smile turned into a scowl. 'I told you it was a joke, to surprise Janey.'

'It was no joke. You terrified me. And her. And you said if I phoned the police, she'd suffer.'

'I deny saying that, but I did make a misjudgement and if I frightened you, I apologise.'

He turned to Janey. 'As I've been telling you, your father sent me. He wants me to persuade you to go home. Since you wouldn't speak to me or let me in, I used my initiative.'

He turned to the officer. 'Her father's Lionel Dobson. I'll give you his address and phone number. He'll confirm what I've told you.'

'In the meantime, sir, I'm afraid I'll have to ask you to come down to the station till it's all sorted out.'

'You'll have egg on your face if you insist on that. Just ring him now.'

'No egg on my face from doing my duty, sir. If you'll please come with me?'

'You'll be sorry. You're too inexperienced to recognise a liar when you see one, and this sweet young lady is a very accomplished liar, as her father will bear out.'

When Yarford had left with the police officer still smiling, Janey sank into a chair and tried to stop crying. 'He'll get away with it. You'll see. He persuaded my father that I was lying after he raped me. He always gets away with things.'

Miss Fairbie sighed. 'She's right. Sods like him usually escape.'

'We'll see about that,' Kieran said grimly.

'I'm going to ask to go into a women's refuge,' Janey said. 'The only thing I can do now is get right away from this part of the country. I don't understand why he won't leave me alone.'

'Even if you leave, you'll always be looking over your shoulder,' Miss Fairbie said quietly. 'I know because that's what it's like for me, why I don't go out unless I have to.'

She looked at Kieran. 'Don't you have any contacts who can help you nab Yarford? You used to be quite famous for investigative journalism. Surely you can pull a few rabbits out of the hat?'

'We're working on it.'

'Better work quickly, then. His sort are good at covering their tracks.'

He could see tears in her eyes as she turned away. That upset him. There had to be something he could do to help people like her.

'You stay here with Millie,' he told Janey. 'I'll go and find out what's happening at the station, then come back and tell you.'

'No. I'm coming with you. I just have to get Millie ready.'

He looked at his watch. 'I need to get off straight away. Look, phone Dawn and see if she can bring you and if not,' he fumbled through his wallet and shoved a couple of notes in to her hand, 'catch a taxi again.'

★ ★ ★

After the police had gone, Winifred called a cleaning company and arranged for them to come round and go through her house as a matter of emergency. The upstairs was in a bad way too and had sickened her. She didn't know what the intruders had used to make the bath dirty, or what they'd poured down her toilet, but she didn't want to go near it.

'Do you want to stay with me tonight?' Haze asked as they watched the cleaning company pack up and leave. 'I've got a spare bedroom.'

Winifred hesitated, then gave in, just this once 'That'd be nice.'

'I think it'd be better if we all stayed here unti you've got a proper security system fitted anc new window locks put on,' Dan said. 'I reckor that nephew of yours is desperate. He migh burn the place down to get you out.'

Winifred looked at him in horror. 'But he'; offshore now.'

'Is he? Are you sure of that? Who does he worl for? Give them a ring and check. There shoulc still be someone in the office. It'd not take ; minute.'

'You're very shrewd,' she said. 'And I'll dc that, just to set my mind at rest.'

Five minutes later she put the phone dowr and filled in the gaps in what they'd heard 'Bradley hasn't worked for them for over a year They wouldn't say why, but from the tone of tha woman's voice, she didn't like him.'

'So we're staying here,' Hazel said. 'I'll ge Dawn to bring a few of my things round.'

'I can run you home,' Dan offered. 'I'm stil able to drive a car, thank goodness. It'll not take more than half an hour. It'll be light for a whil yet, so you should be safe, Winifred. Then I car get my things, too. And we'll order a Chinese takeaway tonight for tea after we get back. I'n feeling peckish even if you ladies aren't.'

'I've never had Chinese food,' Winifred said

My mother only liked plain food and cakes and afterwards — well, I didn't bother to try new things. I should have. I will from now on.'

'Good for you. And you're in for a treat tonight,' he said. 'They do great food.'

While the others were away, Winifred started setting the table. She thought she heard a sound and stopped moving to listen, but everything was quiet and she'd locked the doors again. Then she heard a door closing with a quiet snick and knew she wasn't alone in the house. If this was Bradley . . . She picked up a rolling pin and waited, with her back to the wall. The door of the kitchen swung open slowly and her nephew appeared in the opening.

He laughed. 'All ready for battle, are you?'

'What do you want?'

'To get you out of this house, Auntie, dear. It's the only asset I've got left.'

'It's not your asset, actually. It's mine.'

'What does an old woman need with a place this big?'

'It's my home. Everyone needs a home. Why should I give it up for you?'

'Don't you have any family feeling? I can make sure you live in modern comfort, which at your age should count for something, and still make a fortune from this place.'

She didn't reply, because she didn't want to risk driving him to violence.

'I can do much worse things, though, if you won't play ball,' he said in a voice suddenly harsh. 'You'll not feel safe here from now on, not for a minute. And don't think changing the locks will keep me out, because it won't.' He breathed heavily. 'When did you change that damned power of attorney?'

'After your last visit. I also changed my will then.'

'What?'

'Nothing has now been left to you, so if you hurt me in any way, you'll not only be committing a crime, but sending my estate to someone else.'

'You're lying. You must be. You don't have anyone else to leave it to. And anyway, if you've changed your will once, you can change it again. I warn you — '

'I think you've said enough, young fellow.'

Bradley spun round and Winifred could see Dan standing in the hall behind him.

'Do you think you're going to change my mind, old man?'

'No, but the police will.' He gestured behind him and the same two police officers who'd been round earlier came forward. 'They've been listening to you threatening your aunt.'

'Bradley Parfitt, you're under arrest . . . '

Winifred watched stony-faced as her nephew was led away, then turned to Dan. 'How did you know?'

'After we drove away, I realised I'd left my wallet in my jacket here. I saw that fellow fiddling with the front door lock and knew he was up to no good.' He took out his mobile phone and looked at it in admiration. 'To think I used to complain about these things.' He gave Winifred a severe look. 'And you're not wearing that pendant, which you said you would do. You could have called for help if you had been.'

She could feel herself blushing as both Dan and Hazel looked at her accusingly. 'You're right. I have to get used to it.'

'And now, since the police have taken away your nephew, we'll lock the place up, collect Hazel's and my things, then I'm taking you both out for a Chinese meal. It tastes so much nicer if you eat it in the restaurant.'

'Our Dan's a bully, isn't he?' Hazel said with a grin.

'A dreadful bully,' Winifred agreed. 'You don't need to stay now Bradley's been arrested.'

'Don't you want company?'

She didn't hesitate. 'Yes, I do. Very much. Look I'll show you to your bedrooms and get some clean sheets out, then I'd like to change my clothes. It'll only take me five minutes.'

She felt a sense of exhilaration as she got out a dress her mother had always hated, in a dull rose shade. The style was a bit out of date, but the colour suited her.

And tonight, she vowed, she was going to try every new dish offered her. This was the start of a new life for her. She hadn't many years left, so every single day had to count from now on.

Beaming, she went carefully down the stairs and joined her friends.

* * *

Before Kieran got into his own car to go to the police station, he pulled out his phone and called his friend Jim to bring him up to date on what had happened now.

'I'll go down to the police station too and help you keep an eye on things there,' Jim said at once. 'I've been having some fun and games today. That social worker you told me about was up to her nasty tricks again.' He outlined briefly what had happened to Miss Parfitt. 'She's a feisty old lady, that one. I don't think they'll get the better of her. But what if she was in poor health or losing it just a little? They could have cheated her out of everything she owned.'

'I hate people who do that. Look, I'll meet you at the station. I want to find out about Nicole's son, as well as keeping tabs on Yarford.'

'How do you always manage to find trouble?' Jim teased. 'You're supposed to be retired now.'

And Kieran suddenly realised with a surge of joy that his life hadn't changed all that much, injuries or not. Even if he never walked properly again, he could still do what he'd been doing all his life: seek out injustice and fight for the underdog.

As he drove, he decided he'd been very lucky in a way that had eluded him for most of his life — because he'd also found a woman to love. Not one to have an affair with — he'd had a few of those — but one he wanted to share a life with.

So many things were going to change for the better once Nicole was in a fit state to think about her future.

Strange how quickly he'd fallen for her — and her son. Paul was a great kid. No need to rush things, though. She'd need to take things slowly.

He had no doubts about the outcome, none at

ll. He and Nicole were good friends already and he was quite sure from the way she responded to his touch that she found him as attractive as he found her. They could take their time, get to know one another properly.

He'd always gone with his hunches and this one said things would work out for them.

As for Paul, that lad was as hungry for a father figure as Kieran was for a son.

He wondered if her older son was treatable or if William would stay in la-la land. You never knew with drug users. Some drugs could damage the brain permanently. It'd take a while to get William back on track, and even then he might never reconcile with his mother.

Well, whatever happened, Nicole would not be facing it alone.

23

At the police station, Kieran saw his friend Jim standing to one side and went towards him first.

'What's the news?'

'They won't tell me any details.' He grinned as he added, 'But I've got good hearing and voices echo into this part of the waiting area. I gather they're waiting for someone to back up Yarford's story.'

'Janey's father. It must be. She says the two of them are thick as thieves.'

'He'll testify against his own daughter?'

'Apparently.'

Just then the door opened and an overweight man came in, followed by a thin woman who didn't meet anyone's eyes.

'That's him,' Kieran said. 'And that must be his wife.'

'Looks a right slob. As for her, if I ever saw a downtrodden woman, she's it.'

'He's a nasty sod. I've a photo of him smashing up a perfectly good printer rather than let his daughter have it.'

'I've got an old printer she can have.'

'I'll hold you to that.'

They watched what was happening.

★ ★ ★

Lionel Dobson walked up to the counter. 'I'm here on behalf of my friend Sergeant Yarford.'

'If you'll just wait a moment, sir, I'll get someone.'

Jim stepped forward. 'Could I have a word, sir?'

'Who are you?'

'Press.' He held up his identity card.

'Good. You can see what this country's come to when someone doing a favour for a friend gets accused of sexual harassment. It's a crying shame.'

His wife shot him an embarrassed glance and Kieran realised from his overloud voice and the way he was swaying that he'd been drinking.

A woman officer came into the waiting area. 'Will you come this way, sir? I'll just fetch Sergeant Yarford.' She led the Dobsons into a room at the side, glancing at Kieran and Jim, but not saying anything to them.

Shortly afterwards Yarford came strolling in, stopping to scowl when he saw the two journalists. 'Don't let these two anywhere near the interview room,' he called to the officer on the desk.

The man nodded, but didn't say anything and from the look he gave at Yarford's back, he wasn't a big fan of the sergeant's, either.

*   *   *

In the interview room the officer explained what had happened and Lionel immediately grew angry.

'Yes, I did ask him to see my daughter. She

391

won't listen to us. It was the only way I could get a message to her.'

'What message was that, sir?'

'That doesn't matter,' Yarford said. 'It's private.'

'Not if Janey's complaining about harassment, it isn't. It might be relevant. She's a tart, officer. On the streets. How do you think that feels? My friend Gary agreed to tell her she could come back home if she mends her ways.'

Dorothy murmured a protest.

'Did you want to say something, Mrs Dobson?' the officer asked.

'No, she didn't,' Lionel said immediately. 'She's just here to bear out what I'm telling you.'

'Mrs Dobson?'

The woman shook her head.

After they'd gone over all the details several times and Mrs Dobson had winced but not said a word, the officer sighed. 'It seems that Sergeant Yarford was doing just what he said.'

She looked at her companion, but the male officer shook his head. 'We thank you all for coming here voluntarily. It's always best to get these things sorted out properly.'

Yarford leant forward. 'And sometimes it's best to listen to older and more experienced officers and not go down the official track.'

'Just doing my duty, sir.'

The look he gave her was not friendly.

'We'll go and take care of the paperwork at the front desk,' the male officer said.

As they walked across the waiting area, Kieran looked at them and the woman gave a small shake of the head. He felt sickened to think of

Yarford getting away with this.

Just then the outer door opened and Janey came in, pushing Millie in her buggy.

Lionel roared, 'It's all her fault for causing this trouble and telling such lies about my friend and I hope you'll charge her for wasting police time. You should take that baby away from her. It'll stand no chance in life with a mother like that. The Social Services are already looking into it. It's a crying shame.'

Janey let out a cry of anguish and started to back out. Kieran began to walk across to her.

Just then Dorothy darted forward to the desk and said loudly, 'My husband's lying and so is Yarford. I can't let you do this to her, Lionel. You know Yarford raped her and even that didn't upset you . . . ' She burst into tears, sobbing so loudly, her husband's shouts were drowned.

The officer behind the desk smiled just once, then walked round to the waiting area. 'Miss Dobson, is that true? Did Yarford rape you?'

'Yes, he did.' Janey winced as her father made a threatening gesture.

'Gary Yarford, I'm arresting you for rape.' The officer repeated the caution as Yarford stood there stunned.

Kieran put an arm round Janey while the female officer tried to comfort a hysterical Dorothy.

Protesting and demanding a lawyer, Yarford was taken away. Dobson managed to get past the police officers and thump his wife. In the struggle with the police, he managed to punch one of them too, so was also arrested and taken away.

'He'll murder my mother when he gets out,' Janey whispered.

'Do you want to go and see her?'

'No, I don't. She knew all the time that it was Yarford and still let me take the blame, let my father throw me out. I don't want anything to do with her.'

'Are you sure? She *is* your mother.'

'She was always *his* wife first. I don't care if I never see her again. But you'd better tell them to put her in a women's refuge if they want to save her life. My father's put her in hospital a couple of times already, but she refused to press charges.'

Kieran let out his breath in a long, low whistle.

It was a couple of hours before they could leave the police station, then just as they were about to leave, Kieran suddenly remembered William Gainsford.

He walked across to the desk. 'Sorry to trouble you when I know you're busy, but you brought in a young fellow called William Gainsford. His mother is a close friend of mine, so I was wondering if you had any information about him.'

'You can't report on this. He's a minor still, by a few days.'

'I won't.' Kieran smiled. 'I'm doing this as the man who hopes to marry his mother.'

'Ah. Someone's caught you at last, have they Jones? I've seen articles where you said you didn't intend to marry.'

'I must have been crazy.'

'I admire what you've done. You've sorted out

394

cases the police didn't dare touch, so we were rooting for you — well, those of us who care about justice were.' He cast an angry glance towards the door through which Yarford had been taken away, then looked back at Kieran.

'They had to get the doctor in to that young fellow, he was behaving so wildly. The doctor got him admitted to a psychiatric hospital. It took three people to get him out to the ambulance even with sedatives pumped in. He's in a bad way.'

'Yes. I'd guessed that.'

'I hate drugs.'

'Me, too.'

Kieran drove Janey home, feeling tired now. 'I don't think you're going to need to leave town. Yarford won't come near you again. I should think he'll spend quite a lot of time in prison. Don't cry.'

She smiled at him through the tears. 'It's the relief. I can get on with my life now.'

'And stay in Peppercorn Street?'

She nodded. 'Oh, yes. It's a wonderful place to live. Unless you think I'm too troublesome a tenant?'

'No, you're a perfect tenant, just the sort I like to have in my building. But if I can, I'll put you in a ground-floor flat. I'll see if the tenant in the flat next to me will change.'

'I like where I am. It feels safer than the ground floor and I like looking out of the window. And Millie won't always be in a buggy.'

Only when he'd seen Janey to her flat and told Miss Fairbie what had happened did Kieran go down to his own flat, feeling utterly exhausted now.

He could leave the reporting of this case to Jim, who would help the police unpin other details, he was sure. From what Mrs Dobson had sobbed out about that Stevenall, and the bribes they'd had to pay, the woman would be losing her council job.

He picked up his phone. 'Nicole? How are you? Want to know what happened to William and Janey? Right. I'll be round in a few minutes. Is it really only nine o'clock? It seems later. Yes, I'd love something to eat, and a glass of wine would be perfect.'

* * *

Nicole opened the door to him, smiling, looking much better than she had earlier. He couldn't help it, he pulled her into his arms and kissed her.

As she melted against him, he closed his eyes and when the kiss ended, simply held her close for a few moments. 'I needed that,' he said huskily into her hair.

'So did I.' She laughed shakily. 'I don't know why we're standing in the hall. Come in properly and sit down.'

He sat on the sofa, accepted a glass of wine and watched Paul switch off the television and turn to look at him enquiringly. 'I'd better tell you about William first.'

Nicole was sitting beside him and her hand fumbled for his as he explained what little he knew. 'We'll ring the hospital tomorrow.'

She nodded.

'Do you think they can help him?' Paul asked.

'I hope so. Nothing's guaranteed, though.'

'Even if they do, he'll still be a bully and I don't want anything else to do with him.'

Nicole looked at him sadly, then admitted, 'I feel the same now, but if they manage to get him back to normal, we'll see.'

After a pause for a few seconds, Kieran changed the subject. 'About Janey, the news is much better.'

They were both smiling when he'd finished. 'She deserves to get her life together,' Nicole said. 'It's going to be hard work rearing that baby on her own.'

'She'll cope. She now has Miss Parfitt, Mr Shackleton and Dawn's mother as adopted grandparents, not to mention Dawn on her side. Not a woman to tangle with, our Dawn.'

After they'd eaten, Paul went to bed and Kieran pulled Nicole closer to him on the couch. 'So . . . what about you and me?'

'What about us?' Her voice sounded breathless and girlish, and the little he could see of her cheek was faintly flushed.

'Do you think I can start courting you now?'

She raised her eyes then, meeting his and smiling slightly as she nodded. 'That sounds an excellent plan. Paul's already given his approval.'

'He has?'

'Oh, yes.'

He smiled. 'I hope that means he'll accept me as a stepfather one day. He's a great kid.'

'Nearly a young man now.' She cuddled up and they didn't say anything for a while, just sat and enjoyed the peace and the feeling of being loved, even if that hadn't been put into words yet.

Books by Anna Jacobs
Published by Ulverscroft:

FAMILY CONNECTIONS
KIRSTY'S VINEYARD
CHESTNUT LANE
SAVING WILLOWBROOK
FREEDOM'S LAND
IN FOCUS

THE KERSHAW SISTERS:
OUR LIZZIE
OUR POLLY
OUR EVA

THE MUSIC HALL:
PRIDE OF LANCASHIRE
STAR OF THE NORTH
BRIGHT DAY DAWNING
HEART OF THE TOWN

LADY BINGRAM'S AIDES:
TOMORROW'S PROMISES
YESTERDAY'S GIRL

SWAN RIVER:
FAREWELL TO LANCASHIRE
BEYOND THE SUNSET
DESTINY'S PATH

THE WILTSHIRE GIRLS:
CHERRY TREE LANE

ELM TREE ROAD
YEW TREE GARDENS

THE TRADERS:
THE TRADER'S WIFE
THE TRADER'S SISTER
THE TRADER'S DREAM
THE TRADER'S GIFT
THE TRADER'S REWARD

GREYLADIES:
HEIR TO GREYLADIES
MISTRESS OF GREYLADIES
LEGACY OF GREYLADIES

We do hope that you have enjoyed reading this large print book.

Did you know that all of our titles are available for purchase?

We publish a wide range of high quality large print books including:
Romances, Mysteries, Classics
General Fiction
Non Fiction and Westerns

Special interest titles available in large print are:
The Little Oxford Dictionary
Music Book
Song Book
Hymn Book
Service Book

Also available from us courtesy of Oxford University Press:
Young Readers' Dictionary
(large print edition)
Young Readers' Thesaurus
(large print edition)

For further information or a free brochure, please contact us at:
Ulverscroft Large Print Books Ltd.,
The Green, Bradgate Road, Anstey,
Leicester, LE7 7FU, England.
Tel: (00 44) 0116 236 4325
Fax: (00 44) 0116 234 0205

Other titles published by Ulverscroft:

HEIR TO GREYLADIES

Anna Jacobs

1900: The death of her father forces Harriet out of her home to escape the advances of her stepbrother and the rule of her stepmother, and into service at Dalton House. Over time, Harriet develops a friendship with the Daltons' crippled son Joseph — but her life is changed completely when she inherits Greyladies, an old and possibly haunted house. Greyladies could be the answer to Harriet's dreams; but will it be enough to protect her from her family — and can she forge a new life?